# Mirraccino Marriages

*Royal weddings in the Mediterranean*

by Jennifer Faye

Siblings Annabelle and Luca DiSalvo have grown up in the gilded shadow of royalty. Now they're breaking free of palace protocol to find their own happy-ever-afters!

*The Millionaire's Royal Rescue*

Lady Annabelle's father didn't approve of her globe-trotting ways. He thought a job would teach her some responsibility, but it gets her tangled up with renowned tycoon Grayson!

*And look out for Luca's story, coming soon…*

Earl Luca needs to settle down and produce an heir. An unexpected arrival from his past seems to be the answer, but the journey down the aisle is far from smooth!

For more royal romances
from sunny Mirraccino read

*A Princess by Christmas*
*The Prince's Christmas Vow*

Available now!

# THE MILLIONAIRE'S ROYAL RESCUE

BY
JENNIFER FAYE

All rights reserved including the right of reproduction in whole or in part in any form. This edition is published by arrangement with Harlequin Books S.A.

This is a work of fiction. Names, characters, places, locations and incidents are purely fictional and bear no relationship to any real life individuals, living or dead, or to any actual places, business establishments, locations, events or incidents. Any resemblance is entirely coincidental.

This book is sold subject to the condition that it shall not, by way of trade or otherwise, be lent, resold, hired out or otherwise circulated without the prior consent of the publisher in any form of binding or cover other than that in which it is published and without a similar condition including this condition being imposed on the subsequent purchaser.

® and ™ are trademarks owned and used by the trademark owner and/or its licensee. Trademarks marked with ® are registered with the United Kingdom Patent Office and/or the Office for Harmonisation in the Internal Market and in other countries.

First Published in Great Britain 2017
By Mills & Boon, an imprint of HarperCollins*Publishers*
1 London Bridge Street, London, SE1 9GF

© 2016 Jennifer F. Stroka

ISBN: 978-0-263-92281-3

23-0317

Our policy is to use papers that are natural, renewable and recyclable products and made from wood grown in sustainable forests. The logging and manufacturing processes conform to the legal environmental regulations of the country of origin.

Printed and bound in Spain
by CPI, Barcelona

Award-winning author **Jennifer Faye** pens fun, heart-warming romances. Jennifer has won the RT Reviewers' Choice Best Book Award, is a Top Pick author and has been nominated for numerous awards. Now living her dream, she resides with her patient husband, one amazing daughter—the other remarkable daughter is off chasing her own dreams—and two spoiled cats. She'd love to hear from you via her website, www.jenniferfaye.com

For Mona and Louie

Thanks for the smiles and the reminder
that there's more to life than work.

I hope your dreams come true.

# PROLOGUE

ANOTHER DISASTROUS DATE.

Lady Annabelle DiSalvo's back teeth ground together as memories from the night before came rushing over her. It was tough enough finding a decent guy who liked her for herself and not for her position as the daughter of the Duke of Halencia, but then to expect him to put up with her overzealous security team was another thing altogether.

And so when her date had tried to slip away with her for a stroll beneath the stars, her bodyguard had stopped them. Heat rushed to Annabelle's face as she recalled how the evening had ended in a heated confrontation between her, him and her unbending bodyguard. It had been awful. Needless to say, there'd be no second date.

The backs of Annabelle's eyes stung with tears of frustration. She couldn't stand to live like this any longer. Her friends were all starting to get married, but she was single with no hope of that changing as long as her every move was monitored. She just wanted a normal life—like her life had been before her mother's murder.

If only her mother were here, she could talk some sense into Annabelle's overprotective father. She missed her mother so much. And the fact that her father rarely spoke of her mother only made the hole in Annabelle's heart ache more.

She clutched her mother's journal close to her chest. Maybe she shouldn't have been snooping through her mother's things, but her father had left her no other choice. How else would she ever really get to know her mother?

Annabelle slipped the journal into her oversized purse and rushed down the sweeping staircase of her father's vast estate in Halencia. At the bottom of the steps her ever-vigilant bodyguard, Berto, waited for her. There was actually a whole team of them, all taking turns to protect Annabelle.

Ever since her mother had died during a mugging, Annabelle had been watched, night and day. And since her mother's murderer had never been caught, Annabelle had understood her father's concerns at the time. But now, eleven years later, the protective detail assigned to her felt claustrophobic and unnecessary.

She'd thought by moving to Mirraccino, her mother's home country, that things would change, but with the king of Mirraccino being her uncle, she was still under armed guard. But Annabelle had a plan to change all of that. And she was just about to put that plan in motion.

"Berto, I'm ready to go."

The man with short, dark hair and muscles that were obvious even with his suit jacket on, got to his feet. He was the quiet sort and could intimidate people with just a look. Annabelle was the exception.

She'd known him since she was a teenager. He was a gentle giant unless provoked. She thought of him as an overprotective big brother. They moved to the door. Annabelle was anxious to get back to Mirraccino for a pivotal business meeting—

"Not so fast," the rumble of her father's voice put a pause in her steps. The Duke of Halencia strode into the spacious foyer. His black dress shoes sounded as they struck the marble floor. "I didn't know you were leaving so soon." He arched a brow. "Any reason for your quick departure?"

"Something came up." Her unwavering gaze met her father's.

He tugged on the sleeves of his suit, adjusting them. "What's that supposed to mean?"

"It means I have responsibilities in Mirraccino. Not that you would understand." Her voice rose with emotion as memories of last night's date flashed in her mind.

"Annabelle, I don't understand where this hostility is coming from. It's not like you."

"Maybe it's because I'm twenty-four years old and you will not let me live a normal life."

"Of course I do—"

"Then why do you refuse to remove my bodyguards? They're ruining my chances of ever being happy. Momma's been gone a long time. There is no threat. All of that died with her."

"You don't know that." Her father's dark bushy brows drew together and his face aged almost instantly.

Her patience was quickly reaching the breaking point. "You're right, I don't. But that's nothing new. I've been asking you repeatedly over the years to tell me—to tell both myself and Luca why you're worried about us—but you refuse."

Her father sighed. "I've told you, the police said it was a mugging gone wrong."

"Why would a mugger come after us?"

"He wouldn't."

"But?" He couldn't just stop there.

"But something never felt right."

At last some pieces of the puzzle were falling into place. "Because her jewelry and wallet were taken, the police wrote it off as a mugging, but you know something different, don't you?"

Her father's lips pressed together as his dark brows gathered. "I don't know any more than the police."

"But you suspect something. Don't you?" When he didn't respond, she refused to give up. This was too important. "Poppa, you owe me an explanation."

He sighed. "I found it strange that your mother phoned me from the palace to say something was not as it seemed, but she wouldn't go into details on the phone. And two days later, she...she's killed in a mugging."

"What wasn't as it seemed?"

"That's it. I don't know. It might have been nothing. That's what the police said when I told them. All of the evidence said it was a mugging."

"But you never believed it?"

He shook his head. "When the king didn't know what your mother had been referring to, I hired a private investigator. He combed through your mother's items and talked with the palace staff. He didn't come up with anything that would have gotten her killed."

"Maybe the police were right."

Her father shook his head. "I don't believe it."

"Even though you don't have any evidence?"

"It's a feeling." His face seemed to age right before her. "And I'm not taking any chances with you and your brother. You two are all I have left."

"I know you're worried but you can't continue to have us followed around and spied upon like we're criminals. It's so bad Luca never comes home anymore. And—" She thought of admitting that was why she still lived in Mirraccino, but the pain reflected in her father's eyes stopped her.

"And what? You just want to go about as though nothing happened? There's a murderer still on the loose."

Annabelle had placated him most of her life because she felt sorry for him as he continued to grieve for her mother. However, living in Mirraccino for these past couple of years had given her a different perspective. If she didn't stand up for herself, she would never gain her freedom. She would never be able to experience a lot of her dreams. She would forever live under her father's thumb and that was not truly living.

Many people were put off by her security detail. She ended up refraining from doing things just because it was easier than following security protocol and having people send her strange looks, not to mention the whispered comments. Most guys she might have a chance with quietly backed off after meeting Berto. The ones that persisted, she'd learned the hard way, were trouble, one way or the other. And so her dating life was sporadic at best.

"I'm not backing down, Poppa. I'm twenty-four now. I deserve to have my own life—"

"You have a life."

"No, I don't. My every move is analyzed before I do it. And then it is reported back to you. That is not a life."

Her father sighed. "I'm sorry you feel that way, but I'm just doing what I must to protect you and your brother. I don't hear him complaining."

"That's because Luca doesn't care what you or anyone says. He does exactly what he wants."

Her father ran a hand over his clean-shaven jaw. "I know. I know."

"Is that what you want me to do?"

"No!" Her father's raised voice reverberated off the walls.

"Then maybe you need to back off. I'm not wild like Luca, but if that's what you want—"

"Don't you dare. I have enough problems with your brother, but that's going to come to an end. If he wants to inherit my title, he has to earn it."

She couldn't help her brother, not that Luca would want or accept her help, but they were getting sidetracked. "My brother can fight his own battles. This is about you and me. I need you to back off or..."

Her father's gaze narrowed. "Or what?"

She didn't have an answer to that question. Or did she? There was something that had come to mind more than once when she'd felt smothered.

"Or else you'll leave me no choice. I'll leave Halencia and Mirraccino." She saw the surprise reflected in her father's eyes. She hated to do this to him, but perhaps that's what it would take to get her father to understand that she meant business.

He didn't say anything for a moment. And when he did speak, his voice was low and rumbled with agitation. "Your threats won't work."

"Poppa, this isn't a threat. It's a promise. And it's not something that I take lightly."

Her father stared at her as though gauging her sincerity. "Why don't you and your brother understand that I just want to protect you?"

"I know you are worried about our safety after…after what happened to Momma, but that was a long time ago. It was just a mugging—there's no threat to us. You can relax. We'll be safe."

He shook his head. "You don't know that. I can't remove your security detail. I… I have to be sure that you're mature enough—competent enough—to take care of yourself."

The knowledge that her father thought so little of her stabbed at her. But she refused to give in to the pain. This was her chance to forge ahead. "I will prove to you that I'm fully capable of taking care of myself and making good decisions."

Business was something her father understood and respected. She told her father how she'd taken over the South Shore Project. With the crown prince now occupied with his new family and assuming more and more of the king's duties, he didn't have time to personally oversee the project. And Annabelle had happily stepped up. And she almost had the entire piazza occupied. There was just one more pivotal vacancy that needed to be filled. And not just by anyone, but a business that would draw the twentysomething crowd—the people with plenty of disposable cash that would keep the South Shore thriving long into the future.

"And you think you can do this all on your own?" There was a note of doubt in her father's voice.

Her back teeth ground together. Her father was so old-fashioned. If it were up to him, she'd be married off to some successful businessman who could help sustain her father's citrus business.

Annabelle lifted her chin as her gaze met his. "Yes, I

can do this. I'll show you. And once I do, you'll remove the bodyguards."

Their gazes met and neither wanted to turn away. A battle of wills ensued. Obviously her father hadn't realized that he'd raised a daughter who was as stubborn as him.

All the while, she wondered if there was any truth to her father's suspicions about her mother's death. Or was he just grasping for something more meaningful than her mother had died over some measly money and jewelry?

# CHAPTER ONE

THIS DAY WAS the beginning of a new chapter…

Lady Annabelle DiSalvo smiled as she walked down the crowded sidewalk of Bellacitta, the capital of Mirraccino. Though the day hadn't started off the way she'd hoped, she had high hopes for the afternoon.

With a few minutes to spare before her big meeting, she planned to swing by Princess Zoe's suite of offices. They had become good friends since Zoe and the crown prince had reconciled their marriage. Annabelle admired the way Zoe insisted on being a modern-day princess and continued with her interior design business—although her hours had to be drastically reduced to accommodate her royal duties as well as being a wife and mother. If Zoe could make it all work, so could Annabelle. She just had to gain her freedom from her father's overzealous security.

It wasn't until then that Annabelle recalled the email Zoe had sent her. Zoe had left town with her husband on an extended diplomatic trip. And with the other prince in America, visiting with his wife's family, the palace was bound to be very quiet.

Someone slammed into her shoulder. Annabelle struggled not to fall over. As she waved her arms about, the strap of her purse was yanked from her shoulder. Once her balance was restored, her hand clenched the strap.

No way was this guy going to get away with her purse—with her mother's final words in a journal lying at the bottom of the bag. For the first time ever, Annabelle regretted forcing Berto to walk at least ten paces behind her. This was all going down too fast for him to help.

Knowing the fate of the journal was at stake, she held on with all of her might. But the short lanky kid with a black ball cap was moving fast. His momentum practically yanked her arm out of its socket.

Pain zinged down her arm. The intense discomfort had her fingers instinctively loosening their grip. And then they were gone—the purse, the journal and the thief.

"Hey! Stop!" Annabelle gripped her sore shoulder.

"Are you okay?" Berto asked.

"No. I'm not. Please get my purse! Quick!"

The man hesitated. She knew his instructions were to stay with her no matter what, but this was different. That thief had her last connection to her mother. Not wasting another moment while the culprit got away, Annabelle took off with Berto close on her heels.

"Lady Annabelle, stop!" Berto called out.

No way! She couldn't. She wasn't about to let another piece of her past be stolen from her. The hole in her heart caused by her mother's death was still there. It had scar tissue built up around it, but on those occasions when a mother's presence was noticeably lacking, the pain could be felt with each beat of her heart.

Annabelle's feet pounded the sidewalk harder and faster. "Stop him! Thief!"

Adrenaline flooded her veins as she threaded her way through the crowd of confused pedestrians. Some had been knocked aside by the thief. Others had stopped to take in the unfolding scene.

It soon became apparent that she wasn't going to catch him. And yet she kept moving, catching glimpses of the kid's black ball cap in the crowd. She wouldn't stop until all hope was gone.

"Stop him! Thief!" she yelled at the top of her lungs.

Frustration and anger powered her onward. Berto remained at her side. She understood that his priority was her, but for once, she wished he would break the rules. He had no idea what she was about to lose.

Annabelle's only hope was that a Good Samaritan would step forward and help. *Please, oh, please, let me catch him.*

"Stop! Thief!"

* * *

So this was Mirraccino.

Grayson Landers adjusted his dark sunglasses. He strolled down the sidewalk of Bellacitta, admiring how the historical architecture with its distinctive ornate appearance was butted up against more modern buildings with their smooth and seamless style. And what he liked even more was that no one on this crowded sidewalk seemed to notice him much less recognize him as…what did the tabloids dub him? Oh, yes, the slippery fat cat.

Of course, they weren't entirely off the mark with that name. A frown pulled at his lips. He jerked his thoughts to a halt. He refused to get lost on that dark, miserable path into the past.

He scratched at the scruff on his face. It itched and he longed to shave it off, but he really didn't want to be recognized. He didn't want the questions to begin again. The minor irritation of a short beard and mustache was worth his anonymity. Here in sunny Mirraccino he could just be plain old Grayson Landers.

In fact, in less than a half hour, he had a meeting for a potential business deal—a chance to expand his gaming cafés that were all the rage in the United States. Now, it was time to expand into the Mediterranean region.

And Mirraccino offered some perks that had him inclined to give it a closer look. He couldn't imagine that it'd be hard to attract new employees to the sunny island. This island nation was large enough to offer them a choice between city life or a more rural existence. And there was plenty of room on the South Shore for a sizable facility.

His board would love the revenue growth from the international venture. Adding Mirraccino as the hub would give them diversification. It could be the beginning of great things.

"Stop! Thief!" screamed a female above the murmur of voices.

The next thing Grayson knew a young lanky guy bumped into him as he ran up the walk. Grayson reached out, grabbing him as he passed.

The kid yanked, trying to escape the solid hold Grayson had on his upper arm. Between his grip on him and the fact that Grayson had almost a foot on the guy and at least thirty pounds, the kid wasn't going anywhere.

"Thief! Stop him!" again came the female voice and it was growing closer.

Could this guy be the person in question? Grayson gave the teenager a quick once-over. "I'm guessing that's not yours." Grayson gestured to the purse in the kid's hand.

"Yes, it is."

"It's not exactly your color." The purse was brown with pink trim and a pink strap.

The guy continued to struggle, obviously not smart enough to realize that he wasn't going anywhere until the cops showed up. "Let me go!"

Grayson narrowed his gaze on the guy. "If you don't stand still, you won't like what I do next."

"Dude, you don't understand." The kid glanced over his shoulder. "They're after me."

"Probably because you stole," Grayson snatched the purse while the guy wasn't paying attention, "this."

The kid with a few scrawny hairs on his chin turned to him. "Hey, give that back." He glanced over his shoulder again as a crowd formed around them. "Never mind. You keep it. Just let me go."

"I'll keep it and you."

"I called the cops," someone in the crowd called out.

Inwardly, Grayson cringed. The very last thing he wanted to do now was deal with more cops. A little more than a year ago, he'd answered enough questions to last him a lifetime. He was really tempted to let the kid get away and then Grayson could quietly slip into the thickening crowd.

Before he could make up his mind whether to do the right

thing for some stranger or protect himself from yet another interrogation, the whoop-whoop of a police car blasted into the air. Then there was the slamming of a car door.

The suspect in Grayson's hold fought for his freedom with amazing force for someone so slight. The punch that landed in Grayson's gut made him grunt. Anger pumped in his veins. No matter what it cost him personally, this guy needed to learn a lesson.

The crowd parted, allowing the police officer to make his way over to them. Thankfully the officer immediately took custody of the feisty young man and restrained him.

"Move aside." A deep gruff voice shouted. "Let the lady pass."

Grayson glanced up to find the most beautiful young woman standing at the edge of the crowd. Immediately he could see that there was something special about her. Maybe it was her big brown eyes. Or perhaps it was the way her long flowing dark brown hair framed her face. Whatever it was, she was definitely a looker.

It was only then that Grayson noticed the big burly man at her side. Her boyfriend? Most likely. The stab of disappointment assailed him.

Not that he was interested in starting anything romantic. He'd learned his lesson about affairs of the heart—they made you do things you wouldn't normally do and in the end, you got your heart broken, or in his case ripped from his chest. No, he was better on his own.

He was about to turn away when he realized the young woman looked familiar. And then it came to him. She was Lady Annabelle DiSalvo—the very woman he was here to meet with.

The police officer turned to the crowd. "There's nothing here to see. Everyone, please, move on."

Lady DiSalvo didn't move. Was she that fascinated? Or could she be the victim in this case?

This was not the way he'd planned for their relationship

to start—their business relationship that was. And then her gaze moved to him. He waited, wondering if she recognized him. Nothing appeared to register in her eyes. And then she turned to talk to the man at her side.

A camera flash momentarily blinded Grayson.

*Seriously? Could this day get any worse?*

*Where is it?*

*It has to be here.*

Annabelle craned her neck. Her gaze frantically searched for her purse. *Oh, please, let this be the right person. Let him still have my purse.* And then she realized that during the foot chase he could have ditched it anywhere along the way. Her elation waned.

Her gaze latched on to the tall, dark and sexy man standing in the center of the scene. She'd sensed him staring at her earlier. But with those dark sunglasses, she couldn't make out his eyes. He was tall with an athletic build. Her gaze took in the heavy layer of scruff trailing down his jaw, and she couldn't help wondering what he'd look like without it. The thought intrigued her, but right now she had more pressing matters on her mind.

She was about to glance away when she noticed that he was holding her purse. Her gut said he wasn't the thief. The young man next to him giving the policeman a hard time was wearing a dark ball cap. That had to be the culprit. The kid had the right build as well as a smart mouth.

"Hey you! That's my purse!" Annabelle called out, hoping the stranger would hear her. "I need it back."

A reporter positioned himself between them. The man with her purse began backing away and turning his face away from the camera. What was up with that?

She had to get to the man with her purse. And it'd probably go better if she didn't have Berto in tow. Even though she knew he was a gentle giant, strangers found his mammoth size and quiet ways a bit off-putting.

While Berto glanced over the crowd for a new threat, she quietly slipped away. She threaded her way through the lingering crowd. There was a lot of *pardon me* and *excuse me.* But finally she made her way over to the man with her purse in his hand just as the officer was escorting the thief to the police car.

Annabelle had to crane her neck to gaze into the man's face.

"Thank you so much. I didn't think I'd ever see my purse again. You're quite a hero."

The man looked uncomfortable with her praise. "I'm glad I could help."

"Well, I really appreciate it."

"No big deal."

It was a huge deal, but she didn't want to get into any of that right now. "If you'll just give me my purse, I'll be going."

Even standing this close to the man, she couldn't make out his eyes through the large, dark sunglasses. His brows rose in surprise, but he didn't make any motion to give it back.

"Is there a problem?"

"I can't hand it over." The man's voice was deep and smooth like a fine gourmet coffee.

He couldn't be serious. She pressed her hands to her hips. "I don't think you understand. That's my purse. He," she gestured to the thief, who was struggling with the police officer, "stole it from me."

"And it's evidence. You'll have to take it up with the police."

Really? He was going to be a stickler for the law. "Listen, I don't have time for this. I have a meeting—"

"I have to give this to the police. I'm sorry." There was a finality to his tone.

What was it with this day? First, there was the scene with her father. Then she missed her flight. And if that wasn't enough, she'd nearly lost her mother's journal. And now, this man refused to return her belongings.

Maybe she just needed to take a different approach. "If it's a reward you want, I'll need my purse back in order to do that."

The man frowned. "I don't need your money."

This couldn't be happening. There had to be something she could say to change his mind before the policeman turned his attention their way. At last, she decided to do something that she'd never done before. She was about to play the royalty card. After all, desperate times called for desperate measures. And right now, she was most definitely desperate.

But then she had a thought. "If I don't file charges, it's not evidence."

"You'll have to take it up with the officer."

Seriously. Why was the man so stubborn?

"Do you know who I am?"

Before the man could respond, the policeman strode over to them. "I'll be taking that."

The mystery man readily handed over her purse. She glared at him, but she didn't have time to say anything. Her focus needed to remain on getting the journal back.

"That's my purse. I need it back," Annabelle pleaded with the officer. "All of my important things are in there."

"Sorry, miss. Afraid it's evidence now." When the young officer glanced at her, the color drained from his face. "Lady Annabelle, I didn't know it was you. I… I'm sorry."

She smiled hoping to put him at ease. "It's all right. You're just doing your duty. As for my purse, could I have it back now?"

Color rose in the officer's face. His gaze lowered to the purse in his hand. "The thing is, ma'am, regulations say I have to turn this in as evidence. My captain is always telling us to follow the regs. But seeing as it's you, I guess I could make an exception—"

"No." The word was out of her mouth before she realized what she was saying—or maybe she did realize it. She didn't want this young man getting in trouble with his captain because she had him break the rules. "You do what you need to do and I'll come by the police station to pick it up later."

The officer's eyes widened in surprise. "Much appreciated, ma'am, especially seeing as you're the victim. I'll need you to file a complaint against the suspect."

"I… I'm not filing charges."

The officer frowned at her. "That would be a mistake."

He went on to list the reasons that letting the kid get away with this crime would be a bad idea. And he had some good points. In the end, she had to agree with him.

"Okay. I'll need you and the man who caught the thief to make statements down at the station." The officer glanced around. "Where did he go?"

She glanced around for her hero, but there was no sign of him. How could he vanish so quickly?

"I didn't get a chance to catch his name much less take a statement." The officer shook his head as he noted something on the pad of paper in his hand.

Why had the man disappeared without giving his statement? Was he afraid of cops? Or was it something else? Something that had him hiding behind dark sunglasses and a shaggy beard?

Or perhaps she'd watched one too many cop shows. She'd probably never know the truth about him. But that didn't stop her from imagining that he was a bad boy, maybe a wrongly accused fugitive or a spy. Someone as mysterious as him had to have an interesting background. What could it be?

# CHAPTER TWO

AT LAST SHE'D ARRIVED.

Annabelle checked the time on her cell phone. Luckily, she'd had it in her pocket or it would have been confiscated with her purse. She had two minutes to spare before her meeting with an executive of the Fo Shizzle Cafés. Her name was Mary and they'd corresponded for the past few weeks. It seemed Grayson Landers, the CEO and mastermind behind the hip cafés, was only hands-on once a site had been vetted by a trusted member of his team.

Annabelle took a seat at one of the umbrella tables off to the side of the historic piazza in the South Shore. She glanced around, but there weren't any professional young women lurking about.

Annabelle looked down at the screen of her phone. Her social media popped up. There were already numerous posts about the incident with her purse. There were photos of her, but no photos of her hero's face. Too bad.

And then a thought came to her. Perhaps a phone call to the police station would hurry along the return of her possessions. Her finger moved over the screen, beginning the search for the phone number—

"You're seriously not going to let me through?"

The disgruntled male voice drew Annabelle's attention. She glanced up as Berto blocked a man from getting any closer. She swallowed hard. It didn't matter how many times it happened, she was still uncomfortable having security scrutinize everyone that came within twenty meters of her.

Berto stood there like a big mountain of muscle with his bulky arms crossed and his legs slightly spread. Annabelle had no doubt he was ready to spring into action at the slightest provocation. He'd done it before with some overly enthusiastic admirers. Okay, so having him around wasn't all bad, but she did take self-defense classes and knew how to protect herself.

"You'll have to go around. The lady does not want to be disturbed." There was no waver in Berto's voice.

"I'd like to speak to the lady."

"That's not happening."

Annabelle couldn't see Berto's face, but she could imagine his dark frown. He didn't like anyone messing with his orders and that included keeping strangers at a distance.

Annabelle's gaze moved to the stranger. She immediately recognized him. He was the man who'd rescued her purse from that thief. What was he doing here?

He was a tall man, taller than Berto, but not quite as bulky. The man's dark hair was short and wavy, just begging for someone to run their fingers through it. And those broad shoulders were just perfect to lean against during a slow dance.

He was certainly handsome enough to be a model. She could imagine him on the cover of a glossy magazine. He didn't appear threatening. Perhaps he was interested in her. What would it hurt to speak to him?

Annabelle slipped her phone in her pocket. "Berto, is that any way to treat a hero? Let him through."

There was a twitch of a muscle in Berto's jaw, letting her know he wasn't comfortable with her decision. If it were up to him, her father or even the king, she'd never have a social life. It was getting old. And if this man was bold enough to stand up to Berto, she was intrigued.

Without another word, Berto stepped aside.

The man approached her table. He didn't smile at her. She couldn't blame him. Berto could put people on edge.

"I'm sorry about Berto. He can be overprotective. I'd like to thank you again. You're my hero—"

"Stop saying that. I'm no one's hero."

"But you stopped that thief and without you, I probably

wouldn't have gotten my purse back." Or more importantly, the journal.

"I was just in the right place at the right time. That doesn't make me anything special."

"Well, don't argue with me. It's all over social media." She withdrew her phone. She pulled up the feed with all of the posts that included photos of this man holding her purse, but his head was lowered, shielding his face.

She noticed how the muscles of his jaw tensed. He took modesty to a whole new level. What was up with that? She was definitely intrigued by this man.

"I'm guessing you didn't track me down to claim a reward."

The man in a pair of navy dress shorts and a white polo shirt lowered himself into a seat across the table from her. "You don't recognize me, do you?"

Was this man for real? "Of course I do."

He shook his head. "I meant, do you know my name?"

She was definitely missing something here, but what? "I take it you know me."

"Of course. You are Lady Annabelle DiSalvo, daughter of the Duke of Halencia and niece of the king. Also, you are in charge of the South Shore Project."

If he was hoping to impress her, he'd succeeded. Now, she had no choice but to ask. "And your name would be?"

"Grayson Landers."

*Wait. What? He was the genius multimillionaire?*

Surely she couldn't have heard him correctly. He removed his sunglasses and it all came together. Those striking cerulean blue eyes were unforgettable—even from an online photo. At the time, she'd thought they'd been Photoshopped. They hadn't been. His piercing eyes were just as striking in person—maybe even more so.

Somehow, someway she'd missed a voice mail or an email because the last she knew she was supposed to be meeting Mary. She swallowed hard. She should be happy about this change of events, but her stomach was aflutter with nerves. She resisted the urge to run a hand over her hair, wishing that she'd taken the time to freshen up before this meeting.

"Mr. Landers, it's so nice to meet you." She stretched her hand across the table.

His handshake was firm but brief. She had no idea if that was a bad sign or not.

"I, uh, wasn't expecting you."

"I know. You were expecting Mary, but my plans changed at the last minute, making it possible for me to attend this meeting."

"I see. I… I mean that's great." She sent him a smile, hoping to lighten the mood.

There was just something about this man that made her nervous, which was odd. Considering who her uncle and her father were, she was used to being around powerful men.

But most of the men in her life wore their power like they wore their suits. It was out there for people to see, maybe not flaunting it, but they certainly didn't waste their time trying to hide who and what they were. But this man, he looked like an American tourist, not a man who could buy a small country. And that beard and mustache hadn't been in any of the photos online.

His brows rose. "Is there something wrong with my appearance?"

Drat. She'd let her gaze linger too long. "No. No. Not at all. In fact, you look quite comfortable."

Her words did nothing to smooth the frown lines marring his handsome face. "Do I need to change for today's meeting?"

"Um, not at all." She jumped to her feet. "Shall we go?"

He didn't say anything at first. And then he returned his sunglasses to the bridge of his nose as he got to his feet. There was something disconcerting about not being able to look into his eyes when they spoke.

The sooner she got this presentation under way, the sooner it'd be over. "Would you like a tour of the South Shore?"

"Yes."

Short and to the point. She wondered if he was always so reserved. She started to walk, thinking about where she should begin. Of course, she'd given this tour a number of times before to other potential business owners, but somehow it all felt different where Mr. Landers was concerned. Everything about him felt different.

Annabelle straightened her shoulders as she turned to the small piazza where an historic fountain adorned the center. "I thought we would start the tour here. The South Shore is a historic neighborhood."

"I see that. Which makes me wonder why you think one of my cafés would fit in?"

"This area has had its better days." She'd hoped her presentation would make the answer to his question evident, but she hadn't even started yet. She laced her fingers together and turned to him. "Where buildings had once been left for nature to reduce them to rubble, there is now a growing and thriving community."

"That's nice, but you haven't answered my question."

She moved closer to the ancient fountain where four cherubs in short togas held up a basin while water spouts from the edge of the fountain shot into the basin. At night, spotlights lit up the fountain, capturing the droplets of water and making them twinkle like diamonds. Too bad she couldn't show him. It was a beautiful sight.

"If you will give me a chance, I'm getting to it."

He nodded. "Proceed."

She turned to the fountain. "This is as old as the South Shore. The famous sculptor Michele Vincenzo Valentini created it. It is said that he visited Mirraccino and fell in love with the island. Wanting to put his mark upon the land he loved, he sculpted this fountain as a gift to its people. The sad thing is that not long after the project was completed, he passed on."

"Interesting." Grayson glanced over his shoulder at Berto. "Will he be coming with us?"

"Yes." Without any explanation about Berto's presence, Annabelle moved toward one of her favorite shops lining the piazza, the bakery. She inhaled deeply. The aroma of fresh-baked rolls and cinnamon greeted her, making her mouth water. Perhaps they should go inside for a sampling. Surely something so delicious that melts in your mouth would put a smile on her companion's handsome face.

"This bakery is another place that's been around for years. In fact, this family bakery has been handed down through the generations. And let me tell you, their baked goods can't be surpassed. Would you care to go inside?"

He didn't say anything at first and she was starting to wonder if he'd even heard her. And then he said, "If that's what you'd like."

Not exactly the ringing endorsement that she'd been hoping for, but it was good enough. And the only excuse she needed to latch on to one of those cinnamon rolls. She yanked open the door and stepped inside. The sweet, mouth-watering aromas wrapped around her, making her stomach rumble with approval. It was only then she realized that due to her flight delay not only had she missed an opportunity to freshen up but she'd also missed her lunch.

After Grayson had enjoyed a cannoli and some black coffee and she'd savored chocolate-and-pistachio biscotti with her latte, they continued the tour. They took in the new senior facility that was housed in a fully refurbished and modernized historic mansion. They walked along the waterfront and visited many of the shops and businesses where Annabelle was friends with most everyone.

"This place must be very special to you," Grayson said.

At last, he was finally starting to loosen up around her. She knew fresh pastries and caffeine could win over just about everyone. “Sure. I’ve been working on the project for two years now. It’s given me a purpose in life that I hadn’t realized before.”

“A purpose?”

She nodded. “I like helping people. I know from the outside it might seem like I’m doing the crown’s bidding, but it’s a lot more than that. I’ve been able to help people find new homes here in the South Shore. We created that new seniors’ residence. Wasn’t that seashore mural in the ballroom stunning?”

“Yes. It was quite remarkable. And it’s very impressive how you’ve taken on this project and found a deeper meaning in it than just selling parcels of land. But I meant you personally—you seem to have a strong link to this place. When you talk about it, your face lights up.”

“It does?” Was this his way of flirting with her? If so, she liked it.

“Did you spend a lot of time here as a child? The way you describe everything is way more personal than any sales pitch I’ve ever heard. And trust me, I’ve heard a lot of them.”

“Well, thank you, I think.” She smiled at him, still not quite sure how to take him or the things that he said. “But I didn’t spend much time here as a kid. I grew up in Halencia. It’s a small island not too far from here.” But he was right, this place did have a very familiar vibe to it. She’d noticed it before when she was working but had brushed off the sensation. “My mother grew up here. When she talked about her homeland, it always seemed as though she regretted having to leave here. But as for me, until recently, I only came here for the occasional visit.”

“Really? Hmm… I must have been mistaken.”

“I think it must just be from me working so closely on this project.”

“Of course. Mirraccino seems like it would be a great place for a young family. And that fountain, I can imagine kids wanting to make wishes there. And that bakery, it was fantastic…"

Grayson's voice faded into the background as Annabelle latched on to a fuzzy memory of her mother. They'd been here, in this very piazza the day before her mother was murdered. The memory was so vague that she was having a hard time focusing on it. But she did recall her mother had been upset. She definitely hadn't been her usual happy, smiling self.

"Annabelle? Are you okay?"

Grayson's voice jarred her back to reality. Heat rushed up her neck and settled in her cheeks. She was embarrassed that in the middle of this very important meeting she'd zoned out and gotten lost in her memories. "I'm sorry. What did you say?"

"I can see something is bothering you." He led her over to one of the benches surrounding the fountain and they sat down. "I know we barely know each other, but maybe that's a good thing. Sometimes I find it easier to talk to a stranger about my troubles."

What did she say? That she had some vague flashback? And why did she have it? What did it even mean?

It was best to deflect the question. "What troubles do you have?"

He glanced away. "We…um, aren't talking about me right now. You're the one who looked as though you saw a ghost."

So he did have a skeleton or two in his closet. Was it bad that she took some sort of strange comfort in knowing that he wasn't as perfect as she imagined him to be, not that she'd done any digging into his past. When she'd done her research on Fo Shizzle, she'd been more interested in his company's financial history and their projections for the future—all of which consisted of glowing reports.

"Annabelle?"

"Okay. It's not that big of a deal. I was just remembering being here with my mother."

His brows drew together. "I don't understand. Why would that upset you?"

She'd told him this much; she might as well tell him the rest. After all, it wasn't like the memory was any big deal. "It's just that the memory is from a long time ago and it's vague. I remember that day my mother wasn't acting like herself. She was quiet and short-tempered. Quite unlike her."

"Was your father with you?"

Annabelle shook her head. "I don't know where he was. I'm assuming back home in Halencia with my brother."

"You have a brother?"

She nodded. "He's six years older than me. But what I don't get is why I'd forgotten this."

"It's natural to forget things that don't seem important at the time. Do you think the memory is important now?"

"I have no idea."

"Why not just ask your mother about it?"

"I can't." Though Annabelle wished with all of her heart that she could speak with her mother.

"You don't get along with her?"

In barely more than a whisper, Annabelle said, "She died."

"Oh. Sorry. If you don't mind me asking, how old were you at the time?"

"I was thirteen. So I wasn't really paying my mother a whole lot of attention."

"I remember what it was like to be a kid. Although I spent most of my time holed up in my bedroom, messing around on my computer."

"So that's how you became so successful. You worked toward it your whole life."

He leaned back on the bench and stretched his legs out in front of him. "I never set out to be a success. I was just having fun. I guess you could say I stumbled into success."

"From what I've read, you learned to do quite a bit as far as computers are concerned."

"Coding is like a puzzle for me. I just have to find the

right connections to make the programs do what I want." He glanced at her. "It's similar to the way you have snippets of a memory of your mother. You need to find the missing parts for the snippets to fit together and give you a whole picture."

Annabelle shrugged and glanced away. "I'm sure the memory isn't important."

"Perhaps. Or maybe it is and that's why you've started to remember it."

"It's not worth dwelling on." Who was she kidding? This was probably all she'd think of tonight when she was supposed to be sleeping. Was there some hidden significance to the memory?

Just then she recalled her mother raising her voice. Her mother never shouted. Born a princess, her mother prided herself in always using her manners.

"You remembered something else."

Annabelle's gaze met his. "How do you do that?"

"What?"

"Read my mind."

"Because it's written all over your face. And just now, you went suddenly pale. I take it whatever you recalled wasn't good."

"I'm not sure."

"Maybe it would help if you remembered a little more. Perhaps it's not as bad as you're thinking."

"Or maybe it's worse." She pressed her lips together. She hadn't meant to utter those words, but the little voice in her head was warning her to tread lightly.

"Close your eyes," Grayson said in a gentle tone.

"What?"

"Trust me."

"How can I trust you when I hardly even know you?"

"You have a point. But think of it this way, we're out here in the open and your bodyguard is not more than twenty feet away. If that isn't enough security, there are people passing by and people in the nearby shops. All you have to do is call out and they'll come running."

"Okay. I get the point."

"So do it."

She crossed her arms and then closed her eyes, not sure what good this was going to do.

"Relax. This won't work otherwise."

She opened her eyes. "You sound like you know what you're doing. Are you some kind of therapist or something?"

"No. But I've been through this process before."

"You mean to retrieve fragmented memories?"

"Something like that. Now close your eyes again." When she complied, he said, "Recall that memory of your mother. Do you have it?"

Annabelle nodded. All that she could see was the frown marring her mother's flawless complexion and the worry reflected in her eyes.

"Now, was it sunny out?"

What kind of question was that? Who cared about the weather? "How would I know?"

"Relax. Let the memories come back to you. Do you recall perhaps the smell of the bakery?"

"I've heard it said that smell is one of the strongest senses—"

"Annabelle, you're supposed to be focusing."

And she was dodging the memories, but why? Was there something there that she was afraid to recall?

She took a deep breath and blew it out. She tried to focus on any detail that she could summon. Together they sat there for countless minutes as she rummaged through the cobwebs in her mind. Grayson was surprisingly patient as he prompted her from time to time with a somewhat innocuous question. These questions weren't about her mother but rather about sensory details—she recalled the scent of cinnamon and how her mother had bought her a cinnamon roll. The sun had been shining and it had taken the chill out of the air, which meant that it was morning.

"And I remember, my mother said she had to speak to someone. She told me to wait on a bench like this one and she would be right back."

"She left you alone?" There was surprise in his voice.

"No. She stayed here in the piazza, but she moved out of hearing range. There was a man that she met."

"Someone you know?"

"I'm not sure. I never saw his face. I just know their conversation was short and he left immediately after they spoke."

"What did your mother say to you?"

Annabelle opened her eyes. "I don't know anymore. I don't think she said much of anything, which was unusual for her. She was always good at making casual conversation. I guess that's something you learn when you're born into royalty—the art of talking about absolutely nothing of relevance."

"At least nothing bad happened."

"Thanks for helping me to remember."

"I wonder what it was about that day that the memory stuck in your mind."

"I'm not sure."

The truth was, it happened a day or two before her mother died. Could it mean something? Had the police been wrong? Was her mother's death more than a mugging? Or was she just letting herself get caught up in her father's suspicions?

Annabelle didn't want to get into details of the murder with Grayson. As it was, she'd exposed more of herself to this stranger than she'd ever intended. It would be best to stop things right here.

# CHAPTER THREE

GRAYSON HAD RESERVATIONS.

The site for Fo Shizzle was not what he'd been envisioning.

Sure, what he'd seen so far of Mirraccino was beautiful. Maybe not as striking as Annabelle, but it definitely came in a close second. The South Shore was a mix of history and modernization. The view of the blue waters of the Mediterranean was stunning. But it just didn't seem like the right fit for one of his Fo Shizzle Cafés.

"So what did you think?" Annabelle's voice drew him from his thoughts.

"I think you've done a commendable job with this revitalization project. I think it's going to be a huge success." Now how did he word this so as not to hurt her feelings? After all, she'd been a wonderful hostess. And to be honest, he didn't want this to end. This was the most relaxed he'd felt in more than a year...ever since the accident and the ensuing scandal.

"But...?"

"What?" He'd let his mind wonder and hadn't heard what she'd been saying.

"You like the South Shore, however I detect there's a but coming. So out with it. What isn't working for you?"

He paused, struggling to find the right words. "I was under the impression that the site of the café would be in the heart of the city. This area is nothing like the locations of the other cafés. The way the South Shore was described in the proposal was that it was an up-and-coming area. This," he outstretched his arms at the varying shops, "is very reserved. It's an area that would be frequented by a more mature clientele."

"We are in the process of revitalizing the area—the proposal was a projection. I was certain if I could get a representative of Fo Shizzle here that they would see the potential.

I'm sure your café will be a huge draw. I've spoken with the tourism department and they can insert photos and captions prominently in their promo."

His brow arched. He had not expected this bit of news. He couldn't deny that free advertising would help, but would it be enough? "The thing is, my cafés are designed for younger people, high school, college and young adults. The cafés do not cater to a more mature audience. They can be a bit loud at times, especially during an online tournament. The decor is a bit dark with prints of our most popular avatars. Do you know much about our games?"

She shook her head. "Since you can only play on a closed circuit within one of your cafés, I've never had the opportunity. But the research looks intriguing. And I think it would be a hit here with the young crowd."

"To be a success, this area would have to be heavily frequented by young people—"

"And that's what we want." She smiled at him as though she had all of the answers. "I have research studies broken out by demographic."

He liked numbers and charts. "Could I take a look at them?"

She nodded. "Most definitely. I had a copy in my purse, but I also have them at the palace along with an investment package with detailed figures and projections. I wanted you to have a feel for the area before we dove into the numbers."

He glanced around the piazza. "I'm just not sure about this setting. Don't get me wrong—it's beautiful, but it's not quite as urban as our other locations."

"In the reviews I've read about Fo Shizzle, they say young people come from miles away just to hang out and take part in the high-stakes gaming tournaments. You've definitely latched on to a great idea. And I hear the coffee's not so bad either."

"The coffee is actually quite good." He'd made sure of that. Being a coder, he lived on a steady stream of caffeine when he was on a roll. And he was picky about the flavor. He wouldn't have anything less than the best for his cafés—just as he would only have the top-of-the-line games. The newest titles. And the best quality.

Annabelle gave him a speculative look as though figuring out his unshaven appearance and his longer-than-usual hair. It was not his standard appearance—not unless he was on a deadline for a new program rollout. When it came to business, all else came in a distant second, third or lower ranking.

When she didn't vocalize her thoughts about his appearance, he added, "I'm usually a little more cleaned up." Why was he making excuses for his appearance? It wasn't like he was going to ask her out on a date or anything. Still, he heard himself say, "It's just with the media and all, sometimes it's easier to travel incognito."

She nodded but still didn't say anything.

He hated to admit it, but he really did want to know what she was thinking. Did he really look that bad? His hand moved to his jaw. His fingers stroked his beard. It was quickly filling in. Soon it would start to get bushy. He didn't warm to the thought.

Beards were okay on some guys, but not him. It just wasn't his thing. "Is it really that bad?"

She shrugged. "It's okay."

Definitely not a ringing endorsement for his new look.

"I guess it doesn't matter much if I shave or not now that my picture is all over social media. And it's not like I'm going to be here much longer—"

"What? You mean you're leaving? Already?"

He nodded. "I have to keep scouting for a headquarters for my Mediterranean expansion."

"But this is it. The South Shore will be perfect."

Was that a glimmer of worry reflected in her eyes? Surely she couldn't be that invested in doing business with him. And if she was, he had to ask himself why. What was driving her to close this deal?

He cleared his throat. "I'm not ready to make a decision of this magnitude. I have plans to visit Rome, Milan and Athens next."

"And when will you be leaving?"

"In the morning—"

"But you can't." She pressed her lips together as though regretting the outburst.

"Why not?"

"Because you still have to file a report with the police. There's the theft and…and you're an eyewitness. They'll probably want you to testify."

She had a point. And as much as he would like to fly off into the sunset, he wouldn't shirk his duty. "You know, the only reason I walked away is because you said you weren't going to press charges so I figured there was no reason for me to stick around."

"I was truly considering it, but the policeman convinced me it wouldn't be in anyone's best interest. So it looks like you'll be hanging around Mirraccino a bit longer. And I would love to show you more of this beautiful land."

How much more was there to see? And did she really think another day of playing tourist was really going to change his mind?

"I don't know." He glanced at his wristwatch. It was getting late. "Maybe I could swing by the police station now and give them my statement."

"It's Friday. And it's late in the afternoon. I'm sure the people you'll need to speak with will be gone for the weekend or at least have one foot out the door."

"Can't I just give my statement to an officer? Surely the whole police force doesn't go home early for the weekend."

Annabelle smiled. "Funny. But I meant you'll probably have to speak with some of the clerical or legal people."

He nodded. "I suppose they might do things a bit differently from what I'm accustomed to in the States."

Annabelle nodded. "Now let's see about getting you situated."

"I have a room at the hotel in the city."

"I was thinking of something different. How about being a guest at the royal palace?"

Had he heard her correctly? She was inviting him to stay in the palace with the king? "Are you serious?"

"Of course I'm serious. The king is my uncle."

"And you live there—at the palace, that is?"

"At the moment, I do. I've been living there while working in Mirraccino for the past couple of years."

There was a lot about Lady Annabelle that intrigued him. And honestly, what would it hurt if he took a few more days before moving on?

Annabelle was the first person to interest him in a long time—just not romantically. It wasn't that he didn't find her exceedingly attractive. He did. But he refused to get sucked into another relationship. He'd been through enough. His heart was still mending.

"Oh, please say that you'll stay. I've already had a suite made up for you. And…and the King is expecting you at dinner tonight."

"The king wants to meet me?"

Her cheeks bloomed with color and her gaze didn't quite meet his as she nodded.

He suspected she was just saying anything to get him to stay. He had to admit no one had ever dangled an invitation to meet a king before him in order to help with a business deal. What made this amazing woman feel as though she had to jump to such lengths to get him to close this deal?

"Tell the truth," he said. "The king, he isn't expecting me at dinner, is he?"

Her gaze finally met his. "No, but I'm sure it won't be a problem. The suite truly is prepared and awaiting your arrival, as well as the financial projections. We can go over them together if you like."

He couldn't help but smile at the eagerness reflected on her face. "You know, I've never stayed in a palace before." When her eyes widened and her glossy lips lifted into a smile, he said, "We'll just need to pick up my luggage at the hotel and then I'd very much enjoy staying with you—erm, staying at the palace."

A visit to a royal palace, what could possibly go wrong?

Security would be heavy and the paparazzi would be non-existent. It would be a win-win.

But who would keep him from getting lost in Lady Annabelle's brown eyes?

At last, Annabelle got through on the phone to the police department.

And without playing the royal card, she was able to speak with someone in authority. They told her to stop by in the morning and they'd see about getting some of her possessions back to her. She wasn't sure what *some* consisted of, but it was a start.

"Everything okay?" Grayson asked.

She nodded. "They'd like you to stop by tomorrow and give them a statement."

He didn't say anything as he turned to stare out the window as they approached the palace gates. She chose to take his silence as a good sign, but she couldn't help but worry just a bit about the impression he'd gotten of Mirraccino. She could only hope the financial projections packet she'd put together would outweigh everything else.

Annabelle sat in the back of her sedan with Grayson as Berto ushered them past the security gates and onto the royal grounds. Annabelle had to admit that after living here for the past couple of years she'd begun to take the palace's beauty for granted.

She turned to Grayson to find him staring out the window. He seemed to be taking in the manicured lawns, the towering palm trees and the red-and-white border of flowers lining the long and winding drive.

"This place is remarkable." Grayson said, drawing her from her thoughts. "We have nothing like this where I come from."

"You're from California, right?"

He nodded, but he never took his gaze off the colorful scenery. "I couldn't even imagine what it must be like to live here."

"You get used to it." As strange as that might sound, this big place felt like home to her. "Is this your first visit to Mirraccino?"

"Yes." He still didn't look at her.

The turrets of the palace were first to come into view. They were colorful with stripes of yellow, pink, aqua and gold. Annabelle found herself looking at them through new eyes.

And then the palace in its entirety loomed. It was enormous, even compared to her family's spacious mansion back in Halencia. While her home in Halencia was all white, the palace was created in warm shades of tan and coral with some accents done in aqua. It was simple and yet stunning.

And with the afternoon sun's rays, the palace practically gleamed. When she was a little girl, she'd thought the palace was magical. She'd always wanted to be a princess, but her mother assured her that she didn't need to be a princess to be special.

Being the daughter of the Duke of Halencia, she was addressed as Lady Annabelle. It gave her recognition in high society but not much else. Her father's estate would eventually revert to her older brother, the Earl of Halencia. She used to think it was unfair, but now she appreciated having choices in life.

The car pulled to a stop outside the palace. Berto rushed to get the car door. Annabelle alighted from the car followed by Grayson.

Grayson turned to her. "Why is the South Shore so important to you that you'd go out of your way for me?"

She schooled her features, trying to hide any hint of her desperation. "The South Shore was a pet project of the crown prince. He brought me in on the project at the beginning. When his responsibilities drew him away, I promised to see that it was finished."

"So you're keeping a promise to the prince?" Grayson arched a brow.

"He's my friend as well as my cousin," she was quick to clarify.

"That's right. You did mention the king was your uncle. So this is a family favor of sorts?"

"Yes. You could put it that way." If that's what he wanted to believe, who was she to change his mind? Because in the beginning that's all it had been. Now it was her way to prove herself to her father. "But in the process, I've really come to care about the people of the South Shore and I want to see it flourish."

He smiled at her, making her stomach quiver with the sensation of butterflies. "In that case, lead the way."

She didn't normally enter through the main door, but Grayson was a special guest—pivotal to her future. It wouldn't hurt to give him the VIP treatment.

Berto swung open the enormous wooden door with the large brass handle. They stepped inside the palace and once again she consciously surveyed her surroundings from the marble floor of the grand entryway to the high ceiling with the crystal chandelier suspended in the center. As a little girl, when there was a royal ball, she'd sneak down here and dance around the table in the center of the floor. She'd pretend that she truly was a princess attending the ball. Oh, the silly things kids did.

Grayson took in the opulent room. "I couldn't even imagine what it must be like to live here."

She shrugged. "It has its protocols and a system that it's

best not to tamper with, but other than that I imagine it's like most other homes."

Grayson laughed. "I don't think so."

Just then, Alfred, the butler, came rushing into the room. "Lady Annabelle, I'm sorry. I didn't hear you arrive."

"No problem. I was just showing Mr. Landers around."

The butler gave her guest a discerning once-over. "Yes, ma'am. Is there anything I can do for you?"

"No, thanks. I was just going to show Mr. Landers to his suite of rooms so he can freshen up. Could you let the kitchen know that there will be one more for dinner?"

"Yes, ma'am. Shall I inform the king?"

Normally, she would say yes, but seeing as Grayson was a special guest who could make such a difference to her future, she said, "I'll speak to my uncle. Thank you."

Annabelle showed Grayson to the sweeping steps to the upstairs. A comfortable silence engulfed them as Grayson continued to take in his surroundings. She had to admit the palace was a lot more like a museum than a home. There were so many priceless works of art and gifts from other nations.

But more than anything, she wondered what thoughts were going through Grayson's mind. There was so much she wanted to know about him. As her uncle said often, knowledge was power. And she needed the power to push through this business deal.

She tried to tell herself that was the only reason she wanted to know more about Grayson. After all, it had nothing to do with his good looks or the way he was able to connect with her back at the piazza.

No. It was none of those things. It was purely business.

# CHAPTER FOUR

*OKAY. SO MAYBE this isn't so bad.*

*A vacation in a Mediterranean palace.*

*In fact, the palace is the perfect inspiration for a new game for Fo Shizzle.*

Grayson sat in the formal dining room at a very large table. Did they really eat here every day? He might be rich, but he'd come from a humble beginning. He didn't stand on airs and most of the time his dinner was eaten alone in front of his desktop computer.

Meeting the king had been a great honor. Thankfully Annabelle had instructed him on the proper protocol while they were in the car. He wondered how he should have greeted her considering she was the daughter of a duke. He'd hazard a guess it wasn't to argue about what to do with her purse after the theft.

And try as he might, he couldn't help but like Annabelle. Not that he would let her sunny smiles get to him. He'd learned his lesson about love, especially about loving someone in the spotlight. And Annabelle, with her constant bodyguard, was definitely someone who was used to living in the spotlight—a place where he felt uncomfortable.

"Mr. Landers, you picked an optimal time to visit Mirraccino," the king said as their dinner dishes were cleared from the table.

How exactly did one make small talk with a king? Grayson swallowed hard. "Please call me Grayson." When the man nodded, Grayson continued. "If you don't mind me asking, why is this an optimal time?"

The king turned to Annabelle. "You didn't tell him about the heritage festival?"

"It slipped my mind." Color rushed to her cheeks. "I mean, there was so much going on this afternoon. I apologize. You are most definitely welcome to stay and partake in the festivities."

"No apology is necessary." Grayson could understand that the theft had shaken her up.

"Annabelle," the king said, "you need to slow down. I think you're becoming a workaholic."

Feeling bad for Annabelle, Grayson intervened. "I'd love to hear more about this heritage festival."

The king leaned back in his chair as the wait staff supplied them with coffee and a dessert plate of finger foods. "The heritage festival is an annual event. It's held in Portolina, which is a small village within walking distance of the palace. The villagers get together—actually people from all over the nation make the pilgrimage to Portolina for the four-day celebration."

Grayson took a sip of his coffee and then gently set it back on the fine china saucer which had tiny blue flowers around the edge. He didn't think he'd ever used such delicate dishes. With his big hands, he was afraid of touching such fragile items. He had no doubt that they were antiques. And he didn't even want to imagine their value. He might be wealthy, but there was a vast difference between his wealth and that of the king.

Grayson pulled his dessert plate closer. "I actually don't know if I'll be here that long."

The king picked up a mini pecan tart. "You really don't want to miss the event. Maybe you could extend your vacation. You would be my guest, here at the palace."

"Thank you, sir. I… I'll see if I can adjust my schedule."

"Good. You'll enjoy all of the activities." The king acted as though Grayson had said yes. The king added some sugar to his coffee and stirred. "You are here to determine if the South Shore is appropriate for your business. I hope you found it as beautiful as we do."

"I did, sir." That was certainly not one of the reasons he was hesitant to put in one of his cafés. But he really didn't want to get into the details with the king. "I'd like a chance to check into a few more locations before I commit my company. And as soon as this situation with Annabelle and the police is wrapped up—"

"Police?" The king sat up straight. A distinct frown marred his face as he turned to his niece. "Why is this the first I'm hearing of an incident with the police?"

Color flooded Annabelle's face. "It's not a big deal."

"I'll be the judge of that." The king turned back to Grayson. "What exactly happened?"

"Uncle, I'll explain." Annabelle sent Grayson a warning look. "There's no need to drag Grayson into this."

"It appears he's already a part of it. He at least knows what happened, which is more than I do." The King turned back to him and gestured for Grayson to spill the details.

Grayson swallowed hard. "It really isn't that big of a deal."

"If it involves my niece, it's a very big deal."

Grayson glanced down at the small plate filled with sweets. He suddenly lost his appetite. He launched into the details of his first meeting with Annabelle. He tried to downplay the events, realizing how much the king worried about her. And Grayson knew what happened when a high-profile person didn't heed safety protocols.

When Grayson finished reciting the events as best as he could recall them, the king gestured for the phone. He announced that he was going to speak with the police.

"Uncle, I have everything under control."

The man sent her a pointed look. "It doesn't sound like it. You don't have your purse and you don't know what's going to happen to that thief." He shook his head as he accepted the phone that had already been dialed for him. "What is this world coming to when you can't even walk down the street without being accosted?"

"Uncle, it was nothing. I don't know who is worse. You, or my father?"

"We just want you to be safe." The king pressed the phone to his ear and began talking.

Grayson found the whole dynamic between these two quite interesting. They were comfortable enough with each other even though they were in opposition. Annabelle was noticeably seething under all of the fuss, but she restrained her emotions. And her uncle looked worried. These two obviously loved each other deeply.

The king didn't say much during the phone conversation. It seemed as if he was getting a blow-by-blow explanation of the chain of events. Grayson glanced at Annabelle, who looked miserable. He was sorry that he'd opened his mouth. He had thought the king would have been informed. After all, Annabelle was his niece.

"There. That's resolved," the king said as he disconnected the call. "You and Grayson are to go to the police station tomorrow morning. They will be expecting you. Grayson needs to give his statement, as do you. As for your belongings, they should be able to give you your wallet but the rest is evidence."

"I know," Annabelle said.

The king's eyes widened. "What do you mean, you know?"

"I'd already called and made arrangements to go to the station in the morning."

For a moment her uncle didn't say a word and neither did anyone else.

Finally, the king got to his feet. "Now, if you'll excuse me. I am needed elsewhere."

Grayson didn't know whether to stand or remain seated. When Annabelle stood, he followed her lead. They didn't sit back down until the king was out of sight. Once seated again, Grayson took a sip of coffee and waited until Annabelle was ready to speak.

"I'm sorry about that," she said while staring at her coffee cup.

"It's no big deal."

"But you didn't come here to witness some family drama."

"It's okay. I understand." Grayson didn't. Not really. His parents lived in rural Ohio and were so caught up in their own lives that they never gave him a second thought. He didn't know what it was like to have your every move under a microscope. He imagined that it would be quite oppressive.

"No, you don't," Annabelle said wearily. "My life…it's complicated."

If he were smart, he'd get to his feet and head for his suite. They'd done enough sharing for one day, but he couldn't turn his back on her. She obviously needed someone to lend her an ear.

He cleared his throat while searching for some words of comfort. "Everyone's life is complicated. It's how you get through it all that matters."

She arched a fine brow. "Even yours?"

He nodded. "Even mine."

"But you're rich and you run your own company. You don't have people telling you what to do and thinking they know better. You get to call all of the shots."

Grayson laughed. "If that's what you think, then you've got it all wrong. My name may be on the company letterhead, but I have a board and shareholders to answer to. A lot of those shareholders think they have all of the answers, even though they are far removed from our target clientele and know nothing about our product and its design."

"Oh. I didn't realize." She paused as though letting this information sink in. "But you only have to deal with it as far as your business is concerned. At least, they aren't involved in your personal life."

Grayson rubbed the back of his neck. Now she was heading into exceedingly uncomfortable territory. Time for a change of subjects. "Should we go to the police station together in the morning?"

"After what happened with my uncle, I didn't think you'd want anything to do with me."

"Seriously? That was nothing. Trust me, my father ruined more dinners than I could ever count. What your uncle did was just his way of showing that he cares about you and is worried about your safety."

Her eyes widened with surprise. "You really believe that? Or are you just trying to make me feel better?"

He wasn't going to feed her a line. Other people had done that to him and he knew it wasn't helpful. "How about a little of both?"

A small smile pulled at her lips. "Thanks for being honest. I really appreciate it."

"You're welcome."

She studied him for a moment, making him a little uncomfortable.

"Do I have something on my mouth?" When she shook her head, he asked, "My nose? My chin?" She continued to shake her head but a smile had started to lift her lips. "Then what is it?"

"You look tired. Is it jet lag?"

"Actually, it is. I can't sleep on planes." He always envied those people who could snooze after takeoff and wake up at landing.

Annabelle got to her feet. "Why don't we call it an evening?"

"But the financials?"

"Can wait until tomorrow." She started for the door and he followed.

It wasn't until she paused outside his room that he realized she hadn't answered his question. "About the police station—"

"Oh, yes. We can go together. Is first thing in the morning all right?"

"It's fine with me. Just ignore the jet lag."

Then hesitantly she asked, "Will it be a problem if my bodyguard accompanies us?"

"Not a problem at all." A question came to his mind although he wasn't sure if he should ask, but seeing as they were starting to open up to each other, he decided to go with it. "Are you always under protection?"

"Yes. Ever since my mother was murdered."

"Murdered?"

Annabelle averted her gaze and nodded. It was obviously still painful for her. He couldn't even imagine the pain she'd been living with.

Grayson cleared his throat. "I'm sorry."

Her gaze finally met his. "Thank you."

"Your father, he thinks the person is going to come after you? After all of this time?"

"I don't know what he thinks. The official report says that she died during a mugging. My father doesn't believe it, but he has no proof of anything to the contrary. And it isn't just me that my father has a protective detail on. It's my brother too. But Luca doesn't let it bother him. He still keeps up with his globe-trotting, partying ways. Maybe that's his way of dealing with everything. I don't know. We've grown apart over the years."

"I take it you don't believe your father's suspicions?"

"Quite honestly, today is the first time he's shared this information with me. And I don't know what to make of it."

"So your brother doesn't know?"

She shook her head. "I wouldn't even know what to tell him."

The look in her eyes told Grayson this was all very troubling for her. It was best to change the subject. "I always wanted a brother or sister, but fate had other ideas. And now looking back on things, I guess it was for the best. They were spared."

"Your home life was that bad?" She pressed her lips together as though realizing she was being nosey. "Sorry. I shouldn't have asked."

"It's okay. I started this conversation. As for my family, we saw things differently. My father grew up working with his hands, tilling the ground and planting seeds. I was never interested in that sort of life and it infuriated him. He thought I should do the same as he'd done and follow in the family tradition of farming." Grayson shifted his weight from one foot to the other. "Let's just say those discussions became heated."

"And your mother?"

"She always sided with my father. They were always so worried about what I should be doing with my life that they never stopped and asked what I wanted to do with it."

"I'm sorry. That's tough. But somehow you overcame it all and made yourself into a success."

"Trust me. It wasn't easy. And I wouldn't want to do it again."

"Do you still speak with your parents?"

"I haven't seen them in years. When I walked out, my father told me that if I left I would never be welcome again. I guess he meant it because I've never heard from them."

"That's so sad."

"The reason I told you that is because I don't want to see the same thing happen with you and your family."

"But this is different—"

"Not that much. You are struggling for your freedom and they are struggling to keep you safe. You can't both have your own way. Someone is going to win this struggle and someone is going to lose. The key is not to destroy your relationship in the process."

"You sound so wise for someone so young."

"I don't know about that. Maybe I just wish someone had given me some advice along the way instead of me always having to learn things the hard way."

"Well, don't worry. Things are about to change." She

pressed her lips together and glanced away as though she'd just realized she'd said too much.

"Ah, you have a plan."

"It's nothing. I should be going. I've forgotten to give the king a message from my father." And with that she rushed off down the hallway.

Grayson watched her go. He couldn't help but wonder about this plan of hers and if it was going to get her into trouble. It was obvious that she wasn't ready to share the details with him. But that didn't keep him from worrying about this *plan*. His mind told him it was absolutely none of his business, but his gut told him that she might get herself into trouble trying to prove a point.

And he might have just met her, but he already realized she was stubborn. Stubborn enough not to ask for help? But what was he supposed to do about any of it?

# CHAPTER FIVE

ALONE AT LAST.

The next morning, Annabelle hurried to her suite of rooms as soon as she'd returned from the police station. Grayson had stayed behind in Bellacitta to meet with a business associate. They'd agreed to meet up later to go over the financial projections for the South Shore Project.

She'd been relieved to have a little time to herself. At last, she'd recovered her mother's journal, and she had some privacy to look at it. And if she'd had any qualms about invading her mother's privacy, the police had remedied them. They had her open the journal and read just a bit to herself to verify it belonged to her. She didn't correct their assumption that it was her journal.

Alone in her room, Annabelle sat down at her desk in front of the window that overlooked the blue waters of the Mediterranean. And though usually she took solace in the majestic view, today her thoughts were elsewhere.

As the hours ticked by, she turned page after page. There were old snapshots stuffed between the pages. Some of her mother and father. Some of Annabelle and her brother. There was so much history crammed between the leather covers that it floored her.

And thankfully, there was nothing scandalous or cringeworthy within the pages. Not even anything blushworthy lurked in the passages, which was a gigantic relief to Annabelle. It was almost as if her mother had known that one day one of her children would be reading it.

Instead, the journal read more like the highlights of a royal's life. There were mentions of birthday celebrations, picnics, holidays and countless other events that Annabelle had either been too young to remember or hadn't bothered to really notice. But her mother had remembered and made note of colorful details that brought the passages to life. And it had been a nice life, not perfect, but the bad times were smoothed over and the good times highlighted. That's how she remembered her mother—always trying to fix things and make people smile.

Annabelle didn't even notice lunchtime coming or going. At some point, she moved from the desk chair to the comfort of her big canopied bed with its array of silken pillows. She couldn't remember the last time she'd curled up in bed with a book in the middle of the day. It felt so decadent. She continued devouring word after word, feeling closer to her mother than she'd felt in a very long time.

*Knock. Knock.*

Annabelle's gaze jerked to the door, expecting one of the household staff to enter with fresh flowers or clean linens. A frown pulled at her lips. She really didn't want to be disturbed. She still had a lot of pages to read.

*Knock. Knock.*

"Annabelle? Is everything okay?"

It was Grayson. And something told her he wasn't going to leave until they spoke. With a sigh, she closed the journal and set it off to the side of the bed. Hating to leave her comfy spot, she grudgingly got to her feet.

She moved to the door and then paused to run a hand over her hair. Deciding that it was good enough, she reached for the doorknob.

"Hi." She couldn't help but stare at his handsome face and piercing blue eyes. Now that he'd shaved, his looks were a perfect ten.

He frowned. "Why do you keep looking at me that way?"

"What way?" She averted her gaze. She was going to have to be more covert with her admiration in the future.

He sighed. "Never mind."

She stepped back, allowing him to enter the room. "Come in."

He stepped into her spacious suite and glanced around. She followed his gaze around the room, taking in the settee, the armchairs, a table with a bouquet of flowers and her desk. She noticed how his gaze lingered on the king-size bed.

At last, his gaze met hers. "You missed lunch?"

"Did we have plans?" She didn't recall any. In fact, Grayson had said he planned to remain in the city for most of the day.

"No, we didn't. But I wrapped up my meeting early and returned to the palace. I thought I would see you at lunch and when you didn't show up, I… I just wanted to make sure everything was all right."

"Oh, yes, everything is fine. I was reading." She gestured toward the now rumpled bed.

Grayson's gaze followed her hand gesture. "It looks like I must have startled you."

"What?"

He moved toward the bed where he knelt down and picked up the journal from the floor. But that wasn't the only thing on the floor. The precious pictures were scattered about.

"Oh, no." She rushed over.

"No worries. Nothing's ruined."

"You don't have to pick that up," Annabelle said, kneeling down next to him. "I can get it."

"I don't mind." He picked up a photograph and glanced at it. "Is this you as a child?"

She looked at the photo and a rush of memories came back to her. "Yes. That's me and my brother, Luca."

"You were a cute kid."

"Thanks. I think." Her stomach quivered as Grayson's gaze lingered longer than necessary. She swallowed hard. "I can't believe my mother kept all of those pictures stuffed in her journal."

"Ah…so that's your mother's. It explains why you're so protective of it. I thought you were going to jump across that desk at the police station when the officer said he couldn't release it to you."

Heat rushed up Annabelle's neck and settled in her cheeks

as she realized how that incident must have looked to others. But she'd been desperate to hang on to this link to her mother. And by reading the pages, she already felt as though she knew her mother so much better.

"Thanks for stepping up and reasoning with the officer," Annabelle said. "I just couldn't get him to understand my urgency."

"You're welcome."

"You know, you're not such a bad guy to have around."

His voice grew deep and gentle. "Is that your way of saying you'd like me to stay for the heritage festival?"

"Maybe." Did her voice sound as breathless to him as it did to her?

His head lifted and their gazes met. There was something different about the way he looked at her. And then it struck her with the force of an electrical surge—there was desire reflected in his gaze. He wanted her.

It was like a switch had been turned on and she was fully aware of the attraction arcing between them. Annabelle had never felt anything so vital and stirring with anyone else in her life. Maybe she'd led a more sheltered life than she'd ever imagined. Sure there had been other men, but those relationships had never had this sort of spark and soon they fizzled out.

With them kneeling down on the floor side by side, their faces were only mere inches apart. Did he have any idea what his close proximity did to her heart rate, not to mention her common sense?

His gaze dipped to her mouth and the breath hitched in her throat. Was he going to kiss her? And was it wrong that she wanted him to?

Not waiting for him to make up his mind, she leaned forward, pressing her lips to his. If this was too bold, she didn't care. She'd been cautious all of her life, while her brother had been reckless. If she wanted things to change, then *she* had to change them, by taking more chances.

His lips were smooth and warm. Yet, he was hesitant. His mouth didn't move against hers. Oh, no! Had she read everything wrong?

Her problem was her lack of experience. She hadn't gotten out enough. She didn't know how to read men. Here she'd been thinking that he desired her and the thought had probably never crossed his mind. She was such a fool.

She started to pull back when his hand reached up, cupping her cheek. Her heart jumped into her throat. Then again, maybe she had been right. As he deepened the kiss, her heart thump-thumped. He did want her. And she most definitely wanted him.

Her hands slid up over his muscled shoulders and wrapped around the back of his neck. All the while, his thumb stroked her cheek, sending the most delicious sensations to her very core, heating it up and melting it down.

She didn't know where this was headed and she didn't care. The only thing that mattered was the here and now. And the here and now was quite delicious. Quite addictive—

Footsteps echoed in the hallway. Annabelle recalled leaving the door wide open.

She yanked back. Grayson let her go. It was as though they both realized that what was happening here wasn't practical. They came from different worlds and worse yet, they were involved in a business deal. She couldn't lose her focus.

Annabelle averted her gaze as she ran a shaky hand over her now tender lips. How could she face him again after she'd initiated that kiss—that soul-stirring kiss?

She glanced down at the mess still on the floor. Focus on anything but how good that kiss had been. Annabelle began picking up the papers when there was a knock at the door. She glanced up. "Come in."

A member of her uncle's staff appeared, holding a tray of food. "Excuse me, ma'am. The king asked that this tray be brought to you since you missed lunch."

"Oh. Thank you." She forced a smile. "You can leave it on the desk."

"Yes, ma'am." The young woman deposited the heavily laden tray and then turned for the door.

The door snicked shut as Annabelle turned back to Grayson. He was picking up the last of the photos and papers. They were now sorted into two piles. One of snapshots and one of scraps of papers.

"I think I got it all," Grayson said but his gaze never quite met hers.

So he regretted what just happened between them. She couldn't blame him. She'd let the attraction she'd felt since she first met him get the better of her. Now, she had to somehow repair the damage if she had any hope of getting him to bring his state-of-the-art gaming café to Mirraccino. And it wasn't just the café Grayson would bring to the area, but it would also be the headquarters for the Mediterranean arm of his business—an employment opportunity that would help Mirraccino.

"I'm sorry." They both said in unison.

The combined apology broke the tension. They both smiled—genuine smiles. Maybe this situation wasn't beyond repair after all. A girl could hope, couldn't she?

"I shouldn't have kissed you," Annabelle confessed.

"You didn't do it alone."

"But still, I initiated it. This is all on me."

He arched a brow. "I don't think so. I could have stopped you…if I'd wanted to."

Had she heard him correctly? Or was she just hearing what she wished to? "Are…are you saying you didn't want it to stop?"

His gaze searched hers. "If we're to continue to do business together that probably shouldn't happen again."

"Agreed." She averted her gaze. "And I think you're going to be impressed with the incentives we're willing to offer you to bring your business to Mirraccino."

"I'm looking forward to seeing the package."

As Annabelle continued to gaze down at the Oriental rug covering the wood floor, she noticed a cream-colored slip of paper sticking out from the edge of the bed. It must have come from the journal. She bent over and picked it up.

"Sorry," Grayson said. "I must have missed that one."

"It was most of the way under the bed. It's no wonder you missed it."

Wanting something to distract her from the jumble of emotions over Grayson's pending departure, she unfolded the slip of paper. Inside was a message. A very strange message.

"What's the matter?" Grayson asked.

"It's this note. It seems odd. Why would my mother have a note addressed to Cosmo? I don't even know any Cosmo."

"Do you mind if I take a look?"

There certainly wasn't anything personal in the note so she handed it over. It honestly didn't mean anything to her. Why in the world had her mother kept it? And why would she have placed it with her most sacred papers?

Grayson read the note aloud:

*Cosmo, tea is my Gold. I drink it first in the morning and at four in the afternoon.*

*for you. I hope you enjOy. Am hopiNg The Queen Is weLL. Visit heR oftEn? Nate is Well. yOu muSt see Sara. She's growN very much. Everything is As you requesTed. Don't terry. Get goin noW. WishIng you all of tHe best.*

"What do you make of it?" Annabelle asked.

Grayson stood up and turned the paper over as though searching for more clues as to why her mother had kept it. "You're sure it doesn't strike any chords in your memory?"

"None at all. In fact, can I see it again?" Annabelle examined the handwriting. "That's not even my mother's handwriting."

"That's odd. You're sure?"

"Positive." She moved to the bed and retrieved her mother's journal and flipped it open to a random page. "See. Very different handwriting."

"I have to agree with you. Perhaps it wasn't in the journal. Maybe someone who stayed here before you dropped it."

"Impossible. I've been in this room for a couple of years and trust me when I say they clean the palace from top to bottom without missing a thing. No, this had to have come from the journal. But my question is why did my mother keep such a cryptic note?"

Grayson backed away. "I can't help you with that."

She folded the note and slipped it back in the journal. It was just one more mystery where her mother was concerned. Annabelle would try to figure it out, but later. Right now, she had to convince Grayson that Mirraccino was a good fit for Fo Shizzle.

"We should go over those financial projections now." She glanced at him, hoping he'd be agreeable. "Unless you have other plans."

He shook his head. "I'm all yours."

His words set her stomach aquiver with nervous energy. She knew he'd meant nothing intimate by the words, but it didn't stop her mind from wondering *what if*?

A couple of hours later, Annabelle stared across the antique mahogany table in the library at Grayson. She'd successfully answered all of his questions about the financial projections and the future of the South Shore.

He was still reading over the material. There was a lot of it. She'd worked hard to present a thorough package. But she had one other idea up her sleeve.

Grayson straightened the papers and slid them back in the folder. "You've certainly given me a lot to think about.

Between the proposed national advertising campaign and the tax reduction, I'm impressed."

"Good." But he still didn't seem thoroughly convinced and that worried her.

He picked up the folder. "I appreciate your thoroughness."

She refused to stop while she was on a roll. If she could bring this deal about, the South Shore would have an amazing facility for seniors in need of assistance. It would have decent-priced housing for young families. And this café would give young people a reason to hang out in the South Shore without causing a ruckus. And from the reviews she'd read about the cafés in other cities, it would provide a popular tourist destination.

"Why not hang out with me today?" she asked in her best cajoling voice. When his gaze narrowed in on her, she smiled.

"I have some reports to review and emails to answer."

"Can't they wait just a little bit?" She had to think fast here. "After all, it's a beautiful day in Mirraccino. And this is your first and perhaps your last trip here. And you haven't seen that much of the island."

"I've seen enough—"

"To know that it's beautiful. But I haven't yet shown you other parts of it. Mirraccino is a complex nation. It has a rich history, but it is also a thriving community with a technology base that tops the region. And there are lots of young people—young people who would like the opportunity to remain here in Mirraccino when they complete their education."

Grayson rubbed a hand over his clean-shaven jaw. "I don't know."

The way his eyes twinkled told her he was playing with her. She asked, "Are you going to make me beg?"

Surprise and interest lit up his handsome face. "I—think—"

"You'll be a gentleman and accept my invitation without making me go to such great extremes."

He smiled and shook his head. "Boy, you know how to take the fun out of things."

"I thought fun was what we just had before we were interrupted." She was blatantly flirting with him, something she rarely did, but there was something about him—something that brought out the impish side of her.

"Is that what we were doing?"

He wanted her. It was written all over his face and as much as she'd like to fall into his arms, they'd both agreed it wasn't a good idea. There was work to be done. And she wasn't about to confuse her priorities again.

Before lunch, she'd had the forethought to set up some appointments at the university with the faculty and some of the computer science students. She had a feeling if he were to see this island nation for all of its benefits, he'd change his mind about expanding his business here. At least she hoped…

And what was in it for her? Besides helping her community once their business was concluded, she wouldn't mind another of those mind-blowing kisses. Not that she was anxious for anything serious. She didn't have time for a relationship. But if he were to set up a business in Mirraccino, she might be able to make time for a little fun. As it was, all work and no play made for a dull Annabelle. That's what her brother always used to tell her. Maybe he wasn't all wrong.

Grayson quietly studied her for a moment. "Okay. You've won me over. Let's go."

Yay! This plan would work. She knew what he wanted and now she could show him that Mirraccino could provide it. "Just give me a second to freshen up."

"Do you mind if I take another look at that cryptic note?"

His question surprised her, but she didn't see how it would hurt. While Grayson read over the note, Annabelle touched up her makeup and swept her hair up into a ponytail. She knew that it was fine just the way it was, but she had an impulse to look her best. Not that she was trying to impress anyone of course…

# CHAPTER SIX

"WELL?"

Grayson couldn't help but smile at Annabelle's enthusiasm. Her eyes twinkled when she was excited and she couldn't stand still. She stared at him with rapt attention.

"It'd been a long time since someone had looked at him like he was at the center of their world. He'd forgotten how good it felt for someone to care about his opinion. Was it wrong that he didn't want it to end?

"Grayson, please, say something."

"I really enjoyed today. Thank you."

Her smile broadened and puffed up her cheeks. She was adorable. And a business associate—nothing more. It was for the best. "How much?"

"How much what?"

"How much did you enjoy today?" She clasped her hands together. "Enough to seriously consider Mirraccino for your new headquarters?"

He couldn't help but laugh at her eagerness. "How could I say no to that pleading look?"

"You mean it?"

He nodded. What he didn't tell her was that he'd made up his mind after reviewing the financial package. "I sent the figures to my team to consider."

"I knew you'd like it here."

Grayson began walking along the sidewalk of the great Mirraccino Royal University with Annabelle by his side. He didn't say things that he didn't mean. And he wasn't truly impressed that often, but today he had been.

He was glad that he'd relented and decided to give Annabelle…erm… Mirraccino another try. Annabelle had arranged for a most impressive tour of the up-to-date campus. He'd talked with the professors in the computer science department. And he'd even agreed to give a spontaneous guest lecture.

To his relief, the lecture had gone well and the students had been quite receptive to his talk on his company's cloud technology and how they'd harnessed it to make their café games relevant and constantly morphing into something bigger and better.

"Really? You were honestly impressed?" Annabelle came to a stop in front of him. Hope reflected in her eyes.

"Yes, I meant it. Why do you sound so surprised?"

"I don't know. I'm not. It's just—"

"You weren't so sure about today, were you?"

She shrugged. "Not really. I wanted to believe you'd see the full potential that Mirraccino could offer you—offer your company, but yesterday you seemed to have made your mind up about everything."

He couldn't let her stop there. "And what have I decided about you?"

Annabelle glanced away. "That I'm spoiled and over-protected."

"That isn't what I think. That is what *you* think, but it shouldn't be. I think you work hard for what you want. Setting up everything today couldn't have been easy, especially when it was done at the last minute."

Her gaze met his. "I called in every favor I had here at the school. But to be honest, when I spoke to the head of the computer science department and told him who I wanted to bring for a visit, he was more than willing to help. You have quite an amazing reputation in your field."

"I don't know about that, but I appreciate your kind words."

When she gazed deep into his eyes, like she was doing now, it was so hard to remember that they were supposed to be doing business together and not picking up that kiss where they'd left off. His gaze latched on to her tempting mouth. What would she say? His gaze moved back to her eyes. Was that desire he spied glinting within them?

He didn't know how long they stood there, staring into each other's eyes. In that moment, there was nowhere else he needed to be—nowhere else he wanted to be. There was a special quality about Annabelle that sparked life back into him. She filled in all the cracks in his heart and made him want to face whatever life threw at him.

A motion out of the corner of his eye reminded him they weren't alone. Today there was a female bodyguard escorting them. She was not the friendly sort—always on guard. He recalled Annabelle calling the woman Marta.

Having a bodyguard watch over them dampened his lusty thoughts. He didn't like an audience and he preferred not to end up in one of those reports sent off to the Duke of Halencia. But that didn't mean their outing should end just yet.

"How about we go to dinner? I'd enjoy trying one of the local restaurants."

Surprise lit up Annabelle's eyes, but in a blink her enthusiasm dimmed. "Um, sure."

"What's the matter?"

"Why does anything need to be the matter?"

"Because it was written all over your face and it was in your tone."

"It's nothing. You're just imagining things." She glanced away and pulled out her phone. "I know the perfect spot. I'll just call ahead and let them know we're on our way."

He didn't believe her protests. There was something weighing on her mind, but he didn't push the subject. If she wanted to confide in him, she would have to do it of her own accord. Once she made the call, they started across the campus toward the parking lot.

After touring this university with its state-of-the-art facilities and cutting-edge technology, he realized there was a lot more to this island nation than its obvious beauty and rich history. The university was surprisingly large, drawing students from all over Europe and there were even some Americans in the mix.

There was a wealth of knowledge here. Some of the students had heard of his cafés and had pleaded with him to build one in Mirraccino. And there were other students who were anxious to work for him.

It would mean his company wouldn't have to go outside Mirraccino every time they needed to hire personnel for the technological portion of the business. And with some combined initiatives with the university, word about the café would reach the targeted demographic.

"What has you so quiet?" Annabelle asked, interrupting his thoughts.

"I was just going over the events of the day."

"I'm glad you enjoyed your visit. You know, I graduated from this university with a business degree. I never knew what I'd do with it, but the South Shore Project has been good for me. I like getting up in the morning and having a purpose. Too bad the project is winding down."

"Then why don't you find another job?"

She shrugged. "It's hard to have a normal job when you have someone shadowing your every move."

"Maybe your circumstances will change and you'll be able to do as you please."

Annabelle lowered her voice. "That's my plan."

Again the warning bells went off in his mind. He couldn't resist asking, "What plan?"

She glanced over her shoulder as though making certain her bodyguard wasn't within earshot. "I plan to show my father that I'm fully capable of caring for myself and that he no longer has to watch over me. And when you sign on with the South Shore, he'll have to acknowledge that fact."

"And if your father doesn't agree? Then what?"

"Then I'm leaving. I've always wanted to travel. Maybe I'll go to London, Paris," she paused and stared at him, "or perhaps I'll go to California."

He didn't believe she'd actually do it. "Could you really walk away from your father and uncle?"

"Why not?" she said with bravado. "It'll make their lives easier. After all, you left your family. Why shouldn't I?"

"My circumstances were different." There was no comparison between their situations. He had to make her understand. "Your father and uncle love you very much. That's why they worry so much. I never had anyone worry about me."

"I'm sorry. I... I shouldn't have said anything."

He couldn't leave off there. He had to stop her from making a big mistake. "When I left, my parents didn't try to stop me. When I rejected their way of life, I became dead to them. But if you leave here, your father and uncle will never stop looking for you."

"So they can stick their security detail on me—"

"No, because they love you and your absence would make them sad. Please tell me you understand what a gift you have here."

"I... I do." She twisted her purse strap around her fingers. "But somewhere along the way that love started to smother me. My father doesn't accept that my mother has been dead for eleven years and if there were any lingering dangers, something would have happened by now."

He sure hoped she was right. Still, there was an uneasy feeling in his gut. But then again he probably wasn't the best judge of danger. His thoughts strayed back to his last girlfriend. A harmless day of fun had turned deadly. And he'd missed all of the signs. So maybe he was just being overly sensitive now.

They rounded the corner of the administration office when a group of reporters rushed them. Grayson's whole body tensed. He'd known this moment would come sooner or later. He'd been hoping for later.

Annabelle's bodyguard rushed in front of them, waving off the paparazzi.

Members of the press started yelling out questions. "Lady Annabelle, is it true? Do you have a new love interest?"

"Does the king approve?"

"How long have you two been involved?"

The questions kept coming one after the other in rapid succession. Thanks to social media, they couldn't even visit the university without the whole world knowing.

He glanced over at Annabelle and was surprised to find her keeping it all together. But then again as a member of the royal family, she was probably used to these occurrences. Now he better understood her father's reluctance to lift the security detail.

Campus security quickly responded. Grayson guessed that the bodyguard had alerted them. With help, they made it to their car. Marta drove as he sat with Annabelle in the backseat. But when they took off out of the parking lot, they were followed.

As their speed increased so did Grayson's anxiety. His fingers bit into the door handle. His body tensed as memories washed over him. Usually he only visited this nightmare when it was late and he was alone. But now it was happening right before his wide-open eyes.

His past and present collided. He recalled the moments leading up to the hideous chain of events. It was like a horror movie playing in his mind and he was helpless to stop it.

"Grayson, are you okay?" Annabelle asked.

He nodded, not trusting his voice at that moment.

"No, you're not." She pressed a hand to his cheek. "You feel okay, but you're pale as a ghost."

"I'm fine," he ground out.

Just then there was a bang. He jumped, nearly hitting his head on the roof. In the next instant, he was leaning over to Annabelle and pulling her as close as possible with seat belt restraints still on.

"Grayson, let me up." She pushed on his chest.

He hesitated. Not hearing any further gunfire, he moved, allowing Annabelle to sit fully upright.

"What was that?" she asked, uneasiness filling her voice.

Grayson didn't dare say what he thought it was. He didn't

want to scare her any more than necessary. Sadly, he knew what a gunshot sounded like from inside a vehicle.

"A vehicle backfired," Marta said from the driver's seat.

Annabelle's hand slipped in his and squeezed.

*A backfire?* That knowledge should make him feel better and put him at ease, but it didn't. There were still paparazzi in cars and motorcycles swarming all around them. Their chaotic and unwanted caravan was flying down the highway now.

"Marta, take us back to the palace," Annabelle ordered.

The bodyguard never took her gaze off the road. "Understood. I'll let the palace know we're coming in hot."

Annabelle leaned her head against Grayson's shoulder. "I'm so sorry. Don't worry. We'll be at the palace soon."

"I'm fine." Why did he keep saying that? He was anything but fine. It was just that he wasn't ready to open up about his past. He didn't want to see the disappointment in Annabelle's eyes when she knew that he wasn't such a great guy after all.

"No, you're not. If it's the paparazzi, I'm sorry. I guess I didn't think about them getting wind of us being at the university. But I'm sure some of the students got excited and were posting pictures and messages about the visit on their social media accounts."

They remained hand in hand the rest of the way back to the palace where there was a heavy contingent of armed guards. There was no way any reporter was going to get past the gates.

As the gates swung closed behind them and their speed drastically reduced, Grayson could at last take a full breath. He felt foolish for letting the incident affect him so greatly. It'd been a while since he'd had a panic attack. There'd been a period after the accident when he'd stopped leaving his Malibu beach house for this very reason.

It'd been more than a year since the accident. He'd thought that he would have been past it by now. But the idea of the same thing happening to Annabelle shook him to the core.

When the vehicle pulled to a stop in front of the palace, he immediately jumped out. He'd made an utter fool of himself. How could he not tell the difference between a gunshot and a car backfiring? What was the matter with him?

He needed some fresh air and a chance to pull himself together before he faced Annabelle's inevitable questions. He couldn't blame her for wondering what was going on with him, but he didn't know what to tell her. He'd never discussed that very painful episode with anyone but a counselor. And he wasn't going to start now.

He took off in the direction of the beach. He knew from talking to Annabelle that it was private. He would be safe from prying eyes there.

"Grayson, wait," Annabelle called out.

He kept moving.

"Let him go," Marta said.

"But he…" Annabelle's voice faded into the breeze.

The more he walked, the calmer he got. And his jumbled thoughts smoothed out. Needing a diversion, he pondered the strange note that Annabelle had found among her mother's things. There was something about the message that continued to nag at him.

He pulled his phone from his pocket. On it was an image of the note. He'd taken the photo because his gut was telling him there was something about it that wasn't quite right. But what was it?

He read the note once, then twice and a third time. Was it the misspelled words that bothered him? Or perhaps the mix of lowercase and uppercase letters? Or was it the fact the message just didn't say much of anything?

Who in the world would write such a cryptic note?

And why would Annabelle's mother place it in her journal?

There was more going on here than they knew. But what was it?

## CHAPTER SEVEN

THIS WAS HER FAULT.

Annabelle felt horrible about the paparazzi's appearance at the university and the ensuing chase. Though Grayson was a multimillionaire and famous, he didn't appear used to the hounding press.

She hadn't thought of that aspect when she'd made arrangements to take him there. She'd been so anxious to show him how well his business would fit in here that she hadn't taken time to plan a rear exit from the campus to avoid the press.

If it hadn't been for Grayson's adverse reaction, she might have turned the situation around and given a public statement about the pending contract with the Fo Shizzle Café chain. But on second thought, she would have been rushing things. There was no verbal or paper contract…yet.

And after today, there might not be one. Unless she could turn things around. First, she needed to get the press off their trail. And then she needed to smooth things over with Grayson.

She called the palace's press secretary and set up a brief statement to be given just outside the palace gates where the paparazzi were lying in wait. She knew from past experience that they wouldn't go away until they got a story—whether it be the truth or a bit of fiction that they conjured up.

And next, she called the kitchen and requested a candlelit dinner to be served on the patio overlooking the sea. She didn't know if Grayson would be in any mood to join her, but she wanted to make the effort since their prior dinner plans had been ruined.

With all of the arrangements made, she put on a pair of dark jeans, a white blouse and a navy blazer. She piled her hair atop her head. She wore a modest amount of makeup and chose gold hoop earrings and a necklace to match. Simple and presentable.

Her stomach churned with nerves. She never liked talking with the press. Some would say that she should be used to it, being part of a royal family. But she was the same as everyone else and longed for a private life.

Knowing she had to do this if she wanted the press to lay off, she made her way down the grand staircase. In her mind, she went over and over what she would say to the reporters. It was her intention to give a statement and not accept questions because quite honestly, she wouldn't know how to answer any questions about her relationship with Grayson. It was very complicated to say the least.

This time not only was her bodyguard present, but a bunch of palace security met her in the grand foyer of the palace. And then she spied her uncle talking with the palace guards. She inwardly groaned.

Knowing there was no way to avoid the king, she walked directly toward him. "Hello, Uncle."

"Don't hello me. What's going on?" His voice grew husky with concern. "I heard there was a high-speed pursuit with the paparazzi today. You know that's dangerous. You should have used the protocols that we have in place if you are going to do something high profile."

"But it wasn't high profile. It was a visit to the university."

"The university?"

Annabelle explained what had led her and Grayson to the school. And she admitted to the fact that she hadn't anticipated the students making a big deal of the visit via social media. It was her slipup and no one else's.

The king nodded in understanding. "You have to be careful. Your life is not like other peoples'. You must take precautions."

"You know, sometimes when you say that you sound just like my father."

"Well, that's because your father is right."

"Right or wrong, I have to go talk to the press."

"You could let the press secretary handle it. That's what we pay her to do."

Annabelle shook her head. "I started all of this and if there is to be any peace for the remainder of Grayson's stay, I must fix it."

Her uncle sighed. "You always were a stubborn girl. So much like your mother. Do what you must, but a full security team will accompany you."

She knew better than to argue with the king. There was only so much he was willing to concede and she knew she'd hit that limit. She was fine with the escort as long as they hung back.

She gave her uncle a hug. "I'm sorry I worried you. That was never my intention."

"I know. Though some may think otherwise, it's not always an easy life. There are limitations to what we can or should do."

"I understand. I will be more cautious."

And with her uncle's blessing she set off down the drive to address the media. Though her insides shivered with nervous energy, she kept moving. She would fix this and then she would speak with Grayson.

The household knew to alert her when he returned from his walk. So far she hadn't heard a word. Surely he'd be back soon.

# CHAPTER EIGHT

IT WAS A CIPHER.

Grayson picked up his pace as he retraced his footsteps back to the palace. The calming sound of the water and the gentle breeze had soothed his agitation as he'd hoped it would.

And now he had to find Annabelle. He had to tell her what he'd uncovered. Something told him that she'd be just as intrigued as he was.

As the last lingering rays of the sun danced over the sea, Grayson took the steps trailing up the side of the cliff two at a time. He knew she'd also want an explanation for his peculiar reaction in the car.

And as much as part of him wanted to avoid her and those uncomfortable questions, there was another part of him that was excited to tell her what he'd figured out. And yet, the conclusions he'd arrived at only prompted more questions. Hopefully Annabelle would have the necessary answers. He just had to find her.

When he reached the patio area overlooking the beach, he stopped. There before him was a beautiful dinner table set with fine linens and china. It was lit with candles, giving it a warm and romantic atmosphere.

He inwardly groaned, realizing that he'd stumbled into someone's special plans. Someone was going to have a nice evening—a very nice evening. He couldn't even remember the last time he'd wined and dined someone.

Thankfully no one appeared to be about. He made a beeline for the door, hoping to get away without being noticed.

"Mr. Landers," the gravelly male voice called out.

He stopped in his tracks, feeling as though he were back in elementary school. The principal had more than once caught him pulling pranks on his classmates. Sometimes he'd done it just to make them smile, but more times than not it was because he was bored senseless. No one had recognized that he had excelled far beyond his class. Not his teachers and not his parents. As long as he maintained good grades, no adult paid him much attention.

Grayson turned to find out what he'd done this time. "Yes."

The butler stood there. His face was void of emotion. Grayson couldn't help but wonder how many years it'd taken the man to perfect that serious look. Grayson didn't think he could mask his emotions all day, every day. It definitely took skills that he didn't possess.

"Lady Annabelle requested that you wait here for her. She will be here momentarily."

"You mean the table, it's for us?"

The man nodded and then withdrew back behind the palace walls.

Grayson wasn't sure what to make of this scene. He moved to the wall at the edge of the patio. He stared off at the peaceful water while a gentle breeze rushed over his skin. This whole thing felt like a dream, but it wasn't.

He turned back to the table. It was most definitely real. What exactly did Annabelle have in mind for this evening? It was obvious he hadn't scared her off with that meltdown in the car. But how was that possible? Was she used to people freaking out when the paparazzi were in hot pursuit?

"Grayson, there you are," Annabelle crossed the patio to where he stood next to the wall. "Listen, I'm so sorry about earlier. But no worries, I took care of it."

"You took care of it?" He sent her a puzzled look.

"The press. I gave them a statement. I'm sorry that I had to out us."

Out them? His gaze moved from her to the candlelit table with the rosebud and the stemware. What exactly did she want to happen this evening?

He cleared his throat. "You told them about us?" His voice dropped an octave. "What exactly did you tell them?"

Her eyes widened. "Not that."

He breathed a little easier. Sure, the kiss wasn't anything scandalous. Far from it. But he didn't need any more sparks fanning the flames with the media. He had enough rumors following him about and not only did they conjure up horrific memories for him, but they also put his board on edge as it reflected poorly on the leadership of the company.

"Then I don't understand," Grayson said. "Why did you talk to them?"

"So they would leave us alone. I told them we are in negotiations over the South Shore property."

"Oh." That was so much better than anything that had crossed his mind.

"I know that it was presumptive, so I made it clear that no deal has been reached and that we are still in the negotiating stage."

He nodded. "I understand. Did they go away?"

"Actually, they did. They seemed disappointed that it was all about business. Can you believe that? This is a huge deal for Mirraccino. I thought they'd be excited and asking for an exclusive, but nothing."

Grayson's mouth drew upward at the corners. "I think they were hoping for some romance and the promise of a royal wedding."

She shook her head. "That's not happening. Besides, my cousin just got married a couple of years ago. They don't need another wedding already. I have other things on my mind right now."

"You mean dealing with your father?"

She nodded. "But I don't want to talk about that now. I'm hungry."

He thought of what he'd discovered about the note, but he decided it could wait for a bit. Some food did sound good. He glanced over at the candlelit table and wondered if Annabelle was hungry for food…or was she hoping for more kisses?

* * *

Dinner was amazing.

Annabelle hated to see the evening end. This was the most enjoyment she'd had in a long time. Grayson had opened up more about his childhood in Ohio. She wasn't surprised to find out that his IQ was genius level and that he'd grown bored of school. Her heart had gone out to him when she learned that his parents had done nothing to nurture his special gift.

With the dinner dishes cleared, every bit of crème brûlée devoured and the hour growing late, they headed inside. She noticed Grayson had grown quiet. Perhaps he was just tired. They had had a long day. Or perhaps he was still rattled by the paparazzi and the chase back to the palace.

Annabelle had made a point of avoiding the topic during dinner, not wanting to ruin the meal. But perhaps it would be best to clear the air.

"Grayson, about earlier at the university, I'm sorry. I hadn't considered that the press would show up. I know I should have, but I was distracted."

"It's not your fault. I shouldn't have let it bother me."

It did a whole lot more than bother him. "Do you want to talk about it?"

Grayson's gaze didn't quite meet hers. He shook his head.

"I understand." She didn't. Not really. "Have you decided what you'll do about tomorrow?"

This time he did look directly at her with puzzlement reflected in his eyes. "What about tomorrow?"

"You're supposed to leave. But I was hoping after the visit to the university that I'd convince you to stay and give the South Shore and Mirraccino more consideration. Of course, I hadn't counted on the press messing up everything."

He reached out to her, but his hand stopped midway. He lowered his hand back to his side. "They didn't ruin anything. It was no big deal."

She didn't believe him, but she wasn't going to push the

matter. "Does this mean you'll accept my uncle's invitation to stay for the heritage festival?"

A small smile pulled at his lips. "How could I turn down an invitation from a king?"

"He will be pleased." She started to turn for the door to her suite, wishing he were staying for her instead. "You should get some rest."

"Annabelle, wait. I'm staying for more than just that."

She turned back to him, hesitant to get her hopes up. "What reason would that be?"

"Do you have to ask?"

"I do."

"I'm staying because of you."

Though she tried to subdue her response, it was impossible. Her heart fluttered in her chest and a smile pulled at her lips. "You're staying for me?"

He nodded. "I think you did a terrific job today swaying my decision on the viability of establishing my Mediterranean headquarters here. The projections and incentives were impressive and well thought out. And the programs at the university were current and cutting-edge."

"Thank you for the compliment. I hope it all works out." And that he spends a lot more time in Mirraccino. "It's getting late. We should call it a night." Before she did something she might regret—like kiss him again.

"Oh, okay. It's just I had something I wanted to talk to you about."

"Do you mind if it waits? I need to be up early tomorrow. I have a couple of things I need to do for my uncle first thing."

"Um, sure. I'll see you in the morning." For a moment, he didn't move. It seemed as if he was considering whether he should kiss her or just walk away.

Was it wrong that she willed him to kiss her again? Her gaze sought out his lips, his very tempting lips. She'd never been kissed quite like she had by him. It had rocked her world right off its axis. What would one more kiss hurt?

Her heart pounded harder, faster. Her gaze focused on his. Was it her imagination or were their bodies being drawn toward each other? If she were just to sway forward a little, their lips would meet and ecstasy would ensue.

Grayson backed away. "I'll see you in the morning."

Maybe she shouldn't have rushed him off. Maybe she should have said that she'd talk to him as long as he wanted. But he was already walking away. She sighed. Tomorrow was another day. Hopefully it would go smoother than this one.

"Good night."

She turned to her suite. Something told her that sleep was going to be elusive that night.

# CHAPTER NINE

HAD HE BEEN imagining things last night?

Grayson assured himself it had been a bunch of wishful thinking on his part. It was the best explanation he could come up with for that tension just before he'd walked away from Annabelle. After all, she was royalty and he was just a techno geek from Ohio. Definitely worlds apart.

Grayson ate his breakfast alone. So far there'd been no sightings of the king or Annabelle. Before coming to breakfast, Grayson had checked her room, but she hadn't been there. She must have urgent things to do. Grayson couldn't even imagine what it must be like having your uncle be the king. The responsibilities must be enormous.

But he had to gain Annabelle's attention long enough to ask her some questions about the cryptic note. And no one he'd spoken to seemed to know where she might be. After breakfast, he checked the gardens and the beach. No sign of her.

He was about to head back upstairs to check her room again when he passed through the grand entryway. It was then that he noticed a folded newspaper sitting on a table. If he couldn't find Annabelle, perhaps he'd do a little reading about Mirraccino. The more he learned about this Mediterranean paradise, the easier time he'd have selling the idea to his board of directors.

He glanced around for one of the many staff to ask them if he could borrow the paper, but no one was about. He picked up the paper and unfolded it. The breath caught in his throat when he saw a picture of himself.

His gaze frantically scanned the picture. It was of him and Annabelle. They were staring at each other. The photo made it look like they were about to kiss. But that wasn't possible. The only kiss they'd shared had been in the privacy of Annabelle's room. And this photo, it was taken outside, and from the looks of it at the university.

His gaze scanned up to the headline—Hero To The Rescue!

He was not a hero. Why did people keep saying that? He inwardly groaned, his hands clenching and crinkling the newspaper. If he were a hero Abbi wouldn't be dead.

Blood pulsated in his temples. Why couldn't the paparazzi find someone else to torment? He'd had enough of it back in California after the car accident.

Grayson's attention returned to the brief article. It was pretty much what he'd expected. Innuendos and assumptions. But what he didn't expect was a quote from Annabelle.

"We are together."

She'd said that? To the media? Why would she tell them such a thing? It wasn't true. He'd made sure to keep his distance since their one and only kiss—no matter how tempting he found her. What was she up to?

"Grayson, there you are." Annabelle's voice called out behind him. "I've been looking everywhere for you."

He choked down his outrage at the headline. He could only be thankful that the Mirraccino media hadn't dug into his past, but something told him they would soon. "Apparently you didn't look hard enough." He closed the paper along the fold. "I've been right here."

"I'm sorry things took so long this morning. There was more to do than I anticipated."

He nodded. His mind was still on the newspaper article. "Really? It seemed like you took care of everything last night."

She sent him a strange look as though she didn't know what he was talking about. "I, ah, had some last-minute details to take care of for the heritage festival."

His gaze lowered to the photo of them. It had to have been digitally altered because there was no way he'd looked at Annabelle like...like that—like they were lovers.

"Grayson, what's the matter?"

He wondered if she'd seen the photo yet. "Why do you think something is the matter?"

"Because you've barely said a word to me. And you keep scowling. Now what's the matter? Have I done something to upset you?"

"You might say that." He held out the newspaper. "When were you going to tell me about this?"

She retrieved the newspaper from his hand. Her mouth gaped open. He wanted to believe that this was as much a surprise to her as it was to him, but he couldn't let go of the fact that there was a quote from her.

"Aren't you going to say anything?" His voice came out more agitated than he'd intended.

"You think I did this?" Her free hand smacked off the paper.

"It has you quoted in the article."

"I'm surprised you took time to read it." She tossed the paper back on the table. "For the record, I didn't imply that you and I are lovers. They did that all on their own. I don't know why you're making such a big deal about this. Surely someone of your position must be used to the media by now."

That was the problem. He was all too used to them. He knew how much their words could cut and he thought at last the rumors had died down. But there hadn't been a word about the accident in the paper. Maybe he was being oversensitive.

He shouldn't have been so quick to think the worst of her. Is that what he'd let happen to him? Had his bad experience jaded him?

"I thought you and I were friends, but obviously I was wrong." Annabelle's voice drew him from his thoughts. "I won't make that mistake again." She turned to walk away.

He couldn't let her walk away. Not like this.

Grayson cleared his throat. "Annabelle, wait."

She hesitated but didn't turn around. Her shoulders were

rigid. And if he could see her eyes, he'd bet they were glowing with anger.

"I'm sorry," he said. Those words didn't often cross his lips. But he truly owed her an apology. He couldn't take out what had happened to him in the past on her. "I shouldn't have accused you of anything. I know the media can turn the most innocent of comments around."

She turned to face him. Her expression was stony cold. "I appreciate the apology."

He couldn't tell if she truly meant that or not. He'd really messed things up. He raked his fingers through his hair.

"I've got things to do." Annabelle walked away.

He picked up the paper again and held it before him. He studied the photo of them. Is that really how she looked at him? There was a vulnerability in her gaze as her body leaned toward him. This knowledge started a strange sensation swirling in his chest.

Then his gaze moved to the image of himself. He looked like he was ready to sweep her into his arms and have his way with her. Was that really what he'd felt in that moment? He recalled the desire to taste her sweet kisses once more, but he'd thought he'd covered it up. Obviously, he'd failed. Miserably.

Footsteps sounded in the hallway. He glanced up hoping to find Annabelle returning so that they could smooth things over—so they could resume the easy friendship that they'd developed. But it wasn't her. It was Mr. Drago, one of the king's men.

"Can I help you, sir?" The man was always so formal.

"Uh, no." Grayson returned the paper to the table. "I was just going to look for Annabelle."

"I believe I saw her go out to the patio."

"Thank you." Grayson walked away.

Part of him told him to leave things alone. It was best that they didn't reconnect. After all, it wasn't like he was ready for anything serious. He didn't know if he ever would be. He'd already failed so miserably.

And since that deadly car accident, he'd cut himself off from everything outside his board of directors, and his assistant. He'd forgotten how much he'd enjoyed laughing with someone and just sharing a casual conversation.

Annabelle had given that back to him and he wasn't ready to give it up. He wasn't ready to give her up. Not yet.

What was he supposed to do now? He just couldn't leave things like this. And then he thought of the cryptic note. He hadn't had a chance to tell her his suspicion about it. Maybe that could get them back on friendly terms.

He picked up his pace.

*Insulting.*

*Insufferable.*

*Annoying.*

Annabelle muttered under her breath as she strode down the hallway with no actual destination in mind. She just needed some space—make that a lot of space—between her and Grayson before she said something she might regret. How dare he accuse her?

Like she would do anything to help the media. What did he take her for? A fool? Or was he just another man who thought she wasn't savvy enough to take care of herself and watch what she said to the press?

Her back teeth ground together as she choked back her exasperation. What was it with the men in her life? She found herself headed for the patio. It was her place of solace, well, actually the beach was. The sea called to her. She stared out at the peaceful waters as the sunshine danced over the gentle swells.

She longed to go for a walk and let the water gently wash over her feet. It was so therapeutic. The more she thought about it, the more tempted she became. After all, she didn't have anything else that needed her attention. Why not go for a walk on the beach?

Without any more debate, she set off down the steps. The warm breeze rushed through her hair, brushing it back over her shoulders. Later, she might go for a dip. It'd been a long time since she'd gone swimming, too long in fact.

She slipped off her shoes and walked to the water's edge. She enjoyed the feel of the sun-warmed sand on her feet and then the coolness of the water as it washed over them.

"Annabelle!" The all-too-familiar voice called out to her.

Grayson.

She groaned inwardly. She wasn't ready to deal with him. Not yet.

She started walking like she hadn't heard him. Maybe he'd get the hint and leave her in peace, but something told her that man hadn't gotten to the position of head of his own multinational company by letting people brush him off.

"Annabelle, wait up!"

He definitely wasn't going to relent. She stopped and turned, pausing for him to catch up. What did he want now?

He jogged up to her. "Mind if I walk with you?"

"Suit yourself."

They walked for a few minutes in silence. Surprisingly it was a comfortable silence. Maybe she'd overreacted too. It just hurt when Grayson thought she'd betrayed his trust. When had he come to mean so much to her?

"I wanted to talk to you about that note you found in your mother's journal. There's just something about it that's not quite right."

That's what he wanted to talk about? A little smile pulled at her lips. "What doesn't seem right to you?"

"It's not any one specific thing. It's more like a bunch of small things. You said the handwriting wasn't your mother's, right?"

Annabelle nodded. "My mother was a perfectionist when

it came to penmanship. She would never abide by that mix of upper and lowercases in every word."

"Do you know of your mother keeping secrets? Or sneaking around?"

"My mother? Never." And then the memory of that day at the South Shore came back to her. "Then again, there was that strange man that she was arguing with."

"Maybe your mother was holding the note for someone else. Do you think that's possible?"

Annabelle shrugged. "At this point, I guess most anything is possible."

"Then I'm about to tell you something and I don't want you to freak out."

"Now you're worrying me."

"I just told you to stay calm."

"You can't tell someone not to freak out and expect them to remain calm." She stopped walking. She drew in a deep breath of sea air and blew it out. "Okay. Now tell me."

His gaze met hers. "I think the note is some sort of cipher."

"A cipher?"

"Yeah, a code. A secret message."

"I know what a cipher is. I just don't know what my mother would be doing with such a thing. Surely you must be wrong."

"I don't think I am. Back in college, my buddy and I would write them just to see if we could outsmart each other with some unbreakable code."

"Seriously? That's what you did for fun?"

Grayson shrugged. "Sure. Why not? The party scene just wasn't for me."

"You'd rather exercise your brain."

"Something like that."

"How good were you?"

"Let's just say the government got wind of what we were up to and wanted to recruit us out of college."

"I take it you didn't accept their offer."

"I didn't. But my buddy did. He works for one of those three-letter agencies."

Wow. She'd never met someone so intelligent that they sat around writing coded messages for fun. Who did that? A genius of course. And Grayson was the cutest nerd she'd ever met.

"So what did this message say?" Annabelle asked, more curious than before, if that were possible.

"I didn't start working on it. I mean, I wanted to, but I wanted to check with you first."

"Yes, decode it. I need to know what it says."

Grayson's brows drew together. "Are you sure? I mean, it could be anything. Something innocent. Or it could be something about your mother that you never wanted to know."

"You mean like she was having an affair?"

He didn't say anything, just nodded.

Annabelle didn't believe it. "I realize there's a lot about my mother I don't know, but there is one thing I do know and that is my parents truly loved each other. She wouldn't have cheated on my father. Whatever is in that note, it's something else. And it just might be what got her killed."

"Have you recalled meeting anyone by the name of Cosmo?"

"I've thought about it a lot and I have nothing."

"You mentioned that you have a brother. Could you check with him?"

She pulled out her cell phone and pulled up her brother's number. Thanks to palace security, they made sure that cell service was available down on the beach.

"What are you doing?" Grayson asked.

"Calling my brother like you asked." The phone was already ringing. She held up a finger for Grayson to give her a minute.

Her brother's familiar voice came over the phone. "Hey sis, now isn't a good time to talk."

"Is that any way to greet your only sibling?"

He sighed. "Sorry. It's just that I'm late to meet Elena."

"Is there something going on with you two?"

"Why do you always insist that something must be going on with me and Elena? Can't we just be friends?"

"When Elena is gorgeous, not to mention an international runway model, no, you can't just be friends. Her days as a tomboy are long gone. Don't tell me you haven't noticed because then I'll have to take you to the eye doctor."

"Sis, enough. We're friends. Nothing more. Besides, you know I don't do serious relationships."

"And that's what Elena wants?"

"I don't know."

"Are you in Paris?"

"Perhaps. Now, why did you call?"

She went on to ask him about the name on the note but made sure not to mention the cryptic message. Her gut told her to hold her cards close to her chest until she knew more.

Her brother didn't recall meeting or hearing of anyone with that name. But it spiked his curiosity and she quickly diverted his attention. He might have his issues with their father, but that didn't mean he wouldn't inform their father of her activities if he thought it was for the best. He was yet another protective male in her life. She was surrounded by them.

As soon as she disconnected the phone, Grayson asked, "So what did he say?"

"He's never heard the name. So does that help or hinder us?"

"It doesn't help us. But it shouldn't hurt us if it truly is a code."

"Oh, good. At last, my family will have some answers."

"Don't go getting your hopes up." Grayson looked very serious in that moment. "I've been known to be wrong. I haven't started working with it."

Annabelle stopped walking. "Well, what are you waiting for? The note is back the other way."

"You mean you want to work on it now?"

"Maybe my father was right. Maybe there is more to my mother's death than a mugging. Either way, I need to know. I owe my mother that much."

# CHAPTER TEN

EVENING HAD SNUCK UP on them.

It was nothing new for Grayson. There were many days that came and went without much notice by him as he pounded away on his keyboard. He couldn't help it. He loved what he did for a living. In fact, he thrived on developing software. Watching a program he'd written from scratch come to life was a total rush.

Running a corporation, well, that was something that didn't exactly excite him. There was a lot more paperwork and decisions that had nothing to do with his computer programs or the functioning of the cafés. And administrative issues seemed to crop up when he was right in the middle of a big breakthrough.

But squirreled away in the palace in this enormous library with just about every edition of the classics on the shelf, he found himself distracted. And it wasn't the moonlight gleaming through the tall windows. Nor was it the priceless artwork on the walls or the artifacts on display. No, it was the beautiful woman sitting next to him.

Annabelle yawned and stretched.

"Getting tired?"

She shook her head. "No. I'm fine."

He didn't believe her. It was getting late and they should call it a night.

"Okay, so it isn't all of the capitalized letters," Annabelle said. "And it's not any of the other combinations we've tried. What else could it be?"

"Let me think." He shoved his fingers through his hair. He'd run the note through a program he had on his computer and searched for different variables. Nothing came up…at least nothing that made the least bit of sense.

She sighed and leaned back in her chair. "Are you sure there's something here?"

"You sound skeptical."

"I am."

"If you want, we can forget I ever said anything."

She didn't respond for a moment, as though she were weighing her options. "It won't hurt to work on it some more."

"There's a message here. I know it. Those random capital letters must mean something."

"I guess I should let you know that I already signed us up for some of the games at the heritage festival tomorrow—"

"You did what?" Grayson frowned at her. "You probably should have checked with me first. I'm not that sports oriented unless it's on a digital screen."

"Good."

That certainly wasn't the response he was expecting. "Why good?"

"Because then you can't show me up at the games."

He shook his head. "You're something else."

"I hope that's good." She smothered another yawn.

"Let's just say you keep me guessing."

Her eyes lit up. "Good. I never want to be accused of being boring. Now what should we try next?"

"We're obviously spinning our wheels right now. Maybe if we take a break for the night something will come to one of us by morning."

With Annabelle in agreement, they turned off the lights in the library and closed the door behind them. The palace was quiet at this hour. But then again, Grayson had noticed that for the most part the palace was quite tranquil. He didn't know if that was due to the large size and the noise not carrying throughout or if it was a request of the king. It was a lot like living inside a library and every time Grayson went to speak, he felt as though he should whisper.

They stopped outside Annabelle's suite. Grayson really didn't want the night to end. All afternoon and evening, he'd envisioned running his fingers through her long, silky hair. And showering kisses over her lips, cheeks and down her neck.

"What are you thinking about?" Annabelle sent him a smile as though she could read his mind.

He cleared his throat. "I was just thinking some more about the note."

She nodded, but her eyes said she didn't believe him. "Well, you better get some rest. We're going to be very busy tomorrow."

"I'd be better off here, working on deciphering the note."

"And I think you need to get out and experience a bit of Mirraccino. After all, the contract isn't signed yet. I still need to give you a good impression of our nation."

His gaze strayed to her lips before returning to her eyes. "I have a very good impression already."

"Why Grayson, if I didn't know better I'd think you were flirting with me." She sent him a teasing smile. "I must be more tired than I thought. Good night." And with that she went into her room and closed the door.

He stood there for a moment taking stock of what just happened. He'd been soundly turned down. That had never happened to him. In fact, he was normally the one who turned away women.

Annabelle was most certainly different. And it had nothing to do with her noble birthright. It was something deep within her that set her apart from the other women who'd crossed his life.

"I can't believe you talked me into this."

The next morning, Grayson stood in the middle of the road. He hunched over at the starting line of the chariot race. His hands wrapped around the handles of the wooden cart. Why exactly had he agreed to this? And then he recalled Annabelle's sunny smile and the twinkle of merriment in her eyes. That had done in all of his common sense.

And now he was the horse and she was the driver. Go figure. What part of not being athletic didn't Annabelle get? And worst of all, the king was in attendance. Grayson could feel the man's inquisitive gaze following him.

"What did you say?" Annabelle asked. "I can't hear you from back here."

Before he could answer a horn was blown.

"Hold on!" Grayson yelled and then he lifted the front of the wooden chariot and set off.

Annabelle of course got to stand in the rustic chariot. He could hear her back there shouting encouragements. It wasn't helping. Why did people find getting all hot and sweaty so exhilarating? He jogged each morning, but that was for the health benefits, not because he enjoyed it. His favorite part of running was when it was over. He was more than fine with a tall cold drink and his laptop.

Lucky for him Annabelle didn't weigh much. He kept his gaze on the finish line. He'd told Annabelle not to get her hopes up for winning. He was definitely not a sprinter, but now that the race was under way, his competitive streak prodded him onward.

He looked to his right. They'd passed that team, leaving only one other team in this heat. He quickly glanced to the left to find two guys. They were slightly ahead.

"Go, Grayson!" Annabelle cheered. In his mind's eye he could see her smiling. "We can do this!"

She was right, he could catch them. Adrenaline flooded his veins.

He just had to push harder. This wasn't so bad. In fact, he kind of liked it.

"Grayson, straighten up."

He glanced forward and realized that he'd listed to the left. Oops. But it wasn't such an egregious error that it couldn't be fixed. He just had to stay focused. The further they went, the heavier his load became. His leg muscles burned, but he refused to slow down. Annabelle was counting on him.

His breathing came in huffs. He really needed to take his

running more seriously in the future. Who knew when the next chariot race would pop up? He'd laugh, but he was too tired.

He was running out of energy. Still, he kept putting one foot in front of the other. The finish line was just a little farther. Keep going. Just a little farther.

*He.*

*Could.*

*Do.*

*It.*

When his chest struck the ticker tape, a cheer started deep in his chest and rose up through his throat. He lowered the cart. He drew in quick, deep breaths.

The next thing he knew, Annabelle ran up to him. With a great big smile, she flung her arms around him. "We did it! We did it!"

He wasn't so sure how much of a "we" effort it was, considering all she'd had to do was hold on, but he wasn't about to deflate her good mood. He wrapped his arms around her, pulling her close and enjoying the way her soft curves molded to his body.

But then she pulled away—much too soon. She was still smiling as she leaned up on her tiptoes and swayed toward him. She was going to kiss him. That would make this torture he'd gone through totally worth it.

And then something happened that he hadn't expected; her lips landed on his cheek. His cheek? Really? He deserved so much more than that.

Totally deflated, he struggled to keep the smile on his face as the official made his way over to congratulate them and let them know that they would be racing later that afternoon in the final heat.

Yay! Grayson couldn't wait. Not. But when he looked back at Annabelle, who was still grinning ear to ear, his mood lifted. How could he complain when it obviously made her so happy? Besides, it meant that he didn't have to go running later this evening or tomorrow morning. He could deal with that.

When they set off to get drinks, Annabelle glanced his way. “See, that wasn’t so bad, was it?”

“If you say so.” He refused to tell her that she was right. If he did, he worried about what she’d come up with next for them to do.

“And I bet you thought all of these old games would be boring. Sometimes you don’t need technology to have a good time. Doing things the old-fashioned way can be fun too.”

There was something in what she said that struck a chord in his mind. While Annabelle got them some cold water to drink, he thought about what she’d said about not needing technology and doing things the old-fashioned way.

“Here you go.” She held the water out to him.

He readily accepted it. He could feel the icy-cold liquid make its way down his parched throat. It tasted so good that he ended up chugging most of it.

“You know, you’re right,” he said.

“Of course I am.” Then she paused and sent him a puzzled look. “About what exactly?”

“Not needing technology. Sometimes old school works.”

“I’m not following you.”

He lowered his voice, not wanting to be overheard. “The note. I was trying more modern ways of cracking it but I need to try a more old-school method.”

“Oh.” Her eyes lit up. “That’s great.” Then the smile slipped from her face.

“What’s the matter now?”

“You won the race.”

Leave it to Annabelle to confuse him once again. “I thought that was a good thing.”

“It was until you figured out what to do with the note. Now we have to stay for the final heat and the note is back at the palace.”

“Stop fretting. It isn’t going anywhere.” He glanced

around. "Why don't you show me around the village before lunch?"

She hesitantly agreed and set off. He found it interesting that the streets within the village were blocked off to cars and trucks. The cobblestone paths were for two-legged and four-legged passersby only.

Annabelle pointed out historic buildings with their stone-and-mortar walls. Each building was unique, from their materials to the layout, and even the doors were all different shapes. There were no cookie-cutter replicas anywhere.

Walking through Portolina, Grayson felt as though he'd stepped back in time—at least a couple of centuries. He enjoyed visiting, but he definitely wouldn't want to stay. He had a soft spot for all things technological starting with his computer and microwave.

The villagers were super friendly. Many of them made a point of greeting Annabelle. They didn't treat him as an outsider but rather drew him into the conversation. He'd never visited such a friendly place.

The cobblestone path wound its way through the village, past the tailor, baker and schoolhouse. Whatever you needed, it was within walking distance. It was such a simple way of life. The exact opposite of his high-tech, state-of-the-art existence.

But not all of Mirraccino was locked in the past. This island nation had the best of both worlds. It tempted him to consider purchasing a vacation home here.

He glanced over at Annabelle. She was all the incentive he needed to spend more time here.

He halted his thoughts, startled that he was beginning to feel something for Annabelle. But that couldn't be. He wouldn't allow himself to get emotionally invested.

If he were smart, he'd catch the next plane to Rome. But he'd already obligated himself to decipher the note and there was the pending proposal for the café. He was stuck.

He'd just have to proceed carefully and not risk his scarred heart.

# CHAPTER ELEVEN

SHE HAD TO HURRY.

That evening, Annabelle rushed out of the kitchen. She paused in front of an ornate mirror in the hallway to run a hand over her hair. She considered going back to her room to touch up her makeup, but she didn't want to waste any more time. She was already ten minutes late to meet Grayson.

The day had rushed past her in a heartbeat. In between the chariot races, the tour of the village and the quaint shops, they'd sampled many of the local culinary treats. Truth be told, she'd had a fantastic day. She'd had more fun with Grayson than she'd had in a long time. She hadn't realized until then how much she'd let her work take over her life. And that had to stop.

She promised herself that once she finished the South Shore Project she would start living her life and having some fun. If she'd learned anything from her mother, it was that life was too short not to enjoy it. And she enjoyed it a lot more with Grayson in it. He'd been such a good sport that day with the chariot races. And she had a surprise for him tomorrow at the festival.

But now it was time to puzzle over that note again. It wasn't like she could make anything of it. She honestly didn't think there was anything to it. However, she didn't mind spending more time with Grayson while he worked on it.

Annabelle rushed into the library to find Grayson already there. "Sorry I'm late. Things took longer than I'd planned."

He glanced up from where he was sitting on the couch. "No problem. I haven't been here that long. I had a lot of emails to answer and a couple of phone calls to return."

"Sounds like you were busy. I hope there aren't any problems with your business."

"No. Nothing serious. Just the usual things that need answering or approval. If it isn't one thing, then it's something else. I also did some thinking about that note. Do you think Cosmo is some sort of nickname that your mother had?" Grayson asked. "Maybe something from her childhood?"

"Not that I know of. Does this mean you think the note was written to her?"

"It's just a thought."

She stood behind him as he sat on the couch. She leaned over his shoulder, getting a better look at the note. "But if this note was written to her, I'm confused. So she gave someone tea who must have known her when she was a child? It just doesn't make any sense."

"Which is why I think it's a cipher."

She picked up the note and stared at it, wishing something would pop out at her. "In the beginning I thought the chance of this note being some sort of cipher was a bit far-fetched."

"And now?"

"I'm still skeptical but the mix of random upper and lowercase letters is odd. And then there's the strange wording. I mean, do people really say that tea is their gold. Isn't that a bit of overkill?"

"What do you think?"

She moved around the couch and sat down. "Maybe Cosmo is some sort of code name."

Grayson smiled. "Have you been watching a lot of 007 movies?"

She shrugged, not really in a jovial mood. Maybe it was just exhaustion settling in. Or maybe it was her rising frustration. "I just want to know the truth. I want to know if there's more to my mother's death than anyone has acknowledged. Maybe unraveling what exactly happened to her and who killed her will help my father. I don't think he's ever really recovered from the event. He's always worried about me and my brother."

"And you think that if you can figure out what happened then your family can have a normal life?"

"Maybe not normal precisely. I'm not even sure what that

is anymore, but something less stressful than what we have now. My father is always worried, checking in every evening. And my brother, well, he says that he's fine, but he's never home. He's always on a new adventure. Last I heard he was in Paris, visiting an old friend of ours. It seems like my family is never in the same place at the same time."

Grayson reached out and took her hand in his. "I'm sorry. I hope you're able to change things. I know what it is to live without any family around. It can get pretty lonely, especially around the holidays."

"Why don't you try talking to your family?"

He shook his head. "That chapter of my life is over."

"A lot of time has passed since you've spoken to them—tempers have cooled, expectations have adjusted and regrets have set in." She didn't want him to pass up a chance to reconnect with his parents. If she could have one more day with her mother it would mean the world to her. "When was the last time you spoke with them?"

He cleared his throat. "When I got a scholarship to college. I was sixteen."

"Sixteen. Wow. How did you make it on your own?"

"I worked. Hard. I took every job I could find. I ate a lot of ramen noodles and cans of tuna."

"Surely they miss you."

He shook his head. "They made their feelings bluntly obvious."

"A lot of time has passed. Maybe you could try again."

"Annabelle." There was a definite warning tone to his voice.

She understood this was a sensitive subject for him, just as her mother's murder was sensitive for her. If she could pay him back for all of his assistance by helping to find a bridge back to his family, she had to try.

"I'm sure they regret the way things ended."

"Stop." Grayson's body grew visibly stiff. "Now, do you want to go over this note or not?"

Perhaps she shouldn't have pushed the subject of his family so much. "I only meant to help."

"I know." He turned his attention back to the note and then began typing on his computer.

She glanced at the monitor. "Your idea of this being old-school coding, what did you mean?"

"I think this note could simply be a case of letter replacement or taking every other letter or so."

"What can I do to help?"

He explained his plan to unravel the note. It sounded simple enough. She just wondered if it'd work.

Annabelle made a stack of photocopies, even though Grayson offered to write a computer program to sort out the correct letters. She said they could do it just as quickly by hand. And she wanted to be able to contribute. So with copies of the note and highlighters, they started going through the note, highlighting every capital letter without success. Then they tried every other letter, every third letter and so on.

"This isn't working," Annabelle said in exasperation.

"I agree." Grayson studied the note for a bit. "Maybe we're jumping ahead."

"What do you mean?"

He continued staring at the copy of the note. "Perhaps the note is telling us something."

*Knock. Knock.*

Who could that be? Annabelle sent Grayson a worried look. No one in the palace knew what they were up to and that's the way she wanted it to remain. She quickly turned all of the pages over.

"Come in."

The door opened and Mr. Drago stepped into the room. Annabelle had known him all of her life. He was a quiet man, who never gave any outward signs of what he was thinking. Annabelle had always felt like they were strangers.

"Excuse me, ma'am. The king would like to know if you are done in his office."

"Yes, I am." Did her voice really sound off? Or was she just being a bit paranoid. "Please thank my uncle for me."

"Yes, ma'am. Is there anything I can do for you?"

"Thank you, but I think Grayson and I are good."

"Very well." He looked at her like he wanted to say something else, but then he quietly backed out of the room, closing the door behind him.

Once he was gone, she breathed easier and unclenched her hands. "Do you think he suspects something? Or worse, do you think my uncle is suspicious?"

"Why? Because he asked if you needed anything?"

She nodded. Her mind raced with potential scenarios, none of them good.

"The only reason anyone would be suspicious is because you look like you're ready to jump out of your skin. Relax," Grayson said. "I'm serious. You look like you just stole the crown jewels."

"Not me." She sat down on the couch next to him. "I'd crack under the stress."

"I don't know about that. You seem to be doing fine with our secret investigation."

"But that's different. If this note proves to have something to do with my mother's death, what we're doing is about uncovering the truth about my past—a chance for my family to heal. I'm not out to hurt anyone. Unless you consider the killer being exposed and punished."

"And for any of that to happen, we need to decode this note." Grayson paused and gave her a serious look. "Are you going to be okay if this turns out to have absolutely nothing to do with your mother's death?"

"I honestly have no expectations. Okay, that's not exactly true. I'm starting to believe you. But whether the coded message has something to do with my mother's death is questionable. And we won't know unless we get back to work."

"It's getting late. Maybe we should pick this up in the morning."

"About that…we can't." This time she avoided his gaze.

"And why would that be?"

"Because we have plans."

"Oh, no. Not another chariot race. I refuse. I ache in places that I don't think are supposed to hurt. You'll have to find yourself another horse."

Annabelle failed to suppress a laugh. "I promise it's nothing like that."

"Good. Then what plans would these be?"

"I promise no physical effort will be required, but I'm going to make you wait until tomorrow to find out the details."

"Oh, no. I don't think so." His determined gaze met and held hers. "You have to tell me or else."

She couldn't stop smiling. "Or else what?"

He reached out and started tickling her. His long fingers were gentle, but they seemed to gravitate to all of her ticklish spots. Laughter peeled from her lips as she slid down on the couch. She tried shoving him away, but he was too strong for her.

And then suddenly she realized that he was practically on top of her. He smelled spicy and manly. And her hands were still gripping his shoulders that were rock hard with muscles.

Their gazes met and her heart leapt into her throat. Did he have any idea what he did to her body? Or how much she wanted to pick up kissing him where they'd left off before?

He stopped tickling her, as though he were reading her thoughts. Was it that obvious on her face how much she desired him? And in that moment, she wanted him touching her again, not tickling her, but caressing her. And she wanted his mouth pressed to hers.

Not about to let the moment slip away, she reached up and pulled his head down to hers. She claimed his lips with all the heat and passion that she'd kept locked up inside her. His lips moved over hers with a gentleness that surprised her. His approach was much smoother than her inexperienced clumsiness.

She slowed to his gentle, enticing pace. She found the slow kiss allowed her to enjoy the way he evoked the most delicious sensations within her. She could kiss him all night long. A moan swelled in the back of her throat and grew in intensity.

The note and its meaning slipped to the back of her mind. All that mattered right now was the man hovering over her. She'd never felt like this for a man before…ever. He was sweeter than the finest chocolate cake. And he was more addictive than her caramel coffee lattes.

She had no idea how much time had passed, nor did she care, when a cell phone buzzed. Annabelle knew nothing could be as important as this moment. And apparently Grayson agreed as he continued to kiss her. But the phone kept on buzzing.

Grayson pulled back. The phone stopped ringing. Too little, too late.

He ran a hand over his mouth as though realizing the gravity of what had just happened between them. It wasn't just a passing fancy. There was something serious growing here. Annabelle wasn't anxious to examine it too closely. Everything would be better if they just kept it light and simple.

The phone began to buzz again. Grayson frowned. "I better get this."

Annabelle sat up and straightened her clothes. "Go ahead."

It was funny how things went from very heated to suddenly awkward in a matter of seconds. What in the world had come over her? She remembered their sweet moment of abandon. It had been so good. And so not what they should have been doing together. After all, she still had a deal to sign with Grayson. The last thing she needed to do was complicate matters even more than they were already.

Still… She sighed, recalling the way his lips felt against

hers. Heat swirled in her chest and rushed up her neck. She resisted the urge to fan herself.

Annabelle lifted a sheet of paper with a copy of the note. This was what she should be concentrating on, not Grayson and his tantalizing lips.

"Sorry about that," Grayson said, turning back to her. "It was business."

"Um, no problem." She pretended to be concentrating on the note, but she was having a severe problem focusing. "I was just thinking some more about this note."

"Oh, no, you don't." He swiped the paper out of her hand and set it on the coffee table.

"Hey, what did you do that for?"

"Because we weren't finished yet."

Again, heat flooded her cheeks. "Grayson, I don't think—"

"Hey, you owe me an answer and I'm not letting you get out of it."

An answer? He wasn't talking about picking up where they'd left off with the kiss? Oops. She averted her gaze, not wanting him to read her thoughts.

"Well?" he prompted.

She glanced at him, surprised to find merriment twinkling in his eyes. So, he didn't regret what just happened between them, but had she read too much into it? That must be it. She needed to lighten up.

Her thoughts were cut off when Grayson's fingers began tickling her sides again. Why did she have to be so ticklish? How embarrassing.

Laughter filled the air and her thoughts scattered. What was it about this man that made her forget her responsibilities and just want to have fun with him?

Having problems catching her breath between the laughter, she finally gasped, "Okay."

He paused and arched a brow. "Okay, what?"

"Okay, you win." She drew in one deep breath after the

other, so relieved that the tickling had subsided. “I’ll tell you.”

“So out with it. What devious plan do you have in store for me?”

“Eating cake.”

His brows drew together. “What?”

“You’re a judge for the baking contest tomorrow.”

It took a moment for her words to sink in and then a smile lifted his very tempting lips. “I can do that. I like cake.”

“There’s more than cake. There will be cookies, bread and some other stuff.”

He rubbed his flat abdomen. “Sounds good to me.”

“I’m glad you approve. So it’s a date?”

The startled look on Grayson’s face alerted Annabelle to her slip of the tongue. She inwardly groaned. If only it were possible to go back in time, she would. In a heartbeat.

# CHAPTER TWELVE

A DATE?

Was she serious?

Grayson's heart was lodged in his throat. Sure they'd had some fun this evening, well, pretty much all day. He hadn't even minded playing the part of her horse for the races. But this was going further than he'd intended.

Granted, he probably shouldn't have given in to his urge to tickle her—to hear her laugh, but hindsight was always twenty-twenty. And then he'd made things worse by kissing her. Or was it that she'd kissed him? It was all a bit jumbled in his mind.

He got up and backed away from Annabelle. Some distance would help them both think clearly. He hoped.

Because there was no way he was dating her—or anyone. He'd sworn off relationships after Abbi had died in that car crash. He couldn't make himself that vulnerable again. He couldn't go through the pain of losing yet another person who he loved.

"I… I'm sorry if you got the wrong idea," he stammered. His heart was pounding so hard now that it was echoing in his ears.

"I didn't." She glanced away and started straightening up the papers. "It was just a slip of the tongue. Honest."

He wanted to believe her, but he recalled the intensity of their kiss. And it sure wasn't just him who had been into it. She'd been a driving force that had kicked up the flames of desire.

Perhaps it was time to straighten a few things out between them. He certainly didn't want her to get the wrong idea and end up getting hurt.

"Annabelle, we need to talk."

"About the note?"

He shook his head. The hopeful look on her face fell and

he knew that he was on dangerous ground. One wrong word or look and things would go downhill quickly.

"Listen, Annabelle, I think I gave you the wrong impression." Boy, this was harder than he'd thought it would be. And with her staring right at him, he struggled to find the right words. "I didn't mean to imply with that kiss that there could be anything between us. I… I just got caught up in the moment."

Her gaze narrowed in on him and he prepared himself for her wrath. He was certain that someone as beautiful, fun and engaging as her was not used to being rejected—not that he was rejecting her. He was just letting her know that he wasn't emotionally available. And he didn't know if he ever would be.

Annabelle got to her feet. "I didn't think that this," she waved her hand at the couch, "was a prelude to marriage. I may be a bit sheltered thanks to my father and my uncle, but even I am not naive. Or perhaps that's what you're worried about, my father and uncle forcing you to marry me." Her eyes grew dark and the room grew distinctly chilly. "Trust me. That would not happen. I wouldn't allow it. And I'm sorry you think so little of me."

"That isn't what I meant."

She turned her back to him and began gathering all of the papers. Oh, boy, had he made a mess of things. Where had the smiling and laughing Annabelle gone? And how did he get her back?

He jammed his fingers through his hair. "Annabelle, that isn't what I meant. It's just that, well, I'm not ready for anything serious. And I didn't want you to get the wrong impression. I like you, but that's all it can ever be."

With all of her papers and pens gathered, she straightened. Her guarded gaze met his. "Thank you for sorting it out. I'll make sure that nothing like that ever happens again. And now, I'm going to bed. Alone."

When she started toward the door, he called out, "But what about the note?"

She paused and for a moment he wasn't sure she was going to say anything, but then she turned back to him. "That's not your problem. I appreciate what you've done. But I won't be needing your assistance going forward."

"Annabelle, I'm sorry. I didn't mean to hurt your feelings."

She turned and marched out the door.

*Great!* Could he have made more of a mess of things?

Frustration balled up in his gut. He felt like throwing something. He'd never felt this sort of overwhelming sense of failure. He'd meant to protect Annabelle and instead he'd done the exact opposite.

Energy built up in his body and he needed to expunge it. But when he glanced around, he knew this was not the place to take out his emotions. This palace was more exotic than any museum he'd ever visited. He might be rich, but he'd be willing to guess that most of the pieces in this room were priceless. He needed to get out of here.

He headed for the door. There was no way he'd be able to go to sleep anytime soon. He was wide awake and he had a decision to make: cut his losses and leave Mirraccino as soon as possible or stay and try to make this up to Annabelle.

Deciding to burn off some of his pent-up energy, he headed for the beach. The sand was highlighted by moonlight, but he barely noticed the beauty of the evening. His thoughts were solely on Annabelle.

He started walking aimlessly. He had to work all of the frustration out of his system so that he could think clearly. He didn't know how far he'd walked when he finally stopped.

He'd known the truth before he'd even set off on this stroll—he wasn't going anywhere. At least not yet. He had too much to wrap up here, from testifying over the purse snatching to judging at the festival. But he knew those were just excuses. He wanted to stay and make things right with Annabelle. At this point, he had to wonder if that was even possible.

By the time Grayson returned to his suite, his body was exhausted. After a cool shower, he stretched out on the king-size bed. He closed his eyes, but all he saw was Annabelle's face with that hurt expression that sliced right through him. He tossed and turned, but he couldn't find any solace or drift off to sleep.

He turned on the bedside light and reached for his phone. Annabelle may have taken all of the paper copies of the note with her, but she'd forgotten that he still had a photo of it on his phone. He pulled it up and stared at it for a moment.

For being a genius, he sure hadn't displayed much intelligence when it came to revealing the secrets of this note. What was up with that? He was usually very good at this type of thing. And then the answer came to him. He hadn't wanted to solve the mystery of the note. He liked having an excuse to spend time with Annabelle.

But now that he'd gone and ruined all of that, there was no reason for him not to finish it. Perhaps it could be some sort of peace offering. After all, he wanted Annabelle to find the truth about her mother. He just hoped it would bring her the answers she craved.

He stared at the message. He believed the key to solving it was more obvious than he'd first surmised.

He read it again. *Tea is my Gold.*

Could that mean *T* equaled *G*?

Grayson retrieved his computer and set to work setting up a spreadsheet to imitate a cipher wheel. In the end, he determined that the capital letters and misspellings were red herrings.

He set the cipher wheel with *T* equals *G*. The other sentence in the message referenced the first and forth. After trial and error, he decided that it was referring to the first letter in the first and fourth words.

In the end, he ended up with: *SUNDIAL. FIVE. TWO.*

Grayson went over the message again and again. It always came back to the same thing. He stared at the message. That had to be right.

What were the chances that he'd got it wrong and the words were so clear?

None. This was it.

He was holding the answer that Annabelle had been seeking. But where was this sundial? And what would they find when they got there?

He wanted to go wake her up, but he didn't dare. She'd been so upset with him earlier that perhaps some sleep would improve her mood.

In the meantime, he searched on the internet for a sundial in Mirraccino, but he couldn't find any. That was odd. Was it possible this mysterious sundial was on another island? Or in a different country?

He yawned. At last, he was winding down. He glanced at the time on his laptop. It was well past two in the morning. If he didn't get some sleep, he'd turn into a big grumpy pumpkin come sunup.

Talk about overreacting.

Annabelle made her way to the village for today's baked goods competition. She'd delivered her entry early that morning and returned to the palace to finish some work on another of the South Shore revitalization projects.

The truth was that she hadn't slept much the night before. Once she'd calmed down and gotten over the sting of Grayson's rejection, she'd realized that she could have taken his words better. A lot better.

Did she really have to storm out of the room? Heat rushed to her face. He was honest with her and that's what she'd wanted. She just hadn't expected him to turn away her kisses. Was she that bad at it?

The thought dug at her. Or was there something wrong

with him? After all, what did she really know about him? That he lived in California. That he was rich. And that he was estranged from his family. In the grand scheme of things, that wasn't a whole lot of information. Perhaps she'd been saved from an even bigger hurt. She clung to that last thought, hoping it would ease the pain in her chest.

She approached the tent where her triple chocolate cake was to be judged. It was then she realized that she'd forgotten to notify the festival officials that Grayson wouldn't be judging. She was certain after the scene last night that he wouldn't waste any time leaving Mirraccino.

And the fate of the South Shore? Her stomach clenched. She hated the thought of letting down her cousin, the king and the students at the university. Everyone was very enthusiastic about the trendy café.

She would reach out to Grayson after the judging and see if he would still consider taking part in the South Shore. If need be, she'd extricate herself from the project. That would make it simpler for everyone and hopefully give him less reason to take his business elsewhere.

Annabelle stepped into the white-tented area and stopped. Her gaze searched for one of the officials. At last she spotted Mr. Caruso.

She made her way over to him. He'd just finished speaking with someone and turned to her. "Good morning, Lady Annabelle. The festival is going along splendidly. I was so happy to learn that you're taking part in it this year. As a representative of the royal family, it really helps relations with the citizens."

"And I was very happy to take part. I had a lot of fun." Her thoughts momentarily strayed to Grayson. It wouldn't have been nearly as fun without him.

"I hope you'll be taking part in the community dinner as well as the masquerade ball."

"I'll definitely be here for the dinner. I wouldn't miss it."

Without Grayson around, it didn't sound nearly as inviting, but she would not let the people down. "As for the ball, I don't think I'll be able to attend."

"That's a real shame, but we're really pleased to have you here for the rest of it."

She forced a smile that she just didn't feel at the moment. This was the moment when she needed to admit that Grayson would no longer be around and there was no one to blame for that but herself. She'd driven him away.

She laced her fingers together to keep from fidgeting. "There is something I need to tell you. I'm sorry that it's last-minute, but Mr. La—"

"Is right here."

The sound of Grayson's voice made her heart skip a beat. She spun around to find him standing a few feet away. The expression on his face was blank. To say she was surprised by his appearance was an understatement. She thought for sure that he'd already be jetting off for Italy.

Regardless of why he'd stayed, she was happy to see him. Very happy.

But just as quickly, she realized that his presence probably had more to do with the South Shore Project and less to do with whatever was going on between them. That thought dampened her enthusiasm a bit.

Annabelle swallowed hard. "Grayson, what are you doing here?"

His brows drew together. "Did you forget? I'm one of the judges for today's contests."

"Oh. Of course."

Mr. Caruso spoke up. "And we're very happy to have you. Trust me, judging today is definitely a treat." The older man turned back to Annabelle. "What did you start to tell me?"

"Oh, it's nothing. Nothing at all."

She walked away, letting Grayson and Mr. Caruso talk about what was expected of him during today's baking competition. She couldn't deny that she was happy to see him. But what did this mean? Did he regret rejecting her?

And if he did, could she trust him not to hurt her again?

# CHAPTER THIRTEEN

"ANNABELLE! ANNABELLE, WAIT UP!"

Grayson had excused himself, telling Mr. Caruso that he'd forgotten to relay a message to Annabelle and that he'd be right back. It wasn't exactly the truth, but it wasn't exactly a lie. He did have something that he had to tell Annabelle, but he hadn't forgotten. He just didn't want to make a scene in front of the man. There was enough gossip going around about them already.

Was she walking unusually fast? Or was he just imagining it? He picked up his pace. He wasn't going to let this awkwardness between them drag on.

"Annabelle." Foot by foot, he was gaining ground on her. When at last he was just behind her, he said, "You can keep going, but just so you know, I'll keep following you."

With an audible sigh, she stopped and turned to him. "Grayson, what are you doing here? I thought we said everything last night."

"Annabelle, I want to apologize."

She shook her head. "Don't. You were honest."

"But there was more I should have said." When her eyes lit up just a little, he knew he had her attention. "I overreacted last night and didn't handle things well. I… I don't know what I was thinking."

"It's for the best." There was a resigned tone to her voice.

"Really?" Surely he hadn't heard her correctly. "You're fine with ending things?"

"Yes. After all, it's not like there was anything serious between us." Her voice was hollow and lacked any emotion. "You made perfect sense."

He made sense? He wasn't sure how to take that.

Her gaze didn't quite meet his. "And don't feel obligated to judge the baking competition. I can make your excuses."

"You aren't getting rid of me that easily." He smiled at her, but she didn't smile back. "I'm looking forward to this."

"I just don't want you to do it out of obligation."

"I'm not—"

"And I hope this won't affect the South Shore deal."

"Business is business. I'm expecting to hear from the board today or tomorrow."

"Good. Now I have to go." She turned and walked away with her head held high and her shoulders rigid.

He blew out a frustrated breath. He'd really messed things up. He stood there watching her retreating form. She'd said all of the right things and yet he didn't believe a word of it.

He might not be in a place for a relationship, but that didn't mean he was okay with hurting Annabelle. He felt awful for his outburst the prior evening. There had to be a way to make it up to her. He wanted to make her smile again. But how?

He thought about the problem for a moment. And then he latched on to the heritage festival. Annabelle had been so excited about it. He thought about the baking contest today. It'd be great if she won, but he didn't know what she'd baked and he wasn't one for cheating. If she won, it had to be on her own merits. That was the only way it would mean anything.

No, there had to be something else. He pondered it some more as he walked over to the tent to get his judging paperwork. He was almost there when the idea hit him. A little payback for Annabelle signing him up for all of these activities. He would now sign her up for an event.

Second place.

Annabelle shook hands with so many people congratulating her on her accomplishment. She knew that it was foolish and petty, but she'd been hoping to take first place. She wanted to show Grayson what he was passing up by brushing her off.

She gave herself a mental jerk. Since when did she worry

so much over what a man thought about her? There had been no one else in her life who had ever affected her so greatly. It was best that he would be leaving soon. She needed to think clearly because she still had a note to decipher. She wasn't giving up…even if Grayson would no longer be helping her.

Having spent a few hours at the festival, and with the baking competition over, it was time she left. She didn't want to have to force a smile on her face any longer. She needed some alone time.

With Berto following close behind, Annabelle was almost to the palace when Grayson came rushing up from behind. His sudden appearance startled her. "Grayson, whatever it is, it'll have to wait."

"Hey, is that how it's going to be from now on?"

She kept walking. "I don't know what you're talking about."

"Yes, you do. You've said all of the right things, but you don't mean any of them."

She stopped and glared at him. "Grayson, what do you want from me? You said there shouldn't be anything between us. I said I was fine with that. And now you're upset because I'm trying to maintain some distance between us. You can't have it both ways."

He frowned as he considered her words. "Would it help if I admitted that I'm confused—that you confuse me?"

"No. It wouldn't." She started walking again. The palace was in sight. Just a little farther.

He reached out, touching her arm. "Annabelle, don't run away."

That stopped her in her tracks. She did not run from anything or anyone. She straightened her shoulders and lifted her chin. She turned to him. "What do you want from me?"

"Nothing."

That was not the response she was expecting. "Then why are you here?"

"It's what I can do for you. I figured out the cipher."

"You did? It really is a cipher?" The longer it'd taken them to crack the code, the more her doubts had mounted.

He smiled and nodded. "I figured it out last night."

"You did?"

"I couldn't sleep, so I worked on it."

He hadn't been able to sleep last night. The thought skidded through her mind, but she didn't have time to dwell on it. She had to know about the note. "And what did it say?"

"That's the thing. It didn't mean anything to me. I hope it makes sense to you."

"How will I know if you don't tell me?"

"It said, 'Sundial. Five. Two.'"

"That's it?" It sure wasn't much to go on. "Do you think it ties in with my mother's death?"

"The more important question is, do you believe it ties in?"

She gave it some thought. How many people possessed a coded message? And perhaps it would explain her father's inability to let go of the past. But what was her mother doing with a coded message? What was she involved in?

"Annabelle, what are you thinking?"

The concern in Grayson's voice drew her from her thoughts. "I honestly have no idea what to make of this. I've got more questions than answers."

"Then if you're willing, I think we should follow the clue. It will hopefully give you some peace of mind."

"I… I don't know. What if it's something bad? I'm not sure my family can take any more bad news."

"If you want, I can investigate on my own. And if I think it's something you should know, I'll tell you."

Her gaze met his. "You'd really do that for me?"

He nodded. "You are stronger than you give yourself credit for. And you deserve the truth."

He was right. She could do this. She slipped her hand into his. "We'll do this together."

"Good." He squeezed her hand. "Do you know where we can find a sundial?"

She stopped to think. A sundial? Really?

"Annabelle, please tell me you know of one."

Her mind raced. And then it latched on to a memory. "There's one in the garden."

"What garden? Do you mean the palace gardens?"

She nodded. "It's overgrown with ivy now. When I was a kid, my cousins, my brother and some others would play in the gardens. It's a great place for hide-and-seek. Anyway, we stumbled over the sundial."

"Do you remember where it is?"

The gardens were immense. It would take a long time to search them without some direction. But she was certain that with a little time, she could lead them to the sundial.

"Come on." She started off toward the palace at a clip.

It was only when they reached the palace gates that she realized she was holding his hand. She assured herself that it was just a natural instinct and the action had no deeper meaning. After all, he'd made his feelings for her known. Rather, that should be, he had made his *lack of* feelings for her known.

She quickly let go and pretended as though their connection had no effect over her. *Just stay focused on the note and the sundial.*

Annabelle led them straight to the gardens and suddenly it all looked the same. Sure, each geometrically-shaped garden had a different flower. But then she recalled the ivy. That's what she had to search for. They walked all through the gardens. Each path was explored. No turn was left unexplored.

"I don't understand it," Annabelle said. "I know there was ivy here at one point."

"Don't worry about the ivy. Try to remember if the ivy was near a wall. Or was it out in the open? Was there a statue nearby? I noticed there are quite a few scattered throughout the garden."

She closed her eyes and tried to pull the memory into focus. It had been a lot of years ago and she'd never suspected that she would need to know where to find the sundial.

“Maybe we should ask someone,” Grayson said.

Her eyes opened. “No way. We’re so close. And I don’t need my uncle or father finding out what I’m up to.”

“But you’re a grown woman. What can they do to stop you?”

She smiled at his naivety. “You obviously have forgotten that my uncle is the king. If he says jump, people ask how high? And my father, he’s a duke. He’s the one who stuck my security detail on me. There’s a lot they can do to make my life miserable. I’d prefer to avoid as much of it as I can.”

“Okay. Point taken. But what are we going to do if you can’t remember where it is? Or worse, what are we going to do if it has been removed?”

“I highly doubt that it’s been removed. If you haven’t noticed, my uncle doesn’t like change.”

“It sounds like you two have a lot in common.”

She stopped walking and turned to him. “What’s that supposed to mean?”

“It means that you stay here and let them influence your life instead of getting out on your own.”

“I left Halencia and my father’s home to come here. I can’t help that he sent his security with me.”

“But you didn’t go very far, did you? I mean how much different is your uncle’s home from your father’s? They both keep a close eye on you.”

She didn’t like what Grayson was implying. “That’s not fair.” And worse, his accusation had a ring of truth. “What do you want me to do? Abandon my family like you did?” There was a flinch of pain in his eyes. She hadn’t meant to hurt him. “I’m sorry. I shouldn’t have said that.”

“No. You’re right. I did leave my family. Maybe they didn’t deserve the way I cut them out of my life. Maybe I should have tried harder.”

“And maybe you’re right. Maybe I took the easy way out by coming here.” Which went back to her thought of visiting the United States. “And once this mystery is unraveled and the South Shore Project is resolved, I just might surprise you and go on my own adventure."

"What sort of adventure are we talking about?"

And then it came to her. "That's it."

"What's it?"

"An adventure. It reminded me that we were role-playing. The sundial was on the helm of our ship." She started walking.

"And..."

"And it was next to a wall that overlooked the sea." She smiled at him. "Thanks."

"Sure." He looked a bit confused. "Glad I could, uh, help."

They made their way to the far end of the garden where there was a stone wall. They walked along it until they found the sundial.

"It's here!" Annabelle was radiating with happiness.

They both rushed over to the historic sundial. It was made of some sort of metal that was tarnished and weathered. It was propped up on a rock. And just as Annabelle recalled, it overlooked the sea.

"What else did the note say?" Annabelle asked.

"Five. Two."

"What do you think that means?"

"If I have to guess, I'd say five down and two across."

They both looked at the sundial. There was nothing there but the big solid rock and the sundial. Annabelle tried moving the dial, but it was not meant to move.

"Try the rock wall," Grayson suggested, already scanning the area for any sign of disturbance.

Together they worked for the next hour trying each and every stone, but none of them would give way.

Annabelle kicked at the wall. "This is pointless."

"Hey, don't give up so easily."

"Why not? It's obvious that none of these rocks are going to move. There's nothing here."

He had to agree. He didn't think this was the spot. But

the note had been so specific. If they could just find the right sundial.

"What makes you think the sundial is here in Mirraccino?" Grayson asked. He couldn't shake the thought that Annabelle and her mother had lived in Halencia and she had found the note in Halencia, yet they were looking here in Mirraccino.

"It's a gut feeling, plus the fact that my mother was murdered here in Mirraccino. It's going to be here." She turned back to the rock wall. "What am I missing?"

"Is it possible there's another sundial around here?"

Just then the butler, Alfred, came up the walk. "Oh, there you are, ma'am." He sent her a puzzled look as she stood in the dirt next to the wall. And then in polished style, he acted as though nothing were amiss. "The king would like to know if you and Mr. Landers will be joining him for dinner."

Annabelle glanced at Grayson. She didn't know where their relationship stood and she had absolutely no idea if Grayson would even be here come dinnertime. And more than anything, she didn't want to stop for dinner. She wanted to keep hunting for the other sundial.

"I had plans to take Lady Annabelle to dinner," Grayson said to her utter surprise. "But if that's a problem, we could go another time."

"No, sir. Not a problem. I will let the king and staff know that you have other plans." The man turned to walk away.

"Alfred, do you have a moment?" Annabelle made her way back to the sidewalk with Grayson right behind her.

The butler turned to her. "Yes, ma'am."

"Grayson and I were just talking about the sundial. Do you know how old it is?"

"No, ma'am, I don't. It could very well be as old as the palace."

"See," Annabelle turned to Grayson, hoping he'd play along. "I told you it was really old."

Grayson's eyes momentarily widened before they went

back to normal. "Yes, you did. I just love all of these historical artifacts. Sundials happen to be a favorite of mine."

"Alfred, do you know of any other sundials on the island?"

The butler paused for a moment as though surprised by the question. She hoped he would give them the clue they needed to find the next piece of this puzzle that her mother had left behind for her.

"Actually, ma'am, there is one other. It's in the old park in the city."

"That's wonderful." Annabelle couldn't help but smile. The butler watched her carefully and then just to cover her tracks, she said, "I'll have to show it to Grayson before he leaves the island."

"Anything else, ma'am?"

"No. Thank you."

The butler nodded and then turned and strode off.

"Do you think he suspects anything?" Annabelle asked. Her gaze trailed after one of her uncle's most trusted employees.

"Does it matter? You didn't know about the other sundial, right?" When she shook her head, Grayson added, "Without you asking him about it, we might never have found it."

"You're right." She just couldn't shake this feeling that she'd made a mistake. "Let's go into the city."

"You know, I wasn't lying when I said I wanted to take you to dinner this evening."

"Oh, but I thought you said you didn't want to get involved."

"It's dinner. I want to make it up to you…you know, for the way I acted last night."

"So what does this mean? Have you changed your mind?"

"How about, I want to be your friend?"

Friends? That wasn't so bad. There were even friends with benefits, but that was for another time. Right now, she wanted to find that sundial.

## CHAPTER FOURTEEN

FIVE DOWN. TWO ACROSS.

"This is it! This is it!" Annabelle struggled not to shout it to the world. Instead, her excitement came out in excited whispers.

She worked to loosen the stone just as her phone rang for about the tenth time. And again, she ignored it. After dinner in the city at a small Italian restaurant, she'd grabbed Grayson's hand and snuck out the back while Berto waited for them by the front door.

With the darkness of evening having settled over the city, they'd been able to move quickly down the sidewalk. It was only a five minute walk to the oldest park in Bellacitta.

The hard part was searching in the dark for a sundial. Thank goodness cell phones also made good flashlights. And Grayson found the sundial on the north side of the park near a rock wall.

Once again, her phone rang. And just like before, she ignored it.

"Aren't you ever going to answer that?" Grayson asked.

"Not until I'm ready."

"Annabelle, this isn't safe. You shouldn't have ditched your security detail."

The truth of the matter was that she felt bad about slipping away without a word, but knowing Berto's allegiance was to his employer—her father—what else was she to do?

She and Berto were friendly, but he'd never let that get in the way of doing his job. And he was very good at what he did. She'd make sure to protect him from her father's wrath and somehow make this up to him.

"You do know that they're able to trace the cell phone signal?" He glanced around as though expecting an army of royal guards to arrive.

"I know I told you that my father keeps a close eye on me

and my activities, but relax a little. I don't think even he'd go to that extent. At least, not yet." She smiled at Grayson, hoping to put him at ease.

He didn't return the friendly gesture. "This isn't safe. What if your father is right and there's a real threat on your life? And your bodyguard, I'm sure he won't be happy about you giving him the slip."

"He never is. And besides, I have you to protect me."

"Wait. You've done this before?"

"Ditch Berto to go treasure hunting? No. Ditch him so I could have some semblance of a normal life? Yes. But not very often—only for really important things." She'd gone through a bit of a rebellious stage as a teenager, but unlike her brother, she'd realized there was more to life than partying. She'd wanted an education and a career. So she'd settled down to study and bring up her grades.

"I don't like this." Grayson glanced into the shadows. "We're going back."

She pressed her hands to her hips. What was it with the men in her life bossing her around? She'd been hoping Grayson would be different. "I'm not leaving here until I do what I intended."

His hard gaze met hers. For a moment, there was a mental tug of war, but she refused to give in. She had a plan and she was going to see it through to the end. She owed her mother that much.

"Okay." Grayson conceded with a frown. "But we have to hurry up."

That was good enough for her. She turned and counted out the rocks, but when she went to remove the stone, it wouldn't budge. The tips of her fingers clenched as tight as possible and she pulled, but it wouldn't move.

"Come help me. This rock is stuck."

Grayson glanced around. "You know if we're not careful, we'll be going before that judge for our own crimes."

"What crime? All I'm doing is moving a stone. And I promise to put it right back."

Grayson sighed but he moved next to her and wiggled the stone out of its spot in the wall. "See. Nothing to it."

She glared at him. "That's because I loosened it for you."

"Uh-huh. Sure."

Any other time, she'd have continued the disagreement, but not today. The important thing was solving this clue. They looked at the stone, but they didn't see anything suspicious about it. It looked like your basic stone. So what now?

Annabelle wasn't about to give up. She moved to the wall and in the dark, she ran her hand around the hole in the wall until her fingers felt something smooth in a groove. The more she ran her fingers over it, the more she realized that it was plastic. She pulled it out.

"It's here!"

"Shh... Do you want us to get caught?"

"Sorry." Annabelle glanced around but there was no one in this part of the park.

Grayson replaced the stone in the wall and joined her on the sidewalk. "Let's go."

"Don't you want to see what it says?"

"It's too dark here. Let's go back to the palace and read it there."

There was no way Annabelle was waiting any longer. Just then her phone buzzed again. She figured she'd better get it before her uncle called out every police officer on the island to search for her. She withdrew her phone. She didn't get a word out before Berto started shouting at her. She could hear the worry in his voice. She apologized profusely and promised it wouldn't happen again.

"So how much trouble are you in?" Grayson asked as she disconnected the call.

"I'm not." When she met the disbelief reflected in Grayson's eyes, she said, "Okay. Maybe just a little."

"And I'm sure your father will hear about it. What will you tell him?"

She grinned at him. "The truth."

"The truth? I didn't think you wanted your father to know about the note."

"Who said I was going to mention that? I was going to tell them that I wanted some alone time with you."

"Oh. Good idea. That will make him happy," Grayson said sarcastically.

And then without any warning, Grayson leaned down and pressed his lips to hers. At first, Annabelle didn't respond. Where had that come from? She'd thought he didn't want this. Perhaps all day he'd been trying to tell her that he'd changed his mind.

Annabelle had no idea what was up with him but she wasn't going to complain. She enjoyed feeling his lips move over hers. And soon she was kissing him back. Her heart thump-thumped in her chest.

Perhaps he truly did regret what had happened the other night. Maybe it was a lot to compute for both of them. And the evening had been beautiful…in a way. A walk in the royal gardens. Dinner in one of the local restaurants. And now a walk through the park beneath the stars.

Okay, so maybe that hadn't been exactly how the day had unfolded, but who said she couldn't use some creative license and remember the fun parts. And with Grayson's lips pressed to hers, this was the best part of all.

When he pulled back, she looked up at him. "What was that for?"

"So you don't have to lie to anyone. When they ask why you slipped away, you'll have a very good reason." His voice was warm and deep.

She wasn't quite sure what to say. In that moment, she wasn't sure she trusted herself to speak. Her heart was still beating wildly in her chest.

"What?" He studied her for a moment. "You don't have anything to say?"

She swallowed hard. "Yes. Let's look at this note."

Under a light along the sidewalk, they stopped. Annabelle carefully removed the note from the plastic, afraid the paper would disintegrate in her hands, but luckily it didn't.

When she had it unfolded, she asked, "Can you tell what it says?"

Grayson studied the paper. "There's something there, but in this light I can't make it out. We'll have to look at it when we get back to the palace."

And so they set off for home. Annabelle didn't know which had her stomach aquiver—the new message or the very unexpected, very stirring kiss.

This was impossible.

The next morning, Grayson sighed and leaned back on the couch in the palace's library. They both studied the note.

The paper was old and weathered. And worse yet, some of the ink had faded. But Annabelle refused to give up. And he couldn't blame her. If he were in her shoes, he wouldn't give up either.

"What are we going to do?" Annabelle asked, sitting down beside him.

"Find a solution." He opened his laptop and started typing keywords into the search engine about recovering writing from a faded document. Surprisingly, results were immediately available. "At last an answer."

He turned the computer so Annabelle could read the instructions. It certainly seemed easy enough. But would it work for them?

"Let's do it," Annabelle said.

"Are you sure?" he asked.

"Of course. Why not?"

"Because those are some serious chemicals. They could ruin the paper beyond repair."

"And what good is that note the way it is? We can only make out bits and pieces of the message. Certainly not enough to figure out what it says. I say let's do it."

"Okay then. Can you get the chemicals they mention in the article?"

"I think everything should be here at the palace. The trick is knowing who to ask or where to look."

He nodded in understanding. "You find what we need and I'll meet you out on the balcony."

"The balcony?"

"You surely don't want to use those chemicals in here. Do you?"

"You're right." She started for the door.

"Annabelle," when she paused and turned to him, Grayson asked, "you did read the part where the blog post said to let the paper dry for a few hours before trying to read it?"

She frowned but nodded. "This is going to be the longest few hours of my life."

"Hey, no worries. I'll keep you distracted. After all there's the heritage dinner in the village and we have to be at the courthouse soon—"

*Knock. Knock.*

Annabelle opened the door. The butler stood there holding a big package.

"Ma'am, this was just delivered for you."

"For me? But I'm not expecting anything."

"I assure you, ma'am that it has your name on it. But if you don't want it, I'll take it away."

"Oh, no, I'll take it." She lowered her voice. "I always do enjoy a good surprise."

Grayson couldn't help but wonder why there was only one box. He'd expected at least two boxes. Something was amiss, but he'd straighten it out later.

She moved to the table and set down the big box. The outside cardboard shipping package had already been opened. Grayson guessed that was typical protocol for the palace.

He couldn't blame them. In this day and age, one couldn't take chances when they lived in the public eye.

Annabelle lifted out a big white box with a large red ribbon. She glanced at him again. "You know what this is, don't you?"

"I'm just watching."

He enjoyed the childlike excitement written all over her face. Who'd have thought a member of royalty, who could have pretty much anything she wished for, would get so excited over a present. Or maybe the excitement was due to her utter surprise and wonderment. Whatever it was, he wanted to put that look on her face again.

She slid the ribbon from the box. She didn't waste any time and she wasn't exactly gentle. She was certainly anxious to see what was inside. Grayson stood back and smiled.

Annabelle lifted the lid and looked inside. At first, she didn't say anything. His heart stopped. That couldn't possibly be a good sign. The breath caught in his lungs as he waited.

Annabelle lifted the black sequined tulle gown from the box. He'd read the description of each gown on the internet until he found the one he thought would look best on Annabelle. He just hoped he'd guessed correctly about the size. After all, he'd never bought a gown before. But what was the good of being rich, if you didn't splurge once in a while?

She turned to him. Her mouth gaped open, but her eyes said it all.

At last, Grayson could breathe. "You like it?"

She nodded vigorously and smiled. "It's amazing. But I don't understand."

"You will. There should be more in the box."

She turned around and lifted out a Venetian mask with an intricate detail and feathers. "But I… I'm not going to the masquerade ball."

"You are now. It's called payback."

Her puzzled gaze met his. "Payback?"

"Yes, you signed me up for the chariot races and the judging. By the way, I really enjoyed the last part." When a smile lifted her lips, he knew he could get her to agree to go the masquerade ball…with very little persuasion. "And I thought it was time I signed you up for something."

Just then his phone buzzed. He wanted to ignore it, but he couldn't. He was expecting a decision from the board. As he checked the caller ID, he realized it was them.

He moved to the other end of the room to take the call. If it was bad news, he didn't want Annabelle to overhear. He'd need a moment to find the right words. But he sincerely didn't believe that it'd come to that.

A few minutes later, he returned to Annabelle. She sent him a curious look but she didn't pry.

"Aren't you curious?" he asked.

"I figured if you wanted me to know that you'd tell me."

"What would you say if I told you the board unanimously approved the South Shore Project?"

Her eyes widened. "Really?"

"Really."

She cheered and then rushed to him with her arms wide open. She hugged him tight. Her soft curves pressed against him and at that moment, he only had one thought on his mind—kissing her.

He pulled back just far enough to stake a claim on Annabelle's glossy lips. He just couldn't help himself. No other kiss had ever been so sweet. He just couldn't get enough of her.

He lowered his head—

*Knock. Knock.*

Grayson uttered a curse under his breath as he released Annabelle.

Her fine brows drew together. "Do I even want to know what else you're up to?"

"Me?" he said innocently. "Why are you blaming me for someone knocking on the door? Do you want me to get it?"

"No, I've got it."

She swung the door open and the butler was standing there with another large box. Annabelle immediately took it. A grin played upon her very kissable lips.

"Thank you." She started to close the door.

"Ma'am."

She turned back to Alfred. "Yes."

"The box is for Mr. Landers."

"Oh." Pink tinged her cheeks. "I'll give it to him. Thanks." When the door closed, Annabelle sent him another puzzled look. "What's this?"

He approached her and took the box from her. "This is what I'll be wearing to the ball."

"You're going?" The surprise in her voice rang out, making him smile.

"Of course. I wouldn't make you go alone." When her mouth opened in protest, he held up a finger silencing her. "And before you complain, just remember that you owe me. And be grateful that there'll be no chariots involved and that you won't have to pretend to be a horse." As she broke out in laughter, he'd never heard anything so wonderful. "By my way of thinking, you definitely win."

She subdued her amusement. "When you put it that way, I have to agree with you."

"Good. I'll take that as your acceptance. We'd better get ready to leave for the courthouse."

"I almost forgot." She checked the clock. "We don't have long. I just need to change."

"I think I will too. I'll meet you back down here."

Her gaze moved to the note. "What about this?"

"We don't have time to do anything with it now. Do you have someplace safe to keep it?"

She nodded. "My room will be safe enough." She lowered her voice even though they were the only two in the library and the doors were shut. "As a little girl, I found a loose piece of molding with space behind it. It will be the perfect place."

"Sounds good."

He knew that he shouldn't be so eager to spend time with her. After all he'd gone through after Abbi's death, he'd sworn off letting anyone get that close to him again. But if he could just maintain this friendship with Annabelle, they'd be all right.

# CHAPTER FIFTEEN

WHO'D HAVE GUESSED that he could be so charming?

Annabelle's feet barely touched the floor as she made her way back to her room with her ball gown in her arms. She wondered if it'd fit. She wasn't worried. There was a woman on staff at the palace who could work magic with a needle.

She couldn't believe Grayson had bought her a ball gown. No one had ever done anything so thoughtful for her—ever. Annabelle spread the gown out over the bed. It was simply stunning, with a crystal-studded bodice. The man certainly had good taste. A smile pulled at her lips.

If he didn't want to get involved with her, he was certainly sending out the wrong signals, from the kiss in the park to this gown. Maybe he was changing his mind. And she didn't see how that would be so bad.

There was a knock at her door. She rushed over, thinking that it was Grayson. She wondered what he'd forgotten to tell her. She opened it to find a new member of the household staff standing there holding a silver tray.

The young woman smiled. "Ma'am, your mail."

Annabelle accepted it and closed the door. She was about to set the mail aside when she noticed that the top envelope didn't have a postage stamp.

She stared at it a little longer. It had her name typed out but no address. And the longer she stared at it, the more convinced she was that someone had actually used a typewriter. She was intrigued. She didn't know of anyone these days who used a typewriter.

She placed the other two envelopes on the desk before picking up a letter opener and running it smoothly along the fold in the envelope. She withdrew a plain piece of paper. When she unfolded it, she found a typed note:

*This is your only warning.*
*Leave the past alone.*
*Nothing good will come of you unearthing ghosts.*
*You don't want to end up like your mother.*

Annabelle gasped. She'd been threatened. Adrenaline pumped through her veins. The implications of this note were staggering.

She backed up to the edge of the bed and then sat down. This verified her father's suspicions. He'd been right all along. Suddenly, guilt assailed Annabelle for thinking all these years that her father was paranoid.

Her mother's killer was alive and here in Mirraccino. And this cipher was somehow tied in to it all.

She had to tell Grayson. She rushed out of her room and down the hallway to Grayson's door. Please let him be here. She knocked, rapidly and continuously.

"Okay, okay. I'm coming."

Grayson swung the door open. He was wearing a pair of black jeans and his shirt was unbuttoned. The words caught in the back of Annabelle's throat. He looked good—really good.

"Annabelle, what's the matter?" Grayson's voice shook her out of her stupor.

"I, ah…" She suddenly realized that telling him about the note probably wasn't a good idea. She moved the envelope behind her back.

The more she got to know about Grayson, the more she realized that he was cautious like her father and uncle. He'd probably want to tell the king about the note and she didn't intend to let that happen until she discovered the truth about her mother's death.

"Annabelle?"

"Sorry." Her mind rapidly searched for an answer that wouldn't raise his suspicions. She glanced up and down the hallway, making sure they were alone. Then she lowered her voice. "I just wanted to let you know that I stashed the note." Then she made a point of checking her bracelet watch. "Shouldn't we be going?"

He frowned at her. "I didn't think you'd be anxious to get to the courthouse early."

She shrugged. "It never hurts to make a good impression."

"Annabelle, there's something else. Tell me."

She frowned at him. How could he read her thoughts so easily? The truth was that she really did want to share the contents of the note with him. She'd trusted him this far, surely she could trust him with this too.

"There is one other thing." She glanced around again to make sure they were still alone. She really didn't want anyone to overhear them and report back to the king.

"Would you like to come inside?"

He didn't have to ask her twice. She stepped inside and closed the door behind her. "I received something very strange in today's mail."

"The mail? What is it?"

She held out the envelope. "Here. Maybe it'd be better if you read it yourself."

His brows drew together as he accepted the envelope. He glanced at the front which only had her name, Lady Annabelle. He withdrew the note and started to read.

He didn't say anything as his gaze rose to meet hers. And then he read it again. The continued silence was eating at her. Why didn't he say something?

At last, not able to contain herself, she said, "Well, what do you think? This is a good sign, isn't it?"

"Good? How do you get that?" His voice rumbled with emotion. "This is far from good."

Why wasn't he seeing this as a good sign? Maybe if she explained her reasoning. "Don't you see? If we weren't getting close, whoever this is wouldn't be scared that we're going to reveal the truth."

"And I think you're taking this too lightly. Annabelle,

this is a threat to your safety. You have to tell your uncle and the police."

She shook her head. "No way. This is proof that my mother's murder was something more than a mugging."

"Which is another reason to bring in the authorities."

"No." She would not bend on her decision. "They won't take it seriously—"

"They will. They'll make sure you're safe."

"But they won't reopen my mother's case."

"You don't know that for sure."

Her unwavering gaze met his. "We have no proof of foul play. Until we do, this stays between us."

Grayson blew out a deep breath as he raked his fingers through his hair. "You think we'll find the proof we need by following the clues?"

She nodded. "I promise, as soon as we have proof of my mother's murder we'll go to the police."

"Can I trust you?"

She swiped her finger over her heart, making an *X*. "Cross my heart and hope to die."

"Okay. I don't think you have to go that far. But if I agree to go along with this, you have to do something for me."

"Name it."

"You have to promise not to go out of my sight. Someone has to keep you safe—someone who knows there's a legitimate threat lurking out there."

The implications of his words struck her. "When you say not out of your sight, are we talking about sleeping and showering together?"

He frowned at her. "Any other time I'd welcome your flirting, but not now. This is serious. You get that, don't you?"

She did, but she refused to let that note scare her off. "I was just trying not to let the threat get to me, but you just went and ruined that."

"You can't pretend your safety isn't at risk." He pressed

his hand to his trim waist. “You should back off this search and let me handle it.”

“That’s not going to happen.” She leveled him a long, hard stare, making sure he knew she meant business. “I’ll take the threat seriously, but we’re in this together.”

“And when I tell you to do something to keep you safe, you’ll do it without arguing?”

“Now you’re pushing your luck.” When he looked as though he was about to launch into another argument, she said, “Stop worrying. I won’t do anything dangerous. Besides, you’ll be right there to protect me. Now, we should get going.”

There was no way Grayson was cutting her out of this hunt. They were close to solving her mother’s murder. Really close.

“What’s wrong?”

Annabelle’s voice cut through Grayson’s thoughts. They had just finished at the courthouse and had returned to the palace. She’d maneuvered her car into a parking spot off to the side of the palace with the other estate vehicles.

Grayson cleared his throat. “I didn’t think you knew how to drive.”

It wasn’t what he was thinking about, but it gave him time to think of how to word the next thing he had to tell her.

She sent him a puzzled look. “Why would you think that? Doesn’t everyone know how to drive?”

He shrugged. “It’s just that since I’ve known you, one of your bodyguards has driven you everywhere.”

She shrugged. “I guess it all depends on my mood. But as you noticed, they were right behind us.”

“I only noticed because you said something.”

“Someday that’s all going to change. As soon as we figure this mystery out.”

This was his cue to speak up. “I’ve been thinking.”

"I know. You've been quiet ever since the judge gave the kid probation."

That wasn't what had him quiet, but the judge's sentence did give him pause. "Did you think that was a fair sentence?"

She shrugged. "After hearing the kid's side of it, I can see where desperation might have led him to do something stupid."

The teenager had been trying to help his mother financially. She'd just lost her job and he was scared of how she would make ends meet. It would be a tough position for anyone.

Grayson rubbed his clean-shaven jaw. "I'm just worried the kid might not have learned his lesson. And if he were to be put in a tough spot again, he might make the same poor choices."

"Let's hope not. But doesn't he deserve a chance to prove himself?"

Grayson glanced away. "I suppose."

Annabelle's gaze bored into him. "There's something else that's bothering you and I know what it is."

"You do?"

She whispered. "It's the note, isn't it?"

Needing some air, he got out of the car and she joined him. She kept looking at him, waiting for an answer. He had to find just the right words so she'd give credence to what he was about to say.

He held his hand out to her. "Let's go for a walk."

"But we need to take care of the note and then get ready for the festival dinner—"

"This is important. Come on." He gave a gentle pull on her arm.

For a moment, he thought that she was going to resist, but then she started moving and he fell in step with her. She was headed for the royal gardens, the exact place he had in mind. The gardens were enormous and would allow them plenty of privacy.

With the golden sun of the afternoon shining, it lit up all of the flowers from reds and yellows to purples and pinks. Plenty of greens were interspersed to offset everything. He never considered himself a flower kind of guy, but there was something truly beautiful about this place.

When they came upon a bench along one of the walkways, he stopped. "Let's sit down. We need to talk."

"I'd rather be treating the note so that we can read it."

"That can wait. This can't."

She wasn't listening to him about the threat and he had to find a way to reach her. He needed her to be cautious. But he understood her hesitation to tell her father or uncle. After all, she'd been living with security dogging her steps for years now unless she was on the palace grounds. He couldn't imagine what they might do to protect her if they found out about the note. Before he made the decision of whether to tell anyone about the threat, he had to know that Annabelle was taking it seriously.

"Okay. I'm listening." Annabelle's gaze met his.

"That's the problem. I don't think you're hearing what I'm trying to tell you. This note, it's serious."

"It's proof that we're close to the truth about my mother's murder."

"It's much more than that and you know it." He really didn't want to scare her with the stark possibilities, but what else did he have to knock sense into her?

Annabelle sighed. "I know you're worried. But I can't stop—"

"I know. I know." He understood how important this endeavor was to her.

Annabelle's determination reminded him of Abbi's. That was not a good thing. Warning bells were going off in his head. Maybe if he'd been more insistent with Abbi then they wouldn't have been in that horrible car accident that stole her life far too soon.

He took Annabelle's hand and guided it to his face. He

ran her hand down over the faint scar trailing down his jaw. "Do you feel that?"

"It's a scar?"

He nodded. "I'm going to tell you something that I've never told anyone. I mean, it was written up in the papers, but they invariably got the facts wrong. Way wrong."

Annabelle sat quietly as though waiting until he was ready to go on. The horrific and painful memories washed over him. He'd locked them in the back of his mind for so long that it was almost a relief to get them out there—almost.

He cleared his throat, hoping his voice wouldn't betray him. "When my company went public and I ended up with more money than I knew what to do with, I gained instant fame. I could have easily become a partying fool with a girl on each arm, but that just wasn't me."

"Let me guess—you preferred to spend your time working on your computer."

"Something like that. I guess when you grow up with your nose in a book or gaming on your computer, it's tough to change. One night, after a particularly successful deal was signed, a couple of friends talked me into going out to celebrate. Of course, I'm the lone guy at the table while those two were off chatting up some beautiful girls. And that's when Abbi stepped into my life. Literally. I was on my way out when she stepped in front of me."

"And it was love at first sight."

Grayson shrugged, not comfortable talking about his feelings for Abbi with Annabelle. "She was leaving too. I offered to grab some coffee with her and she agreed. There was an all-night coffee shop a couple of blocks away. I had the feeling that I should know her, but I didn't. And she was actually okay with that. She told me she was an actress. She'd just had her first box office hit. But she wasn't like the others who'd passed through my life. She didn't want anything from me. She was down-to-earth and actually interested in my games."

It'd been a long time since he was able to think about

Abbi without seeing the horrific scene of the accident with the blood and her broken body. Those images were the ones that had kept him up many nights. But these memories, he found comfort in them. He remembered Abbi smiling and laughing.

"We became fast friends."

"Uh-huh." The look in Annabelle's eyes said she didn't believe that they were just friends. And there was something else. Was it jealousy?

"Trust me. In the beginning, neither of us were looking for anything serious. We both just needed a friend—someone who treated us like normal people. And so when she wasn't filming or doing promo spots, she came and crashed at my place. We gamed a lot."

Annabelle frowned.

"What's the matter?" Grayson asked.

"I just never had anyone like that in my life. Sure, there's my brother, but other than that my father succeeded in isolating me."

"What about female friends? Didn't you have some close ones?"

She nodded. "I did. But then we grew up and went our separate ways. In fact, my brother is visiting one of our old friends right now. She's a model on the Paris runways. Who'd have guessed, given that she started off as a tomboy contrary to her mother's best intentions? She and my brother were best friends as kids. They'd fish together and go boating. You name it and they probably did it."

"But not you?"

"I guess I was too much of a girly girl. I was not into getting dirty or touching creepy, crawly things." Her face scrunched at the mere thought and he couldn't help but smile.

So once again, she'd been left out. Grayson's heart went out to her. He knew what it was to be alone and never know if the people who were in your life were there because they liked you or because they liked what you could do for them.

He couldn't blame her for doing everything she could to solve her mother's murder and to regain her freedom.

When Annabelle spoke again, her voice was soft. "Did you and this Abbi get romantic?"

"Eventually. At the same time, she got nominated for a prestigious award for outstanding supporting actress. Her fame grew exponentially overnight. In the process, she gained what she called a superfan. I called him a stalker from the get-go, but she didn't want to believe it."

Annabelle remained quiet.

"Eventually, she told her agent and the studio where she was working on a new film. They hired her a bodyguard until they could do something about the stalker. And everything quieted down. No notes. No roses. No photos. Everyone assumed the guy had given up and moved on." Grayson felt like such a fool for letting himself believe that someone that obsessed would just give up. If only he had done something different.

Grayson leaned forward resting his elbows on his knees. He stared straight ahead, but all he could see were flashbacks of the past. A nightmare that would never fully leave him.

"We felt suffocated and needed some time alone without any security watching Abbi's every move. So we snuck off to the beach—alone." The breath caught in the back of his throat as he recalled how things had gone from fun to downright deadly. "It…it was like something out of a real-life horror movie." The pain and regret stabbed at him. He lowered his head into his hands. "I keep asking myself, what was I thinking?"

Annabelle didn't say anything. Instead, she placed her hand on his back, letting him know she was there for him. The funny thing was that he was supposed to be here for her—to help her see reason. And yet here she was being supportive to him.

When he found his voice again, he said, "At first, I couldn't even believe what was happening. At a red light on the way to the beach, gunshots rang out from the car beside us. The windows shattered."

Annabelle let out a horrified gasp. "Were you hit?"

He shook his head. "I punched the gas and luckily didn't hit anyone as we cleared the intersection. It turned into a high-speed chase, but I just couldn't shake the guy. And then..."

The scenes unfolded before his eyes. To this day, he still kept thinking "what if?" scenarios. If only he'd made a different decision, Abbi might still be here.

He swallowed hard. "I came upon an intersection with heavy cross traffic. I stopped...the stalker didn't. He...he plowed into the back of my car. It sent us airborne. I can't remember anything other than Abbi's scream. The rest is a blank. The first responders said that I was thrown free, but Abbi, she, uh, was pinned under the wreckage."

"I'm so sorry." While her one arm was still draped over his back, her other hand gripped his arm. "You don't have to go into this—"

"Yes, I do. You have to understand."

"Understand what?"

He had to keep going. He had to make Annabelle understand that risky decisions had major consequences. "Abbi died on the way to the hospital. And it was my fault."

"No, it wasn't." Annabelle's voice was soft and gentle like a balm on his scarred heart.

Grayson turned to face her. "I wish I could believe that. I really do. But it was my idea to go to the beach. It...it was my idea for us to spend some time alone. I just never thought that guy was still sticking around. I failed her."

Annabelle pulled him close and held him. He knew he didn't deserve her sympathy when he was sitting here while Abbi was gone. Life wasn't fair. That's one thing his father had taught him that had been right.

When he gathered himself, he pulled back. "The media, they got ahold of the story, and they told lie upon lie about me and about Abbi. It got so bad that I didn't leave my house for a long time. I worked remotely. That's when I started working on my plan to take the cafés global."

"I'm very sorry that all of that happened to you, but why did you tell me?"

"Because I need you to take that note seriously. Abbi and I didn't take her threat seriously enough and look what happened."

Her gaze met his. "You are that worried about me?"

"Yes. I couldn't stand for anything to happen to you."

"It won't."

"Promise me that you'll be careful."

"I promise."

And then he claimed her lips, needing to feel her closeness. Her touch was rejuvenating and eased away the painful memories. He'd never forget what happened, but he knew now that he had to keep going forward because his life's journey wasn't complete. Maybe he was meant to be here and keep Annabelle safe.

But as her lips moved beneath his, something very profound struck him. Here he was warning her about unknown dangers and yet, he was the one in imminent danger—of losing his heart, if he wasn't careful.

# CHAPTER SIXTEEN

"THIS IS A MOMENT we've been waiting for." The king's deep voice rang out loud and clear.

Annabelle quietly sat at the heritage dinner that evening. Back at the palace the note had been brushed with chemicals that hopefully would illuminate the print on it. And while she waited, she'd been treated to the most amazing home-cooked food.

She wasn't alone in her enjoyment. Everyone had oohed and aahed over the entrees before devouring them. And the sinfully delightful desserts had just been served, but before people could dive in, the king wanted to make a special toast.

Grayson sat next to her at the long wooden table. They were having dinner in the village streets of Portolina. It was a community affair and this was the only spot big enough for such a large turnout. Annabelle smiled as she gazed around at so many familiar faces.

Her eyes paused on the man next to her—Grayson. He'd surprised her today when he'd opened up to her with what must have been one of the most tragic moments of his life. And the fact that he'd done it because he was worried about her was not lost on her. This man who said that he wasn't interested in a relationship was now throwing out very confusing signals.

And the fact that he'd been willing to keep her secret for just a little while longer made him even more attractive. He was not like the other men in her life. He was not domineering and insistent on having his way. He was willing to listen and consider both sides of the argument. That was a huge change for her. And it was most definitely a big plus in her book.

Not to mention she was getting used to having him next to her—really used to it. She didn't know what she was going to do when he left Mirraccino. Because no matter what was growing between them, she realized that he intended to leave and return to his life in California.

"And that's why I'd like you to help me welcome Mr. Grayson Landers," the king's voice interrupted Annabelle's thoughts.

Applause filled the air as Grayson got to his feet. He smiled and winked at Annabelle before he made his way toward the king. Hands were shaken. The contract for the South Shore Project was signed. And Grayson offered a brief thank-you.

Annabelle hadn't realized how much this moment would mean to her. She thought that it would be monumental because at last she could show her father that she could take care of herself. But she realized that this moment meant so much more because Grayson now had a permanent tie to Mirraccino. He would be housing his Mediterranean operations right here in addition to starting one of his famous cafés. Maybe it wasn't such a far-fetched idea to think that they might have the beginning of something real.

"Annabelle."

She turned to find her father standing behind her. "Poppa, what are you doing here?"

"Is that the way you greet your father?"

"Sorry." She moved forward to give him a kiss on the cheek followed by a hug. "I didn't know you were coming."

"We need to talk." His voice was serious, as was the expression on his face.

She started to lead him away from the crowd. "Is something wrong?"

"Yes, it is."

Fear stabbed at her heart. It had to be serious for him to come all of this way on the spur of the moment. And then a worst-case scenario came to mind. "Is it Luca? Has something happened to him?"

"No."

She let out a pent-up breath. She could deal with anything else. Curiosity was gnawing at her. "What is it?"

"We'll talk about it back at the palace."

Annabelle walked silently next to her father. He was never this quiet unless he was really agitated. She had a sinking feeling that she knew the reason for his impromptu visit. And this evening was most definitely not going to end on a good note.

Annabelle stopped walking. "Let's have it out here."

Her father sighed as he turned to her. "Don't be ridiculous. We're not going to talk out here in public."

"There's no one within earshot. And I don't need the palace staff overhearing this and gossiping." She wasn't about to say that there was someone out there who thought they had a vested interest in anything having to do with her mother's murder. Right now, she wasn't sure who she could trust and who she couldn't.

"Fine." Her father crossed his arms and frowned at her just as he had done when she was a little girl and had gotten into the cookies right before dinner. If only this problem were so easy to remedy. "I know what you did. I know you stole some of your mother's belongings."

"Stole? Really?" The harsh word pierced her heart, but she refused to give in to the tears that burned the backs of her eyes. "She was my mother—"

"And her journal is none of your business."

"I disagree. I was robbed of really getting to know her. And you…you shut down any time I ask about her. How else am I supposed to get to know her?"

Her father's eyes widened with surprise. "Why can't you just leave the past alone?"

"How am I supposed to do that when you can't let go of it?"

Her father's gaze narrowed in on her. "There's more going on here, isn't there?"

"No." She realized that she'd said it too quickly. She'd never been capable of subterfuge and her brother never let her forget it.

"Whatever you're up to, daughter, I want it stopped. Now!" Her father so rarely raised his voice that when he did, he meant business.

"Is there a problem here?" Grayson's voice came from behind her.

She'd been so caught up in her heated conversation with her father that she hadn't even heard Grayson's footsteps on the gravel of the roadway. But she should have known that he wouldn't be far behind. He'd said he'd be keeping a close eye on her.

Her father didn't make any motion to acknowledge Grayson. Instead he continued to stare at her, bullying her into doing as he commanded. And as much as she loved him, she just couldn't abide by his wishes anymore. Their family was falling apart under the strain of what had happened to their mother. She could no longer bear the mystery, the silence, the not knowing. Someone had to do something and it looked like it was going to be her.

"Poppa, I'd like you to meet Mr. Grayson Landers. He has just bought the last property in the South Shore piazza."

The two men shook hands. All the while her father eyed up Grayson. She wasn't sure what was going through her father's mind, but she'd hazard a guess that it wasn't good.

Now was her chance to make her move. "Poppa, now that I've concluded the South Shore Project on my own, surely you must recognize that was quite an accomplishment."

Her father's bushy eyebrows rose. "Yes, you're right. You did a very good job. I'm sorry I didn't say something sooner. As you know, I had other matters on my mind."

"I understand." So far, so good. "Now you have to accept that I can take care of myself. I'd like the security removed."

"No." There was a finality in his voice.

She'd heard that tone before and knew that arguing was pointless. When her father made up his mind, he didn't change it—even when he was wrong. "One of these days you'll have to let go of me."

Her father turned to Grayson. "I see the way you look at my daughter and the way she looks at you. Make sure you take care of her."

Without hesitation, Grayson said, "I will, sir. I promise."

And then her father turned toward the palace, leaving them in the shadows as the sun set. Annabelle let out a sigh.

Grayson cleared his throat. "So that was your father?"

"The duke himself. I take it he wasn't what you were expecting."

"I guess I was just hoping that he would be warmer and friendlier than you'd portrayed."

"He used to be…when my mother was alive. Her death changed us all."

"I'm sorry." And then Grayson drew her into his strong arms. She should probably resist, but right now the thought of being wrapped in his embrace was far too tempting.

The best thing she could do was give her father time to disappear to the study for his evening bourbon and then she would head inside. She was anxious to see if they could read the note yet.

Nothing was ever easy.

Grayson sighed. The initial treatment with the note hadn't worked. Some more research on the internet had them searching for yet another chemical. But it was harder to locate and required a trip into the city. Annabelle had insisted on driving. She'd said it calmed her down when she was worked up. And so with her security in the vehicle behind them, they made yet another jaunt into the city.

This trip had been short and to the point. There had been no time for a walk around the South Shore or a stroll through the picturesque university campus. There hadn't even been a few minutes for some ice cream on this warm day. No, today they both wanted to solve this latest clue.

Like the duke, Grayson was worried about Annabelle's safety. If he could solve this mystery on his own, he would.

But he didn't know the island well enough in order to make sense of the clues—for that he needed Annabelle.

This application just had to work. Annabelle and her family deserved some answers. It wouldn't bring back Annabelle's mother, but it might give them all a little peace.

"Well, come on," she said before she alighted from the car.

Grayson opened the car door and with the necessary supplies in hand, he called out, "Hey, wait for me."

She did and then they headed inside. Annabelle agreed to retrieve the note from her hiding spot and meet him in his room. He had a feeling that the weathered paper wouldn't hold up much longer so they had to get it right this time.

When the lock on his door snicked shut, he noticed how Annabelle fidgeted with the hem of her top. Was she nervous about being alone with him? Was she secretly hoping more would happen than revealing the contents of the note?

Maybe a little diversion would help them both relax. His gaze moved to Annabelle's full, glossy lips. He took a step closer to her. What would it hurt to indulge their desires?

"Don't even think about it." And then a little softer, she said, "We don't have time."

Not exactly a rejection—more like a delay of the game. He smiled. He could work with that.

His gaze met hers. "There's always time."

She crossed her arms and arched a brow, letting him know that she meant business.

He sighed, thinking of the delicious moment they'd missed out on. But then he recalled the ball that evening and his mood buoyed. Soft music, Annabelle in his arms and the twinkling stars overhead. Oh, yeah. This was going to be a great night.

"You're right." He moved to the desk near the window. "Let's get to work."

While Annabelle peered over his shoulder, he applied the solution. All the while, he willed it to work.

At first, there was nothing and then there were the faintest letters. Together they worked, making out the wording of the note. Thankfully the person had used the same key, making decoding it quite simple.

"We did it!" Annabelle beamed.

"Yes, but what does 'Placard. Two. Three.' mean?"

The smile slipped from her face. "I have no idea."

He studied the note making sure he hadn't made a mistake. "What do you think we'll find this time?"

When Annabelle didn't respond, Grayson glanced up at her. Lines had formed between her brows and her lips were drawn down into a frown. Oh, no. There was a problem.

"Annabelle?" She didn't respond as though lost in her thoughts. He cleared his throat and said a little louder, "Annabelle, did you remember something? Do you know what this note is referencing?"

This time her gaze met his and she shook her head. "I haven't a clue."

"But something's bothering you."

She glanced away. "It's just the not knowing. It's starting to get to me."

Was that it? Or was she having second thoughts about unearthing the past? He needed to give her an out. "If you've changed your mind, we can put the note away and forget that we found it—"

"No. I can't. My mother deserves better than that."

But it wasn't her mother he was worried about right now. "You have time to think about it. We can do whatever you want." He consulted his wristwatch. "And now it's time to get ready for the ball."

"I'm not going." She stated it as though it were nonnegotiable.

She might be stubborn, but he was even more so. "You have to." When her gaze met his, he said, "You're my date. And I've never been to a masquerade ball. Look," he walked over to the bed and picked up his black mask, "I'm all set to be your mystery man."

That elicited a slight smile from her, but she was quiet. Too quiet.

"And you can be my seductive lady of intrigue," he said, trying to get her to loosen up so she could enjoy the evening."

"Intrigue, huh?"

He nodded, anxious to see her in the gown. He'd never bought clothes for a woman before. And now he wanted to see if his hard work had paid off. "You'd better hurry. You don't want to be late for the ball."

"But what about the note?"

He frowned. Maybe she needed a dose of reality. "You know how you accused your father of being all caught up in the past?" When she nodded, he added, "Well, you're getting just as caught up in this note. It's not healthy."

Her gaze narrowed. "You don't understand—"

"I do understand. Just remember who has stood by you through all of this. I want you to know the truth, but I also want you to realize that there's more to life than that note, than the past. Tonight we go to the ball. And tomorrow we will work on solving the message. Agreed?"

She didn't say anything.

"Annabelle?"

"Fine. Agreed."

*Knock. Knock.*

When Annabelle opened the door, Mrs. Chambers stood there. Her silver hair was twisted and pinned up. Her expression was vacant, not allowing anyone to see her thoughts about finding Annabelle in Grayson's room. Not that he cared what anyone thought.

The woman said, "Ma'am, I came to help you dress for the ball."

"I'll be right there."

"Yes, Ma'am. I'll wait for you in your room." The woman turned and walked away.

Annabelle waited a moment before she said, "Do you think she overheard us talking about the note?"

He had absolutely no idea, but he knew that Annabelle was already stressed. "I don't think we were loud enough for her to hear us through the door." He moved to her side and brushed his fingers over her cheek. "Just give me tonight and I'll give you my undivided attention tomorrow."

She stepped closer. "Does that mean no laptop?"

He readily nodded, which was quite odd for him. Normally he felt most at ease when his fingers were flying over the keyboard typing code or answering emails. His hands wrapped around Annabelle's waist. But tonight, his hands felt much better right here.

"No laptop." He leaned forward and pressed a quick kiss to her lips.

When he pulled back, her eyes were still closed. They fluttered open. The confusion about why he'd pulled away so quickly was reflected in them.

"There will be more of that later." He had no doubts. "But first you need to change. It wouldn't do for Cinderella to be late to the ball."

"When you put it that way, you have a deal." She lifted up on her tiptoes and pressed a kiss to his lips.

Before he could pull her close again, she stepped out of his reach. A naughty smile lit up her face. "We have a ball to attend."

He sighed. Suddenly the ball didn't sound like that great an idea, but Annabelle was already out the door. He shook his head. This evening was going to be far more complicated than he ever imagined. Because there was more to those kisses than either of them was willing to admit.

And yet this evening was going to be a once-in-a-lifetime experience. A ball attended by a king and a duke. And Grayson would have the most beautiful woman in his arms…all night long.

The answer could wait.

Now that the moment of truth was almost here, Annabelle wasn't so sure she was doing the right thing. What if she learned something bad about her mother?

Annabelle's stomach quivered with nerves. What exactly had her mother gotten herself mixed up in? Did her father secretly know? What if all this time he'd been trying to protect her mother's memory? The thought sent a chill down Annabelle's spine.

She scanned the party guests for her father. At last, she found him talking with one of the village elders. He had come alone to the ball and she knew that he would leave alone too. She did not want to end up like him.

Now wasn't the best time to speak to her father, but she couldn't stand the tug of war going on within herself. She had to know.

She made her way over to him. "Good evening, Poppa."

"Hello, daughter. Shouldn't you be with your date?"

Her stomach churned. She was in no mood to make polite chitchat. The best way to end her agony was just to get it out there. "Do you know why Momma was murdered?"

Instantly the color drained from her father's face. "Annabelle, what's the meaning of this?"

"You said you didn't think she died as a result of a mugging, but do you know what did happen?" And then a thought popped into her mind and she uttered it before her brain could process the implications. "Are you afraid that she did something wrong and it got her killed?"

The color came rushing back to her father's face. His voice came out in hushed tones but there was no mistaking the fury behind each word. "Annabelle, I will not stand for you speaking to me like this. I've done nothing to warrant such hostility and suspicion."

He was right. She'd let her imagination get the best of her. "I'm sorry, Poppa. It's the not knowing. I can't take it anymore."

"Do you honestly think your mother would have done anything to hurt our family? She loved us with every fiber of her being." His eyes glistened with unshed tears. "I miss her so much."

"I miss her too."

"She would have been proud of the young woman you've grown into."

"Thank you."

"For what?"

"Talking about Momma. You never want to talk of her and it hurts because I miss her too. And talking about her keeps those memories alive for me."

Her father cleared his throat. "I'm sorry I failed you in that regard. I will try to do better."

"And I'm sorry my questions hurt you."

They hugged and Annabelle accepted that was the best she could hope for from her father tonight. She decided to go in search of her dashing escort. She didn't care how many balls she attended, they were all magical. But this evening was extra special thanks to Grayson.

Tonight, she would laugh, forget about her problems and kick up her heels. Grayson would make sure of it. And tomorrow, her feet would land back in reality. But tomorrow was a long way off.

Her gaze sought out Grayson, who looked so handsome in his black tux. She was in absolutely no hurry for the sun to rise on a new day because she had a gut feeling that tomorrow would bring her those long-sought-after answers. And she had absolutely no idea if those answers would be good or bad.

"Here you go." Grayson stepped up to her and held out a glass of bubbly. When she accepted it, he held up his glass to make a toast. "Here's to the most beautiful woman at the ball."

Heat rushed to her cheeks as she smiled. The truth of the matter was that she felt a bit overdone. The king had sent along a tiara for her to wear. As far as tiaras went, at least it wasn't big and showy, but it just felt like too much.

"Thank you for the kind words."

"They aren't just words. I mean them." He leaned forward and planted a quick kiss on her lips.

He pulled back before she was ready for him to go. A dreamy sigh passed her lips. If only…

Thoughts of her gown and tiara slipped to the back of her mind. Her heart tap-danced in her chest as Grayson smiled at her. How had she gotten so lucky?

The evening took on a life of its own. She sipped at the bubbly. She talked with the guests. And then Grayson held out his hand to escort her onto the dance floor.

In his very capable arms, she glided around like she was on a cloud. She wasn't even sure if her feet ever touched the ground. And her cheeks grew sore from all of the smiling. But she couldn't stop. This was the most amazing evening and she didn't want it to end…not ever.

Grayson stopped moving.

Annabelle sent him a worried look. "What's the matter?"

"Look up."

She tilted her chin upward. "I don't see anything but darkness."

"And…"

"And a star." She smiled. "Are you making a wish upon that star?"

"Perhaps."

Well, he wasn't going to be the only one to make a wish. She closed her eyes and Grayson's image filled her mind. There was something about him that she couldn't resist. She wished…she wished…

And then his lips pressed to hers. Oh, yes, that's what she wished.

## CHAPTER SEVENTEEN

THE FAIRYTALE WAS winding to a close.

The ball was over, but Annabelle was not ready to lose all of her glittery goodness and turn back into a pumpkin. With Grayson by her side, the magic would continue long after the last song finished and the twinkle lights dimmed.

"What are you smiling about?" Grayson's voice broke into her thoughts as they paused outside her bedroom.

"Nothing." Annabelle continued to smile as she had all evening. She couldn't help it. She couldn't remember the last time she was this happy. And she didn't have any intention of letting this evening end.

Grayson's mouth lifted ever so slightly at the corners. "Oh, you have something on your mind."

"How do you know? Do you read minds now?"

"No. But your eyes give you away."

He was right. She did have something on her mind. And as delicious as the thought was, she wasn't sure she should follow her desires. But then again, what was holding her back now?

The deal for the South Shore had been signed. If she didn't act now, it'd be too late. Grayson would be leaving for California and she'd be left with nothing but regrets.

Her heart pounded in her chest. Tonight the moonlight and the sweet bubbly had cast a spell over her. She was falling for Grayson in a great big way.

But if she were honest with herself, this thing—these feelings—had started when he'd played her hero and saved her mother's journal from the would-be thief. There had been something special about Grayson from the very start.

And now she was ready to take the next step—one that she didn't take lightly. She'd never outright asked a man to spend the night. She wasn't even sure what to say. But tonight she was feeling a little bit naughty, uncharacteristically bold, and a whole lot reckless.

She opened the door.

"Well, I'll see you in the morning." Grayson turned to walk away.

Oh, no. She wasn't letting him get away. She needed to do something quick, but what? "Grayson, wait."

He turned back. "What is it?"

"I need your help." Without any further explanation, she took his hand to lead him into the bedroom.

But he didn't move. "Annabelle, I don't think this is a good idea."

She turned to him, not about to let logic rain on their magical night. "Why Grayson, what do you think I'm going to do?" Her voice lowered to a sultry level. "Take advantage of you?"

He didn't say anything at first. "The thought had crossed my mind."

"Tsk. Tsk." She gave his hand another pull. "Come on. I promise to keep my hands to myself…unless you'd rather I didn't. And besides, you did agree to stay with me until we solve the mystery of the note."

Grayson groaned. And she grinned like a Cheshire cat. Without a word, he followed her into the darkened room. Something told her that his capitulation was out of pure curiosity and the fact that no matter how much he wanted to deny this thing between them, he simply could not.

"You might want to close the door," she suggested without making any effort whatsoever to turn on the light.

"Annabelle—"

"Trust me." She moved toward the bed.

He groaned again and inwardly she laughed. Who knew Grayson could be so much fun? Or maybe the fun was in her being bold and sassy. Her smile broadened.

When the door snicked shut, she could hear Grayson's soft footsteps behind her. He wanted this night as much as she did. He hadn't been with anyone since his girlfriend, which was understandable and even a bit admirable, but it was time he moved on. It was time that she spread her wings with a man who wasn't intimidated by her father or her security team. And a man who took her opinions seriously.

"Can you unzip me?" She wished she could see the look on his face right now.

"I… I shouldn't be doing this."

"If you don't, I'll have to sleep in this beautiful gown," she said as innocently as she could muster. "Mrs. Chambers already went to bed. She never goes to the ball. And I can't reach the zipper."

He stepped closer. In the next moment, his fingers were touching the bare skin of her upper back, sending shivers of excitement tingling down her spine. He sucked in an unsteady breath. Millimeter by millimeter the zipper came undone. His fingertips were surprisingly smooth. His touch was being tattooed upon her mind.

This was the sweetest torture she'd ever experienced. And then her gown floated to the ground, landing in a fluffy heap. With nothing but moonlight streaming in through the tall windows to see by, she stood there in her black bustier and organza petticoat.

She didn't move. She could feel his gaze on her. The breath caught in her lungs. What was he thinking? Did he want her as much as she wanted him?

Desire and anticipation mounted within her. This was the most exquisite moment as they stood at the fork in their relationship. No matter which direction they took, after tonight, things would never be the same again.

And then his hands gently caressed her shoulders. His touch was arousing. She imagined turning in his arms and pressing her lips to his mouth, but she didn't. Not yet. She knew what she wanted, but she wasn't sure if he'd overcome the ghosts from his past. For this to work, for this to be right, he had to be all-in too.

His thumbs moved rhythmically over her skin. "Annabelle, are you sure?"

She blew out the pent-up breath. "I am. Are you?"

His response came in the form of a gentle kiss on her neck. She inhaled swiftly, not expecting such a telling response. Not that she disapproved. Quite the opposite. Most definitely the opposite.

## CHAPTER EIGHTEEN

"HOW LONG HAVE you been up?"

Grayson's deep, gravelly voice came from the doorway of the library. Annabelle was wide awake, showered and working to find the answer to the clue in the latest note. She glanced up from one of the history books of Mirraccino.

When she saw Grayson, memories of being held in his arms came rushing back to her. Along with the memories came the emotions—powerful emotions that sent her heart racing. Last night had been so much more than she'd ever envisioned.

She was in love with Grayson.

And she had never been so scared.

She'd never been in love before. She'd never wanted to let another man into her life. She already had enough men telling her what to do, why add one more? But Grayson was different. He spoke his opinion, but left room for her response.

The truth of the matter was that she could imagine keeping him around, but never once last night or any time since she'd known him had he mentioned sticking around or inviting her to be a part of his life. He'd warned her in the beginning that he wasn't in this for anything serious. She remembered that moment quite vividly. Why hadn't she listened to him then? Now she'd complicated everything exponentially.

"Annabelle, what's wrong?" Grayson approached her, concern written all over his face.

She held up her hand, maintaining an adequate distance between them. She couldn't bear for him to touch her. And she refused to give in to the tears that were stinging the backs of her eyes. This was her problem to deal with, not his. He hadn't done anything but what she'd asked him to do.

"I... I'm fine."

"You don't look fine. Listen, if this is about last night—"

"It's not. And I'd prefer not talking about it." She couldn't stand the thought of him letting her down gently. She could just imagine him giving her some sort of pep talk.

Grayson raked his fingers through his hair. "I knew that last night was a mistake. I didn't mean to—"

"Stop." Then realizing she'd raised her voice while the door to the hallway was standing wide open, she lowered her voice. "It wasn't a mistake. You have nothing to feel bad about." And she just couldn't talk about it any longer. "And I have to go out. If you need anything just ask the staff."

She started for the door, but Grayson was hot on her heels. She needed to shake him. She needed to get away from absolutely everyone. She needed some time alone in order to think clearly.

The only person she really wanted to talk to was the one person missing from her life—her mother.

Not needing protection while she was within the palace walls, her security detail was out of sight. That left Grayson, who was right behind her. She kept moving with no particular destination in mind.

"Annabelle, you can't just walk away."

"Watch me."

"We need to talk."

"No, we don't." She kept walking, wishing he'd give up. "There's nothing to say."

"I disagree."

He refused to leave the subject alone. What did he want her to do? Say something to make it better? That wasn't possible.

Annabelle went out the back door. When she spotted her little red convertible, she headed straight for it. There wasn't anyone around, thankfully. She jumped inside and was relieved to find the keys waiting. The staff routinely left the keys in a strategic spot so that vehicles could be readily available and moved to the front of the palace for their owners.

After all, the palace was heavily guarded. No one was going to break in and steal a car. Not a chance.

The next thing she knew, Grayson was in the seat next to her. *Just great.*

"You need to get out because I really am leaving."

"I'm not moving. You can't just act like nothing happened last night." He turned to her. "Annabelle, we have to talk."

"So you keep telling me." She put the car in gear. "Well, if you're not getting out, then I guess that means you're coming with me."

Grayson put on his seat belt, crossed his arms and then settled back in his seat. She'd never witnessed him with a more determined look.

"Don't say I didn't warn you." She accelerated toward the front gates.

It was then that she realized she didn't have her security detail following her. She also knew the guards would stop her and ask about her lack of security. She had no clue what to say. When she neared the gate, she found them opening it for a delivery truck. Though the guards waved for her to stop, she kept moving.

"Annabelle, what are you doing?"

"Whatever I want." She knew it was a childish answer, but she wasn't much in the mood for a serious talk.

It wasn't until they were on the main road that Grayson asked, "Would you at least tell me where we're going?"

"You'll find out soon enough."

"Annabelle?" Grayson stared into the passenger side mirror.

"I told you, you'll find out the destination soon."

"No, that isn't it." He tapped on the window. "There's no car behind us. Where's your security detail?"

He stared at her, waiting for this information to sink in. Her face paled as her gaze flicked to her rearview mirror. He knew she hadn't planned this little escapade. It'd been a spur-of-the-moment decision, which led him to believe she had been more upset this morning than she was willing to let on. He figured as much.

The thing was he wanted to talk to her. He wanted to tell her how much last night had meant to him, but she refused to give him a chance.

He'd have sworn by her responses and words that last night had been special for her too. So why had the walls gone up in the light of day? And what had she been doing up so early after such a late night?

That was his problem. He didn't understand women. He never had. Abbi used to tease him about it. But there was nothing funny about this situation—not after that threatening note.

"Annabelle, where's your security?"

"Obviously not here."

"I don't understand. Why would you leave without them?"

"Because..."

"Because what?" He wanted a real answer. What was going on with her? She'd been acting strange all morning.

"Because you wouldn't leave me alone. You kept wanting to talk about last night and I didn't. I didn't plan to leave the palace, at least not at that point and so I didn't tell anyone."

"You ran off?"

"No!" She frowned as her grip on the steering wheel visibly tightened. "I... I just didn't stop to tell anyone."

"Isn't that the same thing?"

She took her eyes off the road for a second to glare at him. "No. It isn't."

Grayson sighed. "Okay. I guess I did push the subject this morning. I'm sorry. I just thought we could talk things out." When she opened her mouth to protest, he continued before she could speak. "But no worries. Just turn around. We'll be back at the palace in no time."

Her lips pressed together. She didn't say anything and the car didn't slow down. Maybe she didn't hear him.

"Annabelle, turn around."

She eased up on the accelerator and the car started to slow down. He breathed easier. She'd turn around and soon they'd be back at the palace. No harm. No foul.

She put on the turn signal. So far so good. He glanced around. "What is this place?"

"It's a historic landmark. It's where our ancestor's fought to maintain our monarchy and traditions."

Any other time Grayson wouldn't have minded stopping and exploring the site, but not today. When Annabelle didn't immediately turn around, he thought she was just looking for a safe place to maneuver the car.

"You can turn here. I don't think there's anyone around to see if you drive off the road."

"I'm not turning around."

"What?"

"This is our destination."

"Annabelle, this isn't funny." A feeling of déjà vu came over him. "Turn around."

"No. We're here and there's something I need to see. It won't take long."

Arguing with her was proving fruitless so he pulled his cell phone from his pocket. He went to dial, but realized he didn't know the phone number of the palace. And that wasn't his only problem. There wasn't a signal out here in the middle of nowhere.

He held up his phone and waved it around. Not even one bar appeared on his phone. This wasn't good. He had a bad feeling about this whole expedition. A very bad feeling.

# CHAPTER NINETEEN

THEY'D COME THIS FAR; she wasn't about to back away now.

"Come on." Annabelle got out of the car.

She wasn't so sure Grayson was going to accompany her. He was worried and she couldn't blame him, not after what he went through. But this wasn't her first time without a bodyguard and she highly doubted it would be her last. Sometimes she just needed some privacy and that was tough to do with someone always looking over your shoulder.

She glanced around. Hers was the only car in the parking lot. Everything would be all right. They wouldn't stay long. And contrary to her desires, she wasn't alone.

She started up the path leading to the historic landmark. The cipher had said *PLACARD. TWO. THREE.* Which, if this was the place, had to be just up ahead. She prayed she was right. She just wanted this to be over and to finally have the answers that would hopefully bring her family back together again.

"Annabelle, wait."

She paused and turned to find Grayson striding toward her. He wore a frown on his face that marred his handsomeness just a smidgen. And even if he wasn't happy about being here, she found comfort in his presence. Because maybe she wasn't feeling as brave as she'd like everyone to think. But she refused to be intimidated by that note. She was onto something; she just knew it.

"You're going to do this no matter what I say, aren't you?" His concerned gaze searched hers.

"I am."

He nodded. "Then lead the way."

"Thank you," she said, not expecting a response. But she was grateful that he wasn't going to fight her any longer.

They continued down the windy path that led them to a spot near the cliff that overlooked the sea. Here there was a small park area. There was a sign explaining the historic significance of the spot, but Annabelle wasn't up for a history lesson right now. She needed to see if this was the place with the next clue to her mother's murder and if not, they needed to move on.

"The message said there would be a placard. Do you see one?" Annabelle gazed around the circular patio area. There were a few tables and benches scattered about. But she didn't see a placard.

Grayson was making his way around the circle. "Over here."

He was standing near a rock wall that butted up against a hillside at the back of the park. She rushed over to where he was standing. She looked around and found a bronze placard in the rock wall. It was dedicated to all of the heroes who had defended their homeland in 1714.

"Do you think that's it?" Annabelle's stomach shivered with nerves. Part of her wanted the truth but the other part of her worried about what she might learn. After all of this time, wondering and imagining what might have happened to her mother, she was surprised by her sudden hesitancy.

"Annabelle, what's wrong?" Grayson sent her a concerned look.

"Nothing." She was being silly. They had to find the answers. "Let's do this."

Grayson reached for her hand. "You do realize that this might not be the right place?"

She nodded. "But we won't know until we look."

Together they counted out the rocks, not quite sure where the starting point might be. The first try didn't pan out. The rock in the wall was firmly in there and there was no way they or anyone else was moving it without some serious tools. The second rock they tried had the same results.

"I'm starting to think I got the clues wrong," Annabelle said, feeling silly for taking Grayson on this pointless trip.

"Don't give up just yet. I think this rock is loose." Grayson gripped the stone and wiggled it. "Yes, it's definitely loose."

"This could be it." She moved forward, planning to help.

Before she could move into a position where she could reach the stone, Grayson jiggled it free. Her mouth gaped, but no words would come out. They'd found it. Would they at last have answers or find yet another coded message?

Grayson gestured toward the wall. "Well, don't just stand there, see if you can find anything."

His voice prompted her into action. She felt around inside the hole and grimaced when she realized there were bugs, slime and a whole host of other disgusting things in there. But then in the back of the cavity, her fingers ran across something different. Much different.

"I think there's a plastic bag in here."

"That's good. Can you pull it out?"

It was hung up in some soft dirt, but she easily pulled it free. The bag was covered in muck, forcing Annabelle to swipe it off with her hand if she had any hope of seeing what was inside.

"Is there anything else in there?" Grayson asked.

"Just this. It looks like some sort of thumb drive. An older one."

Grayson returned the rock to its spot and then moved next to her. She handed over the bag. All the while, she wondered what could be so important about a computer file that it cost her mother her life.

"What do you think is on it?" Annabelle asked.

"I don't know, but I'm guessing it's very important."

"It is," a male voice said from behind them. "Now turn around slowly."

Dread inched down Annabelle's spine like icy fingers. When she turned, she gasped. The man standing there holding a gun on them was someone she knew—someone the king knew and trusted. It was one of the palace staff, Mr. Drago.

He was an older man with thinning white hair and the gun he held on them looked to be even older than him. The hand holding the large revolver shook, but she didn't know if it was from nerves or age. Either way, she wasn't feeling so good about his finger resting on the trigger.

"Drop the bag to the ground and kick it over here," he demanded.

Grayson did as he said without any argument.

"And now your keys."

Annabelle had those. She pulled them from her pocket and dropped them to the ground. She gave them a swift kick sending them skidding over the concrete patio.

"Why?" Annabelle hadn't meant to speak—to do anything to provoke him, but the word popped out of her mouth before she could stop it. With the damage already done, she asked, "Why did you kill my mother?"

After the man picked up the plastic bag and the keys, he stuffed them in his pocket. "You don't understand." His eyes filled with emotion. "No one was supposed to get hurt."

The tremors in his hand grew more intense. The gun moved up and down, left and right. And yet his finger remained on the trigger.

"Your mother, she just wouldn't quit interfering. Just like you. I warned you to leave the past alone, but you just couldn't."

"I… I just need to know the truth—to understand." Annabelle couldn't believe she was staring at the man who had killed her mother. Nothing about the man screamed murderer to her and yet, he'd almost come right out and admitted it. "Why did she have to die?"

The man expelled a weary sigh as though he were shouldering the weight of the world. "Since I'm leaving this island—my home—and never coming back, I suppose I can tell you. My wife…she was sick. She needed to be flown to the United States for treatment, but I didn't have that kind of money. And then I got an offer. For some information about the country's defenses, I could get the money necessary to save my wife's life. I'd have done anything for her. She… she was my world."

Annabelle helplessly stared at the man who'd murdered her mother. His hand with the gun continued to shake. And his finger remained on the trigger. Anger and disbelief churned in her gut. And worst yet, she'd dragged Grayson into this mess, risking both of their lives. She deeply regretted her rash decision to rush out here without security.

There had to be a way out of this. Maybe if she kept the man talking a bit longer, a plan would come to mind. "So what went wrong?"

"Your mother caught on to the plan somehow. She said she was going to tell the king, and I just couldn't let her ruin everything."

And then a memory fell into place. "It was you that I saw arguing with her in the South Shore piazza the evening before she died, wasn't it?"

He nodded. "I was trying to find out how much she knew. I needed to know if she suspected me. She wouldn't tell me anything, but then the next day we met again. She said she'd intercepted a note to me—"

"Your name is Cosmo?" For as long as Annabelle had been coming to the palace, she'd only ever heard the man addressed by his surname—Drago.

"Yes, it is." His arm slowly lowered as though he was tired of holding up the gun. In the next breath, he lifted it again. "Your mother said that she was taking it to the king. That's when I pulled out this gun. She reached for it. We struggled and…and it went off. There was nothing I could do for the princess. The shot hit her in the chest. She…she died before she hit the ground."

Annabelle's heart jumped into her throat as she envisioned her mother's final moments. Her mother had been protecting the king and this land that she loved. She was a hero and no one knew until now.

Annabelle swallowed hard. “What…what happened next?”

“My wife…she died before I could get the data to sell.”

“And what’s on this thumb drive?”

“Instructions on where to deliver the data. And how I’d get my payments.”

“So you never met the person behind the espionage?”

“No. There were cryptic messages and a couple of phone calls.”

“And they just left you alone after your wife died? Even though they didn’t get their information?”

“I was a man with nothing to lose and nothing to gain by then. I told the man on the phone that I’d go to the king and take my punishment before I’d give in to his blackmail.”

“Funny how you grew a conscience after my mother died.” Annabelle’s hands clenched at her sides as she tried to keep her emotions under control. “How could you do that? Do you know how much we loved and needed her?”

The older man’s eyes grew shiny with unshed tears and his face creased with worry lines. “I told you I didn’t mean for it to happen. It…it was an accident.”

“And then what? You made it look like a mugging gone wrong?”

Drago’s eyes narrowed. “What choice did I have? I couldn’t go to jail. Not with my wife so ill. And it was an accident.”

The man didn’t even hesitate as he spoke. Annabelle’s mouth gaped. The man seemed to think of himself as innocent. No wonder he’d gotten away with it for so many years. Without a guilty conscience to trip him up, it’d been easy.

“What did you do with my mother’s jewelry?” Perhaps it was stashed in the palace and could be used as evidence.

“I buried it.”

“Where?”

“I… I don’t know. It was a long time ago.”

“And you just stayed on at the palace, serving the king and acting like nothing ever happened?”

"What else could I do?" A tear splashed onto his weathered cheek. "The king needed me. I couldn't let him down."

*But you could kill his sister without batting an eye?* Annabelle wanted to tell Mr. Drago about the devastation he'd caused, but she had Grayson's safety to think about. She couldn't agitate this man any further. And there was nothing he could say that would bring her mother back to them.

And that was when she noticed movement behind Mr. Drago.

"What are you planning to do with us?" Grayson asked.

She figured that he must have seen her security team and the police moving into position behind the man. And Grayson was doing his best to distract Drago until they were ready to make their move.

"Do with you?" The man's face broke into a smile. "You think I'm going to kill you too?"

*What did one say to that in this very sensitive situation?* Annabelle glanced at Grayson, willing him not to upset the man, who was obviously not quite all there.

Grayson shrugged. "I don't know."

"I'm just going to leave you stranded out here. No one ever visits this place. I'm surprised you found it."

"How did you discover we were coming here?"

"It wasn't hard to eavesdrop and do a bit of snooping—"

His words were cut off as the police signaled for Annabelle and Grayson to drop to the ground. Grayson leapt into action shielding Annabelle's body with his own. Seconds felt like minutes as she was trapped between the concrete and Grayson's muscled chest.

"All clear," an officer called out.

Grayson helped her to her feet. "Are you all right?"

Annabelle nodded. With unshed tears blurring her vision, she said, "I'm so, so sorry. I never meant for any of this to happen."

He didn't say anything. In fact, without another word, he turned his back to her. She blinked repeatedly as she watched him walk away. She had a sickening feeling that, although no shots had been fired, there had been a casualty today.

Their relationship.

# CHAPTER TWENTY

THE RIDE BACK to the palace was tense and silent.

However, the scene awaiting Annabelle was anything but.

They didn't even make it past the great foyer before her father, followed by the king, confronted her. One glance at Grayson told her that she was in this alone. He wouldn't look at her, much less speak to her. They were acting like she'd planned for all of this to happen. All she'd wanted were some long-overdue answers. Was that so bad?

Speaking of answers, she didn't even get a chance to tell them that she finally had them—she knew what had happened—before her father launched into a heated speech.

"How could you do this?" Her father's face was flushed and his arms gestured as he spoke. "I thought I could trust you. And here you go, sneaking around, risking your safety."

"You don't understand—"

"Oh, I understand." Her father frowned at her before stepping in front of Grayson, who at least had the common sense to stay quiet during this confrontation. "And you, I expected more of you. And yet, you let my daughter go off recklessly without her security—"

"That was not my doing." Grayson's voice rumbled with agitation. "At least it wasn't intentionally. We both got wrapped up in a heated conversation. By the time I realized that Annabelle had forgotten proper protocol, we were almost at the landmark."

Her father's voice echoed throughout the foyer. "How could you not realize you were leaving without any security?"

Grayson and her father glared at each other. Jaws were tight. Hands were clenched.

The king cleared his throat. "We were just really worried about you when your bodyguard reported that you'd slipped off without notifying anyone."

Her father's mouth opened, but before he could utter another angry word, Annabelle said, "And how exactly did you find us if my security wasn't following me?"

Her father paused. He averted his gaze. She knew this reaction. She'd seen it in the past when he'd done something that he knew his family would not approve of.

"Poppa, what is it? What did you do?"

His gaze met hers. "It was for your own good. I knew you were out of control and that things might end badly. I had to protect you."

"Poppa, out with it."

He sighed. "After I learned that you stole your mother's journal—"

"Borrowed."

"Fine. Borrowed. I knew there was a possibility that you'd get caught up in the past and you wouldn't be able to stop yourself—you'd have to follow the clues."

"Of course. How could you expect me not to?"

"Well, I wasn't about to let you go off and get yourself hurt so I installed a tracking device in your purse and your car, as well as a tracking app on your phone. I wasn't taking any chances."

Annabelle checked her phone. "You really did. How could you?"

"What? You're attacking me. My forethought is what saved your life."

Annabelle reached for Grayson's hand, craving his strength and the knowledge that they were in this together. Her fingers brushed over the back of his hand. She was just about to curl her fingers around his when he moved his hand behind his back out of her reach.

When she glanced his way, Grayson was staring straight ahead. She couldn't look into his eyes. She had no way of discovering why he had gone from being so helpful at the landmark to completely shutting down now that they were back at the palace. And the little voice in the back of her mind was warning her this was something different from his confrontation with her father. This thing, whatever it was, had to do with her and her alone.

She turned back to her expectant parent. "Mr. Drago wasn't going to hurt us."

When the king spoke, his voice was hollow as though he were in shock. "Drago, he admitted everything to you?"

Annabelle nodded. "I had to push him a bit, but in the end, it all came out."

"Oh, my." The king's color was sickly white. He stumbled a bit. Grayson and her father rushed to his side and helped him into a chair.

"I'll get help," Annabelle said, afraid this revelation was too much for her uncle.

"No. I'm fine," the king said in an unsteady voice. "I don't believe this. First my wife is murdered and now, my sister—all in the name of the crown." His head sunk into his hands.

Annabelle's heart went out to the man, who had weathered so much during his reign. She'd been so young when her aunt, the queen, was assassinated. The assailant had been aiming for the king but had missed. The whole ordeal had taken a toll on the family, but justice had been carried out. Who'd have imagined a few years later Annabelle's own mother would be killed.

Sometimes she thought being royal was a blessing and other times, she knew that it was a curse. Because the king was right, if not for the crown, both of the women who had meant so much to him—to all of them—would still be here.

"I think that it was an accident," Annabelle said, hoping to lessen the blow for everyone.

"Annabelle, how can you talk like this?" Her father's voice shook with emotion. "He stole your mother from us. Surely you must hate him?"

She shook her head. "No, not hate."

"I don't understand," her father said. "I'm trying, but I just don't get it."

She recalled the time she'd spent with her mother. They hadn't enjoyed many years together but in the time that they'd had, her mother taught her some valuable life lessons. "I don't think Momma would want any of us to hate Mr. Drago. She used to say that hate, and even the word itself, was a more powerful weapon than anything man could ever create. Hate could destroy a man as sure as it could destroy a nation."

Her father's mouth gaped as he tried to absorb his daughter's words. And then he composed himself. "For a moment there, you sounded just like her. I never knew she told you that. I'd almost forgotten that she'd said it. And so you've forgiven this Drago man?"

Annabelle shook her head. "Right now, I'm struggling with the not hating part. Forgiveness, well, it's a long ways off. He stole a very precious person from me—from all of us. And then he nearly destroyed our family by covering it up. He did a lot of damage, but I'm trying to take comfort in knowing he now has to account for his crimes."

"I don't know." Her father rubbed the back of his neck. "I don't think I can be as calm and rational about this as you."

She didn't want to lose her father again to hatred and resentment. Maybe if she explained a little more, it would help. "He said he never meant to hurt her, just scare her. And the gun accidentally fired."

Her father looked at her with disbelief reflected in his eyes. "And you believed him?"

She nodded. "He was leaving the country and never coming back. I'm not even sure that old gun still worked. What do you think, Grayson?"

Instead of answering her, he turned and walked away.

Where was he going? And why wasn't he speaking to her?

She chased after him, following him up the stairs. She couldn't let him get away. Not now. Not after everything that they'd shared. This was the beginning. Not the end.

* * *

Grayson couldn't stand there for one more minute.

It didn't matter what anyone said to Annabelle; she thought that she had done the right thing. He'd only ever been that scared one other time in his life. He'd sworn he would never live through something like it again. And yet just minutes ago he'd been staring down the end of a gun and praying that nothing would happen to Annabelle. And she'd refused to be quiet. She'd kept pushing the man, agitating him.

Grayson's heart pounded just recalling the horrific scene. Why did he think that staying here was a good idea? Why did he think Annabelle would be different?

He strode down the hallway toward his suite of rooms. He needed to get away—to be alone. A headache was pounding in his temples. His neck and shoulders ached. His muscles had been tense since he realized they'd left the palace without her security.

He'd just stepped in his room when he heard Annabelle calling out his name. Couldn't she get the message? He just wanted to be alone.

"Grayson—"

"Not now. Go away." He looked around for his bag. He needed to start packing. He just couldn't stay here any longer.

She didn't say anything for a moment and he was hoping that she'd take the hint and leave. He needed to calm down so he didn't end up saying anything that he would later regret.

"I can't go. I don't understand what's going on." She stepped further into the room.

"You don't understand?" Was she serious?

She sent him a wide-eyed stare. "Why are you so upset?"

"Because of you." At last, he recalled his bag was in the closet. He retrieved it and threw it on the bed. "You're reckless. You think you're invincible. And you don't listen to anyone."

"If this is about earlier, I'm sorry. I was just doing what I thought was best—"

"Best for you. Not best for anyone who cares about you. If that man had shot you..." No, he wasn't going there. He couldn't think about going through that agonizing pain again.

He went to the chest of drawers and retrieved a handful of clothes. The sooner he packed, the sooner he'd be on his way to the airport.

"Grayson, what are you doing?"

"I'm packing. I'm leaving here. I should have left a long time ago."

"But...but what about us?"

He didn't stop moving—he couldn't. He stuffed his clothes haphazardly in the bag. As soon as he was out of here—away from Mirraccino—he'd be able to breathe. The worry, it would cease.

"Grayson?"

He kept packing. In the long run, she'd be better off without him. "There is no us. I can't—I won't—continue this relationship. You take too many needless chances. I can't be a part of your life."

"Seriously?" Anger threaded through her voice. "I did what I had to do. And you know it."

"I know you took a chance with your life—with both of our lives. And it wasn't necessary. The police could have handled it."

Out of the corner of his eye, he spied her pressing her hands to her hips. He didn't dare look at her face. He couldn't stand to see the pain that would be reflected in her eyes—pain he'd put there.

"Don't you understand? The police never would have gotten to the truth. Without it my family would never heal."

Part of him knew she believed the words she uttered. Her entire family was separated with no true hope of coming back together. This discovery would give them a chance to start over.

But he also knew that taking risks and breaking rules was what had cost Abbi her life. He couldn't stick around and wait for Annabelle to take another risk. He couldn't stand the thought of losing her just like he'd lost Abbi.

"Grayson, are you even listening to me?" Annabelle moved to the other side of the bed, trying to gain his attention. "Are you leaving because you never really cared about me?"

It was in that moment he realized he was leaving for the exact opposite reason.

He loved Annabelle.

Normally that revelation would bring someone joy and delight, but it made his blood run cold. He'd cared deeply about Abbi, but he'd never loved her like this.

But with Annabelle, he was head over heels in love. The acknowledgment scared him silly. It didn't matter what she promised, she now had the power to destroy him—to rip his heart to shreds.

"I… I can't do this, Annabelle. I'm sorry." He zipped his bag closed, grabbed his computer case from where he kept it on the desk and headed for the door.

He paused in the doorway. Unable to face her, he kept his back to her. "I know you won't believe this, but I did care. I do care. You're just too reckless. I thought we had a chance but I was wrong. I'm glad you found the truth, but now I have to go."

There was a sniffle behind him, but he couldn't help her now. The best thing he could do for both of them was to start walking and keep going. Because the one thing he'd learned in life was that people let you down, sometimes without even meaning to.

This was for the best.

But it sure didn't feel like it. Not at all.

With each step the ache in his heart increased.

# CHAPTER TWENTY-ONE

ALONE.

Not a soul around.

Annabelle made her way along the deserted beach with the bright moonlight guiding her. She had no destination in mind. There was no place she needed to be. And no one who was expecting her.

She should be kicking up her heels and savoring this moment. Or at the very least feeling as though she'd gained something huge—her freedom. There were no longer people looking over her shoulder. There were no reports filed with her father, detailing any of her activities. And that's because the security detail had been officially dismissed not long after Drago was arrested.

Annabelle stopped walking and turned to the water. It wasn't until that moment she realized her freedom was not what she'd been truly craving all of this time. Because if it was then she wouldn't feel so utterly alone and adrift.

Grayson was gone.

For a moment after he'd packed his bags and walked out the door, she'd thought he might change his mind. She'd prayed that he would come back to her. She'd assured herself that he was just having some sort of reaction to the scene at the landmark. Maybe it was shock or fear and it would pass. It didn't.

But how could he just walk away? He did care about her. Didn't he?

There had been lunches and dinners. The chariot race. The gown he'd given her. Their collaboration over the coded messages. And there were so many small moments…a look here or a touch there. Didn't those all add up to mean something special?

Or had she just been fooling herself?

Maybe if she'd been more open, more honest about her

feelings for him instead of keeping it all locked safely inside. Maybe if she'd have taken a chance, he'd still be here.

A breeze off the water rushed over her skin and combed through her hair. She folded her arms over her chest and rubbed her arms with her palms. At last, she realized that freedom wasn't something anyone could give her. Real freedom came from living her life to its fullest and opening her heart to others—something she'd never done with any man—including Grayson.

She missed him so much that her heart ached. There was a gaping hole in it and she didn't know how to stop the pain. By now, he'd be on his way to Italy or California.

How was it that this man had crashed into her life on a city sidewalk and so quickly, so easily snuck past all of her defenses and burrowed so deeply into her heart? And how did she learn to live without his warm smiles, his deep laughs and his gentle touch?

She groaned with frustration. This was a time when a girl really needed her mother. Tears blurred Annabelle's vision and she blinked them away. What would her mother say to her?

Would her mother ask her how she'd fallen so hard? Would she want to know how Annabelle had mucked things up so quickly? And what would she say to her mother? Would she blame it on the severe restrictions her father had unfairly placed upon her? Or would she take responsibility herself for what had happened?

How had she let all of this happen? How had she let herself fall in love only to lose him so quickly?

And then to her horror, she realized her father hadn't put her in a gilded cage, she'd done that all by herself—she'd done it by keeping everyone in her life at arm's length. If she truly wanted to be free, she had to be willing to open her heart…the whole way.

In that moment, alone on the moonlit beach, she knew

what she had to do next. It was time she took that long-thought-about trip to the United States.

But she wouldn't be running away—she'd be running toward something—or rather toward someone.

# CHAPTER TWENTY-TWO

AT LAST HE WAS on his way.

Grayson had stood for a very long time outside the gates of the palace waiting for the taxi to pick him up, at least an hour, if not longer. When he'd first called for a ride and given them the address, they'd thought he was joking. They had no idea that joking around was the very last thing on his mind.

It was almost as if fate was giving him time to change his mind—time to calm down. Well, he had calmed down. The panic over how close Annabelle had come to being hurt had passed.

But what hadn't passed was his determination to leave here—leave Annabelle. They didn't belong together. They came from very different worlds and he had no idea how to fit into hers. And she was too reckless for him to even consider sharing something serious with her.

He'd thought that by walking away from Annabelle he would start to feel better. After all, he'd cut things off. He'd protected himself and her.

Now, in a taxi, speeding toward Mirraccino International Airport, Grayson leaned his head back against the seat. He assured himself that he was doing the right thing. So why did he feel so awful?

He sighed. He'd already decided to cancel the rest of his Mediterranean trip. The expansion project would go on, but he'd put someone else in charge. He needed some distance from the sunny shores, blue waters and everything else that reminded him of Annabelle.

She was reckless with her safety. He couldn't be with someone like that. He needed someone in his life who was… what? Cautious? Sedate? Anything that wasn't Annabelle.

And why did he need that?

He didn't want to examine the answer too closely. He

worried about what he might find when he pulled back the layers. Because it wasn't Annabelle who had the problems.

It was him.

As the airport came into sight, Grayson could no longer run from the truth. He had to accept that he was at fault here—not Annabelle. The moment of truth had arrived. He could either take the easy way out or he could do what was right.

The taxi pulled up to the curb outside the terminal. "Sir, we're here."

Grayson didn't respond. Nor did he move.

By flying off into the night, he was doing what he'd accused Annabelle of doing—being reckless.

Not that he was being reckless with his safety, rather he was being reckless with his heart. True love didn't come around all that often and for him to turn his back on it was wrong. Because whether it was convenient, sensible, or for that matter logical, he was in love with the duke's daughter.

"Please take me back to the palace."

Would it be too late?

Would she at least hear him out?

He had to hope so.

# CHAPTER TWENTY-THREE

ANNABELLE'S MIND WAS made up.

Now all there was to do was make her flight reservations and pack her bags.

There was no time to waste. Every moment that she knew Grayson was upset with her was torture. She didn't even know if he'd open the door to her, but she had to try. She couldn't live with the what-ifs.

Annabelle trudged through the sand toward the steps that climbed up the cliff behind the palace. As for her father and uncle, she'd have to tell them something, but she didn't know exactly what to say or when to say it—

A movement caught her attention. She glanced up at the top of the steps. She could see the shadowed outline of a person. Who would be coming out here this evening? With her cousins and their families still off on their trips, it didn't leave many people who frequented the beach.

As she studied the figure now moving down the steps at a rapid pace, she made out that it was a man. The breath caught in her throat. Was it possible that it was Grayson? Had he changed his mind? Had he come back for her?

Her heart swelled with hope. A part of her knew that if it was indeed him, then he could have come back for a number of reasons including cancelling his contract for the Fo Shizzle Café.

*Please say it isn't so.*

Not about to wait, she started up the steps. The closer she got to him, the more certain she was that it was Grayson. This was her chance to fix things. Now she had to pray that she'd find the right words to convince him that they deserved another chance.

She moved up the steps as fast as her legs would allow. Breathless and nervous, she came face-to-face with Grayson on the middle landing. Her gaze met his, but she wasn't able to read his thoughts.

"I'm sorry." They both said in unison.

Had she heard him correctly? She wanted to rush into his arms, but she restrained herself. She had to be sure he wanted the same things as her.

"I never meant to scare you," she said. "When I went to the landmark, I never imagined that anyone would find us there. I'm sorry."

He continued to stare into her eyes. "And I overreacted. I was afraid that something would happen to you. And I just couldn't handle that because…because I love you."

Her heart swelled with joy. "You do?"

He nodded. "I do. I love you too much for you to take unnecessary chances with your safety."

"I promise to be more cautious going forward because I always want to be able to go home to the man I love."

Grayson opened his arms up to her and she rushed into them.

"I love you," she murmured into his ear.

"I love you too."

At last, she had the love she'd always dreamed of.

Life didn't get any better than this.

# EPILOGUE

*Two months later...*

"GRAYSON, WHAT ARE WE doing here?"

Annabelle stood next to the water fountain in the piazza of the South Shore. She was all dressed up as she'd been in business meetings off and on all morning. Grayson knew this because he'd had a horrible time trying to reach her. At one point, he'd feared that his surprise would be ruined. But at last, he'd heard her voice on the other end of the phone and begged her to meet him here.

He smiled at her. "Don't you know what today is?"

"Of course I do. It's Wednesday."

"True. But it's something else. Something very special."

"Aren't you supposed to break ground for your new offices?"

"Done."

She clasped her hands together and smiled. "Great. Is that what you wanted to show me?"

He shook his head. He had fun surprising her and he'd made a point of it over the past two months, from flowers to chocolate to the sweetest kitten. But today, this would be the biggest surprise of all.

She sent him a puzzled look. "Grayson, what are you up to?"

"Do I need to be up to something?"

She studied him for a moment. "You're most definitely up to something." She smiled. "Are you going to tell me? Or do I need to keep guessing?"

This was the moment. He dropped down on one knee. "Lady Annabelle, you captured my heart the first time we stood next to this fountain. You've led me on an amazing journey. You've taught me how to love. And you've made me the happiest man in the world."

Annabelle gasped and pressed a shaky hand to her gaping mouth. Her eyes glistened with unshed tears of joy. All around them a crowd of curious onlookers was gathering, but it didn't faze him. All that mattered now was Annabelle.

He pulled a little black box from his pocket. He opened it and held it up to her. "Annabelle, I love you. Will you be my best friend, my partner, my lover, forever?"

The tears streamed onto her cheeks as she nodded and smiled.

He placed the ring on her finger before he swept her into his arms and kissed her. He would never tire of holding her close.

When she pulled back, she gazed up at him. "You really want to do this? Get married?"

He nodded. "Definitely. I'm thinking we'll have a grand wedding. We could have it right here, if you like."

"Here in the piazza?" She didn't look so sure. "How about we think it over? After all, I don't want to rush this. I plan to be engaged only once and I want a chance to savor it."

"Then how would you feel about the grandest engagement party?"

Her face lit up. "I love it! But the size of the party doesn't matter as long as all of the men in my life are there."

"Then it's a plan. I love you."

"I love you too."

* * * * *

**“Don’t expect me to forgive you,” she said.**

“I don’t.” But seeing her again, remembering that they’d once been two halves of a whole, made him wish she could. “I just thought you should know about the divorce.”

“It is kind of important,” she agreed. “Chances are I would have found out the hard way pretty soon.”

“Oh?”

“I’ve been dating someone and it’s getting serious.” She turned away and walked over to the couch, absently rearranging throw pillows. “Lately he’s been hinting about getting married.”

Linc had absolutely no right to the feeling, but that didn’t stop the blast of raw jealousy that roared through him. “I guess it would have been awkward to apply for a marriage license and find out you were still married.”

“You think?”

He detected the tiniest bit of defensiveness in her voice and decided to take a shot. “You never told him you’d been married before?”

“We were married for fifteen minutes.” Ten years ago her eyes took on shades of gray when she was annoyed, and they looked that way now. “It was a long time ago. I’ve been busy. It didn’t seem important.”

“The thing is, you never checked to find out about the divorce,” he reminded her.

“Neither did you.”

“Fair enough. I’ll take care of it now…”

* * *

**The Bachelors of Blackwater Lake:**
They won’t be single for long!

"Don't expect me to forgive you," she said.

[illegible]

[illegible]

"Oh."

[illegible]

[illegible]

"You don't."

[illegible]

[illegible]

[illegible]

[illegible]

[illegible]

*The [illegible]*

[illegible]

# JUST A LITTLE BIT MARRIED

BY
TERESA SOUTHWICK

All rights reserved including the right of reproduction in whole or in part in any form. This edition is published by arrangement with Harlequin Books S.A.

This is a work of fiction. Names, characters, places, locations and incidents are purely fictional and bear no relationship to any real life individuals, living or dead, or to any actual places, business establishments, locations, events or incidents. Any resemblance is entirely coincidental.

This book is sold subject to the condition that it shall not, by way of trade or otherwise, be lent, resold, hired out or otherwise circulated without the prior consent of the publisher in any form of binding or cover other than that in which it is published and without a similar condition including this condition being imposed on the subsequent purchaser.

® and ™ are trademarks owned and used by the trademark owner and/or its licensee. Trademarks marked with ® are registered with the United Kingdom Patent Office and/or the Office for Harmonisation in the Internal Market and in other countries.

First Published in Great Britain 2017
By Mills & Boon, an imprint of HarperCollins*Publishers*
1 London Bridge Street, London, SE1 9GF

© 2017 Teresa Southwick

ISBN: 978-0-263-92281-3

23-0317

Our policy is to use papers that are natural, renewable and recyclable products and made from wood grown in sustainable forests. The logging and manufacturing processes conform to the legal environmental regulations of the country of origin.

Printed and bound in Spain
by CPI, Barcelona

**Teresa Southwick** lives with her husband in Las Vegas, the city that reinvents itself every day. An avid fan of romance novels, she is delighted to be living out her dream of writing for Mills & Boon.

To my sister-in-law, Rose Boyle.
I borrowed your name for the heroine in this book because she's as smart and sweet as you.
Thanks for marrying my brother, sole sister!

## *Chapter One*

"Rose, this might come as a shock, but we're not divorced."

Lincoln Hart looked around the room to make sure there was nothing pointed, heavy, or sharp enough to take out an eye, bash in his skull or maim a fairly important body part. Satisfied, he studied the woman he hadn't seen in ten years and realized Rose Tucker was even more beautiful than she'd been then, when she took his breath away every time he saw her. When he was so in love that being apart from her was almost a physical ache.

*Rose*. Even her name was lovely. She was more polished than the young woman he'd walked away from. And more hostile, but he couldn't blame her.

After what he'd just said she was going to hate him even more than she had a decade ago, and she'd hated him quite a lot then.

"What? Not even a hello?" The hostility in her dark blue eyes wavered to make way for surprise, then suspicion.

"I thought it best to lead with the headline, make sure you got the information before slamming the door in my face."

"You're telling me we're still married? I don't believe you. What kind of game are you playing now? What in the world would you have to gain by pretending we're still married?"

"I'm not pretending. And I'm as thrown by this as you are."

"I doubt that." She put a hand to her forehead as if feeling dizzy.

Linc reached out and curved his fingers around her upper arm to steady her. "Let's sit down."

Apparently his touch snapped her out of it because she yanked her arm away. He half expected her to take a swing at him and wouldn't blame her if she did. This whole mess was his fault from start to finish. If there was anything at all positive about his screwup, it was that his family knew nothing about his brief, whirlwind marriage.

His brothers, Sam and Cal, would rag on him relentlessly, which was bad enough. Katherine and Hastings Hart, his mother and her husband, and his younger sister, Ellie, would be disappointed in him for the way he'd handled the situation. But none of that mattered now. He and Rose had a problem and it was all on him.

"We should probably sit—"

"Don't be nice to me, Linc. We both know that's not who you are."

"What I did to you was lousy, Rose, but that's not who I am." He wasn't the man she thought she'd married, but he wasn't a complete jerk, either.

They stood in the postage-stamp-sized living area of her apartment, which was upstairs from her small interior design studio in an old, redbrick building on one of Prosper,

Texas's, side streets. The fact that this one-room place had charm was a reflection of her skill as an interior designer. The paint was pale gold except for one olive-green accent wall in the living room. The kitchen and living areas were set apart by the clever placement of the love-seat-sized sofa. Wall hangings, knickknacks, lamps and throw pillows added color without being stuffy and formal. It was homey and warm. He liked her taste very much.

"You must have questions," he said.

"How do you know we're not divorced?" She tucked a strand of long black hair behind her ear.

"My lawyer passed away after a short illness and I had to hire a new one to handle my personal affairs. He insisted on looking over all of my official documents. There was a marriage license but no divorce decree. After researching the situation, he discovered that the papers were never filed with the court."

"How could that happen?"

It was hard not to cringe at her bewildered tone, especially since he'd assured her he would handle everything. "I hired a half-price lawyer and got what I paid for—half a divorce."

"Why would you do that, Linc? Your family is worth millions and Hart Industries must have a platoon of the best and brightest legal minds around. It doesn't make sense that you would get an attorney from outside the company, especially someone incompetent. The Harts don't do things like that."

Leave it to Rose to zero in on the core of the problem. It wasn't something he wanted to talk about, but she had a right to know. "I'm not a Hart."

"Excuse me? You're what now?"

"Hastings Hart isn't my father."

"No way." She shook her head.

"It's true. Hastings and Katherine confirmed it. I found out right after we got married."

"How?"

"My biological father came to see me. He confessed he had a…thing with my mother."

"You told me your parents were deliriously happy," Rose said with equal amounts of accusation and defensiveness in her voice.

"That was their story. Turns out there was a rough patch. My older brothers were born nine months apart—twins the hard way, she always said. The fact is she had her hands full raising them and Hastings wasn't around much. He was traveling, working long hours to build Hart Industries into something he could leave to his sons."

"So she turned to another man and had an affair?"

"He and my mother were legally separated and headed for a divorce, so technically it wasn't an extramarital affair."

"And you never knew? Never suspected?" There was skepticism in the questions.

"No. They worked through their problems and he promised to give me his name. Both of them agreed there was no reason for me to know."

"And your biological father was all right with the arrangement?"

"He was a lawyer on the partner track at an ultraconservative law firm that specialized in divorce. Sleeping with a client and getting her pregnant would have caused a scandal that might have cost him his career, so keeping it secret was fine with him."

"Yet he told you all those years later. Why?"

"Midlife crisis, I guess. He never had children." He stopped, waiting for the anger to roll through him so he could continue the act and pretend he was reconciled to the ugly secret. "No one to carry on the family name got to him, probably."

"You don't know?"

"It was a short conversation. At that moment I didn't know whether or not he was lying." Turned out the guy was the only one who *hadn't* lied. "Hastings and Katherine confirmed."

"And you haven't talked to your father since? Asked him why he finally came forward?"

"No." The man ruined his life. Sharing DNA didn't make that okay. "The narcissistic bastard only thought about the fact that he had a son, not what the revelation would do to that son."

"Oh, God. Linc—" Shock and resentment were replaced by pity in her eyes and that wasn't much of an improvement. "I guess it hit you hard."

"Let's just say finding out your parents lied to you about Santa Claus is nothing compared to learning your father isn't who you thought." Linc had had no idea who he was and his only thought was to protect Rose, even from himself.

He remembered that time as if it was yesterday. She'd been hired for the summer at Hart Industries in the real-estate development branch of the company he was taking over. They fell madly in love, had a whirlwind romance and he swept her away to Las Vegas, where they got married. It was the best time of his life and he'd never been happier. Then everything went to hell.

He shook his head and met her gaze. "You thought you married a Hart but I'm not one."

Understanding dawned in her eyes. "You think that was important to me?"

Intensity rotated through him and was nearly as powerful as what he'd felt ten years ago. He recalled the anguish and pain in her voice when she'd pleaded with him to tell her why he was leaving. What she'd done. It was an understatement to say he hadn't been thinking clearly. He left the Harts, too, and stayed away for a long time. "It mattered to me."

"So you had to split from me and got a half-price lawyer to do it."

"I didn't feel it was right to use a Hart attorney since I wasn't really part of the family. And in the spirit of full disclosure, I walked away from everyone." He backpacked through Europe, although it would be more accurate to say that he drank his way from one country to the next. "After two years I came back." But he never forgot that he was the bastard son who always needed to prove himself.

"And your father? The biological one?"

"What about him?"

"What's he like?"

"Good question. Like I said, I don't see him. And if it's all the same to you I don't want to talk about him. I only brought it up for context."

"Don't expect me to forgive you," she said.

"I don't." But seeing her again, remembering that they'd once been two halves of a whole, made him wish she could. "I just thought you should know about the divorce."

"It is kind of important," she agreed. "Chances are I would have found out the hard way pretty soon."

"Oh?"

"I've been dating someone and it's getting serious." She turned away and walked over to the couch, absently rearranging throw pillows. "Lately he's been hinting about getting married."

Linc had absolutely no right to the feeling but that didn't stop the blast of raw jealousy that roared through him. "I guess it would have been awkward to apply for a marriage license and find out you were still married."

"You think?"

He detected the tiniest bit of defensiveness in her voice and decided to take a shot. "You never told him you'd been married before?"

"We were married for fifteen minutes." Ten years ago her eyes took on shades of gray when she was annoyed and they looked that way now. "It was a long time ago. I've been busy. It didn't seem important."

"The thing is, you never checked to find out about the divorce," he reminded her.

"Neither did you."

"Fair enough. I will take care of it now. Mason, my new lawyer, will handle the details and send the papers to you for your signature. Then it will be behind us." At least the paperwork part. His feelings were a lot more complicated than he'd expected.

"Okay." She frowned. "How did you know where I was?"

"How does anyone find anyone? I looked you up on the internet."

Also he'd checked her out, found out what she'd been doing all these years. First college, then five years working with a prestigious design firm in Dallas before opening her own business not quite two years ago. And it wasn't doing well. If she was, she'd still be located in Dallas, not thirty-five miles away, where office and living spaces were combined and cheap.

She ran everything herself, no hired help and therefore no payroll. There were a few flooring, window-covering and paint samples in her downstairs studio, but not what you'd see in a larger, successful company.

Her reputation was good, but her business was going

down with a whimper. Unless someone gave her a high-profile opportunity.

"Look, Rose, there's another reason I came to see you."

"What else could there possibly be? Isn't the fact that we're not legally divorced enough?"

"This is a good thing. Trust me."

"Seriously? You have the nerve to ask me to trust you? Getting involved with you was the worst mistake of my life."

"Right." He refused to react, to let her know the arrow hit its mark. "You have no reason to trust me. And that doesn't bode well, because I want to offer you a job."

"Doing what?"

"Decorating." He moved closer. "My condo in Blackwater Lake, Montana."

"And why would I want to do that?"

"Because the town is about to be on the rich-and-famous radar when a new hotel, condo and retail project opens. The hotel is entering the last phase of construction and will need decorating. I know the developer. Use my condo for your résumé and dazzle them. I'll put in a good word." Linc pitched her the rest of the details, then asked, "What do you think?"

"I think I want to know what your angle is."

"No ulterior motive." Except giving her business a helping hand might earn him some redemption points.

"I don't need your charity."

"That's not what this is." He slid his fingertips into the pockets of his slacks. "I don't deserve a favor, but I'm asking for one. Just think about it."

"Why?"

"Because you're good at what you do." He pulled a card from his wallet and set it on the coffee table. "Call me in a few days with your decision. And before you think about *not* calling, you should know that I'll contact you."

"Okay."

Linc was reluctant to leave but decided not to push his luck. The weird thing was he'd never planned to offer her a job. That changed when he saw her.

Accepting his proposition would mean traveling to Blackwater Lake with him and he really wanted her to do that. For old time's sake. For her business. To make things up to her so he would feel better about what he'd done.

Ultimately the reasons were about him, which did, in fact, make him a self-centered bastard like his father.

"What do you mean you're married? More important—why do I not know this about you? And don't even get me started on why I wasn't invited to the wedding."

Rose stared at her BFF, Vicki Jeffers. After Linc left she couldn't stop shaking. He was a ghost from the past and she'd barely held it together when he showed up out of the blue. She'd really needed to talk to someone and begged her friend to come over. Apparently her shocked and shaky tone had convinced the other woman to break a date. So Rose told her story and the other woman was now staring at her as if she had two heads.

"I'm not married so much as not quite divorced." She took another sip of the wine Vicki had brought. It was a nice vintage, more than Rose could afford. The business she'd launched eighteen months ago wasn't exactly setting the world on fire. Paying her bills was a challenge and left no room in the budget for an expensive bottle of cabernet.

"So you've been married for ten years."

"Not technically," Rose objected.

"Yeah, technically," Vicki countered. "Because if you're

not divorced, you're still married. And you just said that happened almost ten years ago."

"It ended after a nanosecond, so not really married that long."

"Might not feel that way but legally you've been his wife all these years." Vicki sighed and held up a hand. She was sitting at the other end of the couch and tucked her legs up beside her, settling in for a marathon heart-to-heart. "Why don't you start at the beginning?"

Rose blew out a long breath as the highs and lows of that emotional time tumbled through her mind. "It was the summer before I started college. I got a clerical job at Hart Industries. Lincoln Hart had just finished his master's degree in business and was taking his place in the company his father started." Although now she knew Hastings Hart wasn't his biological father.

"So... What? He hit on you? Used his position of power to sexually harass you?"

"Why would you think such a thing?"

"Because I'm a lawyer," Vicki said.

"A very cynical one." Rose shook her head. "He was a perfect gentleman. The truth is we fell madly in love and got married."

"And you never saw fit to say a word about it when we met at school? I thought we shared all of our secrets." There was just a tinge of hurt in her friend's brown eyes. Vicki wrapped a long strand of silky blond hair around her finger and stared accusingly. "But you kept the secret that you were Rose Hart."

The name had a nice ring to it, but she'd never even had a chance to change the last name on her driver's license. "Linc abruptly ended things and said he would handle the divorce details and a lawyer would contact me if he needed anything from me. No one did, so I thought it was done."

"And you didn't wonder why you never heard anything about signing the settlement papers?"

"What did I know about a divorce?" And if she was being honest, there'd been a lot of denial going on. And she'd been so hurt. The pain of not being with him was almost more than she could bear. So many awful feelings. The shock of being dumped without an explanation. Overwhelming bewilderment. Now she knew what happened but still didn't understand why he had to leave her. She would have done anything for Lincoln Hart—or whatever his name was. "I was practically a baby."

"You weren't too young to get married."

"He swept me off my feet. I couldn't say no to him. And he—"

"What?" Vicki's eyes narrowed. "Did he do something?"

"Not what you're probably thinking. He was incredibly sweet and understanding." Not to mention sexy and handsome and completely irresistible. Unfortunately the "sexy and handsome" part hadn't changed. But he was totally resistible to her now. "I was a virgin."

Vicki nearly choked on her wine. "How is that possible?"

"You make me sound like a weirdo. I was only eighteen."

"And crazy in love," Vicki reminded her. "You just told me that you couldn't say no."

"To marriage," she amended. "My mom drilled into me that a man has no need to buy the cow when he gets the milk for free. And if you give it away, he'll just mosey on down the road to another cow. That's what happened to her. Unfortunately when my father moseyed, she was stuck with a baby." Rose pointed to herself. "Yours truly."

"Ah."

"She was determined that the same thing wouldn't happen to me and never let up with the warning not to sleep with a man until I had a ring on my finger. I thought I got really lucky that the man of my dreams was determined to marry me. Of course I couldn't say no."

"So he married you to..." Vicki tapped her lips. "Pop your cherry?"

"That's what I believed for ten years." Rose recalled every word of what he'd said before walking out of her life. She remembered him telling her that he couldn't be with her because he wasn't in her league. She'd thought that was about him having more money than God and her not fitting into his world. Now she knew he'd been talking about himself because his father wasn't who he'd thought. "He had a crisis of identity."

Vicki rolled her eyes. "Yeah, I can see how that could happen. Must be tough figuring out which billions belong to you or your brothers when you're a Hart."

That's just it. At the time he'd recently learned he wasn't biologically a part of the family. But she didn't feel comfortable revealing that.

"Things aren't always what they seem." Rose knew that statement was cryptic, but it wasn't her secret to share, not even with the friend who was like a sister to her.

"A case could be made," Vicki said pointedly, "that he proposed because he was after one thing. Correct me if I'm wrong, but he got what he wanted, then said adios."

"You're not wrong." But there was more to it.

"And you're not divorced? Seems to me someone from the legal department at Hart Industries should be canned over this."

"You'd think." Rose shrugged. "It's probably not a stretch to say that my vow of chastity could have impacted the haste of his proposal. But, I am my mother's daughter." Although she'd made up her mind to be different from Janie Tucker and not play the victim card for the rest of her life.

"So, how was it?" Vicki sipped the last of the wine in her glass. "Seeing him again, I mean?"

"It was surreal. He hasn't changed, other than being ten years older. But it looks good on him." And she hated that. If he was fat, bald and irritating the trauma of having her heart ripped out and handed back would have been worth it. But her luck wasn't that good.

His eyes were still a mesmerizing shade of dark blue. He was tall, lean and broad-shouldered. Walking, talking animal magnetism that was so powerful she could hardly remember what she'd said to him. "And, darn him, like all men he just looks better. Call me shallow, but this would be so much easier if he looked like a troll."

"Very annoying of him." Vicki shifted her position on the couch. "Were there still sparks between you?"

Not unless anger counted. Or maybe it never went away. It had been hard, but ten years ago she pulled herself together and patched the hole Linc left in her life. There was a good possibility that anger had filled up that empty space. "Nope. No sparks."

"So, he came to personally inform you that your divorce never happened." Her friend tilted her head. "That means your tenth wedding anniversary is coming up soon."

"Since we haven't lived together, I don't think there will be an exchange of gifts." Sarcasm was good, Rose thought. It was a sign that she was rebounding.

"I wonder what you give for ten years of marriage."

"A divorce, hopefully." Yay her. A pithy comeback. She was on a roll.

Vicki shook her head, still trying to take in the situation. "How could you never tell me about all this?"

"Haven't you ever done something that is so completely mortifying and humiliating that you didn't want anyone to know about it ever?"

"Of course." Her friend grinned. "But nothing this spectacular. And you know all of my mortifying and humiliating escapades. Yet you kept this to yourself."

"I'm sorry."

"No, no. Don't give me those big, blue Kewpie-doll eyes. You're only sorry you got caught. I want to know why I didn't hear about this until crisis time."

"At first I just wanted to forget. Start college and put it behind me." She'd thought not talking about it would make the pain go away but she'd been wrong. Time had been the cure. "You and I met, and clicked, but I didn't really know you that well. Then the longer I didn't say anything, the more I didn't know how to bring it up. Besides, I thought I was quietly divorced and no one ever had to know."

If no one knew, it wouldn't hurt as bad, right?

"Speaking of that… It's probably a good thing that you found out. Otherwise, when you and Chandler went to get a marriage license, that could have been a shock," Vicki commented.

"That's what Linc said."

"Good. He knows you haven't been pining for him."

If she'd never seen him again Rose would accept that as true. But the rush of emotions when she'd answered her door and instantly recognized him stirred memories of that brief, shining moment when she'd had everything she ever wanted. Had there been pining going on and she wasn't aware of it?

Vicki set her empty glass on the coffee table. "How did Chandler take this 'being married and not divorced' thing?"

"He doesn't know."

"You haven't told him yet?" Her friend looked more shocked about that than any revelation so far.

"No."

"Keeping important details to yourself is starting to form a disturbing pattern. Why haven't you told him?"

"It just happened a few hours ago," Rose protested.

"You called me. It's not a stretch that you could have clued Chandler in on this."

"I needed to wrap my head around it before dumping this kind of news on him. And—" Rose loved her friend, but this rational side could be annoying. Mostly because Vicki was right. "The situation got even more complicated."

"I don't see how."

"Linc offered me a job decorating his condo. A very high-profile project that will generate a lot of attention and publicity."

"There's more, right?" her friend asked suspiciously.

"If it goes well, there's a chance I could get more work in the area. These guys—the Holdens—are building a hotel and resort, all of which will need decorating. This is a once-in-a-lifetime opportunity."

"Obviously you didn't say no."

"You're a lawyer. If someone offered you a case that was the equivalent of this, would you walk away from it? No matter who was doing the asking?"

"I see your point," Vicki reluctantly agreed.

"This could be really lucrative. A career maker." She filled in even more details about the development and the area with luxury homes cropping up. "We both know if I don't get a break Tucker Designs is finished."

"Maybe not—"

Rose's look stopped the words. "I'm going down, Vee. You're my attorney. You've seen my financials. I don't even want to think about that loan from the small business association. And then there's my mom. She raised me completely by herself and worked so hard all her life to take care of me. Waitressing isn't easy and I'd like her to be able to cut back. Enjoy herself more. You know?"

"Yes, but—" Vicki stopped and shook her head.

"How do you think Chandler would take it?" Rose asked.

"Let me think about this." Vicki hummed the *Jeopardy* theme. "You tell the man you're all but engaged to that you're going to Montana with the man you married ten years ago and aren't quite divorced from to do a job in order to save your business."

Rose nodded. "Yes."

"I think any man's head would explode given that scenario."

"That's what I figured, too." This was what Rose really wanted to talk to her friend about. She'd revealed her history with Linc because it had a direct bearing on her decision. As Linc would say—context. "What do you think I should do?"

It didn't take Vicki very long to come up with an answer. "Tell Chandler and don't take the job."

Rose nearly choked on her wine. That's not what she'd expected. "What? I thought you understood."

"I do. But I also saw your face when you talked about Lincoln Hart." There was sympathy in her friend's expression. "I've known you for a long time and you've never looked like that before. Tell me I'm nuts but whether you're willing to admit it or not, you have feelings for the man."

"Of course I do. All of them bad."

"Take it from me. Accepting that job will dredge up more feelings and all the crap comes up, too. Just leave it alone. You're doing fine. Don't give him a chance to hurt you again."

"He can't."

"Okay." Vicki's tone was full of "if you say so but I think you're wrong." "For what it's worth, my advice is to talk this over with Chandler. I'm sure he'll tell you the same thing. Do not take this job."

"Wow, don't hold back. Tell me how you really feel."

"I always do." Her friend smiled. "And just so you know, I want to look over those divorce papers before you sign anything. This time things will run smoothly or you'll know why."

"Thank you, Vicki."

"So you're not mad at me?"

"Why would I be?" Rose protested.

"For telling you what I thought. I know you didn't want to hear that."

"I count on you."

"So we're okay?" her friend asked.

"Absolutely."

That was completely true and Rose valued this woman's opinion more than she could say. But she was going to break the unbreakable rule about automatically taking your best friend's advice. Rose just hoped there wouldn't be an "I told you so" in her future.

## *Chapter Two*

"So you're really moving to Blackwater Lake, Montana?"

Linc was standing by the side table in his office, where there was a bottle of exceptional single malt Scotch, and glanced over his shoulder. It was precisely six thirty and Mason Archer, his attorney, stood in the doorway. Right on time.

"Would you like a drink?" Linc asked.

"Yes." The other man walked closer, passing the desk piled with papers, and went directly to the conversation area with its leather furniture and sleek glass-and-chrome coffee table.

After handing Mason the tumbler of Scotch, Linc said, "You know my sister, Ellie, lives there, right?"

"I do."

Linc grinned because there was no missing his friend's clipped tone. "Don't take her rejection personally."

"How do you take it when a woman says there's nothing that could compel her to have dinner with you?"

"That was a bad time. She'd been burned and swore off men," Linc said. Mason had worked for Hart Industries while Ellie was still there. The man once had a thing for her but that was before she met her husband. However, bringing it up never failed to get a rise out of his friend. Linc liked to get a rise out of him because it almost never happened. "Trust me, it wasn't personal."

"Okay."

"That's it? You're a lawyer who makes arguments for a living. It's like air to you."

"Knowing when not to argue is just as important. Ellie is happily married and has a child. I'm glad for her."

"So you're over her," Linc persisted.

"There was never anything to get over."

"If you say so."

Mason sighed before taking a sip of his drink. "There are many, many other clients I could work for."

"You'd lose a lot of money if you left me," Linc reminded him.

"The peace and quiet would be worth it." Tough words but the other man was smiling.

"You're going to miss me when I'm in Montana."

"Tell me again why it is that you're going," his friend said.

"I'm buying in to my brother-in-law's construction company. It needs an infusion of capital to expand in Blackwater Lake. The town is one of the fastest growing places in the country and there's a lot of opportunity."

The one at the top of his list was getting out of the Hart family shadow. He'd insisted on being treated as an employee of the company and not an heir apparent, like his half brothers. In the last ten years he'd worked his ass off, partly to prove himself to them and partly to stay too busy to think about how his personal life had imploded. The other day he'd seen the anger and resentment in Rose's eyes but that was better than having her grow to despise him because he wasn't a Hart.

He didn't tell her because she would have said she fell in love with the man and not his last name. But the truth was it would have been like marrying the prince who would be king, then finding out he'd been switched at birth for the peasant who owned a pigsty. Walking away saved her from having to deal with that. It was the right thing to do but that didn't get him off the restitution hook for how he'd treated her.

The upside of keeping too busy to brood over lost love was making a lot of money. And he was going to take that money to Blackwater Lake and build more success on his own terms.

Linc remembered telling Rose that it was about to be on the "rich and famous" radar. A place for her to build success too but he had yet to hear from her. It was amazing how much that bugged him. And it's not like he hadn't known there was a better-than-even chance she would tell him to stick his offer where the sun didn't shine.

"Opportunity in rural Montana?" Mason drained the rest of the Scotch in his glass. "There's nowhere to go but up when you're in the sticks."

"It has an airport now." A thought popped into Linc's mind. "You should think about opening a law office there."

"I'm not licensed to practice in Montana."

"You could be. It's probably not a big deal to make that happen." Linc sat on the leather love seat. "There's no competition right now. Could be a good move for you, my friend."

"Not so bad for you, either." The attorney's tone was wry.

This man was an outstanding lawyer. Principled, meticulous, conscientious and smart. They'd met while working for Hart Industries, then Mason had opened his own law firm. When Linc's personal attorney passed away Mason was the guy he wanted. "I'll admit having legal counsel close by would be convenient, but your success and happiness are a concern."

Mason laughed. That was worth mentioning because it didn't happen often. He was far too serious. Linc figured a woman would find him good-looking and wondered what Rose would think. For a split second there was a white-hot flash of jealousy. Not unlike the feeling he'd experienced when she'd mentioned dating someone and that it was getting serious. Again he had a flicker of annoyance at her not getting back to him about the job offer.

"Seriously?" The other man set his empty glass on the silver tray beside the Scotch bottle. "My happiness?"

"Blackwater Lake is a great place. Nice people. Beautiful scenery. Lots to do all year round with the lake and the mountains. You could have a hand in shaping its growth in a positive way. And do something good for yourself at the same time."

Mason's eyes narrowed. "Correct me if I'm wrong, but didn't you once call it Black Hole, Montana?"

"That was a different time."

Linc remembered it well. Ellie had called him, upset because she was pregnant and things were not going well between her and the baby's father, Alex McKnight. The man had eventually won over Linc as well as Sam and Cal. He married Ellie and they had a daughter, Leah, who was two. Moving to the small town in Montana was the best thing ever, she often said to him. Now he was going to see whether or not she was right.

"So, Mason, before we grab dinner, you're probably wondering how the meeting went."

"I'm assuming you're talking about the one with your wife," the attorney clarified.

That took Linc by surprise. The wife part. It had been ten years and as Rose had pointed out, they were married for fifteen minutes. Not nearly long enough to think about her being his wife. Regret about that coiled inside him. And in the decade that had passed no woman had gotten close to him again. Ellie had said more than once that he used women like cocktail napkins and threw them away because he'd never fallen in love. The truth was exactly the opposite. Because he'd loved so deeply and had to let her go he wouldn't ever risk it a second time.

"Linc?"

"Yeah. Right. How did it go with Rose." He shook his head to clear it and thought for a moment. "Better than I expected."

Mason waited, then finally said, "Care to give me the highlights?"

"She didn't throw anything."

"You were at her place." It wasn't a question.

Since Linc hadn't given him the when and where, he asked, "How did you know?"

"She didn't want to break any of her stuff."

"Ah." He hadn't thought of that when picking the venue for his bombshell. His only thought had been that the last thing she'd ever said to him was that she never wanted to see him again. There wouldn't have been a meeting if he'd tried to set one up. Surprise had been the only option. And it worked, sort of. He'd expected to feel nothing and got a surprise of his own at the flood of emotion, the explosion of memories that was like being pelted with hail.

"And after she didn't throw anything?" Mason prompted. "What did she say?"

"She didn't believe it." Linc had revealed everything

to his attorney, including the fact that Hastings Hart was not his biological father. "I explained what happened and convinced her it was true. Of course she wanted to know how the divorce screwup happened."

"You get what you pay for." There was an ironic tone in the other man's voice.

"I already told you that was before your time. Rose seemed…sympathetic after I told her about what happened."

Sympathy was so much more palatable than pity. And he would never be sure whether or not his standing in a financial dynasty mattered to her because he'd taken that choice out of her hands. It was impossible to know for sure if she fell in love with *him*, or the him that was part of the Hart family fiscal package. But in the last ten years he'd learned women were attracted to money even when it came from a bastard.

"What did she say?"

Linc met the other man's gaze. "That I should have told her what was going on."

"You have no idea how hard it is for me not to say 'duh.'"

"Don't think I didn't notice you just did." Linc sighed. "No one is disputing the fact that I'm an ass."

"It's not too late to change."

"Sometimes it is."

"You're ten years older and wiser," Mason reminded him.

"True. But age and wisdom can't undo what I did to her. Only reparation can do that."

"It's true that I haven't worked for you long, but I'm sensing something." Mason's attorney expression returned. "Did she mention retaining legal counsel?"

"No."

"She should," Mason pointed out. "To protect her rights."

"I have no intention of treating her unfairly in the divorce settlement."

The other man's eyes narrowed. "Then what did you do?"

"I offered her a job."

"Doing what?"

Linc hadn't shared his research on Rose. "She has an interior-design business and it's not doing well. She needs some help."

"So, you're giving her money?" There was no approval or judgment in the other man's voice, he was just seeking clarification of facts.

"No. I want to hire her to decorate my place in Blackwater Lake. With the possibility of future high-profile projects to strengthen her résumé and get more work."

Mason thought that over, then nodded approvingly. "Smart move. Keep her happy to avoid an ugly and public divorce. In the long run a goodwill gesture could be less expensive than a lawsuit for retroactive alimony. Alienation of affection."

"This has nothing to do with dodging back–spousal support. She's entitled to a generous settlement." Pain and suffering came to mind and Linc winced. He hated that he was the one who'd hurt her. "But you should know that she hasn't agreed to my offer yet."

It had been long enough and Linc was beginning to wonder if Rose planned to ignore his proposition. He wasn't sure what constituted a decent length of time to allow her for consideration, but time was almost up. He'd give her another twenty-four hours, but if there was no word, he planned to make good on his promise to contact her.

"You're a good man, Linc."

"Don't tell anyone. No one would believe you but it could be bad for my business reputation if that rumor got out."

"There's this handy thing called attorney-client privilege and it means I'm not allowed to reveal your confidential information."

Even if Mason swore on a bible, Linc was pretty sure Rose wouldn't believe him. Leaving her had ripped out his heart and if she hurt even half that bad it made what he'd done unforgivable. So, the longer it took for her to get back to him, the more determined he became to hire her. If necessary he would sweeten the deal. Somehow…

His cell phone rang and he picked it up, checking the caller ID. What a coincidence. Before it sounded again, he answered. "Rose."

"Hello, Linc. I've been thinking about what you said."

Her voice was businesslike with just a hint of sultriness in the slight lisp. It took a lot of self-control to hold off on a hard sell. "And?"

"I'd like to discuss it in more detail."

"Okay. I'll meet you for dinner. In say…" He looked at the watch on his wrist. "An hour?"

"Tonight?" She sounded surprised.

"Yes. I'm free." He met Mason's gaze and shrugged.

"Tomorrow at my studio would be fine," she said.

Did she have a date? With the guy she was "almost engaged" to? A knot tightened in his gut. "Do you have plans?"

"No, but—"

"Then I'll pick you up in about an hour," he said. "What do you say?"

There was hesitation on the other end of the line that was just about to turn awkward. Then she said, "I'll meet you at the diner. There's only one in Prosper so you can't miss it."

"Okay. See you then."

After he ended the call Mason cleared his throat. "So, I get bumped for dinner with your wife. Should my feelings be hurt?"

"Come on, Mason. We both know lawyers don't have feelings." He grinned at the other man. "You said yourself this was a smart move. I have to close the deal on my goodwill gesture."

And if this was a little more than goodwill that would just be a secret not even his attorney knew.

Rose didn't know what to make of the fact that Linc was able and, dare she say it, eager to have this meeting on such short notice. She hesitated to say he dropped everything but it kind of felt that way.

She'd intended to be at the diner first but got a call about a potential job and had to take it. She wanted to be the one watching him make the long walk past the counter and swivel stools to the booths and tables at the far end. In a perfect world they would both have arrived at the same time, but why should her world start being perfect now? A world where she was in control and not nervous about what the man who'd walked out on her was up to.

Now she was late and moving toward a table in the back, where he was sitting and staring at *her*.

If only she knew what he was thinking. On the upside… She was ten years older and less likely to give a rat's behind what Lincoln Hart was thinking. It had taken her a long time to get to a place where she didn't care and no matter what Vicki thought, she really didn't.

She slid into the red-padded booth seat and met his gaze across the gray Formica table. "Sorry I'm late."

"No problem." There was a nearly empty coffee mug in front of him. Apparently he'd been here long enough to drink it.

Rose waited to feel guilty about keeping him waiting, but couldn't quite manage. "I had to take a work call."

"Of course," he said reasonably. "I hope it wasn't a crisis situation."

As opposed to sitting across from the man who once broke her heart and trying to pretend that same heart wasn't pounding so hard it might give out?

She shook her head. "No crisis."

"Good."

Again she cursed the unfairness of him looking even better than he had ten years ago. She didn't remember his eyes being such a dark shade of blue or that his shoulders were quite so wide. Could be the white dress shirt he was wearing, with the long sleeves rolled up to midforearm. It was a look she'd once loved on him and that thought didn't do much to slow her pulse.

"So I'm glad you called," he said.

"Hmm?" She blinked, suddenly realizing she'd been staring at his chest while her mind skipped down memory lane, very close to the point where she wondered how he looked without a shirt now. "Right. My call. Thanks for meeting me."

"You wanted to discuss the job offer."

"Yes."

Before she could say more, the waitress came over to take their orders. Rose had been hungry until seeing Linc put knots in her stomach the size of a Toyota. But she figured a half-sandwich-and-salad combo would work. He asked for a burger and fries so obviously his appetite was totally unaffected by seeing her. That was irritating.

When they were alone again she asked, "Where is this condo again? The one you need decorated?"

"Blackwater Lake, Montana. It's a picturesque town that's being compared to Vail and Aspen in Colorado."

"And what are we talking about? Paint? Furniture? A theme?"

He nodded. "Everything. Flooring, fixtures, carpet. Right now it's just a shell and the builder left it that way at my request."

"It's my understanding that you can't get a mortgage unless the flooring is installed."

"I don't have a mortgage."

Of course he didn't. His family had buckets of money. Whether or not he was a Hart by blood, clearly Linc was one of their own. Rose refused to wonder what it would have been like to be married to him and not have to worry about the money to pay her rent. It would be dishonest to say she hadn't been dazzled by the glitz and glamour of the Hart name and all it represented, but that's not why she'd fallen in love with him.

"So you're talking about cupboards, sinks and everything?"

"Yes."

"Then you're not living there yet."

"No," he replied.

Rose waited for him to fill in the blank of where he *did* stay but that didn't happen. "Are there accommodations in this picturesque place?"

"I'll handle that and pay all of your expenses."

There was a question she just had to ask because it would be stupid not to. "What's in this for you, Linc?"

His easygoing expression didn't waver. "I get a beautifully decorated condo. What else would there be?"

"That's what I'd like to know. You led me on once and

even married me to get what you wanted, so I'd just like to know if I should be worried."

"I can't stop you. But I give you my word that I only want to take advantage of your decorating expertise to make my place a serene and comfortable space to live in."

"So this time you're not planning to get me into bed and have your way with me under false pretenses?"

His gaze narrowed, a sign that the barb drew a little blood. "There were no false pretenses the first time."

"I don't believe you."

"There's nothing I can say to change that." His mouth pulled tight for a moment. "But let me add this—I researched your company and it's in trouble. Decorating my place is more than a job. It's an opportunity for the kind of publicity that you can't afford. I feel badly about what happened and this is my way of making it up to you."

So it was pity.

The words made her feel both better and worse. There was some satisfaction in calling him on the crap he'd pulled but he really had all the power. Her business needed help and no one else was offering. "Okay, then. I'll put together a contract with a rough estimate of my time and a price. You can decide if it's acceptable."

"It will be."

"You haven't seen anything yet."

"I don't have to." He took a sip of coffee and met her gaze over the rim of the mug.

She knew he was a successful executive and didn't achieve his level of affluence by making bad deals. "What if the charges are inflated?"

"I have trust."

"That makes one of us because I don't trust you."

"You've made that really clear. And I completely understand." Again with the irritating reasonableness. "I'm happy to pay whatever you want to charge for your services."

"You do realize I'm not a hooker."

Even though it had been a quickie marriage in Vegas that's the way he'd made her feel ten years ago. Her words produced barely a flicker of an eyelash but she knew they'd hit their target again. Well, too darn bad. And the exhilaration she felt right now was proof that she'd deliberately provoked him. Not smart to cut off her nose to spite her face but she just couldn't help it. That's not something she would have said to any other client and she had better try to rein in the sarcasm because there was no telling how far he could be pushed. "I'll rephrase," he said. "Whatever your interior-designer fee is I will pay it, along with travel and living expenses while we are in Blackwater Lake."

"You're going, too? It can all be done in email—"

"I have business there anyway."

Of course she'd suspected he probably would be going but when he put the words out there the reality of it all really sank in. If she was going to back out it would have to be now.

Control was an illusion because she really had little choice. No way her business was going down without a fight. She met his gaze. "Agreed."

"Excellent." He looked decidedly pleased and that was irksome.

Which was why she added, "I'm glad you decided to have this meeting in person. I felt it necessary to emphasize how much I don't trust you and wanted to see your reaction to my terms."

"And?"

"You fooled me once, but this time I'm in the driver's seat." Although it was kind of a pathetic seat since she had very little bargaining room.

The waitress returned with a tray bearing food and she set plates in front of them. "Can I get you anything else?"

"Ketchup," she and Linc said together.

"You know each other pretty well." The woman smiled and pointed to the condiments next to the napkin dispenser. "It's already on the table."

Linc met her gaze when they were alone. "So, you haven't forgotten that I like ketchup with fries."

"If memory serves it was practically a religious experience," she said.

"Yeah. Nice to know some things don't change."

And some do when the man you'd loved with every fiber of your being treated you like a mistake. Anger flared again but she willed it away. Losing control with Lincoln Hart was not an option. "Where does the divorce stand?"

"My attorney is working on it."

"Are you paying full price this time?" Darn. The sarcasm just popped out of her mouth. Apparently he didn't bring out the best in her.

But Linc smiled. "With what I'm paying Mason he could put a child through college and multiple postgraduate degrees as well as buy several vacation homes and probably a boat."

"Does Mason have a child?"

"He's not married. And before you remind me that vows aren't necessary to produce a child, I'll just say no. He doesn't have any kids."

"So one can assume that the dissolution of our marriage is progressing at an appropriately acceptable pace?"

"It is." He took a bite of his hamburger and chewed. After swallowing he said, "Is there some reason you want to accelerate the process?"

"Nothing has changed since we last spoke." She pushed

lettuce around her plate without eating any. "I just don't like loose ends."

He set down his burger and wiped his hands on a napkin before pulling a business card from his wallet. He set it on the table and slid it over to her. "This is my lawyer's contact information. Feel free to get in touch with him anytime and ask anything you want. Or have your attorney get in touch with him."

"Okay." She picked up the card and put it in her purse and made a mental note to pass it along to Vicki. "As long as everything goes smoothly I'll be happy."

"How do you define a not-smooth divorce?"

"You disappearing without explanation would put a speed bump in the divorce road." This saying the first thing that popped into her head was becoming a bad habit that only seemed to happen with Linc.

"Don't worry. I'll be around until the papers come."

That would be an improvement over last time, but doing better than he had ten years ago wasn't setting a very high bar.

In the meantime she had a job. That was the good news. Unfortunately she would be working for the man she was just a little bit married to. Did that make her nervous?

Did beavers build dams?

## *Chapter Three*

"So your dad wasn't using the private plane today?"

Linc stared at Rose, sitting across from him in the cushy leather airplane seat. They'd taken off and reached cruising altitude, and there was a steady hum in the pressurized cabin of the Gulfstream jet. They were on their way to Blackwater Lake and hiring a jet for transportation was the most efficient way to get there. Comfort didn't hurt, either. And there might be a little bit of trying to impress her going on.

"If you're talking about Hastings Hart, he's not my father. This aircraft doesn't belong to his company. And you should let it go. I have."

"Really? It doesn't feel that way to me." She tapped a finger against her lips. "Is the jet yours?"

"Not yet." It would be soon. But her comment had him curious. "In what way do you think I haven't let the paternity thing go?"

"You're awfully defensive. You were a grown man when you found out the truth and never suspected before that, which means you were loved and there's a bond. That doesn't just go away."

"You don't understand."

"Right. My bad."

Hell, how could she understand? He didn't, and it had happened to him. But his defensive response only served to sharpen the wary look in her eyes that never disappeared. It was as if any second she expected him to jump out of the plane and skydive so he could be anywhere but here.

It was on the tip of his tongue to say he'd left for her and she didn't understand, but that retort didn't work a moment ago and wouldn't now. "I don't remember you being this annoying."

"Probably because I wasn't," she said cheerfully. "We were firmly in the adoration stage of the relationship. And your abrupt departure didn't give me a chance to trot out the real me."

"Well, this is going to be fun. A guilt trip from Texas to Montana." They'd settled on her giving him four weeks to get the job going, then periodic trips back when necessary. So, for the next month he was going to let her say whatever she wanted to get off her chest. Redemption wasn't going to come without a price, he reminded himself.

"Suck it up, Linc. My attitude has been ten years in the making."

It was going to be a long flight if he didn't get her off this. And he had just the thing to ask. "What does your boyfriend think about you flying off with your husband for a job?"

Her smug expression slipped and she had no stinging comeback, which was a big clue that there was a ripple in the relationship pond.

"Rose?"

"What?"

"Did you tell—" He stopped. If she'd told him the guy's name he couldn't remember?

"Chandler," she said.

"You did tell Chandler about this job in Montana, right?"

She looked out the airplane window and shifted in her seat before meeting his gaze. "Yes, but before you ask, I didn't tell him about our past."

"Practically engaged and keeping secrets already? Tsk."

"Don't judge. You don't know me."

He'd known her once and she was an open book. Sweet and innocent. Generous and loving. There'd been no cynicism in her then and the fact that she had it now was another black mark on his soul. Another sin to lay at his feet.

However, he couldn't deny that the idea of trouble in paradise was damned appealing. "Should I read anything into the fact that you kept the details of our venture to yourself?"

"You can jump to any conclusions you want. I can't stop you and you're quite good at it." Her look challenged him to deny the statement.

Okay. Battle lines drawn. She was on the offensive so that's where he'd go, too. "What exactly did you tell him? You must have said something. He's bound to notice that you're not around. I certainly would if you and I were involved."

Every day for the last ten years he'd noticed that she wasn't there.

"I told him that I was going to be very busy."

He couldn't tell whether it was guilt or defiance in her tone. A little more pushing couldn't hurt because he'd already damaged her and he had little left to lose. "Too busy to see him?"

"Yes."

"And he's okay with that?"

"I'm so lucky. Chandler is a sweet, understanding man. He's supportive of my career."

"A real saint."

He knew couples made compromises. His mother and Hastings compromised the truth about Linc for their relationship. But unquestioningly letting the woman you loved fly to Montana with another man, even one she was divorcing, seemed wrong to him.

Come to think of it there was something else he wanted to know. "Is Chandler aware that you're a married woman?"

"Oh, please. I'm not—"

"Don't deny it. We've already gone over this. There's no divorce, so technically we are still married." He folded his arms over his chest and couldn't quite keep the "gotcha" out of his voice. "You didn't tell him."

"I don't remember you being this annoying, either." She stared at him and must have realized he wasn't backing down because there was a lot of resignation in her sigh. "No. I never told him about the marriage."

Why? he wanted to ask. Was she afraid that would destroy their relationship? A man who truly loved her wouldn't give a tinker's damn about this. Linc remembered how it felt to love her. In the same situation, if she'd dropped this bombshell on him, he'd have hired the best divorce attorney on the planet to dissolve the union so he could marry her. Making her his was more important than anything. Correction: it would have been, if he was Chandler.

"On the upside," he said cheerfully, "since he doesn't

know about the marriage it saves you the trouble of having to break the news that you're not divorced."

She huffed out a breath. "Not only are you annoying, you're a smart-ass."

"Is that any way to talk to the man who's funneling work your way?"

"We both know you're not the typical client. Other than my expertise on decorating you have an agenda. I haven't figured out what it is yet but we both know there is one."

"You're even more creative than I knew." He knew how smart she was and shouldn't have been surprised she'd guessed. "I look forward to seeing what you come up with for my condo."

"Do you take anything seriously?"

"Of course."

"Like what?" she demanded.

"My business."

"That's not what I meant and you know it. What about your family?" There was a gleam in her eyes now. "Come to think of it, I have no idea what you've been up to and you know an awful lot about me."

"Because you've been very generous in sharing details."

"My mistake," she said. "Let's even the playing field. Tell me about your personal relationship."

"What makes you think I have one?"

She gave him an "oh, come on" look. "I guess a specific question would be better. And before you give me an evasive answer, consider that there's still a lot of flight time left and I can be persistent."

"Okay, I've been warned. What would you like to know?"

She gave him a thoughtful look for several moments. "Since you left me, have you been close to needing a marriage license?"

"Since you, marriage has not once entered my mind."

He'd never let a woman that close because it wasn't fair to lead anyone on. Marriage wasn't a step he would ever take again.

"Hmm. That brings up more questions than it answers." Rose tucked a long strand of shiny dark hair behind her ear as she studied him. "Is that because of what happened with your parents?"

"Hastings isn't my father."

"He still parented you with your mother. Is it that? Or was marriage to me so bad? Did I break you, Linc?"

Leaving her did, but that wasn't her fault. It was the only way he could think of to protect her from the mess that was his life. Eventually he had put the pieces back together and if they didn't quite fit, that wasn't on her.

"You know better than anyone, Rose, that I'm a bad risk."

"At least you're taking responsibility." There was a flash of what looked like sympathy on her face before she shut it down. "But ten years is a long time. I don't quite know what to make of the fact that you're alone."

"Let's just call it a public service." When she opened her mouth to protest, he said, "Want a drink? The bar is stocked. Let's go check out the galley and see what we can find."

"Don't think I didn't see how you just tried to distract me from your love life. And I'll admit it worked, but only because I've never been on a private plane before."

"I'd never have guessed, what with your cool, sophisticated demeanor."

"Don't let that fool you. On the inside I'm giddy with curiosity and excitement."

Until this moment Linc hadn't realized how much he'd missed teasing her. And her honesty. He didn't know any woman who wouldn't have pretended that a lift on anything but a commercial flight happened every day. Her excitement at a new experience was charming and brought back memories of his eagerness to introduce her to all the pleasures life had to offer.

Including sex.

He'd given up the right to her body and the tempting curves in front of him now. Settling for drinks and hors d'oeuvres on a jet paled in comparison but that was all he could hope for. And the remainder of the flight passed quickly with a bottle of wine and snacks that had Rose moaning in ecstasy while he questioned how much pain he could handle on the road to redemption.

The Gulfstream landed at the recently opened Blackwater Lake Airport. A Mercedes SUV was waiting and he stowed their luggage while Rose let herself into the passenger seat. He got behind the wheel and drove into town, pointing out the highlights along the way.

"This is a very small place," she commented, sounding less than thrilled.

"You're observant. I always said that about you."

"Oh—" She pointed out the window. "The Blackwater Lake Lodge. That's the first hotel I've seen. It looks nice."

He drove past and left the city limits. "Right now it's the only hotel in town."

She glanced over her shoulder. "Then why didn't you stop?"

"Because we're not staying there."

"Linc—" There was warning in her voice. "This is where we talk about how much I don't like surprises. You promised that you'd handle accommodations."

"And I have."

"If you're planning to pitch a tent and expect me to

camp out, it would be best if you turned around and put me on the first plane back to Texas."

"Where we're going there are great views and a lot of square footage."

"Wilderness doesn't count. Somewhere in this town there must be a roof and indoor plumbing," she warned.

"There is. Trust me."

"I thought we were clear that I don't trust you."

He was going to do his damnedest to change her mind about that.

Rose was uneasy after Linc bypassed the Blackwater Lake Lodge and kept driving. Finally he turned right and pulled into a long driveway leading to a big house at the top of a rise. The sun was just going down behind the majestic mountains, but there was still enough light to see that the grounds were stunning. A carpet of perfectly manicured green grass was surrounded by flowers and shrubs.

He stopped the SUV by a brick walkway leading to gorgeous double front doors with oval glass insets. "I think this will fit your definition. There's a roof and indoor plumbing. The rest of it isn't bad, either."

"This can't be your place because you said it's a condo and currently unlivable." She left her seat belt buckled. "What's going on? You said you'd handle expenses and accommodations but—"

"This is my sister's place. She lives here with her husband and daughter."

"Why?"

"Because they're married and need a place to raise their child." His tone was wry.

"No. Why aren't we at a hotel?"

"As we established there's only one in town and I

couldn't get a reservation. Late spring is nice here in the mountains and it's becoming a popular tourist destination."

Rose studied him. He was looking awfully darn pleased with himself, but it felt like he'd pulled one over on her and she didn't like it a bit. "I don't know what you're up to, but—"

"And here's my sister now." He pointed to the open front door.

Rose saw a little girl run outside, followed immediately by a man and woman. Linc exited the car and came around to her side to open the door. His family didn't look intimidating but what did she know? These people were related to him.

Rose got out and muttered under her breath, "You should have warned me about this."

"If I did, would you have taken the job?"

That was a good question. Probably she would have but he hadn't given her the chance to decide. Again.

"Linc!" His sister threw herself into his arms.

He grabbed her and lifted her off the ground in a big hug. "Hey, baby sister. You look good."

"You, too." Then she smiled at Rose. "Hi. I'm Ellie McKnight."

"Rose Tucker." She shook the woman's hand as the two men greeted each other.

"This is her husband, Alex, and this munchkin is their daughter, Leah."

"Nice to meet you." Rose smiled at the little girl observing the hectic scene from the safety of her handsome father's strong arms. "She's beautiful."

"Just like her mom," Alex said proudly.

Ellie took the child and said, "Honey, why don't you help Linc bring their bags inside."

"Right."

"Rose, welcome to our home."

"Thank you. I appreciate your hospitality, but if it's too much of an inconvenience I can find something—"

"Absolutely not. It's been too long since I had a good visit with my brother. We're happy to have you and I'm glad you agreed to stay with us."

It would probably be rude to say she hadn't agreed to anything because he hadn't shared the trip details with her. So, she kept that to herself. Linc, however, was going to get an earful.

Ellie led her past the living and dining rooms into the huge kitchen–family room combination. There was a river-rock fireplace on one wall with a big flat-screen TV above. Leather sofas and cloth-covered chairs formed a conversation area in front of it and the thick, neutral-colored carpet was littered with pink toys and dolls. When her mom set her down, Leah plopped herself in the middle of it and started playing.

Moments later the men joined them and Alex informed his wife, "Bags are by the stairway. I wasn't sure where you wanted everyone."

"Thanks, honey. I think Linc and Rose might want to catch their breath."

Rose doubted that would happen, at least for her. Since the moment Linc had showed up in her life again she felt as if she'd had the air knocked out of her. Then on the plane he'd confessed that after her he'd never again considered marriage. What did that mean? Had it been awful with her? Resentment pointed her in that direction, but when he'd said it there was a wistful, sad look on his face. And now he'd brought her to stay with his sister. This must be how Dorothy felt when the tornado dropped her in Oz. Rose was definitely not in Texas anymore.

"Can I get you something to drink? Are you hungry?"

Ellie asked. "I've got some appetizers to put out and we'll have dinner in a little while."

"I hope you haven't gone to any trouble," Rose protested.

The other woman waved away her concern. "It's cheese and crackers and Alex is going to grill. Very easy."

Linc looked at her. "How about a glass of wine?"

"That would be nice. White?"

"Done," Ellie said. "And Linc will want a beer."

"I'll take care of the drinks, sweetie," her husband offered.

Rose stood beside Linc on the other side of the huge kitchen island and watched the attractive couple work together. A smile here, a touch there. A closeness and intimacy she'd never had the chance to form with Linc. Envy and regret mixed with her lingering anger at what he'd done to *them*.

When everyone had drinks Ellie held up her wineglass and said, "Let's drink to me."

Linc grinned and said, "Now why would we do that?"

"Because I talked you into moving to Blackwater Lake, which makes me pretty awesome. You're going to thank me for this."

Alex touched his longneck beer bottle to his wife's glass. "I thought you were awesome even before your brother bought his condo. And I thank my lucky stars every day that you came into my life."

Rose wanted to hold on to her envy and dislike of these two, but she was powerless. They were so cute, so friendly. She tapped her glass to theirs. "I think you're awesome for wanting to put up with your brother as a full-time resident."

There was a funny look on Linc's face when he joined the toast. "To my favorite sister."

"I'm your only sister."

"I knew there was a reason you had to be my favorite because you're a pain in the neck."

"Takes one to know one," Rose said, meeting his gaze as she took a sip of her wine.

"I like her," Ellie said enthusiastically to the two men. "Linc told me you're friends. How did you meet?"

"At work," Linc said, jumping right in.

It took Rose a couple of beats to realize Ellie was clueless about their relationship, the fact that they were married and Linc had left her. Women had a way of picking up details, especially personal ones, so if his sister was clueless it was a good bet that the rest of his family was, too.

"Did you decorate Linc's offices in Dallas?" Ellie persisted.

"No," Linc answered for her again.

Rose didn't miss the fact that he looked more than a little uncomfortable about the turn this conversation was taking. Apparently when he was handling accommodations he hadn't factored in the part where his sister would be curious about them. It wasn't often that someone got what was coming to them so quickly or that the wronged party was around to see. He was getting what he deserved and she was a witness, so karma would have to forgive her for gloating.

She was waiting for more questions, but Leah chose that moment to toddle over and grab her mother's jeans-clad leg. She started to whine and, when picked up, pointed to the crackers-and-cheese plate on the island.

"Someone's hungry," Ellie said, quickly kissing the rosy-cheeked little girl before handing her to her father. "I don't want her to fill up on snacks. Honey, if you could put her in the high chair and feed her that would help. It would be better if she eats before we do."

"Gotcha, little bit," he said, tickling his daughter to make her giggle.

"While you do that, I'll show Linc and Rose to the guest wing so they can freshen up."

The three of them grabbed the bags and took them upstairs, following Ellie to the end of the long hall.

"So, it's a guest wing," Linc said. "Aren't you the grand one?"

"No. Just awesome." Ellie grinned at him, then pointed out the two large bedrooms connected by a bathroom. "Rose, I'm putting you in the one with the window seat that faces the backyard and mountains. Dallas is flat and I thought you might enjoy a different view. Linc, you take the other one." A piercing wail came from downstairs. "I'd better go help Alex. Hungry and tired is not an attractive combination on my daughter. See you two in a few."

Alone in the hall Rose met Linc's gaze. "So, your sister doesn't know we were married."

"No."

"You kept me a secret—"

"No." He took her arm and tugged her into his bedroom, then shut the door. "Not a secret."

"When you withhold significant life details from your favorite sister it kind of falls under the heading of secret."

"That was a complicated time." He didn't look happy.

Tough, she thought. "You were ashamed of me."

"No." His voice was sharp. "Not you. It was all me. My bad. Then I took a long break from everyone and everything. After that there was no point in saying anything."

"So now we're in Blackwater Lake and staying with your sister. Arrangements that you made and didn't see fit to share with me."

"Look, I know you're miffed—"

"That's way too nice a word for what I'm feeling," she snapped. "But there's a silver lining."

"What's that?" There was a wary look in his eyes.

"You didn't think it through about how to explain me."

He nodded grimly. "I thought you were enjoying that a little too much."

"Actions have consequences—even after ten years. Especially if you keep secrets."

"Look, Rose, I was a jerk."

"Was?" She folded her arms over her chest.

"I apologized for it and I'm handling the divorce," he continued, ignoring the dig. "I groveled."

"Yes, you did." She would give him that.

"Ellie and I are close. She's the one who convinced me to come back after I left—"

"And you don't want your favorite sister to know how big a jackass you are," she mused.

"I'm not comfortable with the jackass part," he said, "but essentially you're right. I'd consider it a big favor if you would keep the details of our relationship just between us."

Rose was loving this. Confident and unflappable Lincoln Hart was insecure and uneasy. "You know, this is a very unfortunate time for you to find out that what they say about reaping what you sow is true."

"Could you be a little more specific?" Tension tightened his jaw.

"I don't trust you," she reminded him.

"So you're going to rat me out to my sister?"

Rose shrugged, then walked through the connecting bathroom and closed the door behind her. This was too sweet. She was charging him an arm and a leg for this decorating job, which was pretty great all by itself. But now she had leverage and that was priceless.

## *Chapter Four*

The morning after their arrival at his sister's, Linc waited a decent length of time for a sign that Rose was finished in the bathroom they shared. He'd been a gentleman; ladies first. But the longer it went on the more certain he was that this was revenge.

He knocked lightly on the door. "Are you going to be finished in there sometime in the next millennium?"

"Come in," she answered sweetly.

He did and there she was, putting on makeup and wearing nothing but a satiny pink robe that tied at her small waist and outlined her breasts. For several moments staring was his only option because he was pretty sure he'd swallowed his tongue. Her legs were smooth and tanned. He knew that because a lot of leg was showing due to the fact that the robe stopped way above her knees. Her feet were bare and the pink-polished toes did things to his insides that had never been done before.

Without looking away from the mirror Rose said, "One would think you'd never seen me put on makeup before and we both know you have."

It was true. He had seen her do this ordinary thing that women do, but now this was so much more intense and he wasn't sure why. Rather than directly address her comment he said, "I didn't know you were such a bathroom hog."

"You didn't stick around long enough to find out anything about me. Lucky you. Maybe you dodged a bullet."

He settled a shoulder against the doorjamb. "Putting a finer point on the situation, I didn't dodge you. We're still married."

"Only on paper."

Meaning there was no hanky-panky of the physical kind going on. But looking at her now, leaning forward to brush mascara on her long, thick lashes and watching the way her breasts strained against that pink satin material made him want to scoop her up, carry her to the bed and engage in hanky-panky for a week.

If he didn't know how soft her skin was, how it smelled and tasted, the temptation might have been easy to ignore. But he did know. He'd never forgotten and more than once since leaving her he'd nearly caved, every time barely stopping himself from begging her to take him back.

The same thing that stopped him then stopped him now. Protecting her from the Hart bastard was the most important thing, along with the overriding conviction that dragging her into his mess was wrong. On top of that, considering she thought he was maybe one life form above pond scum, any move he made on her would likely get his face slapped.

And he wouldn't lift a hand to stop her.

She glanced at him. "I can finish up in my room if you have to—"

"You're fine. All your stuff is here." He looked at the collection of brushes, containers, tubes and bottles. "And it's quite an impressive amount of stuff."

"A girl needs every advantage."

"Not you. Your face is naturally beautiful already."

She looked at him and there was a frown in her eyes. "I wasn't fishing for compliments and you don't have to hand them out. Our divorce is on track. Contracts have been signed guaranteeing my lucrative consultation fee on your condo. There's no reason for you to butter me up."

"I wasn't doing that." And he hadn't meant to say it. The words just came out of his mouth because he forgot for a split second all the crap that had happened, that they were no longer newlyweds who were crazy in love. "It was just my honest opinion."

She faced him and put a hand on her hip, the posture a sign that she was still peeved about something. "That's not fair."

"Since my observation was completely sincere I have no clue what the problem is."

"You didn't give me anything for a comeback. How can I say don't be honest or that I don't trust you? Especially when you're saying something nice to me?"

"You have no frame of reference to believe this, but I am a nice man."

"You're right," she agreed.

That was a surprise. "You think I'm nice?"

"No. I have no frame of reference to accept your words as fact." She turned back to the mirror and assessed her appearance before nodding with satisfaction. "The bathroom is all yours. I've done the best I can do with my face."

Her best was pretty damn good.

When he was alone Linc blew out a long breath and knew his shower was going to be colder than usual, courtesy of Miss Rose Tucker. Although technically she was Mrs. Lincoln Hart. They were married and he wanted her possibly even more than he had before whisking her to Las Vegas for a wedding. But she was forbidden fruit and being this close without being able to touch her was his hell to pay.

It didn't take Linc long to clean up and as he started downstairs he hoped to beat Rose. What with seeing her practically naked, he'd forgotten that she hadn't promised to keep their marriage a secret from his sister. The less time Rose and Ellie had alone to talk, the better. Then he heard the female voices coming from the kitchen and realized she dressed faster than she did hair and makeup. There was enough going on right now without his baby sister finding out about his screwup.

Ellie had always looked up to him and more than once called him her hero. When his life had turned upside down she'd been his anchor and he'd been extraordinarily grateful that at least one thing hadn't changed. He wanted to keep it that way.

He walked into the kitchen. "Good morning, ladies."

"Hey, slowpoke," Ellie said. "Hope you slept well."

"Great," he lied. There'd been no restful slumber with only a bathroom separating his room from Rose's. "So you two are all chummy this morning. What have you been talking about?"

"This and that." Rose was standing next to Ellie on the other side of the island with a knife in her hand. There was a pile of sliced mushrooms in front of her. "Girl stuff."

Best not to push that subject. "Speaking of girls, where is my niece?"

"With her father. Alex took her into town for breakfast." Ellie poured coffee into a mug and handed it to him.

"Thanks," he said, then picked up the subject of his

brother-in-law. “Doesn’t he have a job to go to? It was my understanding that his construction company had more work than he could handle and that’s why he and I are going to be partners.”

“He’s going into the office a little late. He does that once or twice a week, if possible. Daddy-daughter bonding. He calls it his Leah time.”

“Aww, that’s so sweet,” Rose said. “He’s really setting a high bar for dads.”

“Every girl should have that.” Ellie nodded emphatically.

Linc knew Rose had been raised by a single mom and recognized the wistfulness in her expression.

His sister must have seen it, too, because she said, “What was your father like, Rose?”

“That’s a good question,” she said. Her tone was indifferent. “My mom told him she was pregnant and he was never seen or heard from again.”

“Jerk. And it’s his loss,” Ellie said.

“You can’t miss what you never had,” Rose commented philosophically.

“In the spirit of full disclosure, I was pregnant before Alex and I got married. Now this is girl talk,” Ellie warned him. “We hadn’t known each other very long but things got complicated pretty quickly. I was so in love and didn’t think he cared. When Linc called to check up on me, which he always does, I told him everything and he was here the next day.”

“Wow.” Rose gave him a “who would have thought that of you?” look. “A sensitive side.”

“Not when he punched Alex.” His sister slid him a rueful look. “He was sure I’d been taken advantage of.”

Rose shot him a skeptical look. “A regular Rocky.”

“You had to be there,” he said.

"It was actually very sweet once all the testosterone returned to normal levels. In the end everything worked out and Alex and I couldn't be happier." She smiled at Linc. "And now you're going to be living here in Blackwater Lake. I'm going to love having you around. So, you'd better be okay with Alex making time in his schedule for his daughter if you're going to partner up with him."

"Of course I am. Why would you even think I wouldn't be?" Linc asked.

"Good question. You and Rose are friends so she probably has a better answer than me. Or at least a theory."

Linc looked at the woman in jeans and pink sweater, unable to shake the image of her bare feet and polished toes. When had pink become such an erotic color? She met his gaze and there was a gleam in her eyes that made him nervous.

Rose cleared her throat. "The thing is, your brother hasn't had to think about anyone but himself for a long time."

"True. Very astute of you to pick up on that." Ellie tapped her lip thoughtfully as she studied him. "Linc, have you ever had to be unselfish and put someone else's needs before your own?"

"Of course I have."

"When?" Rose was clearly relishing her role in turning up the fire on his hot seat.

"Yeah, when?" Ellie asked.

"I have employees. A happy staff is an efficient staff. It's very basic."

"That's business," Rose pointed out.

"She's right, Linc. If you'd ever been in love, you would get what it means to put someone else first."

He got it big-time and had the dings in his heart as proof. But Rose didn't believe he'd put her well-being before his own and Ellie would be crushed and disappointed that he hadn't confided in her. He wasn't willing to lose what he had with his sister.

Since Ellie had made a statement instead of asking a question, Linc felt justified in not addressing her implication that he'd never been deeply in love. "Did anyone ever tell you that two against one isn't fair?"

"So, are you going to tattle on me to Dad?"

"Yours or mine?" The pity in his sister's eyes made him wish he could take back those words.

"Come on, Linc—"

"What? Get over it?" He sighed. "The fact is, Hastings is not my father. I've accepted that. There's no way to get over your DNA. It is what it is."

"But, still—"

"Ow." Rose dropped her knife.

"Did you cut yourself?" Linc was ready to jump in with first aid.

After checking her fingers for several moments she said, "No. Just a near miss."

"Thank goodness. Be careful. Those knives are really sharp." Ellie breathed a sigh of relief. "Okay, I think we have enough veggies. Let's get these omelets going." She went into command mode. "Rose, your help is much appreciated but I'll take it from here. Go have coffee with my brother."

"Yes, ma'am." Rose did as instructed and sat beside him at the island. There was a smug, satisfied expression on her face.

Suddenly Linc got it. His sister was banging pots and pans, so in a tone only Rose could hear he said, "You did that on purpose. Changed the subject."

"You're welcome." She blew on her coffee. "Even though you don't deserve it."

She'd proactively rescued him from his well-intentioned sibling. Would wonders never cease.

This redemption tour was not at all what he'd expected. One minute she was busting his chops, the next she had his back. He wasn't sure whether or not to be afraid of what she would do next.

"Thanks for getting Ellie off my back."

"Don't mention it. I gave you a distraction, you gave me a job. We're even."

"Not even close."

Rose was pretty sure he'd contracted her services to make things up to her, but didn't comment because a confirmation of her suspicions would make this a pity job.

They'd just left the house after breakfast and she sat in the passenger seat of the SUV while Linc drove to the condo. Pity or not she had work to do and wanted to see what she would be dealing with. They'd arrived yesterday just before sundown and she couldn't really see much. Now the sun was shining, the sky was vivid blue and the scenery was stunning. If she'd been behind the wheel, concentrating on the road would have been a challenge.

"You were not wrong," she said.

Linc glanced over. "I like the sound of that. But what are we talking about?"

"It's beautiful here. The mountains from my room… Majestic, stately, lush, tree-covered." She shrugged. "There are no words to adequately describe this place. And the view of the lake from your sister's family room is breathtaking."

He took his eyes off the road for a moment to look at her but aviator sunglasses hid his expression—although he was smiling. "I'm glad you like it."

Rose knew that smile, the one that used to turn her inside out and, unfortunately, still did a little. "I really do."

"Does that mean you trust me now?"

"Seriously? That was observation and opinion, not the basis on which to determine trustworthiness."

"Oh." He lifted one broad shoulder in a shrug. "A guy can hope."

Why in the world would he care? This was a job, not a relationship, and they were getting a divorce. When it was all over, their paths were unlikely to cross again. That thought should have been comforting but it produced a twinge of something that felt a little like regret. She chose not to comment.

Very soon she spotted a complex of buildings and Linc drove up to the guard gate and stopped the car. He pressed the button and his window went down as the private security guy walked out of the small hut and over to them.

"Nice to see you, Mr. Hart."

"You too, Jeff." He angled his head toward her. "This is Rose Tucker."

Jeff leaned over far enough to get a good look at her. "A pleasure, Miss Tucker."

"Hi." She lifted her hand in a wave.

"Can you put her on my list of approved people? She's my decorator and will need access to my place."

"Sure thing, Mr. Hart. I'll take care of it."

"Thanks."

"You folks have a good day."

The gate swung open for them and Linc drove through. There was a lush, grassy area straight ahead that was landscaped with bushes and flowers blooming in shades of pink, yellow, purple and orange. A charming gazebo stood in the center of the park and ornate streetlights were placed at intervals around it.

"This is like being in a different world," she said. "It's peaceful and pretty and perfect."

"That's what I thought, too."

"Can you drive through the whole complex so I can get a feel for it? I want the interior and exterior of your home to flow seamlessly together. Does that make any sense?"

"Not to me, but that's why I hired you." He kept driving around the grassy area. "It's not very big but this is just the first phase. Each successive one will be separated by a landscaped greenbelt and during future construction the existing residents won't be inconvenienced."

"Smart," she agreed. "The debris in the building stage is an eyesore. And the rogue nails are not the least bit tire-friendly."

As he drove around, Linc pointed out the community pool and clubhouse, which had state-of-the-art exercise equipment and facilities for receptions. It was zoned for a golf course and other amenities. This development had *exclusive* written all over it and probably the monthly up-keep costs were a small fortune on top of the no-doubt impressive price tag on his condo.

He slowed and pushed the button on a controller attached to his sun visor. One of the doors on a three-car garage went up. "This is it."

Rose looked around as he pulled the car into the drive-way. "This is an end unit. Very private."

"That's one of the things that sold me. Common walls between units are kept to a minimum. Condo living with the feel of a single-family detached home. Come on. I'll show you around."

She'd seen the floor plan and already had some notes, but knew that the place was over five thousand square feet on three levels. From the garage they walked into the first one, which was a large room with French doors leading to the backyard.

"Media room," she said absently.

"That's what I thought, too."

He led her up the stairs to the main living area. The rooms were clearly defined: kitchen, living, family and dining rooms. A bedroom and bath down the hall would make a great guest suite. But there were no floor coverings or cabinets. Just a lot of open space with numerous ways to configure it. Upstairs he showed her the huge master suite, then led the way into a long, large room that would be perfect as a spacious home office. And three more bedrooms and baths.

When they came back downstairs she stood in the kitchen, studying the dining room. "Again you weren't wrong. This is just a shell. And no, I haven't changed my mind about trusting you."

"Bummer."

"Do you entertain a lot?"

"Some. I wouldn't say a lot. Why?" he asked.

"Because the alcove between the kitchen and dining room is a perfect place for a butler's pantry."

"And that's different from a regular pantry…how?"

"It's where you store china, crystal, silver. The things you'd need for dinner parties."

"Hmm." He slid his fingers into the pockets of his jeans and frowned.

"What's wrong?"

"I'd rather negotiate a real estate deal than have to handle cloth napkins and place settings."

"You can hire a caterer," she suggested.

"Maybe."

"Why maybe?"

"There isn't a caterer in Blackwater Lake." He thought

for a moment. "Although Lucy Bishop might consider giving it a whirl."

Rose felt another twinge but this time it had nothing to do with regret. The sensation veered more into jealousy territory. This wasn't the time and she was in no mood to think about what that meant. "Who is she?"

"There's a place in town called the Harvest Café. She's a co-owner and the chef. Food is good and she might be persuaded to handle a private function."

"Ah."

"What?" He slid his sunglasses to the top of his head and there was sharp curiosity in his eyes. As if he'd seen her jealousy.

"Nothing. I said 'ah'—it was an acknowledgment that I heard and assimilated the information you related."

"Yes, but the tone of that single-syllable acknowledgement was full of…something."

Had he always been so perceptive? Rose remembered a lot about being with him but not that. She'd been blinded by love in their short time together and thought he was perfect. Now she realized that was an unrealistic expectation. A by-product of being so young and idealistic.

But he was waiting for an answer. "It's just…" She looked around the large space that was going to be spectacular when she got through with it and felt sad. "We never even moved into our own place. We weren't together long enough to set up housekeeping."

His frown deepened. "Is that going to be a problem for you? During this job?"

"Absolutely not. I'm a professional."

"I don't know what else to say, Rose. I copped to being a jerk. I've told you how sorry I am. What more do you want from me?"

She met his gaze and could see his words for the sincere

apology they were. But she'd been so young and hopeful and what he did changed her forever. It had to be said. "I guess I want those ten years back."

"If I could give them back to you I would do it in a heartbeat." He blew out a long breath, but it did nothing to take the edge off his intensity. "If there was anything I could do—"

She'd never get a better opportunity to press her advantage. "There is one thing."

His gaze narrowed on her. "I'm not going to like this, am I?"

"Probably not."

"For the record, there won't be any gold tassels or tapestries. I'm not a 'tassels and tapestry' kind of guy."

"Deal." She laughed and realized that was something else that hadn't changed. Linc could always make her smile and feel better about whatever bad thing had happened to spoil her day. "I'm wondering about something."

"Okay." But he looked as if he was bracing for a punch.

"We've established that Ellie doesn't know about us. That we dated. Got married. Split up. Getting around to the divorce now. You two are obviously close, so why would you not tell her?"

"Are you sure I can't just eat quiche? Or agree to a small tapestry somewhere? Maybe open a vein and bleed a little? The carpet isn't in yet."

"You asked what you can do and this is it. I'm curious."

He settled his hands on his hips and stared at the bare floor for a moment. "After I found out about my father, I told you I was gone for two years."

"Where did you go?"

"Europe."

"What did you do?" Did he miss her the way she missed him? Hurt the way she had?

"I did odd jobs. Drank." He met her gaze. "Ellie was the one who got me to come back."

"Not your parents?"

"No." His mouth tightened into a hard line. Not a shred of forgiveness there.

"How did Ellie do it?"

"It wasn't anything she said. I just missed her. My brothers, too, but she's always the one who could get to me."

"I envy you having siblings. You're lucky. That wasn't in the cards for me. And I just don't understand why you didn't tell her about the marriage."

"After so long it didn't seem relevant. And like she said, she always looked up to me."

"Her hero."

"Yeah. I didn't want her to be disappointed in me. The way I handled it."

"Isn't it possible she would laugh and tell you what a doofus you are?"

"You obviously don't know my sister." One corner of his mouth quirked up.

"I like her. She's generous, down-to-earth, funny and she loves you. I think it would take more than finding out about our marriage for her to abandon you."

"You're just saying that because you're dying to tell her what happened."

"Are you kidding?" Rose wanted to say "duh." "Who wouldn't want to?"

"So, why didn't you tell all?" he asked.

She'd once dreamed of having a traditional family with Linc but that wasn't in the cards for her any more than having siblings. He'd had it all—a mother and father who loved him, a family—and distanced himself from all of it, and that made her wonder. She looked around this space he wanted her to decorate.

"This condo is fabulous and it's clear to see why you're attracted to it. So don't take it wrong what I'm about to ask and keep in mind that I don't need to love a space to do a good job."

"Okay. Where are you going with this?"

"You could have bought a house. That would give you a place to live and room to grow. For a family of your own. Why not go that route? You're a bachelor now but that could change."

The teasing look disappeared and he turned serious. "I deeply regret that you got caught up in my personal family problems. I thought I knew what love was before I found out my parents lied to me all my life."

What was he saying? "You don't believe in love now?"

"No, I don't."

"What about Ellie and Alex? They're in love."

"She's a Hart, I'm not," he said, as if that explained it all.

There were so many things she could say. Harts were not the only humans on the planet allowed to find love. He deserved it, too. Flair for the dramatic much? But all the teasing had gone out of him and he was dead serious about this.

"Okay, then," she said, and walked around to hide her reaction. It made absolutely no sense, but Rose felt as if Linc had just walked out on her a second time. "The architect did a good job with window placement and building orientation. Every one has a spectacular view of either the lake or the mountains."

"That was Ellie."

She met his gaze. "What?"

"My sister is the architect." The teasing expression was back in his eyes. "And don't think I didn't notice what you just did there."

"Where? What?" she asked.

"The way you sidestepped answering my question."

His revelation had pushed the conversation out of her mind and she had no clue what he was referring to. "You asked something?"

"I did." He settled his hands on his hips. "Why haven't you told my sister about us being married?"

This was much less complicated than talking about him refusing love. "I haven't said anything *yet* because it's just too good having something to hold over you."

"If I beat you to the big reveal there goes the advantage," he challenged.

She shrugged. "Either way I get to watch. So go ahead and call my bluff."

This was new, she thought. Being in control of anything where Lincoln Hart was concerned. Rose decided that she liked it very much.

## *Chapter Five*

The next morning Linc stepped out of the shower, then heard the bathroom door open and quickly wrapped a towel around his waist. He watched a sleepy Rose walk in like a zombie and his gut tightened at the sight of her—hair tousled as if she'd just had sex. Her eyes were half-closed the way he remembered them in the throes of passion. She'd told him once that in the morning she barely functioned until after coffee. Apparently that was still true because she hadn't signaled any awareness of his presence yet or the fact that he was nearly naked.

From his perspective, he had the better view of nearly naked. She was wearing a see-throughish camisole top and matching shorts that left her legs mostly bare. He wished they were all bare, but that was a thought that needed to stop right there.

"Good morning."

His voice must have worked like a shot of adrenaline

to blast her out of the trance because her eyes went wide and she gasped. She grabbed the hand towel hanging next to the sink and held it over her breasts.

"Linc! What are you doing in here?"

Obviously the adrenaline hadn't activated all her brain cells yet. "We share a bathroom. Remember?"

The part of him throbbing insistently wished they could share something even more intimate than that. Not ever going to happen, though. Even if she forgave him, he wouldn't get married again and she wouldn't settle for less than that. She'd made it clear ten years ago and the expression in her eyes yesterday when he'd answered her question about why a condo and not a house told him her position hadn't changed. Then the pity for him rolled in and he couldn't stand it.

"Sharing," she said. "Right. I'm sorry for barging in."

"No. I'm sorry. Should have locked your side, but I didn't. Just in case you needed something..."

She cocked her thumb over her shoulder. "I'll just leave and give you your privacy."

When she looked this hot and sexy, privacy was highly overrated. "Don't leave on my account."

She swallowed once and seemed to be very deliberately concentrating on looking him in the eyes and nowhere else. Like his chest, for instance. "That's okay. I'm good. Take your time."

In the short span of their marriage they hadn't spent many mornings together. Maybe that's why the memories were so vivid, because there'd been no time to become complacent, take each other for granted. Linc would never forget her fascination with him shaving. She'd explained about being an only child raised by a single mom. It was an all-female environment. But that innocent remark had filled him with so many profound feelings. Her inexperience and growing up without a father to teach her about the world and keep her safe. At that moment he'd promised himself that he would always protect her.

Everything he'd done after that was to honor that vow.

"I'm just going to shave, then it's all yours." He soaped up his cheeks and jaw, then picked up his razor and started the process that had always seemed a little less tedious after Rose.

"Interesting." She was still standing there. Watching.

"What is?"

"You go for the clean-shaven look when the current style for men is scruff."

"I guess I'm a traditional guy." Who was having a hard time not slitting his throat or cutting off an ear with the sharp instrument in his hand. The sight of her holding that ridiculous towel to hide what he'd already seen was too adorable. And distracting. But he'd rather lose an ear than send her away. If it was good enough for van Gogh…

"But you're a traditional guy who has no intention of settling down. That implies you need an infinite supply of female companionship."

He waited for more but she didn't say anything. It seemed she wasn't fully awake yet and he wanted a finer point on the female companionship thing. "What does that mean?"

"Women like a man with scruff. You need women. Therefore you should cultivate the scruff to attract them."

"Like bees?"

"To honey. Yes."

"And if I told you that the traditional look has been working just fine?" Would she be jealous?

She lifted one smooth, delicate shoulder in a shrug. "I'd say your women are uninspired."

Suddenly he was much less interested in women in

general than this one in particular. For just a moment he stopped shaving and met her gaze. "What inspires you?"

The pulse in her neck fluttered faster as she studied him. But when she answered, her voice was cool and even. "There's a lot to be said for a man with a smooth face..."

"But?"

"What?" she asked.

"You stopped. There was going to be more. There's something about a smooth face and I heard a 'but' in your voice. You were going to add..."

"It's not important."

"To me it is." He waited.

"Why?"

"That one little word could be a good or bad thing."

"Oh?"

"Think about it. A single-syllable word that leaves a clear path for a leap into a very bad place." He met her gaze while he thought about that. "Consider this. A smooth face is attractive on you *but* those features could stop a clock so maybe you should grow a beard."

She laughed. "I didn't mean that."

"Then what? You like smooth but if there was scruff on mine you'd be tempted to forgive and forget that I'm the jackass who left you?"

Her teasing smile slowly disappeared. "Look, Linc, I can't walk in your shoes. There's no way for me to understand what it feels like to find out what you did. No way that I can possibly get what you went through. Are still going through. And I won't patronize you by saying that I do. All I can tell you is that I believe you, that you had a reason for what you did." She shrugged as if to say sorry about this. "And that's the best I can do right now."

"Fair enough." He hadn't planned to ask forgiveness but didn't regret that he had. Her response was both less than he wanted and more than he deserved. For some stupid reason, and he did mean stupid, that gave him hope. For what, he didn't know. All he was sure of at this moment was how very much he wanted to kiss her and what a very bad idea it was.

"Let me know when you're finished in here." She started to turn away.

"Wait." He took the hand towel that was hanging beside the second sink and wiped all traces of soap from his face. "I need to talk to you in case I'm gone when you come down for breakfast."

"You're leaving early?"

"Alex and I have business to take care of. He wants me to see some property for development and look at office space for our company."

"When will you be back?"

"Not sure. I might be gone most of the day."

She nodded. "I've got work to do. Now that I've seen your place, I'll need to make sketches of each room and get some ideas put together for you. I do some on computer and others on paper."

"This house has more rooms than the entire von Trapp family could use. I'm sure Ellie can find space for you to work."

"Yeah. She already mentioned that to me and is going to help me set up somewhere."

"Good." That was his sister. Efficient and gracious. "And while I'm gone, don't say anything to her about our little secret."

There was a wicked look in her eyes. "I make no promises."

"You really are enjoying holding this over my head, aren't you?"

"So very, very much." She grinned.

They stared at each other for several moments and neither of them moved. But her smile faded and there was what looked like wistfulness in her eyes. Was it his imagination or wishful thinking that she was as reluctant and unwilling to lose this moment as he was?

So many thoughts flashed through his mind in those seconds. He'd never stopped wanting this woman and his need to kiss her right now bordered on desperate. She didn't hate him anymore, but did it matter since she was in a relationship that could be moving to the next level?

Except how did you take the next step after not telling your significant other you weren't free from a marriage he never knew about and were going to another state to work for your husband?

Linc had never been more painfully aware that she was his wife than right at this moment. But kissing her the way he wanted could destroy this fragile truce and any gains on having his sins forgiven. As much as he despised the thought of her with another man, sabotaging his opportunity to make things up to her wasn't something he was prepared to do.

"Okay, then," he said. "The bathroom is all yours."

Rose couldn't get the image of Linc shaving out of her mind. She was still thinking about it after showering, doing hair, makeup and walking downstairs. Was there anything sexier than a half-naked man dragging a straight-edge razor over his face? The bunch of muscles in his arm and the way his mouth twisted for the hard-to-get places. She hadn't been able to look away, which was something that hadn't changed in ten years.

Neither had her inability to function very well before coffee. She'd been like a sleepwalker, charging into the room and being only dimly aware of where she was and who she was charging in on. If he'd done that to her…

Well, she'd have to call it a lesson in tolerance and humility. Forgive and forget? Not if she was smart. Remembering and resentment were just about all that stood between her and being made a fool of again.

Ellie was the only one in the kitchen… Scratch that—the only adult. Leah toddled out from behind the island and grinned at her.

"Good morning." Rose smiled at the little girl. "Hey there, cutie."

"Did you sleep well?" Ellie asked.

"So good."

Ellie poured coffee into a mug, put in milk and a low-calorie sweetener and set it in front of her. "Linc told me how you take your coffee and said you really needed this."

"Thanks." Heat crept into her cheeks at the reminder of seeing him with just a towel knotted at his waist. She was still a little weak in the knees. "He said he and Alex had to leave early."

"Yeah. You just missed them." Ellie rested her elbows on the island between them, her gaze sharp and questioning. But all she said was "What would you like for breakfast?"

"Coffee is fine. Don't bother on my account."

"It's no trouble. And it's not all about you," the other woman teased. "The guys decided to grab something out so I waited to have a 'girls only' breakfast."

"That sounds wonderful. How can I help?"

"Set the table and keep an eye on Leah?" she asked.

"I can do that."

A short time later the little girl was in her high chair and the two women were eating scrambled eggs, toast and fruit.

Rose took a bite. "Mmm. These eggs are so light and fluffy. You'll have to tell me how to get them like this."

"Having someone watch my daughter so I don't burn them is the secret."

Rose took a bite of toast and sighed. "Why does everything taste so much better in the mountains?"

"No clue, but it's so true." The other woman cut fruit into tiny pieces and put them on the tray for her daughter. The little girl used her small fork to spear one, then maneuvered the food into her mouth. "Good job, baby girl."

As she ate Rose watched mother and child, envious of everything about them. If things had been different she and Linc might have kids now. Regret twisted inside her until she noticed Ellie watching her. The look wasn't quite suspicious, mostly speculation.

"I need to start working on designs for Linc's place. You said there's somewhere I can do that?"

"Yes. An office down the hall off the family room. Alex and I both use it but there's plenty of room and neither of us is in there during the day. After breakfast I'll get you settled."

"Thank you so much." She sincerely meant that.

Ellie put some eggs on her daughter's tray. "So, how long ago did you and Linc meet?"

"Oh..." She hesitated, trying to figure out what to say, then decided to stick to the truth. "Ten years, I think."

"That's a long time. I don't remember him ever mentioning you."

"He sure talked about you." Rose had always liked how much he cared about his sister. It spoke to the good man that he was and she hoped the pivot would take the focus off her and Linc. "He had a problem with your boyfriend at the time."

"He had a problem with *every* boyfriend I ever had. Including Alex, the love of my life. And now they're going to be business partners." Ellie's smile faded. "We talked about everything. Family. Friends. Linc never said anything about you, though. It just makes me wonder…"

Oh, boy. His sister didn't plan to let this go. "I suppose I should be hurt that I was so insignificant."

"That's the thing. I don't think you are."

Rose finished the last bite of food, then set her fork on the empty plate. "Why do you say that?"

"He knows how you take your coffee and was very specific with the details. Bordering on protective. That doesn't happen if a man is indifferent."

"When he told you he was bringing a decorator here, what did he say?"

"Not much," Ellie admitted. "And I didn't ask because I was so happy about him moving here."

"I know you're close." Rose got up and filled her mug with more coffee. She needed to think about what to say. "But why are you so excited about him moving here? Is it about missing family?"

"Some. But it's more than that. Linc went through a hard time finding out he had a different father." Her eyes widened, as if something just occurred to her. "That was ten years ago, in fact, right around the time you met him. So I'm sure he talked to you about it."

Not then, Rose thought. Still, she didn't want to add too many details. "He left and I missed him."

"My brother is so darn stubborn," Ellie said. "He won't speak to our parents about it and refuses to get to know his biological father. He cut the guy out of his life but doesn't get how that gives the man power over it."

Rose's eyes widened. "I never thought about it that way. If he'd only said something when he left—"

"Wait. Said something? If only… What?"

"Hmm?" *Crap and double crap*, Rose thought.

"Linc left you?"

"Did I just say that out loud?"

"Yes." Ellie was staring at her. "Look, something is up between you and my brother. I could see it from the first. And a little while ago when I told you he said you needed coffee, you were blushing."

"I was?"

"Trust me. The red was so bright it could be seen from space."

Rose blew out a long breath. "I guess my game face needs some work."

"If you're planning to hurt my brother, you'll have to go through me—"

"It's not like that, Ellie. He's the one who hurt me."

"I don't understand."

If ever a situation needed context, this one did. She'd teased Linc about holding the secret over his head, but Rose didn't see any other way out of this now. Maybe it was rationalizing, but shouldn't his sister know? The other woman got up and started to clear the table.

"You might want to sit down for this. It might come as a shock."

"What?" Ellie sat. "You're a man?"

"Wow, if that's where you went, I might need to change my brand of makeup." She was trying to lighten the mood but it wasn't happening. Quick was better. The way Linc had told her. "I'm just going to say this. Linc and I were married ten years ago."

"What?"

"We did meet at work. It was love at first sight—for me, at least. We went to Vegas and got married. It lasted fifteen minutes and he told me we were getting a divorce. That it was him, not me."

"Oh, God—" Ellie put a hand over her mouth and stared before adding, "He found out about his father."

"Yes, although he didn't tell me that then. Just that I was better off without him."

Ellie got up and filled a sippy cup with milk, then handed it to her daughter. The woman moved as if she was on automatic pilot and her mind was racing as she connected the dots. "You must have been—"

"Devastated. Hurt. After a while anger set in and got me through. Now?" She shrugged.

The other woman sat down across from her again. "You said he didn't tell you then. When *did* he tell you?"

"Just recently. He probably never would have except he found out that we're not divorced."

"What?" The pitch of her voice went up and got her daughter's attention. Leah started to cry so Ellie freed her from the chair and cuddled her close. "Mama's sorry, baby girl. But Uncle Linc is… I can't even think of a name bad enough to call him. How could you not be divorced?"

Rose explained everything and that he was handling it now. "In all fairness, he had a shock at the time he promised to take care of everything. Maybe you should cut him some slack."

"Slack?" Ellie snapped her fingers. "Slacker, maybe. There's a name and that's what he is. He's the one I'm going to hurt."

"Ellie, it's all right—"

"No, it's not. All this time you believed you were divorced, then he drops by out of the blue and says you're not? 'Oh, and by the way, will you decorate my condo?'"

"There was a little more in between." Although not all that much. "Basically that's what happened."

"Why didn't you slam the door in his face? I would have. I might now."

"Please don't. I really need this job." There was no point in trying to hide the truth so she explained that her business was in trouble. "Linc offered me this opportunity as a way to save it."

"A high-profile job." Ellie nodded as if pieces had just fallen into place. "So that's what he meant."

"About?" Rose prompted.

"Before he and Alex left today Linc said to tell you that he was going to talk to Burke and Sloan Holden about decorating the lobby of their new hotel."

"He did?"

"Yes. It was very specific, too. That you needed to know he was making good on his promise."

Oh, dear God. That made her feel awful and somehow it gave him an advantage. Because he was keeping his word and Rose had just spilled her guts.

## *Chapter Six*

"Linc, please get here soon." Rose had prayed, willing him to walk in the door so she could talk to him before his sister did.

She'd tried his cell phone but only got voice mail. He'd told her service in the mountains was spotty and this was a superbad time to find out for herself that he was right. She'd taunted him about getting to watch the fallout when Ellie learned they were married but she never really planned to say anything.

It was just something to hold over his head for a little payback. In hindsight it had been pathetically easy for Ellie to get the information out of her, but the result was the same. The cat was out of the bag and there were going to be repercussions. All day it was like waiting for the other shoe to drop.

In spite of that hanging over her head, Rose had managed to get some work done on Linc's condo. Themes, sketches, ideas. But it hadn't been easy to concentrate. The office had a window to the front of the house with the long driveway and she kept looking out, waiting and watching.

She hoped to warn him that his sister knew their secret. Ellie had been gone all day; her job as an architect kept her pretty busy in this growing town. Rose only hoped she was a little busier today than Linc.

A few minutes later she heard a car and looked out the window to see his SUV pull in front of the house. He got out, all lean and lithe masculinity. She caught her breath, grateful that she was still sitting in the chair. Sometimes a wave of attraction to the man crashed over her and threatened to buckle her knees. This was one of those times.

"Pull it together," she muttered to herself.

The front door closed and she hurried to meet him in the two-story entryway. He set down his briefcase at the foot of the stairs and draped his navy blazer over the banister. In worn jeans and a long-sleeved powder-blue shirt that brought out the intensity of his blue eyes, he was sexier than sin. That was pretty darn inconvenient since sin was often irresistible. She felt another one of those attraction waves coming on and forced it away.

He smiled his oh-so gorgeous smile. "Wow. This is a nice thing."

"What?"

"You greeting me at the door after a long hard day at the office."

"Don't make this something it's not. And you don't have an office," she said.

"It's just nice to see you. Here at the front door. Just saying..." He walked past her and headed for the kitchen. "How was your day?"

"Fine." She shook off the dreamy thoughts that clouded her mind and caught up with him. "But—"

"Look at us, all domestic and diplomatic." He flipped on a wall switch and the kitchen's recessed lights instantly blazed to life. There was a satisfied gleam in his eyes and that was about to change.

"Linc, we need to talk—"

He put up a warning finger, cutting off her words. "Let me give you some advice. Those are words no man ever wants to hear within five minutes of walking in the door at night."

"Oh, for Pete's sake. Don't make this a thing—"

"I'm not. It's the truth. Ask Alex if you don't believe me. A guy doesn't want to hear it from anyone—man or woman. A conversation starting out like that is going to be a bad conversation. At least let me have a beer first."

"There may not be time for that. Quit being weird and just listen to me."

He reached into the refrigerator and grabbed a longneck. "Do you want one?"

"No." She needed a clear head for this.

He twisted off the cap and took a pull from the bottle, then met her gaze. "I'm in a great mood. You were wrong before. Alex and I now have an office and we looked at an amazing parcel of land. We're probably going to make an offer on it. That's a good thing and I'm just spreading happiness wherever I go."

"Oh, brother." Her voice was wry. "You're just a regular 'rainbows and unicorns' kind of guy. Any second you'll be tossing glitter."

"Make fun if you must. But how exactly is that being weird?"

"You're acting as if we're a couple. All like a husband coming home to the little woman. It's not natural and yet it sort of falls under the heading of what I need to talk to you about."

There was a puzzled look on his face as he studied her. "At the risk of sounding like a ten-year-old, it takes one to know one. You're the one acting weird. How was your day, really? I sincerely want to know. Think about it this way. I have a personal interest in what you're doing."

Even more than he realized, Rose thought. "I don't remember you being this wordy."

He shrugged. "I've evolved."

"Well, just stop it."

Beer bottle in hand he gestured toward her. "Now that's a momentous statement. How often does a man hear a woman telling him not to evolve? Next you'll be telling me *not* to get in touch with my feminine side.

In the background she heard the sound of the garage door going up and a car pulling in, and knew time was running out. "Will you just stop and listen to me. Ellie will be here any second—"

"I suppose so, since this is her house."

The inside door from the garage opened and closed. Moments later his sister came into the kitchen with Leah in her arms. She walked straight up to her brother and poked him in the chest with her index finger. "Lincoln Hart, you have a lot of explaining to do."

Boom. Time was up.

Rose sighed. "Now those are words a guy really doesn't want to hear."

He frowned at her, then met his sister's gaze. "What did I do?"

"You got married, that's what you did. Ten years ago, you took vows."

His mouth pulled tight for a moment, then his niece poked him in the chest, a perfect imitation of her mother. "See what you're teaching your child?"

Ellie set the little girl on her feet and she toddled off to the wicker basket in the family room, where her toys were stored. Her favorite game was to remove every last item from the very large basket and it would keep her busy for a while. That was a good thing, what with the tension arcing between her mother and uncle.

Rose felt horrible and wanted to do something to smooth out the rift. "This is all my fault."

"No," Ellie said. "My brother gets all the blame for this one."

Linc was clearly not happy when he glanced at Rose, and it was the first time she'd ever seen him look like that. Ten years ago there'd never been an angry moment between them. But, as he'd pointed out, he'd evolved. That didn't make her feel better.

He set his beer on the island beside him. "Ellie, calm down. You'll scare Leah."

"You're the one who should be scared. How could you fall in love and not tell me?"

"Really? That's where you're going with this? Because guys don't talk about every detail of their lives?"

Oh, boy, Rose thought. That was really a bad thing to say. Any minute she expected his sister's eyes to shoot fire and reduce him to ashes on the floor.

"That's wrong in so many ways that I don't even know where to start," Ellie said. "You got married. That's not just a detail, it's a life-changer. And I never knew."

"I don't know if it matters, but back then Linc and I agreed to keep us private for a little while," Rose interjected.

She wondered, not for the first time, if he'd suggested keeping it secret because he was ashamed of her and didn't want to tell his family since he didn't plan to stay married. And maybe she'd agreed to keep it hush-hush out of fear that his family would object to him marrying a nobody like her.

"You were so young and probably starry-eyed in love." Ellie gave her a sympathetic look. "I know you're trying to help, but this is all on Linc. He fell in love and took *the step*. That's something you confide to someone you love and have the sort of close relationship we do. Or maybe I'm wrong about that."

"No, you're not. We are close," he protested.

Ellie planted her fists on her hips just as Leah ran over and wrapped her chubby little arms around her mom's jeans-clad leg. "I told you everything and you didn't share anything. I'm very angry."

"Join the club." The fire in his eyes when he looked at Rose was not unlike his sister's expression. "Rose called me a jackass."

"Jackass," the little girl said, clear as a bell. "Jackass."

"Wow, thanks for that. You just taught my innocent little girl to swear." Ellie huffed out a breath. "You get married and separated, then disappear and teach my child to cuss?"

"In all fairness, Rose is the one who has every right to be ticked off at me—"

"So do I." Ellie shook her head. "So do Mom and Dad and the rest of your family. We love you. You grew up and never suspected that you had a different father. Suddenly this stranger shows up and we're dead to you?"

"You're exaggerating."

"I'm not. And you were gone for a long time. Without ever saying a word about the fact that you got married."

"You were the one who talked me into coming back," he reminded her. "Only you could have."

"That's not going to work, Linc."

"Look, Ellie, you don't—"

"If you value your life, do not tell me that I don't understand. You're an ungrateful—"

"The word I think you're looking for is—" He looked down at the little girl who was staring at them with great interest. "J-a-c-k-a-s-s."

"Let's go with that. Leah doesn't need to expand her vocabulary with words that would shock moms and kids in her play group."

"I would never deliberately do anything to hurt you, Ellie. If you believe anything, believe that. I'm so very sorry."

The anger in Ellie's expression cracked. "Did Rose tell you to say that?"

"No." He glanced at her for a moment. "Why?"

"Because it was exactly the right thing to say and I didn't think you could come up with it on your own." She moved closer and put her arms around him, resting her cheek on his chest. "It's impossible to stay mad and keep yelling at you after that."

"Good." He kissed the top of her head, then looked at Rose, his expression unreadable. "I've evolved."

"Miracles do happen."

"Does that mean there's any chance that you're going to keep this to yourself?" he asked tentatively.

Ellie stepped away and started laughing. "Are you kidding? Have you met me?"

Just then Alex walked into the room. "Hi."

"Daddy!" Leah ran to him and he lifted her into his arms.

"Hi, little bit." He kissed and hugged his little girl, then looked at his wife. "How are my girls? Did you have a good day?"

"It was interesting," Ellie told him. "You're taking me

out to dinner so I can tell you all about it. Linc has volunteered to babysit."

"It's the least I can do," he agreed.

"For so many reasons." Ellie took the little girl from her husband and handed her to Linc. "If you say the magic words you just learned, maybe Rose will help. And, FYI, Leah has a dirty diaper."

Linc sniffed and the look on his face said Ellie wasn't lying about the diaper. And moments later her parents had left the building.

On the upside, Rose thought, the secret was out and the world hadn't come to an end. That didn't mean he wouldn't be furious with her for revealing it. The problem now was that she realized she cared whether or not he was angry with her.

Linc had no time to process the fact that Rose not only ratted him out to his sister, but also allowed him to be ambushed by said sibling. The part of his brain not dealing with the potential disaster of changing his niece's dirty diaper acknowledged that wasn't fair. She'd been trying to tell him something but he was—how did she put it?—wordy.

He looked down at Leah, who, thank God, was on the changing table and quietly preoccupied with the car keys he'd given her. "Princess, do you think I'm wordy?"

She nodded, then held out her little hand and said, "Key."

"Right you are. Uncle Linc is going to change your diaper."

"I make poop." She grinned proudly.

"Yes, you did."

He undid the fasteners on her denim overalls and slid them off. Like any good military general planning a mission he assessed supplies. Wipes and spare diapers were stacked beneath the table, at his fingertips. That didn't make him feel any less like a water buffalo at high tea in this pink room with its pictures of fairies and princesses. The furniture was white and the hand pulls were decorated with pink rosebuds. Leah still slept in a crib, but there was a canopy bed just waiting for her to be old enough to sleep in it.

But looking around was just putting off the inevitable. He took a deep breath and held it, then undid the diaper and cleaned off the little bottom. Next to the changing table was a magic container that inhibited odors. He dropped it in there.

"Good news, kid. The worst is done."

"Good job." The little girl clapped her hands.

"Thank you. Obviously you are showered with positive reinforcement."

She was a mirror of her mother. Case in point, poking him in the chest. He knew words of praise were something she heard frequently.

"Linc?"

He glanced over his shoulder. Rose was standing in the doorway. "What?"

"Ellie called and said to give Leah a bath since you're—" She indicated the clean-up operation currently in progress. "You know."

"Yeah."

"She told me where the pajamas are and to make macaroni and cheese and green beans for Leah's dinner. If you're okay with it, I'll handle that."

"Okay. What about food for the adults?"

"For you there's leftover pot roast to reheat. Mine is easy. Bread and water." She moved to the white dresser and pulled out pink pajamas and white socks, then set them on the bed. "I'll go fill the tub for her, then get dinner ready."

Without another word she left and moments later he heard the sound of running water from the next room.

"Okay, kid, I'm flying solo on this and would greatly appreciate your full cooperation in this endeavor. Okay?"

"Okay," she answered enthusiastically.

After hearing the water go off, Linc took her into the bathroom and lifted her into the tub. Sitting on the side was a plastic cup, which she grabbed before plopping herself down. After filling it with water she dumped it over her head.

"'Poo," she said pointing to a bottle beside her.

At first he thought she had to go again but eventually realized she meant the container that proclaimed in no uncertain terms that the shampoo would not sting her eyes. He handed it over and kneeled down beside her.

"Go for it, kid." She responded with a string of words that he was pretty sure meant thank you and said his name. He loved the way it sounded coming from her. "I'll wash your hair."

"No." She shook her head and water went flying. "Me. I big girl."

"Excellent," he said. "An independent woman."

Linc let her handle things, partly because he never said no to her and partly because this bath thing didn't have to be perfect. There was soap, water and he was there to make sure she was safe. He called that a win.

A pink towel was set out by the tub, probably by Rose. Another independent woman. He was still pissed off that she'd sold him out, but had to admit she didn't jump ship on the babysitting. She pitched in and didn't have to. This wasn't in her job description.

He let the water out of the tub and that set off his niece.

"No, Unc 'Inc. Me do."

"Sorry, kid." He put the plug down again, before all

the water was gone and let her do it her way. Not unlike the woman who was now making dinner. He wrapped the child in a towel and lifted her out, noting the tangle of her wet hair. "Can you comb your hair?"

"No. Brush."

"Gotcha." He held her up to mirror height and let her do the job. It wasn't perfect, but no way he was telling her that. "You look beautiful."

In her room he put her back on the changing table. After a couple of tries he managed to get a diaper on her and she insisted on putting herself in the pajamas.

"Are you hungry?"

She nodded. "Go see Wo'?"

"Rose?" When she nodded vigorously he held out his hand and she put her little one into it. "Let's go."

Rose was at the stove filling a three-section plastic plate. She looked at them and a soft expression chased away the frown on her face. "Leah, you look all clean."

"She did it all by herself," Linc said.

"Good job."

Hmm. Was that a chick thing or a mom thing? A puzzle for another time, he thought. "Okay, princess, let's get you in the chair."

It was a joint effort—he set her on it and Rose clicked the plastic tray into place. Then she put the plate and small fork on it and the little girl dug in. The two of them looked at each other and breathed a sigh of relief.

"Thanks for the help," he said. "I didn't expect it."

"I'm not the one who walks away, Linc. That's your default behavior."

This payback was starting to get old. Especially after what she did. "Is that why you told Ellie? To get even with me?"

"Of course not. I—"

"You promised not to say anything, Rose."

"No, I didn't. I only said it was pretty awesome having something to hold over your head."

"And how much you'd enjoy watching when Ellie found out. Well, chalk one off your to-do list. Was it as entertaining as you expected?"

"Actually, no." Her look was defiant. "I didn't like seeing Ellie upset."

"Me, either." He met her gaze. "So why did you spill the beans?"

"She started to ask questions. How long ago we met. She mentioned you never said anything about me and yet you remembered all the details of how I like my coffee. Then she connected that we met right around the time your biological father contacted you." She sighed. "Did you really think we could be here together and your sister wouldn't notice that there was *something* between us?"

"Yes." That was a knee-jerk response because stubborn was his middle name.

Rose shook her head as if to say he was dumb as dirt. "She's smart. She knows you better, I think, than you know yourself and she's a woman. We don't miss much."

"So now she knows and my relationship with her will never be what it was."

"Oh, for Pete's sake. Why is everything with you an absolute?" she demanded. "There can't be a disagreement with your sister and then you both put it away and move on like you were before?"

"No." Again Mr. Stubborn. "This was a major breach of confidence and she'll never get over it."

"Yeah," Rose said drily. "I could tell by the way she hugged you, then left her child in your care."

When she put it like that… "She was just really ticked

off and not thinking straight. When she has a chance to mull it over she's really going to be mad."

"Baloney." Rose shook her head. "If this revelation had pushed her over the edge, she would have kicked you out of her house."

"She didn't because you're here," he argued.

"No, she would have done it and let me stay." Her smile was full of confidence as she folded her arms over her chest. "She likes me. Possibly more than you, at least right now."

"You're probably right about that," he admitted. "Throwing me into the deep end of the pool with a toxic diaper and a bath was the ultimate punishment."

Rose studied the front of him, soaked with bathwater. "I think you're a fraud."

"You've made that pretty clear, but what is it this time?"

"You enjoyed spending time with that little girl. There was laughter and it didn't sound a whole lot like punishment to me. I heard the two of you chattering away."

"She started it."

"Right." Rose smiled, then it faded, replaced by a sad expression. "You'd be a great father, Linc."

"No."

"You refuse to see it, but Ellie's right. The father who raised you did it so well you never suspected you weren't his son. That means he treated all four of his children the same way."

"My sister wants to pretend nothing is different. But it is. I can never un-know the truth."

"It doesn't have to define you. It doesn't have to close you off to loving someone." Her mouth pulled tight for a moment. "But loving is hard. Running is much easier."

"It's not fair to judge." He knew it had been foolish to ask her to forgive and forget. That was never going to happen and it made him angry. "People deal with adversity differently."

"Stuff happens. How you deal with it reveals character," she insisted.

"That's just it. Half of my DNA is a blank. I don't know who I am."

"Then find out." She smiled at Leah, who was using her little princess fork to carefully move macaroni from the plate to her mouth. If there was a mishap she just picked it up off the tray and shoved the food in. Rose met his gaze again and hers held a hint of warning. "If you don't make an effort and do something proactive, you're going to hold back and miss out on the best that life has to offer."

"Now that I'm not being lied to and have all the facts, it's my choice whether or not I pursue this."

"You're right. No one else has a say in what you do." She looked at him for several moments, then sighed. "We can only take responsibility for our own actions. So, in that spirit… I'm sorry I told Ellie. The other alternative was to flat-out lie and I couldn't do that. But I didn't do it to get even with you. That much energy would mean that I still care about you. Just so we're clear, I don't care about you anymore."

She brushed by him then and walked over to the refrigerator, pulling out leftover containers to reheat last night's dinner.

Linc was annoyed again and the reason was even more annoying. He cared that she didn't care about him. Damn it, he really did.

What the hell was that?

## *Chapter Seven*

The next morning Rose was waiting for Linc in his sister's home office. At breakfast she'd explained that input from him was now required to do her job. After what happened last night she wasn't entirely sure he still wanted her on the job, and if not she needed to know that, too.

He walked in at the appointed time. "Let's do this."

"First, we should talk about whether or not you can work with me. I know you're mad about what I said to Ellie—"

"Not anymore." His expression was unreadable and that was irritating.

"I'm not sure I believe you."

"Why is that?" He folded his arms over his chest and met her gaze.

"If you haven't been taken over by aliens and you're the same Lincoln Hart who has held a grudge against his parents for the last ten years, it seems out of character that you would get over the fact that I revealed our secret marriage from a decade ago just yesterday."

One corner of his mouth quirked up. "Ellie seems to be over it and so am I."

"So you still want me to do the interior design on your condo?"

"Yes."

"Good." That was such a relief. She held out a hand and indicated the two club chairs in front of the desk in the home office. Her laptop was there. "Have a seat. I want to show you some living room ideas and get your feedback."

"Why can't you throw some stuff together and I'll pick something out?"

"Do you have somewhere more important to be?" She tilted her head.

"I'm busy and—"

"If you don't want flowers, puppies and flocked wallpaper in your personal space, you're going to want to sit down and work with me on this. It's my goal to see that when the job is complete, you're deliriously happy with your space."

"Fine." He sat, clearly impatient.

That should have bugged her and it did a little, but mostly the behavior reminded her of a little boy who didn't get his way. For an instant, she could picture what a child of theirs might have been like. That made her sad, so she went back to being bugged.

"Okay. The sooner we get started, the sooner you can go be a tycoon." She sat beside him. "I'm going to click through these design ideas and try to pin down what you like. Color schemes. Ambience, setting, that sort of thing."

"I just want it done," he grumbled.

"You can't possibly want that more than I do." It was

hard to be with him and bump painfully into the past every day, to have her face rubbed in what might have been.

Linc lifted an eyebrow questioningly. “Are you anxious to get back to your regularly scheduled life?”

“Yes and no.”

“Hmm.” For some reason those words made his bored look disappear. “I’d like to hear about the *no* part. What makes you not eager to get back?”

“It’s beautiful here. I like the town and people I’ve met so far. And there’s the prospect of more work.”

“Yes. Don’t think it escaped my notice that I kept my end of the bargain and spoke to Burke and Sloan Holden about your job skills while you were stabbing me in the back.”

“I explained that,” she protested.

“Yes, you did.” He relaxed back into the club chair. “So it’s work and nothing to do with me that would keep you here.”

She wouldn’t let it be about him. “Wow, how did I never notice that your ego is the size of a long-haul truck?”

“I’ve never tried to hide who I am.”

True, she thought. His problem was that half his family story was missing and even a guy as confident as Linc would find that disconcerting.

“Then I guess the reason I didn’t notice was my problem. I was starry-eyed and that tends to prevent a girl from seeing clearly.”

“You are refreshing. A woman who takes responsibility.” He grinned suddenly, and it was spectacular. “So if you like Blackwater Lake and are looking forward to more work here, what would make your life in Texas beckon?” The words were barely out of his mouth when he snapped his fingers. “Chandler. I almost forgot about him. He’s why you’re in a hurry to get back.”

"Yes." The answer was automatic and also a lie. She hadn't really thought about him much and rationalized that Linc was bigger than life and dealing with him was a whirlwind that sucked all the oxygen out of the room. There was no time or energy for anything else. "And we need to work."

"Right." There wasn't a lot of enthusiasm in the single word, not like he'd shown when he brought up her personal life.

She directed his attention to the laptop monitor. "I'm going to scroll through these living-room design ideas and I want you to tell me what, if anything, you like." She clicked and brought up an image.

"Too cold."

"Okay." The ceilings and walls were white and there was an area rug under a glass-topped table. "You're decisive. That's good. Next."

He carefully studied a couple of pictures, then pointed to one. "I like the wood-beam ceiling and built-in bookcases."

"Me, too," she said. "But I'm not sure about that in your living room. Let's keep it in mind for your home office."

His expression said great idea. "Sounds good."

She clicked on the next shot. "Now in this one I like the crown molding and the color of the walls. Gray and white are being used a lot right now but I'm not sure about it for you."

"Why?"

"I've been researching pictures of Blackwater Lake, all the seasons. In winter there's a lot of snow and fog in the mountains. I think the interior of your home should be a contrast to a time of the year that some people might find depressing. Earth colors might give you a warmer ambience overall. And there can be variations on the shade in other rooms that make it less gloomy."

"Good point."

She tapped her lip looking at the next picture. "The TV in this one is prominent in the great room. Since you're going to have a media room do you want one in the family room, too?"

He thought for a moment. "Maybe."

"Would it be a distraction there when you're entertaining?"

"I don't do much of that."

"Not even the family? For football games or holidays?"

"No." He met her gaze. "It's saying a lot that I would rather talk paint color and built-in bookshelves than personal issues, so make whatever you want out of it and we can just move on."

"Okay, then. Next picture." It had white fuzzy chairs against a navy blue wall and both of them said together, "No way."

Rose laughed. "That was unprofessional of me. You might have loved and desperately wanted that. I'm not supposed to influence your choices."

"Not even to talk me out of a big mistake?"

"I would point out the pros and cons without making my preference known," she said.

There was a look in his eyes that was both intense and impossible to read. "No, please, reveal preferences. I'm paying you the big bucks so you'll keep me from picking out something hideous. I want you to like it."

"It doesn't matter whether I do or not. I'm not going to live there."

"Right."

Had she just seen something in his face? A vulnerability, or longing? She wasn't sure and didn't want to make a big deal out of it. After clicking on the next picture she asked, "What do you think?"

"Looks cheesy."

"I agree." But she pointed to the wood floor. "That's a nice color. Not too dark or light and it's pine. Seems appropriate for the mountains. What do you think?"

He examined it closer. "Yeah. I'd have missed it because the rest of the room turned me off. You really have an eye for detail."

"It's my job. And occasionally I'm right." The next five shots were unhelpful but the sixth one caught his eye. She could tell by the excitement in his expression. "What?"

"That fireplace. It's classic but simple and warm."

"Look at you throwing around decorating lingo." She studied the white wood and detailed edges of the fireplace. "I'd have figured you for a rock-face kind of guy. And we should look at that, too. Because this is a focal point of the room and the rest of your choices need to complement it if that's most important to you."

"Important to me," he repeated, studying her. His eyes turned intense and their faces were very close together.

Rose felt heat creep into her cheeks and her pulse rate kicked up a notch or two. She would give almost anything to know what he was thinking and thought about asking straight out. But her cell phone on the desk rang. Normally she checked the identity of the caller before answering but she was too grateful for the interruption.

She picked up the device and hit Talk. "Rose Tucker."

"Hey, Rosie."

"Chandler." She met Linc's gaze and saw the "I told you so" wheels turning. Distance. She needed to be away from him. After standing, she moved toward the doorway. "How are you?"

"Missing you."

"That's sweet." This was where she should have said she missed him, too. But she didn't.

"How's it going there?" If Chandler noticed her lack of reciprocation, his voice didn't reveal anything.

She had told him about the out-of-town job and since he knew nothing about her and Linc being married, the question had to be about her work. "Good. Things are fine."

"How much longer will you be gone?"

"Hard to say." She glanced over her shoulder and saw Linc not even trying to pretend that he wasn't listening to every word. "This is a big job."

"Can you get away for a weekend here in Dallas?"

"Not likely."

"What if I put together a couple of days and come to you?"

Oh, that was a very bad idea and she just barely stopped the words from coming out of her mouth. Instead she thought carefully about what to say. "I hate to see you do that. I won't be able to spend much time with you." In a sudden and surprising flash of insight she saw that Linc looked awfully pleased about that. Was she pleased about his reaction? After telling him she didn't care? That would make her a liar.

"Chandler, I'd love to chat longer, but I'm with a client. Can I call you later?"

"Sure. I look forward to it. Love you, Rose."

"Thanks for calling." She ended the call and took a deep breath before turning to Linc. "Okay, where were we?"

"We're where I ask how important that guy really is to you."

"Very." She sat down and met his gaze, stubbornly refusing to look away even though she desperately wanted to do just that. And she had a feeling he could see the blush creeping into her cheeks.

"Very important?" He leaned closer. "I don't think I believe you. That sounded an awful lot like a defensive response ten years in the making."

"Oh, please." She made a dismissive noise. "Chandler and I are practically engaged. I told you that."

"Then why did you discourage him from coming for a visit?" He held up a hand to stop her protest. "It was the part where you said you couldn't spend much time with him that clued me in. So why don't you want to see him?"

"That's none of your business, Linc."

"Funny." He glanced down for a moment, a small smile on his lips. "It sure feels like my business."

"Well, it's not. Now let's get back to work." She reached out and clicked the computer mouse to scroll to the next picture. "What do you think of this one?"

"What would you do if I kissed you?"

Her heart stopped for a second, then resumed beating very hard and fast. She couldn't look at him. "Don't you dare. I have a boyfriend."

"But what if I did? Would you slap my face?"

"You're so unimportant to me it wouldn't be worth getting that worked up over."

"Care to bet?"

Pulling herself together, she finally met his gaze. She didn't care about him, so why not? "You're on."

He reached into his jeans pocket, pulled out a twenty-dollar bill and set it on the desk. Then he stood and reached down to take her hands and lift her to her feet. He cupped her face in his palms and brushed his thumbs over her cheekbones until she thought she couldn't breathe. And when he touched his mouth to hers, she swore fireworks were going off nearby.

He moved his lips over her face with small, nibbling kisses and touched the tip of his tongue to her bottom lip, tracing it slowly, erotically. Dear God, it felt so good. Right now she'd give him another twenty dollars not to stop doing what he was doing. But that wasn't to be. He pulled back and she swore the move was reluctant on his part. At least she wasn't the only one breathing hard.

Linc looked at her, dropped his hands and stepped away. "Okay, go ahead and slap me. After all, you have a boyfriend."

Oh, God! Chandler. One second she'd held him up as a shield, the next he'd been wiped from her mind like an annoying computer virus. This was a problem and she needed to take care of it right away.

In the Prosper, Texas, diner near her design studio and apartment Rose looked at the man sitting across the table. "Thanks for coming, Chandler."

"Are you kidding? No way I'd have missed this." He smiled warmly and settled his hand on hers. "Although I have to admit it was a surprise when you called and asked me to meet you. After our phone conversation the other day I had no idea when I would see you again."

That talk was before Linc kissed her. The kiss had changed everything. It hadn't taken her long to know what she had to do. After letting Linc know she'd be gone for a couple days she caught a flight to Dallas and here she was with Chandler. One look at him confirmed that the simple touch of Linc's lips to hers was more powerful than anything she'd ever felt with this man.

"Well—" she shrugged "—here I am."

"Yes." He turned his hand over and snuggled her fingers into his palm. "Here you are."

The man was handsome, charming, smart, funny and kind. He was terrific and as far as she could tell had only one flaw. He wasn't Lincoln Hart.

She slid her hand from his. "Chandler, we need to talk—"

"I think you felt it, too," he interrupted.

"I'm sorry, what?"

"You know. They say absence makes the heart grow fonder. Since you've been gone, I realized how much I really care about you. I—"

"Hey, you two." Janie Tucker stood at the end of the table. She was working her shift at the diner and seemed pleased. The smile made her look younger and put a twinkle in her blue eyes. Dark hair the same shade as Rose's was cut into a short bob. "Good to see you, Chandler."

"You, too, Janie."

"Can I get you something to drink?"

"I think we need a couple of minutes. Do you mind?" Chandler gave her the smile that broke every female heart except Rose's.

"Sure thing." She walked back to the counter.

Her mom didn't know what was going on and Rose wanted to keep it that way until she broke the news to this man. When they were alone she sighed and met his gaze. "The thing is this job has turned out to be more complicated than I expected."

"I guess that means I'm going to miss you longer than we expected."

If it was just about time and distance, he'd be right. But it was all about that kiss. "There's something else."

"Whatever it is, I'll be there to work it out with you. That's what a significant other does. And I think you know I want to be more than that. I want to marry you."

"Oh, Chandler—"

He smiled, mistaking her distress for something else that encouraged him. "I've been looking at engagement rings and I want to ask—"

"Don't." She held up a hand to stop him.

"What?"

"Don't ask me. Don't say the words. Please, Chandler," she begged.

"I can't help it. I have to. Will you marry me, Rose?"

She shook her head. "I can't."

"Of course you can. The job in Montana won't last forever. We'll figure out a way to make it work. All you have to do is say yes."

"I can't."

"You keep saying that." His excitement slipped, giving way to confusion. "Why?"

She blew out a long breath and it flashed through her mind that Linc must have experienced a little dread like this before he told her about not being divorced. But he was the last person she wanted to think about right now. If he'd just kept his mouth to himself…

"Rose?"

"I'm married."

"You're what?" Chandler blinked at her. "I don't understand. You're joking."

"I wish," she said miserably.

"Married? If you don't want to marry me just say so. There's no need to lie to me—"

"It's the truth."

"I don't understand. Why didn't you tell me before?"

"I didn't know. I thought I was divorced." She explained what happened ten years ago—falling in love, the quick marriage, what felt like a quicker split with very little explanation from her husband. Why there was no divorce, although it was progressing now. "Linc promised he would take care of it this time and get it right."

"And you believe him?"

"Yes." Trust him, no. "He wants this over with as much as I do."

"Lincoln Hart is your husband?" Chandler frowned. "Is he the man you're working for now? In Montana?"

"Yes."

"What's going on, Rose?" It was not a voice he'd ever used with her. "Is there still something between you?"

"No!" At least she hoped not.

"But you agreed to go with him to Montana. And didn't think it was necessary to tell me you're married to him."

"You know my business is in trouble," she said.

"And I offered to help."

"It's something I have to do alone." Every instinct she had told her not to let him, which, in hindsight, was a sign of something not right. "Vicki said I should tell you about the divorce. It was my decision alone to—"

"So your friend knew the truth but you didn't think it was important to tell me?"

"I should have. I know. I just didn't think that—"

"What? I'd ever find out?" He dragged his fingers through perfectly cut dark blond hair. "So he married you under false pretenses to get you into bed and now you lied to me."

"I didn't overtly tell you an untruth." It was a small hair but she split it anyway.

"A lie of omission." His lips pulled tight for a moment. "The two of you should be very happy together. You're cut from the same cloth."

Rose knew he was right, although not about her and Linc being happy together. "Chandler, please listen. Let me try to explain."

"Try? How much more can there be? No. I'm done." He glared at her. "But I have one question and you owe me the courtesy of the truth."

"Anything."

"Why not just tell me this when we talked the other day?"

Because Linc was sitting there listening to every word. "At that moment I didn't plan to break up. There was a lot to think about—"

"Or," he interrupted. "Better yet you could have called it quits in a text."

Rose winced. She probably had that coming. He had every right to be bitter and though she wanted to get up and walk out right this minute, she didn't. Chandler wouldn't want to hear it, but the real reason she was here had to do with Linc. He'd had the decency to tell her to her face that they were over and she couldn't do less.

And she wouldn't make this worse for Chandler by revealing that after kissing Linc she realized if she had forever-after feelings for Chandler another man's touch wouldn't have affected her the way it did. There had been signs that it wasn't right but her mom really liked him and Rose wasn't getting any younger. Wishful thinking collided with reality the moment Linc's mouth touched hers.

"I'm so sorry." She met his angry gaze. "I didn't mean to hurt you."

"Go to hell, Rose."

It was a technicality, but she didn't need to "go" anywhere because she was already in hell. "Chandler—"

He slid out of the booth and didn't look back as he passed her obviously puzzled mother and headed straight to the diner's exit.

Moments later Janie was heading her way. Too late Rose realized she hadn't carefully thought through the location for this meeting.

"What's going on, Rose? Why did Chandler leave so suddenly? He looked really upset." Janie glanced toward the door he'd stormed through just a minute ago. "What did you say to him?"

"I broke things off."

"But why?"

"I'm not in love with him."

"Are you sure? Maybe if you gave it a little longer." Janie sat down in the booth.

"I'm sure, Mom. When you know, you know." With Linc it had been like an electric storm, immediate and powerful. That made it all the more painful when he left her.

"Does this have anything to do with that man you're working for?"

There was a lot of potential here for yet another lie. Ten years ago Linc was the only one who knew she'd married him. Even her mother was in the dark. Rose always intended to tell her but then it was over and she'd believed the heavy burden of foolishness was hers to carry alone.

"Mom, there's something you need to know."

As Rose talked, a series of emotions drifted over Janie's still-pretty face. Shock, anger, sympathy and, worst of all, a mother's helplessness to fix her child's trouble.

There was so much disappointment in Janie's voice when she said, "You could have told me, honey."

"Yeah. I should have. I'm sorry." Apparently it was the night for those two words.

"You didn't have to go through all of that alone. I should have been there for you."

"You always are, Mom." She reached over and took the other woman's worn hand. "It's just— You work so hard. I didn't want to put one more worry on you."

"You're sweet." She squeezed her daughter's fingers. "But I'm tough. And so are you. Always remember if you need me I'm there and together we can handle anything."

"Okay."

"I mean it." She almost smiled. "Don't get me wrong. I'm still pretty mad at you. But that doesn't change the fact that I love you more than anything in this world."

"I love you, too, Mom." It occurred to her that Linc's sister said almost the same thing to him.

"Now tell me about this guy you're working for. The one you're still married to."

"There's not much to say—"

"No. Not getting away with that again." Janie shook her head. "When you left Texas things with you and Chandler were practically perfect. After a short time in Montana you come back here to break up with him? I know there's a few years on me but I'm not that out of touch. Something happened and now is as good a time as any to break the pattern of keeping things to yourself."

So Rose told her mother about kissing Linc and found sharing the burden helped in an unexpected way. It became clear why she hadn't called it quits with Chandler on the phone. She didn't want Linc to know about the breakup. The idea of her being involved with someone might be the only thing that stood between her and falling for Linc again.

That was called making the same mistake twice and only a card-carrying fool would do that. He didn't have to know that she no longer had a boyfriend.

## *Chapter Eight*

Rose had left Blackwater Lake after giving Linc some vague excuse and now he was wandering aimlessly around his sister's kitchen while said sister was preparing dinner. More often than not he was in Ellie's way, but at the moment she stood in front of a wooden cutting board and pounded the living daylights out of a perfectly innocent boneless skinless chicken breast.

It occurred to him that hitting something might be just what he needed. "Hey, El, want me to do that for you?"

She met his gaze. "That offer sounds an awful lot like a cry for help."

"What are you talking about?"

"You look like testosterone central, which is code for wanting to put your fist through a wall."

"I do not."

"Do to. You've had that look on your face ever since Rose left." She smacked the chicken, then looked up. "Where is she anyway?"

"Home. Something about taking care of an issue and seeing her mother." Every time he thought about her evasive answer his gut knotted with irritation.

"Linc?"

"Hmm?" He blinked and focused on his sister.

"I was talking to you."

"Sorry." He didn't bother to share the train of thought that distracted him. "What did you say?"

"Is Rose coming back? Or did she come to her senses and figure out what a toad you are?"

"Funny." His niece came toddling over and held her arms out to be picked up. He was happy to oblige. "Your mom is a funny girl, princess. She called me a name."

A fitting one since he was the frog who'd kissed Rose. Frog? Toad? Same difference. But didn't they say you had to kiss a lot of frogs before finding your prince? Again he thought it best not to share the information.

"So is she?" Ellie persisted. "Coming back, I mean."

"She didn't say she wasn't. And I have a signed contract for her to decorate my condo. I'm going to hold her to it." He looked at Leah. "Right?"

"Wight." She nodded vigorously.

"It's unanimous. If she doesn't provide mutually agreed upon services, I can sue her."

"That's productive. Go straight to the bad place." Ellie gave him her patented "you're an idiot" stare. "Have you called her?"

"Once or twice." He'd struck up quite a friendship with her voice-mail message and now her mailbox was full.

"And?"

"She didn't pick up."

"What did you do, Linc?"

"Why would you go there? Does it have to be my fault?" He looked at Leah. "Does it?"

"Yes," she said.

"See." Ellie looked triumphant. "Even an almost-three-year-old gets it."

"Traitor," he said to Leah, who just grinned at him.

This argument was on shaky footing because he was almost sure that kiss was the catalyst for her disappearance. And it had nothing to do with toads and frogs. He'd challenged her and they kissed. It didn't take a relationship genius to know there was something going on between her and the boyfriend and it wasn't love.

And, yes, he was aware he'd taken advantage of the situation but it was in the spirit of doing her a favor. If the guy was right for her she wouldn't have been affected. And she had been. On the flip side of that coin, he'd been affected, too. It was official. He really, *really* wanted her.

Ellie sighed. "Why is it so hard for you to just admit you still have feelings for Rose?"

"It's not hard. I freely admit to having feelings. Let me count the ways. Annoyance, irritation, vexation, exasperation, frustration—"

"You're just being a stubborn—" She stopped and looked at her daughter. "J-a-c-k-a-s-s."

"Takes one to know one."

"You like her, Linc."

He was feeling backed into a corner. "What is this? Junior high?"

"Clearly not. Those kids have more maturity than you do."

"Wow. Hostile environment," he said.

"The atmosphere here in my home is just fine. You're the hostile one." She smiled at her daughter. "Leah, Uncle Linc could sure use a hug. He's sad."

He wanted to tell his sister what she could do with

her hostile environment, but two chubby little arms came around his neck.

"Don't cwy, Unca 'Inc."

"Okay." He hugged her back as a lump suddenly formed in his throat. He wanted one of these little people but… There was always a damn *but*. He kissed the little girl's cheek. "Thanks, princess."

"Welcome."

He set her down. "I'm going out."

"Me go, too?" Leah looked up hopefully.

"Next time," he promised. "Bar None doesn't allow anyone under twenty-one."

"That's a great idea." Ellie smiled approvingly. "It's ladies' night. Happy hour prices are good for single women all night. You're unattached. Do the math."

"Have I ever told you how aggravating you are?"

"Every day. But you love me anyway."

"I do." He kissed her forehead, then headed for the front door, where his car keys were in the basket on a side table next to it. He called out, "Don't wait up."

Laughter drifted to him. "In your dreams."

A short time later Linc pulled into the parking lot at the local drinking establishment. The sign over the roof had crossed cocktail glasses, while neon lights in a window spelled out Beer. There was no mistaking the purpose of this place.

He got out of the SUV and chirped it locked, then walked up to the heavy double doors and grabbed one of the vertical handles to open it. The bar and grill was crowded. There were a lot of ladies sitting at the bistro tables scattered around the center of the room and couples occupying booths lining the perimeter. He stood just inside the door for several moments, scoping out everything, and didn't see an empty chair or stool at the bar against the wall.

So, to sum up, he was oh for two. He couldn't take out his frustration on the chicken and now every seat in the bar was occupied. He'd apparently ticked off fate and she was getting even with him.

He was about to turn around and leave when a redhead approached him.

"Hi."

"Hi. Is it always this crowded in here?"

"I wish. It's my place. Delanie Carlson." She held out her hand and he shook it. "But I get a good crowd on ladies' night."

"I can see that. Standing room only. I'm Linc Hart."

"Nice to meet you. My friends and I were wondering if you'd like to join us. We can squeeze in another person. Unless you're determined to be by yourself and brood?" She angled her head at a table in the corner, where two attractive women were sitting.

"The brooding can wait," he said. "Lead the way."

She did and stopped at the table where the two women waited. She held out her hand and indicated the one with short, blond hair and blue eyes. "This is Lucy Bishop. She's the cook and co-owner of the Harvest Café."

"Lincoln Hart."

Delanie looked at the other woman, who had auburn hair and really stunning turquoise eyes. She was wearing a navy skirt and matching suit jacket with a white blouse. Very professional. Probably came directly from work.

"Linc, this is Hadley Michaels, manager and events coordinator at the Blackwater Lake Lodge."

"Nice to meet you," she said.

"Same here." He smiled at each of them. "Do you mind if I join you?"

"Absolutely not."

"Please do."

"What'll you have?" Delanie asked.

"Beer. Tap."

"Coming right up." She shrugged. "I have connections. Take my chair. I'll get another one from the back."

She walked away and Linc looked at the two very attractive ladies and thought, Rose who? Coming here was a good idea, not that he would confirm that to his sister. "I appreciate you letting me crash the party."

"It looked like you were going to leave," Lucy said. "If we let a handsome man like you get away, that doesn't say much for our skills. And make no mistake. We do have skills."

Hadley shook her head. "She makes the best quiche I've ever tasted, but her flirting muscles are a little rusty."

"Really? Was it that obvious?" Lucy teased.

"Not to me." He liked straightforward. No games. No lines drawn in the sand. No history. Don't go there, he warned. It was single ladies' night at Bar None.

"Here you go." Delanie put a cocktail napkin on the table, then set his glass of beer on it. One of the employees brought a chair and she settled herself into it and held up her glass. "To a new friend."

"Who's a man," Lucy added.

"And outnumbered in the best possible way." He touched his glass to theirs.

"Now who's flirting?" Lucy gave her auburn-haired friend a raised eyebrow.

"Don't pay any attention to her," Delanie said. "We'll be gentle."

"So this is your night off?" he asked.

"I'm a single lady." She lifted one shoulder. "For this I have part-time help so I can hang out with my friends."

"And pick up men. Ones who look a little lost." Hadley toyed with the stem of her wineglass. "Is there any particular reason you look that way?"

"Does it have anything to do with that interior decorator from Dallas?" Lucy grinned. "I have a restaurant. People come in and talk. And I know your sister, Ellie."

"So much for being gentle with him." Hadley looked sympathetic. "Don't mind them. They can't help themselves. It's what happens when politeness and curiosity bump together."

"It's a small town," he said. "And the best part is that I don't even have to talk. You're handling that for me like the pros you are."

"Nice try." Lucy sipped her pink drink. "Were you looking lost over a lady or not?"

"Or not," he said.

"Okay, then." Hadley nodded and changed the subject to town expansion and his role in it.

Linc ended up ordering food and chatting with the three of them the entire evening. They were all beautiful, smart funny women and he wasn't interested in hitting on any of them. Because not one was Rose.

Apparently this was what poetic justice felt like. Ten years ago he'd done the leaving and felt bad enough. Tonight he found out being the one who got left really sucked.

Rose left Dallas on an oh-dark-thirty flight to Helena, then had to wait half the day for her connection to Blackwater Lake. It was a very different experience from her first trip here on the private jet. She'd texted Linc that she was coming back today, but not the time. So it was a surprise to see him waiting for her in baggage claim.

At DFW Airport she could have easily slipped by him in a crowd, but this newly opened terminal was proportional to the small town. There was no way he would miss her. Besides employees and the few passengers on the puddle jumper with her, she and Linc were the only two people there at just past seven in the evening.

She had no choice but to stop in front of him and get this first meeting over with. If only she could keep her heart from beating so fast. "Hi, Linc."

"Welcome back."

"Thanks. Why are you here?"

"To pick you up."

When she had talked to Ellie and explained about needing a couple of personal days, his sister had teased that a break was understandable. Working with Linc was intense and anyone who did automatically qualified for sainthood. The guest room would be waiting for her when she got back.

Rose hadn't given him the flight information on purpose, hoping to have other people around when she saw him again. "How did you know when I'd be coming in?"

"You told me it would be today. Since all flights come to Blackwater Lake through Helena and there's only one, I connected the dots."

"You didn't have to meet me."

He took the handle of her rolling bag and started walking. "It's the least I could do."

His tone seemed conciliatory, as if he knew working with him was a challenge. And it was. That kiss had been a dare. It was about messing with her and the relationship she had. *Had* being the operative word. The tactic worked because there was no more her and Chandler.

*He* had every right to be hurt and she'd hated doing that to him, especially since she knew how it felt. But letting things go on when she didn't love him would have compounded his pain and resentment. Thanks to Linc, she knew that, too.

"Rose?" He opened the glass door leading to the parking lot. "Why did you go to Texas?"

Oh, boy.

She met his gaze and said, "I'm not going to answer that."

He stared at her as she walked past him, head held high. "Seriously? I expected you to at least say something like… 'it's complicated.'"

"I wish I'd thought of it." The air was crisp and cool, missing the humidity of Texas. There was a faint pine smell, even here at the airport. In spite of the tension with Linc, her spirits lifted as they crossed the nearly deserted street to the parking lot.

"What do you have to hide?" He glanced down.

The thought crossed her mind to tell him she'd visited her mother, which was true. But she knew Linc and there would have been a cross examination, including a question about whether or not she'd seen Chandler. Somehow he would get the truth out of her and she couldn't have that.

"This is really none of your business."

"It kind of is." He hit a button on his key fob and the rear hatch of his SUV lifted, just before they stopped behind it. "Since you work for me."

"Yes, I do." When they were married, she'd been very young and would have done anything for him. Now she was more mature. Jaded from the way he'd tossed her aside and not so easily swayed. He couldn't always have his way and if she gave in now, he would have the upper hand while they collaborated. It was time to let him know that she wasn't backing down. "My physical presence in Blackwater Lake was not required for me to fulfill my contractual obligation to you."

"Is that so?"

"Absolutely. While I was gone, I put together more decorating options and ideas for you to look over. We can do that right now if you'd like."

He lifted her small suitcase into the cargo compartment, then took her briefcase and stowed it, too. There was a puzzled expression on his face when he met her gaze. "That won't be necessary. Tomorrow is soon enough."

"Okay, then."

Without a word he opened the passenger door for her. Darn him. He always did that.

"Ever the gentleman." She sounded like a shrew but was a sucker for the Galahad routine and had to find a way to fight it off. "You don't have to do that for me."

"I was raised this way."

"By your parents?"

He frowned. "Hastings did insist."

"Well, it makes me uncomfortable." In a way she couldn't explain to him. "Probably because my father was a no-show in my life and I didn't have a male role model."

"A psychologist would have a field day with you."

"No kidding." She thought about it. "Aren't we a pair? I had no father and you had two. Maybe a shrink would give us a group rate."

He laughed. "Always a silver lining."

After shutting her door, he walked around the car and got behind the wheel. "Are you hungry?"

"Why?"

"You are prickly tonight." He started the engine and glanced over. The dashboard lights illuminating his features showed he was smiling. "I have no ulterior motive except that it's the polite thing to do. Manners are something the people who raised me insisted on. Also, I haven't eaten dinner yet. I'm pretty sure my sister's kitchen is closed and stopping somewhere would be faster and easier. And I'd rather not eat alone. How's that for justification?"

"Thorough." She nodded. "Okay. I'm hungry."

"Excellent. I know a place."

Twenty minutes later they were seated at a booth in Bar None. It was a cute, rustic establishment that had buckets of character and charm. Literally. Shelves high on the wall had a grouping of antique items—bucket, washboard, pump and handle, lanterns. The bar that took up the wall opposite of where they sat had a brass foot rail and the plank floor was scratched from wooden chairs sliding over it. The walls were decorated with pictures of cowboys and framed newspaper clippings that looked old and delicate, as if they'd crumble in your hands.

"I like it," she said, after taking in her surroundings.

"It's quiet tonight." He followed her gaze to a couple of guys at the bar. Several of the bistro tables were occupied. "On ladies' night this place really rocks."

"I'm guessing you know this because you were here. Trying to pick someone up." The thought was as annoying as a rock in her shoe even though she had no right to the feeling.

Before he could answer, a very pretty redhead walked over. "Hi, Linc. I didn't expect to see you again so soon. Thought we scared you off."

"Takes more than the three of you to do that. I'm made of sterner stuff."

Three women?

Rose didn't have two fathers, but her single mother had raised her to be polite so an introduction would be good before voicing any of her multiple questions. She stuck out her hand. "We haven't met. I'm Rose Tucker. I work for Linc—his interior-design expert. To decorate his condo." She was rambling and decided to stop right there.

The other woman took her hand and grinned. "Delanie Carlson. It's nice to meet you, Rose. I own Bar None. I work for myself since I own Bar None and inherited it from my father."

"Too much information?" Rose said sheepishly, meaning her own long-winded introduction.

"No." Delanie shrugged. "We'd find out all that stuff anyway. You just saved the town rumor mill a lot of time."

"Happy to help."

Delanie looked at Linc. "To what do I owe a visit from you again so soon?"

"I just picked up Rose from the airport. She had an unexpected trip."

The other woman's gaze sharpened with interest. "Mystery solved."

"Which one would that be?" Rose asked.

"Why he looked lost in here on ladies' night."

Linc made a scoffing sound. "That wasn't lost. I always look like that."

"Really?" The bar owner glanced at Rose, then him. "I don't see it now."

"What do you see?" He asked before Rose could.

"A man who's not sorry his interior-design expert has returned." Delanie shrugged. "Just an opinion and worth what you paid for it."

"Do you see hunger here?" Linc said, pointing at his face. He looked just a little bit uncomfortable at being the subject of this conversation.

"I'm guessing yes?" Delanie said.

"Good answer." Rose liked this woman who was hinting that Linc had missed her. The thought lifted her spirits quite a lot. It shouldn't have. It wasn't a good thing, but there was no denying the truth. "I'm starving. What do you recommend?"

"Do you like hamburgers?" She pulled an order pad from her back jeans pocket.

"I'm all about the fries, but if the burger comes, too, I could manage to choke it down."

"One combo it is then." She laughed.

"Make it two. I'll have a beer. You?" he said to Rose.

"Red wine. Cabernet if you have it."

"I do. Be right back with your drinks, then I'll get those burgers going."

"Thanks."

"I like her," Rose said, watching the woman walk away.

"Yeah. You'd like her friends, too."

"Did you like them?"

"Yes." He shrugged. "Ladies' night is crowded. There was nowhere to sit and they invited me to join them."

"I bet they did." He was an exceptionally good-looking man. Of course women would hit on him.

One of his dark eyebrows quirked up. "You sound a little like a jealous wife."

"And you're acting like a husband with a guilty conscience who's trying to justify carousing."

"Carouse," he said, as if taking the word out for a test drive. "That so isn't what happened. But even if it did, we are legally separated. With a divorce pending."

*Pending.* Now there was a word.

One that meant the legalities of their split were not carved in stone yet. "Remind me to call your attorney and find out how that's going."

"I'll have him call *you.*"

He always one-upped her like that. In spite of the fact that she stood her ground and refused to tell him why she'd left. Maybe because she hadn't explained it to him.

That didn't change anything. She was a girl who was raised to believe she should have a ring on her finger before going to bed with a man. Her current situation proved how deceptively simple that concept was.

Technically she and Linc were still married and sleeping together is what married people were supposed to do. That kiss had reminded her how wonderful sex with Linc had been, but going there now was trouble with a capital *T.* After kissing her he'd brought up Chandler, which told her Linc respected the boundaries of her being in a relationship.

And now she was reminded again why it was so important to keep the breakup with Chandler a secret from Linc. Until the subject of them divorcing came up she'd been thoroughly enjoying her soon-to-be ex-husband. He was handsome and charming and very good company.

It was this charismatic and captivating Linc that she was hiding from. The man who could, with very little effort, coax her into his bed. The same man who hurt her ten years ago and could so easily do it a second time. Losing her heart to Linc again could be too high a price to pay for saving her business.

## *Chapter Nine*

The next day Rose set up her laptop in Linc's condo on a card table he'd borrowed from his sister. She had explained to him that the presentation would be better here in order to help him visualize everything in his space. Using a computer program, she'd done a scaled-down model of each room, but it was small and hard for the average person to envision, hence the field trip.

"Last night I told you I'd been working while I was gone." She glanced up at him. "Prepare to be dazzled."

He was dazzled every time he looked at her. "I can't wait."

The feeling was especially strong right this moment, with the morning sunlight streaming through the window to caress her hair and cheek.

"Linc?" Sitting in one of the two borrowed card-table chairs, she glanced up at him again. "Come around and take a look at the first mock-up. This is the kitchen and family room, where we are now. The furniture is contemporary modern, both sleek and curvy."

Like her, he thought, picturing her in the shower with water turning her skin to—

"The tables are glass," Rose said, interrupting the sensuous thought. "They coordinate with those light fixtures hanging over this bar that separates the two rooms but maintains openness. This area needs definition and that will do it. Plus give you a place for serving food. Or extra seating. Your guests can sit and keep you company while you cook."

"Yeah, that's not going to happen," he said wryly.

"What?" She slid him a look. "You don't visit with people?"

"No. Visiting is my middle name. I don't cook."

"Not my problem." She looked back at the computer screen. "Here's the master bedroom. Going with the same contemporary look, I found a modern take on a four-poster bed."

"It looks like a cage." There were definitely four posts, but made of metal.

"The furniture can change. Just look at the whole concept. With coordinated wall color, comforter, pictures and mirrors it has a chic and sophisticated loft look."

He studied each room as she scrolled through and shook his head. "Gotta say, I'm not loving this."

"Can you be more specific?"

"For starters, it just feels cold and impersonal."

"Changing the wall color can warm it up. A shade with more yellow and gold instead of blue and gray. Can you picture it? Something like we talked about before?"

"Yeah. I don't think that's the problem. It's just too—" He searched for a word and couldn't come up with anything.

"Stark?" she said. "I know what you mean. No wow factor. No pop."

"All of the above," he agreed.

"Okay." She deleted that file. "Let's try something else. Something less…streamlined."

Linc looked carefully at the images as she explained her ideas in detail. Squares and angles for an edgy feel. Geometric with splashes of turquoise, orange and yellow in a lamp here, a wall-hanging there. Or throw pillows.

"Nope," he said, then elaborated. "Just not feelin' it."

"Okay." She nodded thoughtfully. "Let's go through each room and tell me what you don't care for."

He decided to humor her although he could have made it fast.

When the critique was finished, she looked at him with one eyebrow raised. "So, there was nothing about that design you liked?"

"Sorry." He shrugged.

"I really thought you'd like that one."

"If you want me to, I can lie."

"Of course not. You have to be honest. I want you to be happy with the finished product. But this one is a lot like your place in Texas. The bachelor pad you had when we were together."

The one he'd planned to sell or rent. He'd already started looking at houses, a place for them to live and raise a family together. Bitterness at the beautiful, broken dream rolled through him. Since then he'd learned it was better not to have dreams. That way you wouldn't be disappointed.

"It was a lifetime ago," he finally said. "Since then I've—"

"Evolved. Yeah, that's the rumor." She deleted that file. "Okay. Third time's the charm."

"I'm sure it will be a winner," he assured her.

But he was mistaken and gave it thumbs-down.

"What's wrong?" she asked, exasperated but trying to act as if she wasn't.

"Everything is too…fluffy. Too padded. There's a lot of, how should I say this…roundness."

"Really?" She gave him a skeptical look. "I don't think I've ever heard one of my clients describe something that way before."

"Feel free to borrow it anytime," he offered.

She stood and blew out a long breath. "What's going on with you, Linc?"

"I don't know what you mean."

"You're being deliberately narrow-minded."

This was a new side of her, he thought. It was evident last night when he picked her up at the airport and she'd gone toe-to-toe with him and refused to reveal the reason for her trip. And now, he was seeing a toughness about her that was different. He'd once found her innocence intoxicating and he regretted that he'd missed everything that made her who she was now. But this strength was pretty damn sexy.

He folded his arms over his chest. "Narrow-minded? What ever happened to the customer is always right?"

"I get it." She nodded. "Designs are like men. You have to kiss a lot of them to find a winner. But I'm sensing something else is going on here. You're elevating *difficult* to the level of art form."

"How can you say that?"

"Oh, I don't know." She tapped her lip. "Could be your critique, and let me give you examples. Orange isn't the new black, it's only for Halloween and maybe not even then. Glass and chrome make you want to wear sunglasses indoors. And my personal favorite—too much roundness."

"What can I say?"

"Admit you were digging deep to reject everything about these designs."

"In creative endeavors isn't a thick skin required? Is it a little possible that you're being just the tiniest bit sensitive?"

"I'll own up to that if you'll acknowledge that you might be dragging your feet just the tiniest bit," she said, imitating his choice of words.

Her assessment struck a chord but he wouldn't go down easily. "Why would I do that?"

"Exactly what I was wondering. Care to hazard a guess?"

He had one but she wouldn't like it. For that matter he wasn't too happy, either. This presentation coming on the heels of her unexpected trip and his realization that he'd missed her a lot while she was gone had led him to a disconcerting conclusion. He might be looking for excuses to delay and keep her in Blackwater Lake a little longer.

"Nope," he said. "No guesses."

She glared at him. "All I have to say is since you and I have completely different visions of how a living space should look, it's a good thing we're not married."

"It's a technicality," he said, "because we are actually married until the divorce papers are signed."

"Yes. Mason filled me in on the time frame." Whatever he'd said didn't make her look happy. She looked down as if something was going through her mind that she didn't want him to see. "About that—maybe our personal limbo is the problem you're having with decorating this place. It's possible that there's underlying tension, what with the divorce hanging over us."

He could have told her that. His tension was off the charts. He wanted her in his arms, in his bed. That was his grim reality. Visions of touching every square inch of her silky bare skin filled his dreams and made him want the reality. The only thing stopping him was that hitting on her while she was committed to another man would prove Linc actually was as big a jerk as she believed.

"Do you feel tension?" It was an effort to keep his voice neutral, normal.

"No." Her answer came a little too fast. "But if *you* want to terminate our contract and hire someone else, I would completely understand."

"Are you trying to get rid of me?"

"Of course not. I need the work. And the referrals. But I also want you to be happy. And if I'm not the one to do that then you should find someone else. Another decorator. For your home," she added.

"The environment here is important to me, too." But for a different reason. When the contract was fulfilled his debt to her would be satisfied. "And I believe you're the perfect person for the job."

"Okay." She blew out a long breath. "So, it's back to the drawing board. What *do* you want, Linc?"

"Your place." He hadn't planned to say that, but it was true.

"I'm sorry. What?"

"Your apartment. I liked the feel of it. Warm and welcoming." The things in it played a part, but he had a feeling the overall effect had more to do with the fact that she lived in it. That wasn't going to happen here. When this job was done, she was gone.

"Okay, here's what we're going to do." She tapped her lip and seemed to be thinking things over.

"Don't keep me in suspense."

"Most of your…*comments* were about furniture and color choices. So we'll start with furnishings. We'll look at styles on the internet and narrow things down, get a sense of what appeals to you."

*She* appealed to him but that's not what she meant. "There's a town about an hour from Blackwater Lake. It's bigger and has a furniture store. We can go look."

"Good idea. If you can spare the time."

"I can." And the idea of an outing with her was pretty damned appealing.

Call him a glutton for punishment, but he couldn't resist the temptation to spend time with her while she was there. But if he'd learned anything from the time she'd been gone, it was this. His punishment wasn't having her here. It would start when she left for good.

Linc had been brooding for a couple of days, since his meeting with Rose at the condo and their trip to the furniture store. The plan to throw some work her way, rescue her business and atone for his behavior ten years ago had seemed so simple before. But putting it into practice after kissing her had been complex and problematic. The only easy decision was the one to keep her on. He didn't want anyone else to decorate his condo.

Looking out the big window of his new office, he savored the sight of Black Mountain. It had been named after the town's founding family and beat the heck out of the view of flat landscape that he saw in Dallas. He had a good feeling about relocating here and hoped his rosy outlook, no pun intended, didn't change when Rose left.

After spending time with her, the prospect of this town without her in it wasn't quite as cheerful. It was entirely possible he'd subconsciously sabotaged her presentation as a delaying tactic. Identifying the problem was half the battle so he would work on being more cooperative.

He'd brought the borrowed card table and chairs to his

newly leased office space and would keep it until the furniture arrived in a couple of days. This retail center built by Burke and Sloan Holden was ninety percent occupied and located a couple miles from their hotel project nearing completion.

Linc had plans with his brother-in-law for several new housing developments and multiple neighborhoods with graduated price points. There would be a population increase following all the new construction in the area and the expanded workforce would need housing.

He was setting up his laptop on the card table when the office door opened. He smiled when the familiar figure walked in. "Well, if it isn't Sam Hart."

"Hey, Linc. Alex said I'd find you here."

"And why were you looking for me?"

"To say hello."

He knew Sam was very soon relocating the Hart financial corporate offices to Blackwater Lake and was here to check on the building. But he had a feeling the move was more than a business decision. "Ellie got to you, too."

"About this town being the best place in the whole world?" There was a twinkle in the other man's eyes. "Maybe. But I'll deny it if you tell her that."

"Me? Betray a brother's trust? As far as I'm concerned it's strictly business." Linc shook his head. But he felt a small twinge of regret. He'd meant "brother" in the sense of male solidarity because you couldn't have it both ways. Either you were a Hart and part of the inner circle or you weren't. He wasn't. "How does the rest of the family feel about this move?"

"You know Mom. There's drama before she gives her blessing to, and I quote, 'whatever will make you happy.'"

"And moving away from Dallas will do that for you?"

"Any place where my ex-wife didn't try to drag out our

divorce and, not only do her damnedest to clean me out but get her hooks into Hart Industries, too, has got to be an improvement."

"That was a hard time for you."

"*Hard?* Such a small, insignificant word to describe the hell that woman put me through." Sam shook his head. "Never again."

"What did Hastings say about branching out?"

"You mean Dad?"

"*Your* dad, not mine."

Not for the first time since learning the truth, Linc studied his half brother. His own height was six feet, but Sam was a couple of inches taller and his hair was quite a bit darker. They both had blue eyes, but Linc's were a different shade. Ellie, Sam and Cal all had their father's chin, but Linc's came from a stranger his mother had slept with. A man who had stooped to taking advantage of a vulnerable woman.

"Dad thinks the expansion is a good way to grow the company and told *our* Mom that Blackwater Lake isn't on another planet." Sam sighed. "I'll be commuting for a few weeks while the finishing touches are completed. The house I'm building here is nearly finished, too."

"You're building? Ellie didn't mention that."

"Shocking lack of transparency since she's the architect and Alex is the building contractor."

"That doesn't surprise me as much as Ellie missing an opportunity to share news and gossip." Although, to be fair, their sister had been preoccupied with the fact that Linc had been married and she didn't know.

"Speaking of gossip and news…" Sam folded his arms over his chest. "She told me about you and Rose."

"What exactly did she say?" Linc had known this would

happen, but didn't want to reveal more detail than his sister already had.

"That you had the shortest marriage in Hart family history. Even more brief than our own infamous Uncle Foster's union with what's-her-name."

"Again. Hastings's brother is your uncle, not mine."

"Doesn't matter who claims him. He's had a colorful and checkered past where women are concerned."

"I'm not a Hart."

Sam held up a hand. "That so isn't where I was going with this."

"I probably don't want to hear that, either."

"Don't care what you want." Sam shrugged. "And I'd put odds on the fact that you're not going to want to hear this, but tough. According to our sister, who, rumor has it, is very good at observing and making accurate assumptions about these things, there is still something going on between you and Rose. Even after all this time."

Linc snorted. "Ellie is a romantic and sees what she wants to see. If you will, through rose-colored glasses. Pardon the pun."

"Look, she told me why you ended the marriage. Also that you screwed up the divorce."

"She'll never let me live that down," Linc grumbled.

"She's not the only one. But that's not my point. I get it, Linc. Why you went into a tailspin after finding out who your dad is. Ellie doesn't understand why you can't shrug it off, join hands with everyone and sing 'Kumbaya,' but I can see how getting information like that would destroy a guy's whole foundation."

"Good." He was glad someone was on Team Linc. "Then you know why Rose is off-limits."

"If you really feel that way, why is she here to decorate your condo?"

Linc explained about her failing business and his intention to make amends by giving her a hand. "So you can understand that other than a business boost, there can't be anything personal between us."

"Actually, I really don't get it."

"Seriously?"

"Yeah." Sam slid his fingertips into the front pockets of his slacks. "It's been ten years, there's still a spark and you're not divorced. Seems like a whole lot of check marks in the 'second chance' column to me."

"After your less than successful romantic track record, do you really think you're the best one to give me advice?" Linc let that sink in, then added, "There isn't anything between Rose and me and there never can be because my situation hasn't changed."

"Sure it has. You've had a lot of years to get over the shock. A lot of years to get over *her*. And if Ellie is right about her power to sniff out the chemistry between you and Rose, it's something you should explore."

"So says the man who vows never again," Linc reminded him.

"We're talking about you, not me." Sam didn't look the least bit offended.

"Did Ellie send you to talk to me?"

"That's classified."

"I'm going to take that as a yes." This was damned irritating. He was having a hard enough time keeping his hands off Rose as it was. He didn't need his older brother, the one he'd always looked up to, giving his blessing to push the envelope. "And since when are you my fairy godmother? Or, for that matter, do what Ellie tells you to do?"

"Since always, little brother. Don't you? At least I'm sensitive. I thought it best to have this, we're on a pun roll,

Hart-to-Hart here at your office, where it's just the two of us. Man-to-man."

Linc figured it was a waste of energy to remind him yet again that he wasn't a Hart. In spite of his irritation, the blatant admission regarding his motivation drew a reluctant smile from Linc. "I try not to let Ellie know how much power she has."

"Good luck with that, little brother."

"I know." Linc dragged his fingers through his hair. "But there are two reasons why our sister is wrong about this."

"And what might those be?" Sam asked.

"Rose is involved with a man. I don't cross that line."

His brother frowned. "It's not crossing a line if you just tell her how you feel. So, I repeat, if you still have feelings for her put them out there."

"I can't."

"Why not?"

"Nothing has changed. I'm still not a Hart. When we got married she thought I was. She thought she knew what she was getting, but she didn't."

"She knows now what happened, so does it really matter anymore?"

"It does to me." Linc started pacing and there was a lot of room to do it since the space was nearly empty. He needed a lot of area because the intensity pouring through him was big. "I don't know who I am."

"Do you even realize what a ridiculous, archaic attitude that is?"

"That's easy for you to say since you're not the one who's a bastard," Linc retorted. "You're completely secure in your DNA."

"You are the same person I grew up with," Sam protested. "The same brother and son you always were."

"No." Linc shook his head. "Now half of me is a mystery."

"Okay," Sam agreed. "Whose fault is that?"

"Off the top of my head, I'd say it's our mother's fault, along with the man who seduced her."

"Not what I meant. Find out about your DNA. Fill in the blanks."

"What are you suggesting?"

"If the unknown is what's holding you back, change it. Get to know your biological father."

Linc stopped pacing and met his brother's gaze. "What if he's a jerk who takes advantage of women?"

"That's his problem, not yours. It's not what you do."

"I did it to Rose ten years ago. I walked out on her. And he did it to our mother. I researched him. He's been married four times and divorced three."

"Poor bastard," Sam said.

"What if I inherited the jerk factor from him?"

"First of all the two situations are completely different." When Linc opened his mouth to protest, Sam held up a hand to stop him. "Trust me. Think about it. You'll figure out how they're not the same. And second, listen to yourself. Do you know how stupid it sounds? You're a good man."

"Easy for you to say."

"Probably. But just as easy for you to put your questions to rest. As far as I know you only saw him that one time, when he told you who he was."

"Just the once," Linc confirmed. He hadn't wanted anything to do with the guy.

"So, reach out. Get to know him, what he's like. Do it for yourself and let go of the ghosts."

Linc nodded. "I'll think about it."

"Good. I expected you to tell me to go to hell," Sam admitted.

"Don't think I didn't consider that." Linc smiled.

There was a spark of the devil in his brother's blue eyes when he said, "I'm looking forward to meeting Rose."

"Don't tell me. You're coming to dinner."

"Ellie invited me." Sam shrugged.

"Maybe she'll come to her senses and uninvite you between now and then."

"Don't count on it, bro."

If Linc counted on anything now it was his brothers and sister. After the big reveal ten years ago he'd thought of his siblings in terms of half, but that was about him, not them. He was the one with a different father but Sam was right. They had grown up together and Linc was glad Sam, Cal and Ellie were still in his life and treated him no differently. He was the one who'd changed and, again, it could be possible that Sam was right. Maybe it was time Linc faced the man who was responsible for ruining his life.

But whatever he found out wouldn't change the situation with Rose. He wouldn't cross the line into personal territory and risk hurting her again. Somehow he had to find the strength to keep from kissing her a second time.

## *Chapter Ten*

Rose was working in the McKnights' home office and deeply involved in coming up with a decorating theme that would impress Linc. Since his negative critique of what she thought of as some of her best work, she really didn't understand why he wanted to keep her on. Anyone else would have fired her. Since he didn't, she was determined to wow him.

He'd said he liked her place so that gave her a starting point, but nothing in it was expensive. Everything had come from thrift stores, antique shops and garage sales because her budget was thinner than a high-fashion supermodel. So she was going to decorate Linc's condo the way she would have done her space if she'd had money.

She completely lost track of everything and tuned out the distant sounds of doors closing and hushed voices. Then there was an unmistakable squeal of happiness from Ellie. Rose glanced at her phone and noted that it was closing in on dinnertime. She should probably come out of the cave. If she was being honest, burying herself in work could have been a coping mechanism, better known as hiding from Linc.

The intense way he looked at her did funny things to her insides, not unlike the way he'd made her feel when she first knew him. Before he broke her heart. She was older and wiser now so why would this be happening to her again? If it was just Linc, she would stay put and not come out, but his sister was involved. Ellie and her husband had been nothing but incredibly gracious. They deserved friendliness in return.

Rose shut down everything and walked into the kitchen. Thc usual suspects were there—Ellie with Leah in her arms. Alex and Linc. And then there was a very good-looking man she vaguely remembered from working at Hart Industries ten years ago.

"Rose, there you are." Ellie shifted a squirmy Leah onto her hip. "I thought we were going to have to send search-and-rescue to find you."

"Sorry. I got caught up in work." She gave Linc a look that said it was all his fault and hoped he got the message. "It's hard to deal with a client who doesn't like anything."

"So, this is Rose." The good-looking man studied her as if he'd never seen her before.

"Guilty." She figured he wouldn't have noticed her ten years ago because a lot of people worked for the company and she was pretty far down the food chain. Her heart fluttered when she glanced at Linc and realized he'd noticed her.

"I'm Sam Hart, brother of Ellie and Linc. Brother-in-law of Alex and uncle of Leah."

"Nice to meet you." She shook his hand. "Rose Tucker,

interior-design expert of Linc and annoying houseguest to the extraordinarily gracious Ellie and Alex."

"I wish Cal was here," Ellie said. "It would be a family reunion."

"In case you're not aware," Sam said to Rose, "Calhoun Hart is our brother. He's in the middle, between Linc and me."

"In charge of the energy research-and-development branch of Hart Industries," his sister explained. "And it would take an act of God to pry him out of his office."

"Why?" She didn't recall ever seeing the elusive Cal Hart when she'd been employed at Hart Industries.

"He's a notorious workaholic." Sam slid his fingers into the pockets of his slacks. The long sleeves of his white dress shirt were rolled to midforearm and his red silk tie was loosened, giving him a carelessly dashing look. "I'm worried about him."

"Me, too," his sister agreed.

"Why?" Rose asked again.

"He hasn't taken a vacation in years. If ever," Sam explained.

"I'm thinking of holding a family intervention." Ellie absently kissed her daughter's soft cheek. "He's going to burn out and that won't be pretty."

"True." Sam stared at his brother. "Look what happened to Linc. He's exhibit A."

"I have no idea what you're talking about," he said. "There was nothing to see."

"Because you went all lone wolf and radio silent," Sam retorted. "After the family secret was spilled you fell off the grid. For how long?"

"Two years," Ellie said.

Linc took the beer his brother-in-law handed him. "I

don't suppose there's any way the two of you are going to let this drop?"

Sam looked at Ellie and they both said, "Not a chance."

"That's what I thought. So," he said, looking at the watch on his wrist, "how about I give you five minutes to rag on me. Get creative. Give it your best shot. Then we never have to speak of it again."

Rose watched brother and sister think that over. There was a part of her still wanting to see Linc suffer a little for what he'd done. "Is it just me, or does having permission to annoy him without mercy take all the fun out of it?"

"Ah, so you're piling on," Linc said. "How about you, Alex? Feel free to sink to their level. I can take it."

His brother-in-law laughed. "Appreciate the invitation, but I'm handing out drinks. I'll just line yours up, partner. You're going to need them."

"Excellent," Linc said.

"It's kind of a brilliant strategy when you think about it," Rose said. "A time limit on teasing."

"Thank you." Linc's tone was a little smug.

"I don't think it was a compliment." Sam studied his brother. "And who can blame your soon-to-be ex-wife. Yeah, Ellie told me you have the sensitivity of a water buffalo."

"I didn't say that," Ellie protested.

"I filled in the blanks. Probably more efficiently than Linc handled the divorce." There was a wicked, teasing look in the man's eyes.

Rose hadn't been sure what to expect from this guy whose loyalty would be to his family, but he was *not* putting a serious spin on the situation. And bless him for taking the awkwardness out of it. The best way to deal with the elephant in the room was to confront it directly and make fun.

"I think I like you, Sam Hart," Rose said. "And yes, this time it will be a full-service dissolution of marriage."

"You might want to rethink the divorce, little brother." The oldest Hart sibling had a thoughtful expression on his face. "Your wife is as smart as she is pretty. Has it ever occurred to her that she's working for a complete idiot? We already knew that after his disappearance. I used to call him the missing Linc."

"Three minutes and counting," Linc said after a glance at his watch.

"Don't you wonder how he kept Rose a secret from us at all?" Ellie asked.

Sam took the beer Alex handed over. "If I met someone as pretty as Rose, I'd have kept her to myself, too."

"No one asked you," Linc snapped.

"Actually, Ellie did," Sam pointed out.

Ellie set down her daughter and the child toddled to the family room toybox. Obviously she was bored with this grown-up talk. Rose, on the other hand, was kind of liking the sibling interaction.

Sam took a sip of his beer, then said, "I never knew you two were dating, never mind the quickie wedding."

"One minute left." Linc met her gaze and there was an apology in his.

"It's interesting to watch the dynamic between all of you," Rose said. "I'm an only child and would have given anything to have a big brother."

"Want mine?" Ellie set corn chips and guacamole on the kitchen island. "I just can't believe I didn't know Linc was serious enough about anyone to get married. Then he disappeared."

Rose understood the sentiment. After all, the love of her life left her with very little explanation. Now she had one and knew Linc had been betrayed in a more profound and basic way than any of them.

"You know, since I found out what Linc was going through right after we got married, I've tried to put myself in his shoes. How would I feel if I found out the man I thought was my father…wasn't." Rose shrugged. "I can't even imagine what I would do in that situation."

"Thank you, Rose." Linc's mouth turned up at the corners. "I appreciate you sticking up for me."

"It wasn't for you," she teased. "I'd have done the same for anyone."

"You're sweeter to him than he deserves. She's also right." Ellie looked at Sam.

"It pains me to say it, but he did have the right to get weird." Sam grinned. "But he's still our brother and we love him. That gives us the right to rag on him relentlessly. It's our way of keeping him from turning into an eccentric recluse."

"So," Linc said. "You're picking on me out of love."

"Exactly," Sam agreed.

"I just got a warm fuzzy," Linc said wryly.

"Now that we've cleared it all up let me continue—"

"Time is up." Linc looked at Sam. "I think we've exhausted the subject. If you care nothing for me, just take pity on Rose. It's entirely possible she doesn't want to rehash this whole dark past."

"I agree," Ellie chimed in.

"You're my baby sister," Sam said. "We don't have to do what you say."

"You do in my house. And I've got backup." She smiled at her muscular husband.

"Just call me the enforcer," Alex said drily. He dipped a chip in the guacamole and ate it.

Rose watched the siblings continue to banter and saw

for herself the love and affection Linc had from his family. She sensed they'd teased him since childhood and were treating him no differently since learning they didn't share a father.

He was the one with the chip on his shoulder. And she felt a great deal of sympathy for him. The past really had a grip and wouldn't let go. The empathy was far different from what she'd experienced when he'd shown up out of the blue at her door.

Obviously knowing the facts of what happened had helped her to get to this place, but that wasn't the only thing.

She was afraid that hot kiss had started melting the ice around her heart.

The next morning Linc was showered, shaved and dressed. He stood in the bathroom he shared with Rose and stared hard at the door to her room. He needed coffee almost as much as he needed a woman and right now his odds of getting a cup of caffeine seemed the best. Something hot would be good after another cold shower. The thought of Rose in the bed just a few steps away never failed to make his body tight and tense. No way was he going to have her, so he headed downstairs and found the kitchen empty and the house unusually quiet.

"Weird," he said to himself.

He was used to the sounds of his niece giggling, crying or squealing with delight over something wondrous to a child. Sometimes he heard his sister laughing in that certain way she did when her husband was getting frisky. They were happy family sounds, the kind that were unlikely to be heard in his condo.

His biological father got marriage wrong three times and Linc had a failure on his own record. That was enough to keep him from another mistake. But staying here with Ellie and watching her so happy with her own family made him envious of being a Hart in name only.

"Enough with the downer attitude." He sighed. "And stop talking to yourself. The neighbors are starting to talk."

He walked directly to the coffeemaker, where he found a note from his sister. It read:

Dear Linc,

Alex and I had early appointments. Help yourself to anything. Coffee's ready to go. Just turn it on. I'm confident you can handle that. If there's nothing in my house to eat that appeals to you…starve. Or take Rose to the Harvest Café. It's awesome. See you at dinner. Love, Your favorite sister.

He turned on the coffeemaker and said, "Bless you, Ellie."

The machine started doing its thing and he heard the shower go on upstairs, telling him that his decorator would be ready for breakfast shortly. So, he checked out the contents of the refrigerator. Eggs, cheese, mushrooms and tomatoes would make an omelet. There was cut-up cantaloupe and English muffins. That all worked for him so he sliced the ingredients and readied pots, pans and utensils for cooking. The coffee was ready and he got out two mugs, then poured some of the hot black liquid in one of them and waited.

Moments later Rose walked into the kitchen. What was it about this particular woman that hit him like a sucker punch to the gut every time he saw her? She had on a white T-shirt and worn jeans that were just tight enough to show off her curvy little body. It was enough to make a man break out in a cold sweat. Her shiny dark hair was carelessly pulled back into a ponytail with wisps caressing her face. If she had on makeup he couldn't tell and it didn't matter. She was still the most beautiful woman he'd ever seen.

She glanced around and suddenly looked wary at the prospect of them being alone. "Where's Ellie?"

"Early appointment." He held up the note. "We have been abandoned and must fend for ourselves.

"Looks like she got everything ready." Rose indicated the preparations underway.

Linc nodded. "Oh, that. All me."

"You're cooking?"

"Don't sound so surprised. I've got skills."

"That's not breaking news," she said. "But I wasn't aware that cooking was one of them."

"There's a lot about me you don't know."

"You're right about that." Her full lips pulled tight for a moment.

As soon as those words were out of his mouth he wanted them back. No one needed a reminder that their short marriage hadn't given him time to find out what would have her laughing in that special way when he got playful. Or to learn all the particular places to touch her and make her cry out with pleasure. He wanted to now and had only himself to blame for that dead end. Time for damage control. He'd had plenty of experience learning about *that.*

"Coffee?" he asked.

"I thought you'd never ask."

"Coming right up." He poured some into the second mug, then fixed it her way and set it in front of her on the island. "The breakfast menu is mushroom, tomato and cheese omelets. I hope that meets with your approval."

There was a vindictive expression in her eyes when she said, "I don't know. I'm not lovin' it. Cold and impersonal.

No wow factor. No pop. Just not feelin' it. Too mushroomy. A lot of roundness. And cheesy."

"Cute." He couldn't help smiling as he stared across the granite-topped counter. "Is it customary for you to punish a client when he or she doesn't approve of your creative ideas?"

"Of course not. That's no way to do business. You're the only one who gets that special treatment."

"Lucky me." If he'd wanted an interior designer without personal baggage he'd have hired a perfect stranger. "So, are you hungry enough to take a chance that I won't give you food poisoning?"

"Normally I'm not a fan of living dangerously but I'll make an exception. Mostly because it looks like you did a nice job cutting up those mushrooms without taking off a finger."

"Okay, then. Prepare to be amazed."

"With you I'm always prepared."

Linc was pretty sure she wasn't referring to his culinary ability, but decided not to make an issue of it. There were hills to die on and this wasn't one of them. All part of the penance package.

It didn't take long until the mushrooms and tomatoes were ready for the egg mixture and cheese. When the muffins were toasted and buttered, they filled plates, then sat at the circular oak table in the nook.

Rose smiled when she looked at the table. "Did you tell Ellie this has too much roundness?"

"Have you met my sister?" He shook his head. "No way."

She laughed and then took a bite of the eggs. "This is really good."

"I'm glad you like it." He liked watching her enjoy it.

They ate in silence for a few moments as he searched

for a topic of discussion that wasn't about food poisoning, severing fingers or anything else that could land him in deep doo-doo. "Thanks for having my back last night. I know you tried to stick up for me when Ellie and Sam were giving me a hard time."

"Don't mention it. Guess I'm a sucker for the underdog."

"A softie." It had surprised the heck out of him when she came to his defense. He expected her to pile on and wouldn't have blamed her if she did. "Just wanted you to know I noticed and appreciated."

"You're welcome. I'd have done the same for anyone."

Anyone she used to be married to? Or any guy she once had a soft spot for? Speaking of guys… "How's Chandler? Have you heard from him?"

"No." All of a sudden she was so intent on her omelet that she wouldn't look up. She just concentrated on moving the food around her plate.

"Is it unusual for you to go a while without talking?"

"We understand each other if that's what you're asking."

Actually it wasn't and she hadn't answered the question. Besides not making eye contact, she now looked as if she was the kind of designer who used substandard materials and charged the client for top-of-the-line things. And got caught.

"What's going on, Rose?"

"I don't know what you mean."

"You're a terrible liar. For what it's worth, that's a quality I admire since I was lied to for most of my life. But there's something you're not telling me. Something about you and Chandler." He hadn't pushed her much about the motivation behind her trip. But a thought occurred to him and the idea made him want to put his fist through a wall. "When you were gone… Did you go to Vegas and marry Chandler?"

That got her to look at him and her jaw dropped. "No!"

He was relieved to hear that. "Then what's going on? And don't say nothing."

She put her fork down and pushed the plate away with half the omelet uneaten. "If you must know, I did go to see Chandler."

"Booty call?" Again those were words he wanted back. But not as much as he wanted to know the answer.

"No."

"Then why?"

"Has anyone ever told you you're irritatingly persistent? Since you won't let it go, I broke up with him." There was annoyance in her tone but not hurt.

Before he did a triumphant arm pump he wanted to be sure he'd heard right. "So that's where you went? To break up with him in person?"

"Yes."

Right after they'd kissed. There had to be a connection and he would bet everything he had it was because that kiss had meant something to her. But she'd been back for a while now and hadn't said a word about this. Why?

"Were you ever going to tell me?"

"You're not entitled to details of my personal life." There was a defensive note in her voice. "Why would I tell you?"

Because the kiss had meant something to him and he wanted to know if he was the only one. "It feels as if you're keeping it a secret. And you don't have to. Not from me."

She toyed with the handle of her coffee mug. "You're the last person I wanted to share this information with."

"Why? You were very happy to share the fact that you and Chandler were moving in the matrimony direction." He met her gaze. "And then we kissed."

She blew out a long breath. "The fact is that I don't trust

you, Linc. That hasn't changed. I thought I made myself clear on the subject."

"Haven't we gotten past that?"

"Look, I believe you're sorry about what happened. But then—"

"What?"

"Like you said. There was that kiss." Her eyes darkened with doubt. For herself? Or him?

"And?" he persisted. "I dare you to say it didn't mean anything. I know differently. And you broke things off with him."

"Like you said. I can't lie. The kiss was nice," she admitted.

"But?" God, he hated that word.

"I can't forget that you betrayed me once and distrusting you is the best defense I have against it happening again."

He wanted to put his fist through a wall and this time it had nothing to do with Chandler. This was all about him. "Rose, I would never deliberately hurt you."

"I know. Not deliberately. I get that. You might not mean to but it could happen."

"So you're not willing to take a risk? Even though you enjoyed it as much as I did?"

"I like chili cheese fries, too, but that doesn't mean they're good for me. Besides, you and I want different things. Let's just leave it at that." She stood up and took her plate to the sink. "I have work to do."

Linc sat there for a long time thinking about what she'd just said. On the upside, she and Chandler were over. Also on the upside, regarding her reaffirmation that she didn't trust him, she'd only said let's leave it at that. A far cry from slamming the door in his face.

And yet, of all the things she could have said to tick him off, not trusting him was by far the winner. He wanted more from her—exactly what, he wasn't sure. And it didn't really matter because there wasn't a chance in hell of more ever happening. But there was a chance of earning back her faith in him. He promised himself that when her work in Blackwater Lake was done she would damn well trust him again.

He was going to make that happen or die trying.

## *Chapter Eleven*

It was a thrift-store kind of day.

After her talk with Linc over the breakfast he'd cooked, Rose had practically barricaded herself in the office and worked on the computer until her eyes ached. It was time to treat herself and get some fresh air, somewhere away from the tantalizingly masculine and intoxicatingly tempting scent of that man. Linc was going to be with Alex all day and left the car for her. She loved poking through second-hand stores and there was one in Blackwater Lake. That's where she was headed.

If only she could head her thoughts away from Linc. The man defied rational thought, at least for her. He'd seemed happy about her breakup with Chandler and that made her nervous. When she got nervous she pushed back. Hence her bringing up the trust issue again when she no longer believed that he'd married her just to get what he wanted. But that didn't mean the pain of it was canceled out. Putting her heart in his hands wasn't a smart move.

Since she'd furnished her own apartment from the thrift store she wanted to see what she could find for him. After pulling into the parking lot, she found a space, then exited the car.

The large building was painted barn-red and had white trim. Probably in another life it had been a barn, but now there was a lot to look at by the big, double-wide entrance doors. Half barrels used as flowerpots dripped with pink, purple, red and yellow blooms. A big, old wagon wheel was propped up against the outside wall. Motivational sayings painted on pieces of metal were hanging there. The Best Antiques Are Old Friends. Live, Love, Laugh. Home Is Where the Heart Is.

"Wonder if Linc would like that," she mumbled, looking things over.

"What was that?"

Rose hadn't noticed anyone standing there and now saw an older woman with short blond hair wearing a denim shirt with the thrift-store logo on it. "Sorry. I was just talking to myself."

"I've never done that before," the woman teased. "My husband, Brewster, says it's because I like to hear myself talk." She held out her hand. "Agnes Smith. Folks call me Aggie."

"Nice to meet you. Rose Tucker," she said, shaking the other woman's hand.

"You're new in town." It wasn't a question.

"I'm not a permanent resident. Just here for a job."

"What is it you do?" the older woman asked.

"I'm an interior designer. Lincoln Hart hired me to decorate his new condominium."

"I hear the units in that complex up by Black Mountain are pretty fancy."

"It's a wonderful floor plan. Well thought out and lots of

square footage. Not so fancy yet, though." Rose shrugged. "It needs paint, cupboards, countertops, flooring and fixtures. And that's before furnishings."

Aggie glanced over her shoulder at the shadowy interior of the store filled with things people no longer had a use for. "Can't imagine what you're doing here then. Seems to me you're in the wrong place. Jumping the gun, you might say."

"I'm actually looking for inspiration. Trying to get ideas. And I think Linc is an old soul."

"Haven't met the man yet, so I couldn't say. But looking doesn't cost anything except time. If you'll excuse me, I'm expecting a truck that was picking up donations. It's my job to figure out what to do with it all."

"Of course. Nice to meet you, Aggie."

"Likewise." The older woman smiled, then headed toward what was probably the back of the building.

Rose decided to start on the first aisle and do a quick overview of what was there, making notes for anything worth another look. After checking out two thirds of the inventory, she concluded a lot of it fell into the category of "one man's trash is another man's treasure." But there were quite a few pieces of glassware that were noteworthy and might just interest collectors. She liked a couple of pictures of the lake and mountains, and since Linc approved of her taste, he might like them, too.

The final third of the store was furniture—dining room tables and chairs, some matching, some not so much. China cabinets, dressers and vanities. A pretty young woman with strawberry-blond hair and brown eyes was intently studying a twin-sized brass headboard.

Rose took a long look at the graceful lines and delicate detail. "That's really a nice piece."

"I thought so, too." The woman gave her a friendly

smile. "I promised my little girl a pretty bed. Maybe for Christmas."

Rose studied the headboard a little more. "How old is she?"

"Eight. I've been tucking away whatever extra cash I can that doesn't go back into my business."

"I'm a business owner, too, so believe me, I understand. What do you do?"

"A florist. My aunt left the shop on Main Street to me. Every Bloomin' Thing. I'm Faith Connelly, by the way."

"Rose Tucker. For what it's worth, I think your daughter..."

"Phoebe," she said.

"Phoebe... Adorable name. She'll love it."

"I think so, too. And I can kill two birds with one stone. Maybe that's nothing more than justification for the expenditure but the money the thrift store makes goes to the Sunshine Fund."

"I saw the sign outside that said all proceeds go to the fund," Rose said. "What is it?"

"A Blackwater Lake thing." Faith smiled and there was a lot of civic pride in her expression. "Mayor Goodwin-McKnight started it to give a helping hand to anyone down on their luck. People donate used items to the thrift store but cash is also gratefully accepted. And there are potluck fund-raising events, usually scheduled around a holiday like Halloween, Thanksgiving or Christmas. Or any other occasion the mayor can come up with for a party."

"That's very cool." Rose knew how it felt to be down on her luck. Her mom could have used help more than once and if working for Linc didn't jump-start her business Rose wasn't sure that *she* wouldn't need a boost from an organization like the Sunshine Fund.

"Yeah, it is. Community spirit here in this town is something special." The young woman smiled. "Speaking of community spirit, I forgot to ask. I haven't heard about a new business opening up here. What do you do?"

"Oh, mine isn't actually here. I'm from Texas. I was hired for a job in Blackwater Lake." And the promise of more work, she thought, mentally crossing her fingers. "I'm an interior designer."

"Do you work for *the* Lincoln Hart?" Faith's warm brown eyes grew very wide.

"Yes. Although I don't think there's more than one. The world isn't ready for two of him." A single Linc was more than she could handle. "How did you know?"

"I put two and two together. People in town are talking about him buying that condo at the base of the mountain and bringing his own interior designer from Dallas." Faith shrugged. "Being honest, the people doing the talking are women."

"Ah." Rose was surprised that her feelings about this information were decidedly *not* neutral.

"I haven't met him yet, so maybe he's not a flower-buying kind of guy."

"He used to be."

"What was that?" the other woman asked.

"Hmm? Oh, nothing." The memory rushed back so strong it threw Rose off balance. Ten years ago, almost every time she saw him, he brought her flowers—everything from a single rose to bouquets so big she could barely get her arms around them. "So he's not a flower buyer?"

"Since I haven't met him yet, I'd have to say no. But others have. He and Alex McKnight are business partners, but you probably already know that."

"Yes." She confirmed the information because it was obviously common knowledge. Normally she didn't talk about clients because it wasn't professional. A reputation for loose lips could kill a business like hers. There was that trust issue again.

"Is he as good-looking as I've heard?"

"Well, that's hard to say." Rose wanted to fan herself every time he walked into a room, but revealing that would be indiscreet. "Beauty is in the eye of the beholder, as they say."

"True." Faith nodded thoughtfully. "Also true is the fact that single women in Blackwater Lake are quivering with excitement at having a wealthy bachelor take up residence in our little corner of Montana. A man who, rumor says, is not hard on the eyes."

"Are you single?" The information about women made Rose a little tense. That was her best explanation for that question popping out of her mouth.

"Yes." Faith frowned. "I mean no. Actually let me rephrase in a more coherent sentence. I'm not married. Divorced, to put a finer point on it. And considering my horrible history with men, well… To mangle a quote from Scarlett O'Hara and *Gone with the Wind*, 'as God is my witness, I'll never fall in love again.'"

Not that she wished a bad relationship on anyone, but Rose relaxed. "Seems to me there's also a song with a similar theme."

"It's my motto and I'm sticking to it," Faith vowed. "But other ladies in this town have different ideas and they all include your Lincoln Hart."

"He's not mine, actually." Although he kind of was until the divorce was done. "And he's no doubt used to all the attention."

"Probably so if the rumors about money and looks are true. But someone said they Googled him and couldn't find anything about his dating history. He's either very discreet or gay."

Rose knew for a fact that the latter wasn't true and she couldn't deny a sliver of satisfaction that he couldn't be connected to one special woman. "I have nothing to share."

"That's okay. I understand. And I'm sure there's more than one determined woman in this town who will use her assets to unlock his secrets." Faith looked at her watch. "Shoot, I have to get going. And I need to see if Aggie will hold this for me if I leave a deposit." She took the tag on the headboard. "Enjoy your stay in Blackwater Lake. I really enjoyed talking to you."

Rose mumbled something appropriate because her mind was racing. She liked Faith and it was nice talking to her, except for the part about women looking to hook up with Linc. It bothered her and she realized two things simultaneously. Her anger toward him was gone and she couldn't hide behind it any more. The second thing was even more troubling.

The idea of women throwing themselves at Linc and him catching them was deeply disturbing. That was the classic definition of jealousy. A prerequisite for that feeling was caring about someone.

That meant she cared about Linc. Now what was she going to do? She had to get this job moving faster and herself out of Blackwater Lake before there was hell to pay.

"Tell me again why we're here."

The "here" in Rose's question was the Harvest Café and Linc had brought her as part of his trust offensive. "You've been working very hard on my behalf and I'm not easy."

"That's not breaking news." The words were mocking but her mouth turned up at the corners.

"I just wanted to say thank you for putting up with me. Dinner is my way of doing that."

They were standing by the Please Wait to be Seated

sign in the restaurant on Main Street in Blackwater Lake. It was a weeknight and the place was crowded. Although Linc had one, a person didn't need a master's degree in business to see that this eating establishment was successful. The summer tourist season was just around the corner and it was likely to be even more hectic in here.

Rose looked up at him, a question in her eyes. "Ellie told you to take me to dinner, didn't she?"

"No." Her dubious attitude didn't bother him. She would see he was a man of his word. A regular Boy Scout. "When I mentioned to her that I wanted to do this for my patient and creative decorator she said she had no idea that I was so sensitive to another person's needs."

"Go, Ellie." Rose laughed.

"So, relax. Stand down. I have no ulterior motive." Other than to win her trust.

A pretty brunette carrying menus walked up to them. She was wearing a name tag that read Maggie.

"Table for two?"

"Yes."

"Right this way. Follow me."

Linc put his hand to the small of Rose's back. The gesture was automatic, some would call it gentlemanly. Both might be true. For him it was an excuse to touch her. The downside was that he wanted to do so much more.

In an intimate corner of the restaurant Maggie stopped by a secluded table. "Is this all right?"

"Great. It's the one I'd have chosen," he said. "But tell me, where would you have seated us if it wasn't okay? The place is full."

"That's a good question. And the answer would depend on how hungry you are because a wait would be involved." The woman smiled, clearly understanding that he was teasing.

"From my experience that means the food would be worth waiting for," he said.

"It is. And I'm not just saying that because I'm the co-owner." She studied them. "I don't think I've seen you in here before."

"Because we haven't been," Rose said. "I'm Rose Tucker."

Maggie nodded. "The interior designer."

"Yes. How did you know?"

"Apparently you were in the thrift store the other day. Aggie Smith came in for dinner with her husband and I saw Faith Connelly in the grocery store."

"I heard that people talk," Rose said, "but didn't expect it to get around so fast."

"It's what happens when you ask someone what's new," the woman explained. "I'm Maggie Potter by the way."

"Lincoln Hart." He shook the woman's hand.

"Welcome to my humble establishment. I hope you enjoy your dinner."

"Thanks." He held Rose's chair while she sat, then took the one across from her.

"We don't see manners like that in here every day," Maggie commented. "Not that our clientele runs to the Neanderthal variety. But that was impressive, Mr. Hart."

"Linc."

"Just saying…" Maggie smiled at them, then walked away.

When they were alone Rose said, "This isn't a date."

"I'm aware."

"Then why did you hold my chair?"

"It's what a guy does."

"Not really," she responded. "I know of no guys who do that."

"Then you're hanging out with the wrong guys. It's the

way I was raised." He sighed. "Really, Rose, you should set the bar higher."

"Speaking of bars… Unless you want women following you around and throwing their panties at you, your bar could use a reset."

Hmm. There was an interesting sort of fire in her eyes and he didn't quite know what to make of it. "Women? Where did that come from?"

"It seems I'm not the only one they're talking about in these parts. The word is spreading about the wealthy, good-looking man who is relocating to Blackwater Lake. And when the word gets out, and it will, that he's polite—" she fanned herself with her hand "—you will be in demand."

"Not if they know I'm married."

"You won't be for much longer," she reminded him.

It occurred to him that he would rather be in this nebulous state with her than single or married to anyone else. His next thought was that he needed a shrink to unravel the previous one. "I don't even know what to say to that."

"All I'm saying is watch your back. You've been warned."

"Got it."

"And don't be showing up the other guys by holding a woman's chair for her. You'll have no friends." She met his gaze. "Although I think you can probably count on family."

"Ellie is my half sister." Again, consulting a shrink crossed his mind.

"Do you only love her halfway?" Rose asked pointedly.

"Of course not." This conversation wasn't headed anywhere he wanted to go. "So, Miss Interior Designer. What do you think of this place?"

She glanced around, her expression assessing. "It's eclectic but that works. The gold, rust and green colors evoke the harvest theme and a subtext of a bountiful feast.

And there's a relaxed, country feel with the artistically placed items on the shelf. The hand pump, washboard, tin mugs and painted footstool are nice touches. It's cozy and comfortable."

"So, is that an endorsement? Or an article for *Better Homes and Gardens*?"

"It is two thumbs-up." She smiled, then said, "Now we need to check out the menu."

"Yeah." Although he would rather look at her. The way her eyes sparkled when she was needling him. And her face lit up when he made her laugh. She challenged his mind and teased his body just by being her.

A few minutes later a waitress came over to take their orders and the service was fast and flawless. He and Rose made small talk and shared a bottle of wine with the best bread and cranberry-walnut salad he'd had in a long time. The entrées—chicken marsala for him, trout almondine for her—would rival the best food he'd eaten in Los Angeles, New York, or Dallas. And then there was the dessert they decided to share.

"Oh, that's sinfully scrumptious." Rose chewed the first bite of the multilayered chocolate cake and closed her eyes in ecstasy.

Linc's body tightened at the expression on her face—she looked as if she was turned on and loving it. He badly wanted to be that man—the one who turned her on.

"So you like it?" He hoped his voice sounded normal to her because it sure didn't to him.

"*Like* is too ordinary a word for the way I feel about this cake."

He nearly groaned out loud when she took another bite and moaned, closing her eyes again. "Love then?"

"You're getting warmer."

That was for damn sure, but he hoped it didn't show.

There was a question in her eyes when she commented, "You're not eating any."

It would sound pretty dopey if he said he was feasting on the sight of her, just watching her pleasure. Not to mention a suggestive remark like that could violate the spirit of trust he was working for.

"I'm waiting to be a little less stuffed," he lied.

"If you wait too long there won't be any left." She took another bite to prove her point that she could eat it all.

He stuck his fork in, took a taste of melt-in-your-mouth goodness and understood her reaction. Almost better than sex. Those words, thank the Lord, did not come out of his mouth. All he said was, "Wow."

"I know, right?"

Maggie walked over to them, followed by the very attractive blonde he'd met at Bar None on ladies' night. "I see you're having the chocolate-cake experience."

"*Experience* is definitely the right word. This is the most delicious thing I have ever tasted in my life," Rose said.

"Then you can thank my friend, business partner and the chef here at the Harvest Café." She indicated the woman beside her. "Lucy Bishop, meet Rose Tucker and Lincoln Hart."

"Nice to meet you," Lucy said. "Linc and I have already met. I've heard a lot about you, Rose."

"From Aggie and Faith?" Linc asked wryly.

"Actually no," Maggie answered. "Your sister, Ellie."

Lucy looked from one to the other. "Rumor has it that you two are not quite divorced."

"Not exactly a rumor," Maggie clarified, "since Ellie flat-out told us."

"My sister is a lovely woman and many other wonderful things, but trustworthy with my personal life isn't one of them."

"Don't be mad at her," Lucy pleaded. "She shared it in a good way."

"It's hard to see exactly in what way that might be good." He looked at Rose and couldn't decide whether she was amused about this or bothered that their secret was out.

"We were talking about my upcoming wedding," Maggie said. "I'm engaged to Sloan Holden and we're planning it soon."

"I've met him. He's a good guy," Linc said.

"He is." Maggie glowed. "The conversation with Ellie turned to all the couples here in town who have recently taken the plunge into commitment."

Lucy held up her hand and ticked them off on her fingers. "There's Maggie, of course. Erin Riley and Jack Garner—"

"The best-selling writer?" There was a little awe in Rose's voice.

"Yes," Lucy confirmed. "And our own sheriff and the town photographer—Will Fletcher and April Kennedy."

"More and more people are calling it the Blackwater Lake effect." Lucy smiled at them as if that explained everything. "No one understands exactly how or why it happens, but relationship-challenged people come here and end up falling in love. Not me, of course, because I've sworn off men and already live here. But other people new to the area seem to fall under its spell."

"So when you say Ellie mentioned it in a good way," Rose said tentatively, "that means she is in favor of me and Linc—"

"Getting back together," Maggie said, finishing her thought. "Emotionally speaking, since you're still kind of married."

"Well, I hate to be a downer on that idea, but I'm only here to work." Rose shrugged.

"Don't write off the Blackwater Lake effect. This is where strange and unexplainable romantic things happen while you're 'working.'" Lucy made air quotes on the last word.

Rose shook her head. "At the risk of bursting the proverbial bubble, I'm not staying. Not relocating. Going back to Texas. There's nothing between Linc and me. He's welcome to cozy up to any and every woman in Montana. With my blessing."

"Famous last words." Maggie gave her friend a knowing look, then smiled at them. "I hope you enjoyed your dinner."

"Very much," Linc and Rose said together.

"Glad to hear it." Lucy nodded. "We look forward to seeing you in here often."

Linc had watched Rose's interaction with the other two women and wondered if she was protesting too much. It crossed his mind that her "nothing between us" comment could be a defensive reaction. There was that fire in her eyes again when she mentioned him in connection with all the women in Montana and the edge to her voice when she said it.

He had a suspicion that she was jealous and liked the thought of that very much.

## *Chapter Twelve*

"You don't believe in the Blackwater Lake effect, do you?" Rose asked when they were in the car and headed back to Ellie's.

"Uh-oh." Linc's grin was visible in the vehicle's dashboard lights. "You're starting to trust and maybe falling a little in love with me. And judging by the tone of your voice, you're not happy about it."

"Oh, please…" Hopefully she'd put enough sarcasm in those two words to keep him from guessing how close he'd come to the truth. "I'm being serious."

"Me, too. Stranger things have happened. Think about it. Ellie came here for work and fell in love with Alex, then stayed." He glanced over for a moment. "Sound familiar?"

One beat passed, then two. Finally she said, "Tell me that you're not saying that I'm going to stay here in Blackwater Lake. With you."

"You have to admit you're attracted to me."

"No, I don't," she said emphatically. But just because she wouldn't admit there was some truth in his words didn't make them wrong.

"See there? You practically agreed with me."

"I did not." She huffed out a breath. "Those two ladies are very nice and the Harvest Café is a fabulous place. I want to try ice cream in the little store connected to it before I go back to Dallas—"

"But?"

"How did you know there's a *but*?"

"Because that's what you do."

"I have no idea what you mean." She stared at him. "What do I do?"

"Before you deliver the *but*, there's always a compliment, another nice comment, then—*bam*. Zinger."

"I do not." Then she laughed because that's exactly what she'd been about to do. "*But* Lucy and Maggie are romantics who own a business. For them talking up the Blackwater Lake effect could be a marketing tool. And part of a public relations campaign."

"Didn't Maggie's fiancé come to town for work? Then he fell in love and stayed."

"Speaking of romantics," she said pointedly, "when did you turn into one? Is there a full moon on Friday the thirteenth? Is it causing a ripple in the Blackwater Lake effect? When those two events intersect a confirmed bachelor turns into a romantic instead of a werewolf?"

"I'm not a bachelor," he reminded her. "I'm your husband."

"But you only recently became aware of that, which means for nearly ten years you've had a bachelor mindset," she argued. "A status you intend to maintain forever-after when the divorce is final."

"And what do you want after the divorce, Rose?"

"A traditional family. Something I never had. Something that looks a lot like what your sister has with Alex and Leah." His sudden switch from teasing to serious and sensitive threw her off balance, startled her. Otherwise she probably would have given him a flippant instead of honest answer.

"Then I'm sorry things didn't work out with Chandler." That didn't sound the least bit sincere. "I hope it wasn't my fault and another sin to add to my long list."

"No."

Again he glanced over briefly. "That doesn't sound very heartfelt."

"It was completely heartfelt." But no way was she going to say more. Otherwise she'd have to admit kissing him had gotten to her. So much so that she knew what she felt for Chandler would never be the kind of love that would be the foundation for what she so badly wanted. "And I'd rather not talk about him."

"You do realize that shutting down the Chandler topic just makes me want to know more."

"What are you? Twelve? You want what you can't have? Or you don't know the meaning of the word *no*?"

"Both." He grinned. "Not about the being twelve part."

"Not chronologically anyway." He was a man. The only one who had ever touched her heart and, she was afraid, the only man who ever would.

He turned right into his sister's driveway. "Looks like Ellie and Alex have a visitor."

Beside the truck and minivan Rose saw an unfamiliar luxury SUV. "I don't remember her saying anything about company coming."

"She didn't to me," he said.

He parked the car and got out, then came around and opened her door. Definitely he was raised with manners, she thought, sliding out. He put his hand to the small of her back as, side by side, they walked in the front door. The sound of voices became louder the closer they got to the kitchen.

Rose felt him tense and looked up. He was frowning. She'd seen him edgy and annoyed, but she'd never seen him look like that. "What's wrong?"

"That's not company." His voice was rough, harsh with emotion.

"How do you know?"

In the kitchen standing by the island was an older couple in their late fifties to early sixties. The woman was beautiful and had probably been stunning in her younger years. The man was distinguished and still handsome. Ellie and Alex were there, too, and everyone stopped talking when they saw Linc.

"Rose," he said, "this is Katherine and Hastings Hart, my mother and her husband." His voice was cold and bitter when he said, "You should have told me they were coming, Ellie."

"Why? So you could have disappeared?" she said. "Everyone is aware of your situation, Linc."

"Including all of Blackwater Lake by now. Because for some reason you felt it was your mission to make sure that the details of my life were available for public consumption."

"Not the public everyone," she said, defending herself. "I meant your family."

The older woman smiled tensely as she moved closer. "It's very nice to meet you, Rose. Hastings and I look forward to—"

"What?" Linc took a half step in front of Rose, almost a protective move. "Getting to know her? What's the point? Why are you really here?"

The older woman looked a little sad and uncertain, but unapologetic as she met his gaze. "We're here because we want to know what's going on. This rift, this silent treatment from you, has gone on long enough. You're married and never said a word to us?"

"You gave up the right to information about my life when you made the decision to lie to me."

"Lincoln—" Hastings Hart snapped out the name in a deep commanding voice. "You will treat your mother with the respect she deserves."

"That's the thing. Respect is earned and—"

"Linc—" Rose grabbed his hand. "Let's take a walk. Now." Before tugging him back the way they'd come in, she looked at the older couple. "Mrs. Hart, Mr. Hart, it's a pleasure to meet you both."

Sometimes retreat was the better part of valor and this was one of those times. She knew Ellie felt the same when she heard the other woman say behind them, "Mom, Dad, let him go."

At the front door she opened it and they walked outside into the cool night air, but the tension came with them. She expected Linc to pull his hand out of hers but he didn't. She could feel the anger and bitterness in the way he gripped her fingers so tightly.

"Why did you drag me out of there?" he demanded.

"First of all, I didn't drag you. You might be acting like a twelve-year-old, but you're too big for me to do that." She took a deep breath of the cool, fresh air. "Second, I thought it prudent to give you a time-out before you said anything else that you'll regret."

"Anything else implies that I regret what I just said. For the record, I don't. They had it coming. And more."

"Isn't it a beautiful view?"

Ellie and Alex's house was on a hill facing the lake.

Across the street there was grass, a sidewalk and railing. A full moon shone down, highlighting the water and mountains and a refreshing spring breeze cooled her hot cheeks.

"I love the ornate streetlights and the lovely benches along the path. Let's walk over there."

Without a word, Linc lifted her hand and settled it into the bend of his elbow, then escorted her across the street to the walkway as if he was accompanying her into an elegant ballroom. Just a short while ago he'd told her he was raised with manners and she'd just met the people responsible for raising him that way.

She wasn't a betrayal virgin but decided not to point out that he was the man who'd initiated her. Part of her understood why he'd left and wanted to hug him and make the bitterness go away. Or be angry at them in solidarity with him. But he'd been running for ten years and it was time to face this head-on.

"Don't you think it's a beautiful night?" she asked.

"It was until they showed up."

"They love you, Linc."

"They have a funny way of showing it."

"Not really." She knew he was going to push back on this. "Nothing says love more than coming all this way to support their son."

"I'm not—"

"Let me stop you right there. Tonight at the café you pulled out my chair and impressed the heck out of Maggie and Lucy. You told me you were raised with manners. Those were your words. You were brought up to be a gentleman—a good man. The woman and man in your sister's kitchen did that and you should thank them."

"For lying to me the whole time?" He sounded incredulous.

"You never knew. They treated all four of their children the same or you would have felt different and known something was up. You are the good and productive man you are because of the decision they made. Would you be what you are today if they'd told you from the time you could understand that you had a different father? Or maybe when you were a teenager?" She made a face. "That would have been ugly."

"They were just protecting themselves," he growled.

"No. They were protecting you."

"It doesn't matter," he said.

"It does. They always had your best interests at heart because they love you." She put her other hand on his arm, holding tight. "I never had one father. You're lucky enough to have two."

"No—"

"You do. One who raised you and one biological. Just because you're a stubborn ass and refuse to talk to either one doesn't make it not true."

He looked down at her for several long moments and his frown eased a fraction as he settled his big hand over both of hers. "You're brutally honest."

"I try." She smiled. "And here's a thought. Forgive them, Linc."

"Why should I?"

"Because they're human and everyone makes mistakes. But don't do it for them. Do it for you. Forgiveness is the only way to move on and find peace."

The moonlight revealed a glint in his eyes. "Are you willing to practice what you preach and forgive me? I'm human."

"No way," she teased.

"Way." He brushed his thumb over the back of her hand. "I made a big mistake when I left you and I regret it very much. Can you ever forgive me for it?"

"Yes. I already have. You were an idiot."

"Don't sugarcoat it. Tell me how you really feel," he said wryly.

"Brutally honest, remember? The mistake you made was in not talking to me about it. Now I can see a little of what you went through, so forgiveness isn't that hard. Don't you think your mother and father—he is your father," she said when he started to protest. "Don't make another mistake and walk away again without talking things over. Don't be an idiot."

The corners of his mouth turned up just a little. "Something tells me if I head in that direction you're going to have a little to say about it."

"Like I said, you're an honorable man. You'll do the right thing."

In some ways that was a bigger problem for her. She believed he *was* a good man and his betrayal had been an isolated incident, a decision made during a deeply personal and chaotic time in his life. She trusted him and now there was nothing standing in the way of her falling for him. That was bad because she believed he hadn't lied to her when he said that he would never marry again.

That meant falling for him was in direct conflict with having the traditional family she'd always dreamed of.

Linc couldn't sleep.

His mother and Hastings were occupying the downstairs guest room. As if that didn't ratchet up his tension enough, Rose was just a few steps away and he wanted her so badly it felt as if his head was going to explode.

The thought of having his hands on her, being able to kiss every square inch of her bare skin, was driving him crazy. When he managed to doze off, dreams of her yanked him out of it. But he wasn't just drawn to her curvy body.

If she hadn't been with him earlier, first to keep him from saying something he'd regret, then talking him off the ledge, it would have been a lot uglier.

The best way to say thanks for the support was to leave her alone. She wanted marriage and family, but he wasn't the guy who could give that to her.

"Damn it." He threw off the sheet and got up.

There was a really good single malt Scotch in the house and he knew where Alex kept it. Very quietly he tiptoed downstairs in his sweatpants and T-shirt. Light from the full moon trickled in through the high family room windows as he made his way to the kitchen.

He turned on the light over the stove so he could see and still not disturb anyone else in the house. As soundlessly as possible he retrieved the bottle from the "useless for much of anything but liquor" cupboard above the refrigerator but had no idea where to find an appropriate glass. He grabbed a coffee mug and splashed some Scotch into it, then started to put the cap back on the bottle.

"Leave it out." The familiar female voice came from behind him.

He turned to face her. There were shadows in the far corners of the room but he saw Katherine Hart on the other side of the island. "Mom."

"I'm glad you're up. I wasn't quite sure how I was going to reach that bottle. Would you pour me a glass?"

"Are you sure? It's the middle of the night."

"I can't sleep," she said. "It helps."

"Yeah. Me, too." He got out another mug and poured her what looked like an appropriate amount, then came around the island and handed it to her.

Side by side they sat on the high bar chairs at the island and stared into the dim kitchen while sipping the liquor.

Katherine finished first and wrapped her hands around the mug. "So, you and Rose are married?"

"Ellie told you all this."

"I'd like to hear it from you."

"Why?" he asked.

"I don't know." She stared into the empty cup, sad and deflated somehow. Very unlike the formidable woman she was. "I guess I've just missed talking to you. About books, movies, what's going on in the world. In your world."

If he was being honest, he would admit to feeling that void, too. "You have three other kids for that."

"I love all of my children." She glanced at him for a moment. "A mother isn't supposed to have favorites and I celebrate all the qualities that make each of you different and wonderful. But I will admit that you have a special place in my heart, Linc."

"Why?" He figured this was her kissing up to make amends for lying to him.

"You brought Hastings and me back together." She met his gaze directly, unashamed.

That surprised him. "I don't believe you. Your marriage was in shambles. Finding out you were pregnant must have made things worse."

"It was hard," she admitted. "But the way your father—and don't you dare say he's not—stepped up made me realize how much I love him. He took responsibility for neglecting me and his children, then promised nothing would take priority over family again. He could have told me he loves me from here to the moon but that would just have been words. He was there for me during the pregnancy and your birth. He held you, embraced you as his son and never in any way treated you differently from your brothers and sister." Her eyes were fierce with protectiveness for her husband. "He showed me then how much he loved me. Because of you. We both love you in a special way for bringing out the best in us, bringing us closer than we'd ever been."

Linc didn't know how to respond to that. So he said, "Ten years ago Rose and I fell madly in love. We wanted to be married and couldn't wait. So we went to Las Vegas."

"Why didn't you say something to us?"

"I didn't want you to judge, I guess. Be disappointed."

"What makes you think I would have been?" she asked.

"Rose was very young."

"So were you."

He shrugged. "And we just wanted to keep it between us for a little while."

"Then your biological father paid you a visit and the world as you knew it changed," she said. "And you ended the marriage."

"I thought so." He sipped some Scotch and wasn't sure if that was the only reason for the fire in his belly. Somehow telling all this to his mother brought everything back as if it happened yesterday. That feeling of being ripped in half when he faced Rose knowing he was a fraud. "I don't know who I am."

"You're my son." It was the mom voice, the one that did not allow for argument.

"That only gives me half the answers. I'm not a legitimate Hart."

"Have you seen your biological father?"

"Just that one time," he said.

Shadows highlighted the absolute and utter regret on her gently lined face. "It was wrong of me to lie to you, son. I won't offer excuses, but you can believe the decision was made with your best interests being the only priority."

He thought about Rose's comment that there was no good time to tell him. But he wasn't quite ready to relinquish the resentment that had supported him all this time. "You could have shared custody with him."

"That was an option," she agreed. "But there were two things that stopped me. Number one, visitations with him would have set you apart from your siblings and made you feel separate from the family."

He could see how that might happen. Not being a part of the Hart domestic unit had never crossed his mind growing up. He'd been secure and happy, had an idyllic childhood. And it wouldn't have been. But still... "And what was the second thing?"

"Your biological father's career. To claim a child that was conceived not only out of wedlock, but with a woman separated from her husband and a client, as well, could have destroyed his reputation. He was willing and relieved to bow out of the picture."

"So you thought I would never find out unless I needed a kidney and none of the Harts were a match?"

"Yes. Then he changed the rules." The bitterness in her voice rivaled his own.

It crossed his mind that was possibly a trait he'd inherited from her. "Why did he tell me?"

"You'll have to ask him that question."

The familiar anger swelled inside him. "And what if I don't want to see him?"

"That's your choice, of course, but there are things only he can tell you," Katherine said gently. "He can fill in the blanks. I know I've lost your trust and along with it the right to offer advice. So I'll just say this. You're caught between two worlds and that's holding you back." Hesitantly she put her hand on his arm.

It didn't escape his notice that he was no longer prepared and guarded, ready to withdraw from her touch. "I'm fine."

"You'll hate me for saying this, but I'm your mother

and you're the opposite of fine." Apparently the maternal contact made her bolder. More like the mother lion he remembered she'd always been. "Since you left Rose, there's been no one you cared about."

"How do you know that?"

"If you'd wanted to get married again, you would have known there was no divorce from her."

"Fair enough."

"I want you to be happy and you're not," she said. "I don't know what's holding you back but I have a suggestion where to start looking. Talk to your biological father. You don't need anyone's permission, especially mine, so take this advice for what it's worth. Don't think about sparing me or being disloyal to your family. Do it for yourself. And keep in mind that there's room for everyone in your life."

"That's what Rose said," he murmured. Actually she'd told him that she never knew her father and he was lucky to have two who cared about him.

For the first time his mother smiled. "Obviously she and I agree on something, so I have to say she's a bright girl. You were a little bit of an idiot to walk away from her."

"That seems to be the majority opinion. In my defense, it has to be said that hindsight is twenty-twenty." But he'd left her *because* he loved her so damn much. His concern had been for her, sparing her the long, slow painful death of love because he was an imposter. Never mind that he hadn't known. "I did what I felt was right."

"I know. But—"

"What?" he asked.

"Never mind." Katherine slid off the bar chair. "Probably I shouldn't stick my nose into your business."

"Why stop now?" The corners of his mouth turned up.

"Don't be fresh," she teased.

"Seriously," he said. "I'd really like to know what you were going to say."

"Okay." She sighed. "Granted I didn't see you and Rose together for very long this evening, but I got the impression that she was protective of you. Call me silly, but there was a spark. Maybe I'm just a romantic."

Maybe a romantic streak was something else he'd inherited from his mother. On the way home from dinner Rose had accused him of having one. It sure hadn't felt that way for the last ten years. But since seeing her again…

"It's really late," Katherine said after glancing at the digital time display on the microwave. "Oh, I almost forgot, what with all the commotion earlier. Ellie signed for a certified packet that came for you and Rose. It's on the desk in the office. I wasn't prying but the return address indicates it's from a law firm."

The divorce papers had arrived. "Thanks for letting me know."

"You're welcome. I need to get some sleep and so do you."

Easy for her to say, he thought. She would climb into bed next to her husband. But he…

Had a woman upstairs who wouldn't be his wife for very much longer. And he still wanted her as badly as he had ten years ago. He'd promised himself that she was going to trust him before this was all over. And the divorce papers in the study were here to end it. That should have made him feel better.

It didn't.

## *Chapter Thirteen*

Rose looked at the clock on the bedside table and groaned. It was the middle of the night and she hadn't slept much. And she wasn't the only one. A sliver of light coming from around the bathroom door indicated Linc was awake, too. It didn't take a genius to figure out that he was restless because of the earlier scene in the kitchen with his parents. That was a side of him he'd never showed her and she couldn't get it off her mind.

When they were together, he was always confident and a little cocky. Ten years ago his proposal had given her pause because she wondered whether or not she would be his equal in the relationship. She'd needed him desperately but wasn't sure he needed her. Then they got married and shortly afterward he'd left and her question was answered.

Or so she'd thought.

Now she knew he was going through a family crisis and chose to deal with it on his own. Earlier she'd walked him away from the ugly scene, then talked him through the resulting feelings. She was glad to do it but the emotion was bittersweet. If only he hadn't underestimated her when they were together, she could have helped him then and how different their lives would have been. They'd missed out on so much.

If only he hadn't shut her out. If only spending time with him hadn't rekindled her attraction. If only he hadn't sworn off commitment.

If only Linc would turn out the bathroom light. She looked at the clock again and frowned. For a man who set speed records for being camera-ready, he'd been in there a long time. Maybe he wasn't as okay after their talk as he'd led her to believe.

After a brief argument with herself, she decided to check on him. If she was wrong, it wouldn't be the first time there'd been bathroom awkwardness.

She threw back the covers and grabbed her robe from the foot of the bed, then slipped her arms into it. Barefoot, she walked to the door that was just barely open.

Knocking softly she said, "Linc?"

"I'm finished. It's all yours."

Something in his voice set off warning signals that he was troubled. "Are you all right?"

"Yes."

"Are you naked?"

"Why?"

"Because I'm coming in. Ready or not." She put her palm to the door and pushed it open wide. He was standing by the sink naked—except for the towel knotted at his waist.

"I'm sorry I woke you." He glanced at her and his mouth tightened before he looked away.

"Don't be sorry. I was already awake." She shrugged. "Couldn't sleep."

"Seems to be a lot of that going around at casa McKnight."

His face was drawn, tired and tense. And completely vulnerable and sexy. An intoxicating combination. A light dusting of hair covered his broad chest and her palms tingled with the need to touch him. His hair was wet and he brushed it back from his forehead with both hands. The movement had the muscles in his arms rippling in a way that made her heart race.

Then her brain kicked back into gear and decrypted his words. "Who else can't sleep?"

"Besides me?"

"That's kind of what you implied." There was something he didn't want to talk about. "Who was up?"

"My mom. We just had a Scotch together in the kitchen."

"Well. I'm guessing you didn't tell her she gave up the right to have a drink with you because of the lie."

"No." One corner of his mouth quirked up.

She waited for him to say more and when he didn't she couldn't hold back the questions. "Did you talk? Did she talk? Or was there only silence?"

"There was talk," he offered.

"From who? You? Her?" Rose was getting frustrated at having to drag the information out of him.

"She apologized for lying. Said they made the decision so my life would be normal. And never expected bio-dad to change his mind and rat her out."

"You know, Linc, it occurs to me that you could debate the pros and cons of their decision and make an excellent case for the choice they made and the one they didn't. But here's the thing. They made the one they did and you grew up to be the exceptional man you are. There's no going back now."

"Is that your way of telling me to just get over it without actually saying the words?" One dark eyebrow went up questioningly.

"I suppose so. You're going to point out that it's easy for me to say and you'd be right. But what's the alternative?" She was being practical, not cavalier.

"I could continue to be hostile toward her."

"That's really mature," she said.

"As you have pointed out more than once I'm pretty good at juvenile behavior." His mouth twitched.

"Sooner or later we all have to grow up. Even you. Maybe it's time to cut her some slack."

"Maybe."

His voice was wistful and she saw the conflict darkening his eyes. That's the only reason she moved closer and put her hand on his arm—to convey her empathy and compassion. She'd expected his skin to be warm after his shower and was surprised that it wasn't. "Are you okay? Why are you cold?"

"Because I took a cold shower." His eyes darkened. "And no, I'm not anywhere near okay. Pretty much in the neighborhood of everything is screwed up."

"What is it? Are you sick?"

"No." He pulled his arm away almost angrily but the irritation was directed at himself. "Go back to bed. I'm sorry I bothered you."

He hadn't, not the way he meant. But she was bothered now. She closed the gap he'd opened between them and put her hand on his arm again. "Linc, why did you take a cold shower?"

"Why does a man ever do that?"

"Please answer my question," she said.

"Don't push it, Rose." He closed his eyes. "You know why and this isn't what you want."

"How do you know what I want?"

"Because I know you." He looked at her then and his gaze was full of frustration and anger and need. "You're sweet and honest. And you don't trust me."

"What if I've changed my mind? What if I do trust you?" She slid her fingers up to his shoulder and heard his quick intake of breath.

"I'm glad." He gripped her upper arms gently and set her away from him. "Believe me, this is the hardest thing I've ever done. I'm a jerk and an idiot, with public opinion swinging toward jackass, too. But I won't be the son of a bitch who's responsible for you hating yourself in the morning."

"I won't, Linc. Tell me you haven't felt what's going on between us."

"Of course I have." His low voice didn't take the edge off the explosive emotion. "But I won't take advantage of you."

"I want this. How is that you taking advantage?"

"Because you want vows and the whole nine yards and I can't make any promises."

Right this second she didn't give two hoots about anything but the knot of need in her belly that only he could relieve. She moved closer and he retreated, literally putting his back against the wall.

"I'm not going to argue with you," she said.

There was stubborn determination in his expression but the effort showed it was ragged around the edges. "Good, because I've made up my mind."

"Well, then this probably won't faze you at all."

She reached between them and released his towel, then felt it fall at her feet. After pressing herself against him, she stood on tiptoe, put her hands on his cheeks and pulled his face down to hers. Their lips came together in a gentle touch that belied the power of the chemistry boiling between them. For just a second she tasted his hesitation.

Then he said, "Damn it."

The words seemed to get rid of all his hang-ups because he wrapped his arms around her and kissed her like she'd never been kissed before. It was filled with ten years' worth of longing and deprivation and the friction of their mouths cranked up the heat, sent it coursing through her.

He slid his fingers into her hair, cupping the back of her head to make the contact more sure. The kiss went on forever and the room was filled with the harsh sound of their breathing. Suddenly he pulled back and looked at her, his gaze full of hunger and yearning just before he scooped her into his arms. This was happening and stopping it now was like trying to slow a locomotive with a spiderweb. Even if she wanted to, she couldn't do that.

"Your place or mine?" he asked, his voice rough with passion.

"Surprise me."

"Mine has condoms." He shrugged. "They're always in my travel bag. Are you judging?"

"Maybe after I'm finished being grateful." She wrapped her arms around his neck, then leaned in and kissed him just behind his ear.

"You're killing me," he groaned.

"Do you want me to stop?" She licked the spot she'd kissed, then blew on it.

"No." He shivered before his body tensed again.

He carried her into his room and set her in the middle of the bed. Her nightgown and robe were gathered up around her waist and he sat beside her, sliding his hand over her knee and higher to her thigh, before he gripped the hem and pulled both of them off in one smooth move.

Linc opened the nightstand drawer and rummaged around for something. With a triumphant grunt he removed a square packet and set it on the nightstand. Then he took her in his arms and together they slowly lowered to the mattress. A hard-charging heat surged through her when he kissed her neck, breasts, belly and hip.

Oh, God, he was killing her, but what a way to go. Her heart was pounding and she could hardly breathe. More important, she had to get closer. She pressed her body to his, arching her hips against him, showing him what she wanted and that waiting wasn't an option.

"I know, baby," he murmured against her neck.

In the next instant he opened the condom and put it on. Then he pressed her body into the mattress with his own and settled himself between her legs.

She held her breath as he prepared to enter her and sighed in satisfaction when he did. He moved inside her and the tension in her belly tightened deliciously with each thrust. Before she was ready, the bubble burst and pleasure rocked through her in wave after unbelievably powerful wave. He held her, kissed her and whispered tender words to her until the tremors subsided.

Then he settled his weight on his forearms and began to move again. She wrapped her legs around his waist and met him thrust for thrust until he buried his face in her neck and groaned as he found his own release.

Slowly their breathing returned to normal and he lifted his head to smile down at her. "I'll be right back. You don't have to go."

"Okay."

Her eyes closed but she felt the mattress dip as he left the bed and went into the bathroom. After a few moments the light went off and he slid in beside her again, pulling her close.

"You're just full of surprises, Rose."

Probably it was fatigue that made her say what she did next. She was tired and satisfied and happier than she could ever remember being. There were no reserves left to hold anything back and she didn't.

"I love you, Linc. I don't think I ever stopped." She felt his body tense and hurried to reassure him. "It's all right. I know you don't want to hear it but I needed to say the words. Don't worry. I don't expect anything. I just wanted to thank you for this."

"No." Tenderly he kissed her temple. "Thank you."

Barely awake now, she smiled and relaxed against his warmth, looking forward to waking up beside him.

Sometime during the night Rose went back to her own room, quietly shutting the two doors between them. As badly as she'd wanted to stay snuggled in Linc's arms, it was the discreet thing to do. Technically they were married but separated and if anyone happened to walk in and find them in bed together it would be awkward. Possibly requiring a clarification about what was going on and that was difficult since she didn't quite understand it herself.

Not the sex part. That was as easy as it was amazing. But the emotional consequences were much more complicated.

Oddly enough she'd gone back to sleep, but she was awake now and threw back the covers, stretching before rolling out of her own bed. In the bathroom she stared at the closed door to Linc's room and sighed. She was in love with him and he seemed to return the feeling, although he hadn't said so.

After turning on the water in the shower to warm it up,

she smiled at the door that separated them and realized she hadn't been this happy in, well…ten years. Should she invite him into the shower with her? Probably it would be best not to disturb him. He needed sleep since they'd been up pretty late. But she couldn't help hoping he would join her and when it didn't happen she was a little disappointed. Still she looked forward to seeing him.

Not so much his sister and parents.

Would she look any different to them? What if they could tell she and Linc had had sex just by the expressions on their faces or the way they acted around each other? Intimacy as powerful as what she'd shared with him changed everything and there was no going back. She needed to talk to him before facing his family.

She showered, dressed, did hair and makeup, giving him as much time as possible to sleep before softly knocking on his door.

"Linc?" She listened for a response and didn't hear anything. He was a sound sleeper so she knocked a little louder. "Linc? Are you awake?"

It was time for him to be up anyway and she needed coffee, so she opened the door, determined to move this along faster. "Ready or not…"

His room was empty and the bed neatly made.

"Hmm," she said to herself. "It would seem that he let *me* sleep in."

Plan B, she thought. There wouldn't be time to coordinate a plan before facing his family so she was going to have to wing it. At least until she could get him alone to talk about last night.

She'd told him she loved him and had never stopped. It was clear now that without him she'd moved on but hadn't really had a life. Being with him was the most important thing and she was pretty sure he felt the same way about her. He'd actually tried to talk her out of sleeping together in order to protect her. How could you not trust a man like that? How could she not love him? The rest would work itself out in time and now they had it.

Rose took one last look in the mirror, giving her tailored jeans, white blouse and loosely crocheted navy sweater the nod of approval. This look was casual enough for Blackwater Lake, but still professional.

"Coffee, here I come," she said to her reflection and hoped Linc would approve of the outfit.

But Linc wasn't in the kitchen. She saw Ellie and his mother sitting at the table with mugs of coffee in front of them. No sign of Mr. Hart or Linc.

Leah ran over and held out her arms. "Up!"

Rose smiled, more than happy to obey the order. "Good morning, Miss Leah. And did you have a good sleep last night?"

"Yes!" Did all children speak in exclamation points? Leah pointed to the two women. "Mama, Gammy. Look! Wo'!"

"She's been waiting for you." Ellie smiled fondly. "And how did you sleep last night?"

"Fine." Was her voice normal? Or did it sound like the voice of a woman who'd had sex with this woman's brother? Should she say more about how comfortable the bed was or just leave it there?

And where in the world was Linc?

She didn't trust herself to say his name without blushing a dozen shades of pink so didn't bring him up. "Good morning, Mrs. Hart."

"Same to you, Rose. But please call me Katherine."

"I will. Thanks."

"I'll pour you some coffee," Ellie said, standing. "And

you can put my spoiled-rotten child down anytime you want."

Rose hugged the sturdy little body close for a moment. "I like holding her."

"She gets heavy."

Katherine smiled as she looked at her granddaughter. "I can't believe how much she's grown since your dad and I last saw her."

"She's a cutie pie." Rose could practically feel her maternal instincts stirring and stretching as she studied the angelic face so close to hers. It wasn't the first time but this was definitely more powerful than ever before.

Was it sleeping with Linc that made her hormones stand up and shout "look at me"? Or just being around this precious little girl who was his niece? A little girl who was now squirming to get down. Rose set her on her feet, holding on until she was steady, and then Leah took off running into the adjacent family room.

"And now she's so over me," Rose said, laughing.

"A child's short attention span is both a blessing and curse." There was a regretful tone in Katherine's voice. "And when they grow up, you wish it was possible to distract them. Make them forget what's painful for them."

"I imagine so." Rose sat at the kitchen table where Ellie had set her mug, an invitation to join the conversation.

"I apologize that you had to see our scene last night, Rose. It wasn't pretty, but I thank you for being there for my son."

"Of course." And she knew that mother and son had talked, but wasn't sure they'd buried the hatchet. As far as attention spans were concerned, hers had been pretty thoroughly drawn in by the sight of his bare chest and muscular arms. Not to mention that he was wearing nothing but a towel, which was so easily removed—

The older woman was taking her measure, something any loving and concerned mother would do. "So you and Linc are married."

"Just a little bit." Rose could feel the dozen shades of pink starting in her cheeks and took a sip of her coffee. Let them chalk the blush up to a hot flash of caffeine. "It's pretty complicated."

"Yes. It would seem so." Katherine nodded. "But I think you still care about each other—"

"Mom, don't pry," Ellie warned. "You know he hates it when you do that."

"Yes. But since he's giving me the cold shoulder I don't have much to lose with Linc, do I?" The older woman sighed wearily.

"He'll come around," Ellie said sympathetically.

"I'm not so sure. It's been ten years," her mother pointed out.

"But you two are finally talking. And drinking together," Ellie said. She looked at Rose. "They couldn't sleep last night and ended up having a Scotch together."

"Ah." Rose was careful not to let on that she already knew about that.

"I'd hoped it was progress," his mother admitted. "But what am I to think with him leaving so suddenly. Obviously I said something wrong."

Rose had the coffee mug halfway to her lips and froze at the words. Linc was gone? Her whole body went cold.

"I already told you—" Ellie patted her mother's hand reassuringly "—his note said he had to go to Dallas."

Why? Rose wanted to ask because he hadn't told her he was going but managed to keep from saying anything.

"And why would he do that?" Katherine asked instead. "Except to get away from me."

*Or me*, Rose thought. Because she'd said she loved him.

"He still has business in Dallas and probably had something that needed his personal attention," Ellie pointed out. "He probably told Rose where he was going and why."

They both looked at her for an explanation and she wanted the earth to open up and swallow her whole. What in the world was she going to say? That she was the reason he couldn't get out of here fast enough?

She pulled herself together and said, "He mentioned something about details he needed to take care of."

"See?" Ellie looked triumphantly at her mother. "Not everything is about you."

Rose managed to choke down some of the breakfast Ellie made for her. She was even able to converse a little bit, laugh in all the right places, in spite of the buzzing in her head.

Linc left without a word after she slept with him.

Finally the ordeal of keeping up appearances was over and Ellie wouldn't hear of her helping to clean up the kitchen. She and her mother would handle it, then they were off for a day at the mall.

"You should come shopping with us," Ellie suggested.

"If only." Rose forced a smile. "I really need to work."

"My brother is a slave driver."

"He is many things," Rose said diplomatically. "Have fun, you two."

She escaped down the hall to her temporary office and closed the door behind her. And that's when she got the final blow. On the desk was a big official-looking packet from Mason Archer. It had been opened so Linc obviously knew what was inside.

Their divorce papers.

A feeling of déjà vu crushed her heart. The marriage was over and this time he hadn't even had the guts to face her before he left. If only she could fault him for taking advantage of her but he'd told her straight out he didn't want commitment and she hadn't asked for one. He even tried to talk her out of sleeping with him, but she'd pushed.

And now he was gone. At least he'd kept his word and stayed around until the divorce papers came. Then he'd reverted to his default behavior and disappeared without an explanation.

She couldn't continue this job and it was going to cost her everything—her business and her heart. And she had no one to blame but herself.

## *Chapter Fourteen*

Linc decided to take his mother's advice and get some questions answered. He'd left Rose sleeping because after she said she'd never stopped loving him he had no fricking idea what to say to her. After taking the private jet back to Dallas, now he was going to talk to the only person who could give him the answers he was looking for.

It was nearing traditional quitting time when he walked into the offices of Pierce and Associates, Attorneys at Law, LLC. The lobby was a combination of rich, dark wood, glass, mirrors and plants. Tasteful elegance that signified wealth and prosperity.

He stopped at a desk where a young man was typing at a computer. The nameplate read Brandon Riggs. He wore a dark suit and blue silk tie, and had his brown hair slicked back off his forehead.

Brandon looked up from the monitor. "May I help you?"

"I'd like to see Robert Pierce."

"Do you have an appointment?"

"No. But I'm pretty sure he'll see me. Would you let him know that Lincoln Hart is here?"

The young man's eyebrows went up as he grabbed the phone and relayed the message. He listened for a few moments, then met Linc's gaze and finally said, "Okay, I'll send him right up."

"Thanks," Linc said.

"His office is on the top floor."

"I know." And not because that's where Linc's would be. The need to do that might be a hereditary thing, but he knew where the office was by gathering all the information available on this guy. Although that was all just facts. None of the data could tell him whether or not he had the DNA of a son of a bitch.

Linc took the elevator to the tenth floor and it opened to a thickly carpeted reception area with a desk in the center. A middle-aged woman was standing behind it.

"Mr. Pierce said to go right in, Mr. Hart. May I get you something? Coffee? Sparkling water? Scotch?"

"No, thanks." He'd had more than enough coffee and another cup might just make his head explode. And a drink? Not a good idea.

"All right then. I'll say good night." She slid the strap of her purse over her shoulder. "Have a good evening."

"You, too." He'd have an evening but whether or not it was good remained to be seen.

There were double, dark-wood doors straight ahead and an ornate nameplate proclaiming, in large letters, Robert Pierce.

"Here goes nothing."

He walked over and took a deep breath before knocking once and opening the door. The man who had loomed large in his mind for ten years sat behind a big desk covered with files and papers. His tie was loosened and the sleeves of his white dress shirt were rolled to midforearm. Linc studied him for several moments—the strong chin, brown hair liberally shot with silver, blue eyes—looking for a resemblance to himself. He wasn't very good at seeing that sort of thing, but wondered if he had any feature that was unmistakably from Robert Pierce.

The man stood and came around the desk, stopping several feet from him. "Hello, Linc. I'm glad you came to see me."

"I didn't do it for you."

"You look like your mother."

"Maybe that's why no one ever questioned my paternity all those years I thought I was a Hart. I never once suspected I had a bio-dad."

"You make me sound like a science experiment."

"Welcome to my world," Linc growled.

The man looked down for a moment, then met his gaze. "You're pissed off about being deceived."

"Hell, yes. Wouldn't you be?" It was so much deeper than anger. "Can you blame me?"

"And you want to know why I broke my word and approached you."

"Yeah, I do. Because you look pretty healthy to me and unless you needed a kidney or bone-marrow transplant from your only living relative, there's no good reason for doing that to me."

"You're right." He held out his arms, showing he was trim, fit all these years later. "I'm a selfish bastard. That's all I've got."

"Are you serious?" The admission enraged Linc. "You turned my life upside down and cost me my wife. And it was all about you? I have the DNA of a selfish, self-absorbed ass?"

"Not just mine. There's hope for you because your mother is in there, too." No anger surfaced in the man's voice, just sadness and the absence of hope.

That made Linc wonder. "Did you make it a habit to sleep with clients who were separated from their husbands?"

"I don't expect you to believe this." His mouth pulled tight for a moment. "But I never did that before her and I haven't done it since."

"Really? Why should I accept that as true?"

"Because I've never met another woman before or since like Katherine."

There was such abject misery and longing in the man's face that Linc figured either he was a very good actor or it was the truth. If he was right about the latter, he felt sorry for this guy. "You're in love with her?"

"Yes."

"But that was thirty-four years ago. You weren't even together that long."

Robert put his hands in the pockets of his slacks. "Do you believe in love at first sight?"

An image of Rose popped into his mind. She was walking toward him down a hallway at Hart Industries and smiled at him for the first time. He felt as if she'd just ripped his heart out of his chest, in the best way possible. From that moment, Linc had been determined to make her his.

"Yes," he finally said.

"Then you know how it feels to put someone else's happiness before your own."

"I do." It's why he'd walked away from Rose, to keep the ugliness of his life from infecting hers.

"Katherine told me she was pregnant and for just a few moments I was on top of the world. Then she said her husband knew about the baby and me. In spite of what she'd done they were reconciling. She said they were willing to work out a visitation agreement if I wanted."

"So it was your idea to pretend I didn't exist?" His mother hadn't lied.

"Yes." There was regret in his blue eyes. "I'd just joined the firm. As you might imagine it's frowned on for an attorney to take advantage of a client and sleep with her."

Linc winced. He'd had the taking-advantage conversation with Rose before sleeping with her. Then she kissed him and he just had nothing left to fight the wanting her. Hurting her was the last thing he'd ever intended but when sanity returned, so had the guilt.

"You bowed out," Linc said.

Robert nodded. "I promised her I would never see you or make a claim on you. Because I knew it would be easier on her that way."

That was a new perspective.

"That doesn't bode well for my positive DNA profile since we both know you didn't keep that promise." Linc dragged his fingers through his hair. "If I inherited your traits, I can expect to be a lying weasel and an egocentric bastard."

The other man didn't even blink. "That's one way of looking at it."

"How would you suggest I look at what you just told me?"

"Let me frame this for you—"

Anger rolled through Linc at the man's absolute composure. "Don't lawyer your way out of this."

"Hard not to when my career is all I have. I've been married four times and number four is about to implode. I'm alone and have no one to carry on my name."

"So you have commitment problems." This was exactly the reason Linc refused to let anyone in.

"It's not about commitment. I kept looking for a woman to be the love of my life. The problem was I'd already met her and there was no way to replace that since she's one of a kind." He sighed. "I never had a chance with her because she left Hastings but didn't stop loving him."

"How did he reconcile what she did?" Linc wondered.

"You'd have to ask him."

Suddenly Linc's anger evaporated and he felt nothing but sorry for this man. "I guess it's safe to say I didn't inherit your way with words because I have no idea what to say to that."

"There isn't anything to say." Robert rested a hip on the corner of his desk. "I, on the other hand, need to apologize for blowing up your life the way I did. I really am sorry and there's no defense for my actions."

Linc knew what loneliness felt like and was magnanimous enough to admit it could make any man a little crazy. "I believe you and accept your apology."

"If I can make it up to you… If there's anything I can do, just let me know."

The man was a divorce lawyer, but the paperwork was already done. He remembered the packet he'd left on the desk at Ellie's. He'd never forget the lonely, empty feeling that rolled through him when he saw them. "My divorce is already taken care of."

Robert looked puzzled. "Did you get married again?"

"No. Same woman." He explained what happened and found himself telling this man about hiring Rose to decorate his condo.

"So, you're still married to the woman you fell in love with at first sight?"

"Yes."

"Do you still love her?" Robert met his gaze for several moments. "Look, I know I'm the last person you'd ever want to confide in, but I have to say this. Just chalk it up to the voice of experience."

"What?"

"If you're lucky enough to find love, don't walk away from it."

Linc nodded, feeling lighter somehow, as if the rock sitting on his chest had just been lifted. Animosity went poof, too. Robert Pierce wasn't a bad guy, just a tragic one. He fell in love and it hadn't worked out for him.

"Thanks for seeing me," he said.

"Anytime." Robert shook the hand he held out. "My door is always open if you need anything. A kidney or bone-marrow transplant."

"That might explain where my smart-ass streak comes from." Linc smiled sheepishly. "Should I apologize?"

"Not on my account."

"Okay, then. I'll get out of here and let you get back to it."

A feeling of peace settled over him as he left the office and took the elevator to the first floor. His biological father wasn't anything like what he'd been picturing all this time. He seemed a decent, honest man—one he would like to know better. Rose was right. There was room in his life for two dads. Just as he stepped onto the street the cell phone in his pocket vibrated. He checked the caller ID and saw that it was Ellie. Again. He'd been dodging her calls and no longer felt the need to do that.

He hit talk. "Hey, sis. I have something to tell you—"

"Me first." That was her mom voice and put the fear of God into anyone who heard it. "You did it again, moron. Are you really that clueless? Or did you deliberately shoot yourself in the foot?"

"What are you talking about?"

"The lone wolf lives." There was a mother lode, no pun intended, of angry sarcasm in her voice. "You get divorce papers, then walk out on Rose without a word. Again. What the heck is wrong with you?"

The meaning of what she said hit him like a brick to the head. Apparently along with the smart-ass gene he'd inherited the selfish one from bio-dad. He'd only been thinking about what he needed. Oh, God… "I have to talk to her."

"Good luck with that. I don't think there's anything you can say that she wants to hear. For the record? That goes for me, too."

"Ellie, wait—" There was a click and he knew she'd just hung up on him.

Crap and double crap. Apparently he was in the lead for the "jackass of the year" award.

"I can't believe he walked out like that." Rose was back in Texas and a whole week had gone by since Linc left without a word.

Her friend Vicki had come over to her apartment for a trash-talking marathon. She'd been in the kitchen pouring two glasses of wine and set one down in front of Rose. "I'm sorry, honey. It was a no-win situation. Damned if you do, damned if you don't."

"Now I'm double damned." Because he broke her heart again. She added, "I quit his stinkin' job."

"You know you signed a contract." Her friend was also her lawyer.

"He can just sue me." She scooted forward on the couch and took her long-stemmed glass, then sipped some wine. "You can't get blood from a turnip. I'm not even worth his trouble."

"If he gets mad enough you might be." Vicki was sitting at the other end of the couch. "Have you heard from him?"

"He's called every day. Multiple times."

"So you've talked to him."

Rose shook her head. "I don't pick up."

"See, that's where the 'not ticking him off' part comes in. He's really holding all the cards."

Not to mention the grip he had on her heart, Rose thought. She knew how this process was going to go, having been through it with Linc once before. Right now anger sustained her. She was mad as hell and calling him every nasty name she knew helped to stoke her fury. But sooner or later it would subside because maintaining this elevated level of resentment took an awful lot of energy.

When it faded, the pain would come rushing in and threaten to overwhelm her. This time it just might and she'd never recover. The satisfaction of getting over him before had kept her going. Now she knew getting over him was nothing more than a pipe dream.

"He's a pig." Rose refused to give up her "stoking the anger" strategy. "Only a pig would throw around his weight like that and hassle a penniless, hardworking interior designer who's just trying to earn an honest living."

"He really hurt you, didn't he?" Vicki's brown eyes brimmed with sympathy.

"I won't let that be true."

"You slept with him." It wasn't a question.

Rose had not revealed that information to her friend. "You don't know that."

"Yeah, I do. You wouldn't have had sex with him if you didn't love him." Vicki shrugged. "This is me. I know you."

She didn't want to talk about that. "His family is incredibly down-to-earth and nice. I met his parents, his brother and his sister, Ellie. You'd like her, Vee. The three of us could have been really good friends if her brother wasn't such a… I've officially run out of words bad enough to call him."

"Just as I thought. You're in love with him."

"Stop saying that. What difference does it make anyway?"

"Well…" Vicki thought for a moment. "There could be a reason he left suddenly. A situation you are not aware of. Mitigating circumstances."

"You're such a lawyer." Rose drained the wine in her glass. "He left without a word to anyone. Not even his sister. If possible, I think she's more upset with him than I am."

"Still, maybe you should hear his side of the story."

"Again with the lawyer point of view," Rose said. "This isn't a court of law and I don't have to listen to anything he has to say. One time walking out and disappearing for a couple of years is something maybe you could shrug off. But twice is a pattern. Fool me once, shame on you. Fool me twice, shame on me. If I listen to anything he has to say now, it makes me too stupid to live."

Vicki sighed. "I get where you're coming from. But, and this is me being your lawyer, you might want to have a conversation with the man. In my experience, not talking is a good way to get sued. Lack of conversation ratchets up tension and animosity. It doesn't have to be personal. Smooth over the breach of contract."

"As much as I hate to admit it, you make a good point." Rose saluted the other woman with her empty wineglass even as every part of her rejected the idea of discussing anything with Lincoln Hart.

"So, return his call. While I'm here to legally advise you."

Rose both craved and dreaded hearing Linc's voice. It

was bad enough listening to the voice-mail messages. The sound of his words in deep, husky tones broke her heart a little more every time. She would rather bury her head in the sand and leave her backside exposed.

She wanted to push back against the legal advice. The problem was Vicki *did* have a point. Rose had terminated her contract without fulfilling her legal obligation. Her signature was on the paper and he had the money to make her life miserable. Legally speaking, since she was already miserable in a very personal way.

"I'll consider it," Rose said. "But in the spirit of full disclosure I should probably tell you that I've already ignored your advice once."

"I know," Vicki said drily. "You took the job."

"Thanks for not saying 'I told you so.'" Rose knew her friend was trying to look sympathetic instead of smug and the effort was much appreciated. "Considering that I did it anyway, I guess you could say that I've not listened to you twice."

"Oh, dear Lord, what else did you do?"

"I signed the divorce papers."

"Please tell me the terms are generous to you," the other woman begged.

"I could do that," she said, "if I'd actually read them."

"Oh, pickles." Her friend groaned. "Kids. They don't call. They don't write. They don't pay attention to excellent professional advice."

"You have to understand. I found them right after he walked out. I was…feeling a lot of emotions. You could probably say my signature was knee-jerk."

Vicki slapped a hand to her forehead. "What am I going to do with you?"

Rose didn't get a chance to respond to the question because her cell phone rang. She picked it up and looked at the caller ID. "It's Linc."

"Answer it."

"I don't want to."

"You wanted to know what you can do for me. That would be to talk to him." It rang again. "Now."

Rose stared at the other woman for several moments, then sighed and hit the talk button. "This is Rose Tucker."

There was a brief hesitation on the other end of the line before Linc said, "Is it really you? Not voice mail?"

"My mailbox is full thanks to you."

"So you got my messages."

"Yes. Did you get mine about terminating my contract with you?" Rose saw her lawyer nodding approval.

"Which one? The condo work or divorce papers?" Linc sounded ticked off. "I just got them from my lawyer with your signature."

"Good." Something inside her came apart and it was all she could do to get out a single word in a normal tone. She took a deep breath, then added, "So that's done. About the design contract—"

"That's not why I called."

"Oh? As far as I'm concerned there's nothing more to say."

"I couldn't disagree more."

Rose heard something in his voice that tugged at her heart, but giving in to the weakness was just asking for more trouble. That's the last thing she needed. "Linc, the only thing we could possibly have to discuss is why I'm unable to fulfill my legal obligation to decorate your condo—"

"Screw the contract. I don't give a damn about that."

"Glad to hear it. Thanks for calling and—" She was about to say "have a good life and don't ever darken my door again." Instead she added, "I'll watch for the final divorce papers with your signature."

"Everything is not even close to being settled."

She heard a deep, dark element in his voice and could picture intensity in his eyes. Her heart started to pound. "Linc, I can't—"

"I need to talk to you, Rose. Face-to-face. I'll come by and… There's a lot I have to tell you."

"No. I'll expect to receive a copy of the divorce papers. Goodbye, Linc." She tapped the end button and felt her anger go poof just before the pain rushed in.

"Way to keep it all about business," Vicki said.

"I tried. But it's always been personal with Linc."

The dam of feelings burst and Rose buried her face in her hands and started to cry. Damn him for doing this to her again.

## *Chapter Fifteen*

After Rose hung up on him Linc stared at his cell phone and had the sinking feeling that he'd lost her forever. He was like his biological father, always losing at love. But unlike Robert Pierce, a lifetime of unhappiness would be his own fault. She could have been his but he blew it, as his sister said, by going all lone wolf.

Now what?

He left his Dallas condo and drove around for a while, somehow ending up in his parents' upscale suburban neighborhood. They probably didn't want to talk to him any more than his sister or Rose, but this was where he'd come all his life to get his head on straight. This time, them talking wasn't required when he apologized for being a jerk. All they had to do was listen.

Once he'd pulled his SUV into the semicircular driveway, he exited the vehicle and walked to the double-door entry of the impressive redbrick mansion. There was light coming through the glass panes so he rang the bell and waited long enough to wonder if he was deliberately being ignored. Not that they weren't justified, but he wasn't in the mood for this.

Then the outside porch light went on and his father opened the door. "Linc. Come in."

"Thanks."

The house hadn't changed since he'd last seen it. A crystal chandelier glittered from the ceiling of the two-story entryway and a circular table holding an impressive fresh bouquet of flowers sat on it.

"Your mother is in the family room." Hastings didn't hesitate and there was no surprise in his voice. No indication of resentment toward Linc for being a jackass.

When Hastings headed for the stairs and it looked as if he was going up, Linc said, "I'd like to talk to you and Mom both. If that's okay."

"All right." The older man led the way to the back of the house with its spacious, state-of-the-art kitchen and family-room combination. The ten-foot-high wall of windows looked out on the pool in the backyard and a golf course beyond. Nighttime lights illuminated the impressive view.

Katherine was sitting in a floral-patterned club chair reading a book. The Dallas newspapers were spread out on the leather corner group sitting in front of the formal fireplace and flat-screen TV above it. The scene brought an instant flash of familiarity and warmth. He'd missed it more than he would let himself acknowledge and regretted the time that could never be recovered. He also knew how the prodigal son must have felt.

"Lincoln." His mother stood and put down her book on the ottoman. She walked over to him and wrapped her arms around him tight. "It's good to see you."

"You, too." And it really was, even though it had only been a short time since that night in Ellie's kitchen. But he knew she meant it was good to see him *here*.

Katherine gave him one last firm squeeze before backing away. There was a puzzled expression on her face. "I don't mean to sound critical or ungrateful that you've come for a visit. But why are you here?"

"Several reasons. I need advice." He looked at his father specifically.

"Happy to help. And I'm touched. More than you'll ever know." He put his big hand on Linc's shoulder.

"I appreciate that, even though I don't deserve it. You have absolutely no reason to be gracious to me after the way I've behaved—"

"Let me stop you right there," Hastings said. "I love you. And I'm not going to qualify that statement by adding like my own son." The man's eyes were fierce with protective paternal pride and affection. "You *are* my son. And I have always tried to be the best father I knew how to be."

"You're the best dad in the world—" Linc's throat grew thick with emotion and he moved closer to embrace the good man who'd taught him to be a good man. "Thanks, Dad."

Hastings hugged him back, then cleared his throat as he stepped away. There was a suspicious moisture in his eyes. "Okay, then—"

"Mom, Dad—" Linc blew out a long breath as he looked at each of them. "I want to apologize to you both for turning my back on you and being a stubborn ass. It was not my finest hour and I deeply regret hurting you both. You didn't deserve that kind of treatment and I'm more sorry than you'll ever know."

"I wish I could tell you I wasn't hurt," his mother said,

"but that would be a lie. Still, I'm so very happy to see you and accept your apology."

"As easy as that? You're not going to make me grovel?"

Katherine shook her head. "It was very painful to see you confused, hurt, angry and blaming me. But the joy I have right this second at this reconciliation is in direct proportion to the love I have for you. It's never-ending and unconditional."

"I don't deserve it."

"Of course you do." She brushed off his denial.

"What made you come around?" Hastings asked.

"Yes," his mother chimed in. "How did this change of heart happen?"

Rose, he thought. When she said she loved him. At first he was frustrated and angry that he'd broken his vow and compromised her. Then some primal instinct took over and he was tired to the bone of not having the answers he needed to move forward with her. He knew he had to deal with the past first.

"I took your advice, Mom." He met his father's gaze. "Dad, I don't want to hurt you, but it's best to be up front. I went to see Robert Pierce."

"It's about damn time, son," Hastings said.

Linc couldn't help smiling. "Wow, okay then. You're not upset."

"How did it go?" His mother looked protective, wary.

"It sounds weird to say great, but it was. He's not the monster I'd made him out to be."

"And by hereditary extension that made you not a monster, too," Katherine said.

"Yeah. He just had the bad luck to fall in love with someone who wasn't free to love him back."

Hastings slipped his arm around his wife's waist. "He's

a fine man, Linc. Smart. Ethical. An excellent attorney and businessman. Pillar of the community."

"I should have gone to see him a long time ago." Before he'd left Rose the first time. His own stubbornness and stupidity made him want to put his fist through a wall. The colossal waste…

"You still haven't explained what made you go now."

Linc looked at his mother. "Something tells me you already have a pretty good idea."

"I have a theory," she confirmed.

"If it involves Rose, you'd be right. She said I was acting like a twelve-year-old. That there's room in my life for all family. She didn't know her father and I was lucky enough to have two."

"A very insightful young woman," Hastings said.

"One of many sterling qualities," Linc confirmed. His chest squeezed tight at the thought that he might never be able to make things right with her.

"So, you needed to see your biological father and make sure he isn't a despicable human being before setting your cap for her, as they say." His father nodded understanding.

"In my head it sounded much nobler than that," he admitted, "but essentially that is correct."

"So you've come to ask our advice about how to propose to Rose." Katherine's eyes sparkled with excitement at the scent of romance in the air.

"Technically I don't have to propose since we're not divorced."

His mother frowned. "Why do I get the feeling this visit is groveling practice? For seeing Rose?"

"Look, you guys, I've made mistakes in my life but this one is off the charts. And I don't know how to fix it." He explained to them about old habits kicking in, his leaving and her refusal to even talk to him now. "I have no idea what to do. How did you guys get past what happened when you were separated?"

Hastings smiled at his wife. "When you love someone, you forgive them. It's that simple."

"I'm not sure Rose can forgive me. The mistake I made is really big."

"Then the apology needs to be big, too," his father said thoughtfully. "This might be hard to understand, but you brought Katherine and I together."

He remembered his mother saying that and still couldn't wrap his mind around it. "But I was a mistake."

"I never want to hear you say that again," his mother said sternly. "You were then, and always will be, a blessing."

"Sorry, Mom. I really wasn't being that spoiled brat again. Just talking out loud." Linc looked at his father. "And I think I get where you're coming from, Dad. Use the personal flaw and turn it into a win."

Hastings beamed at him. "That's my boy."

"I'm glad you two are on the same testosterone wavelength," his mother said. "But can you translate that for little ol' me?"

"I'm still working on the plan," Linc said, "but I'll let you know how it all comes together."

He was going to do something big and bold to win Rose back. If it took the rest of his life he would show her that he'd never walk away from her again.

Rose closed up Tucker Designs for the night and walked up the stairs to her apartment on the building's second floor. She was a little more hopeful about her business after landing a wealthy client who wanted a recently purchased mansion in Highland Park decorated. It was a Dallas suburb where tech and oil millionaires lived and that made her a little suspicious that Linc might have sent her the client. Because he'd been sending other stuff, too.

She unlocked her door, then opened it and walked inside, taking a deep breath to smell the sweet floral fragrance that filled the apartment. There were rose-filled vases everywhere. Beautiful lavender roses. White ones blushing pink. Yellow and coral. Just gorgeous. But looking at them made her heart hurt because of how much she missed Linc.

She missed talking, teasing and laughing with him. She loved him and this apology with flowers was so tempting. How was she supposed to resist that? But how could she let herself trust him? It would destroy her to let her guard down and be abandoned again. There wouldn't just be heart damage; she would need to have her head examined.

Her cell phone rang and she pulled it from the pocket of her slacks and checked caller ID. It was Linc again. Her rational self warned her not to answer but the emotional part of her ignored it. Time to make that shrink appointment, she thought, after hitting the talk button.

"Linc, please, I'm begging you to leave me alone."

"Do you like the flowers?"

His voice, the deep smoothness of it, slid inside and squeezed her heart. This was absolute torture. Like having red velvet cupcakes in the house while struggling to lose that last five stubborn pounds.

And who didn't like flowers, for Pete's sake? Unless you were allergic to them. She was allergic to Linc; he was bad for her and made her eyes water.

"Rose?"

"The flowers are beautiful," she finally said.

"Which color is your favorite?"

It was on the tip of her tongue to say lavender, then she realized he was effortlessly sucking her into his web. "My favorite is of no concern to you. I'm not speaking to you anymore. We have nothing more to talk about."

She ended the call and realized her cheeks were wet from tears. See? Allergic to Linc. The best way to live with it was *not* to live with it. No matter how much she wanted to.

The doorbell rang, startling her out of the "allergy" attack, and she brushed the moisture from her cheeks. If this was another florist delivering flowers from Linc…

She opened the door. It wasn't a delivery person, but the sender himself with a cell phone in one hand and the handle of a wheeled suitcase in the other. *Speechless* didn't even begin to describe how she felt.

"Hi." Without waiting for an invitation he walked inside, as brazen as could be, and shut the door behind him. As if he was staying.

That loosened her tongue. "What are you doing?"

"I'm moving in. Where should I put my stuff?"

"You can't be serious."

"And yet, I am," he said cheerfully.

"This is my place and I most definitely did not invite you into it."

He looked around and nodded with satisfaction at the vases covering every flat surface in the room. "The flowers look great. Not that this place needs them. It's perfect because of your special touch."

Her heart began a steady pounding against the inside of her chest. "I want you to leave, Linc. Now."

"No, you don't."

"You have no right to tell me what I want. No right to come into my home and demand a drawer. You walked away from me. Twice. And we're divorced. I signed the papers."

"That reminds me." He snapped his fingers and pulled

a familiar-looking manila envelope from an outside pocket of his suitcase. He held it out. "Here are the papers you signed."

She lifted the flap and reached inside, expecting a packet of papers but instead pulling out confetti. Her gaze shot to his. "This is shredded."

"I know."

"How could you do that?"

"There's this handy machine and you just feed the paper in and it comes out like that." He shrugged. "Easy."

"You know that's not what I meant." Rose stared at him. "I don't understand."

"Short version? I instructed my attorney not to file the papers with the court. We're still a little bit married."

"That's not the part I don't get," she said through gritted teeth. The urge to brain him with a vase of flowers was strong in her. "Why didn't you sign them? I thought you wanted to divorce me."

"Not you." His expression turned serious for the first time. "I wanted to divorce my past. My biological father and the reality of not actually being born a Hart. I wanted to be the man you thought you married."

"You are," she protested.

"I get that now and I've come to terms with the person I am. Thanks to you and my parents."

"What happened?" She set the envelope containing shredded legal documents on her coffee table.

"I took your suggestion and saw my father." He slid his fingertips into the pockets of his jeans. "He's a decent man who is a victim of tragic love. It's a 'good news, bad news' thing. The bad is he's been married and divorced a few times but it's because he's trying to find a woman like my mother."

"So he's a one-woman man," Rose ventured.

"Exactly."

"You were afraid you'd inherited the player gene from him," she said.

"Yes." He smiled a little uncertainly. "I didn't want to put you through being married to a womanizing jerk."

"You never were that guy," she said again.

"But I didn't know that I wouldn't turn into him. And I couldn't take the chance. Not with you. I'd rather live with the pain of not having you than risk hurting you."

Her heart was melting as surely as ice cream in the sun. "And now?"

"It seems I do take after him, at least in one way."

"Oh?"

"Yeah." He took a step closer, his gaze never leaving hers. "I fell in love with you. You're the only woman for me and there will never be anyone else."

"I can't, Linc—" Emotion choked off her words and she looked away.

"I know I've hurt you and you'll never know how sorry I am for that. But you and I are meant to be together. The universe is telling us so. Look at all the signs. There was no divorce. You never found anyone else and neither did I."

"Linc…" She met his gaze and recognized the intensity of desperation in his eyes.

"Do you know why neither of us connected with someone else? I can only speak for myself, but I'd wager my last dollar that the same is true for you. In fact you told me that you'd never stopped loving me. And I didn't know what to do."

"Talk to me maybe?"

"I get that now and I'm working on my communication skills. Starting with this—I love you, Rose. I always have. There will never be anyone else for me. Unlike my father, I met the woman of my dreams and was lucky enough to marry her. It was the smartest thing I ever did. After that I—" He shrugged. "Stupid mistake after stupid mistake. The best I can say is that my motives were pure. I was simply trying to protect you from the mess of my life. I just hope you can forgive me. Be my wife. Don't condemn me to a life without you in it."

"Oh, Linc—" She caught the corner of her bottom lip between her teeth.

"Before you give me your final answer, you should know that I won't give up. If you won't let me move in here, I'll pitch a tent outside. I'll send flowers, rent advertising space on I-35 proclaiming my love. Along with a plug for your decorating business."

"What about your business in Blackwater Lake?"

"I'll commute. The condo will stay a shell unless you work your magic. No one but you will ever decorate it." He looked down for a moment, then stared into her eyes. "If you can find it in your heart to give me another chance, I swear that I will never give you a reason to regret it."

Rose had never seen him so vulnerable, so not in control of his feelings. That was new and filled her heart with hope. And most importantly, trust.

She took a step closer and could feel the heat of his body even though they weren't touching. "Can I have my job back?"

"Being my wife?" He frowned.

"No." She glanced down at the envelope on the table, then toyed with the button on his crisp, white shirt. "I never quit being married to you. I was talking about decorating your condo. And living there together."

He closed his eyes for a moment and let out a long breath before looking at her again. A small smile turned up the corners of his mouth as he nodded. "With your special touch, it will be like having the essence of you wrapped around me. To my way of thinking that's about as close to heaven on earth as a man can get."

"I love you, Lincoln Hart."

"Words with wow factor." He grinned, then pulled her into his arms and kissed her into more than being just a little bit married.

* * * * *

*Return to Blackwater Lake in August 2017, when Faith Connelly and Sam Hart are forced together by raging wild fires in the next book in* THE BACHELORS OF BLACKWATER LAKE *series!*

MILLS & BOON®

Cherish™

EXPERIENCE THE ULTIMATE RUSH OF FALLING IN LOVE

**A sneak peek at next month's titles...**

**In stores from 9th March 2017:**

- **Reunited by a Baby Bombshell** – Barbara Hannay *and* **From Fortune to Family Man** – Judy Duarte
- **The Spanish Tycoon's Takeover** – Michelle Douglas *and* **Meant to Be Mine** – Marie Ferrarella

**In stores from 23rd March 2017:**

- **Stranded with the Secret Billionaire** – Marion Lennox *and* **The Princess Problem** – Teri Wilson
- **Miss Prim and the Maverick Millionaire** – Nina Singh *and* **Finding Our Forever** – Brenda Novak

*Just can't wait?*
Buy our books online before they hit the shops!
**www.millsandboon.co.uk**

**Also available as eBooks.**

17/23

MILLS & BOON®

EXCLUSIVE EXTRACT


Griffin Fletcher never imagined he'd see his childhood sweetheart Eva Hennessey again, but now he's eager to discover her secret—one that will change their worlds forever!

*Read on for a sneak preview of*
*REUNITED BY A BABY BOMBSHELL*

A baby. A daughter, given up for adoption.

The stark pain in Eva's face when she'd seen their child. His own huge feelings of isolation and loss.

If only he'd known. If only Eva had told him. He'd deserved to know.

*And what would you have done?* his conscience whispered.

It was a fair enough question.

Realistically, what would he have done at the age of eighteen? He and Eva had both been so young, scarcely out of school, both ambitious, with all their lives ahead of them. He hadn't been remotely ready to think about settling down, or facing parenthood, let alone lasting love or matrimony.

And yet he'd been hopelessly crazy about Eva, so chances were…

Dragging in a deep breath of sea air, Griff shook his head. It was way too late to trawl through what might have been. There was no point in harbouring regrets.

*But what about now?*

How was he going to handle this new situation? Laine, a lovely daughter, living in his city, studying law. The thought that she'd been living there all this time, without his knowledge, did his head in.

And Eva, as lovely and hauntingly bewitching as ever, sent his head spinning too, sent his heart taking flight.

He'd never felt so side-swiped. So torn. One minute he wanted to turn on his heel and head straight back to Eva's motel room, to pull her into his arms and taste those enticing lips of hers. To trace the shape of her lithe, tempting body with his hands. To unleash the longing that was raging inside him, driving him crazy.

Next minute he came to his senses and knew that he should just keep on walking. Now. Walk out of the Bay. All the way back to Brisbane.

And then, heaven help him, he was wanting Eva again. Wanting her desperately.

*Damn it.* He was in for a very long night.


*Don't miss*
*REUNITED BY A BABY BOMBSHELL*
by Barbara Hannay

*Available April 2017*
www.millsandboon.co.uk


Copyright ©2017 Barbara Hannay

The perfect gift for

Mother's Day...

a Mills & Boon subscription

Call Customer Services on

**0844 844 1358***

or visit

**millsandboon.co.uk/subscription**

*** This call will cost you 7 pence per minute plus your phone company's price per minute access charge.**

MD16

# MILLS & BOON®

**Congratulations**
**Carol Marinelli**
**on your 100th Mills & Boon book!**

**Read on for an exclusive extract**


How did she walk away? Lydia wondered.

How did she go over and kiss that sulky mouth and say goodbye when really she wanted to climb back into bed?

But rather than reveal her thoughts she flicked that internal default switch which had been permanently set to 'polite'.

'Thank you so much for last night.'

'I haven't finished being your tour guide yet.'

He stretched out his arm and held out his hand but Lydia didn't go over. She did not want to let in hope, so she just stood there as Raul spoke.

'It would be remiss of me to let you go home without seeing Venice as it should be seen.'

'Venice?'

'I'm heading there today. Why don't you come with me? Fly home tomorrow instead.'

There was another night between now and then, and Lydia knew that even while he offered her an extension he made it clear there was a cut-off.

Time added on for good behaviour.

And Raul's version of 'good behaviour' was that there would

be no tears or drama as she walked away. Lydia knew that. If she were to accept his offer then she had to remember that.

'I'd like that.' The calm of her voice belied the trembling she felt inside. 'It sounds wonderful.'

'Only if you're sure?' Raul added.

'Of course.'

But how could she be sure of anything now she had set foot in Raul's world?

He made her dizzy.

Disorientated.

Not just her head, but every cell in her body seemed to be spinning as he hauled himself from the bed and unlike Lydia, with her sheet-covered dash to the bathroom, his body was hers to view.

And that blasted default switch was stuck, because Lydia did the right thing and averted her eyes.

Yet he didn't walk past. Instead Raul walked right over to her and stood in front of her.

She could feel the heat—not just from his naked body but her own—and it felt as if her dress might disintegrate.

He put his fingers on her chin, tilted her head so that she met his eyes, and it killed that he did not kiss her, nor drag her back to his bed. Instead he checked again. 'Are you sure?'

'Of course,' Lydia said, and tried to make light of it. 'I never say no to a free trip.'

It was a joke but it put her in an unflattering light. She was about to correct herself, to say that it hadn't come out as she had meant, but then she saw his slight smile and it spelt approval.

A gold-digger he could handle, Lydia realised.

Her emerging feelings for him—perhaps not.

At every turn her world changed, and she fought for a semblance of control. Fought to convince not just Raul but herself that she could handle this.


Don't miss

**THE INNOCENT'S SECRET BABY**

by Carol Marinelli

OUT NOW

BUY YOUR COPY TODAY

www.millsandboon.co.uk

Copyright ©2017 by Harlequin Books S.A.

CM0317_2

# Join Britain's BIGGEST Romance Book Club

- **EXCLUSIVE offers every month**
- **FREE delivery direct to your door**
- **NEVER MISS a title**
- **EARN Bonus Book points**

---

Call Customer Services

**0844 844 1358***

or visit

**illsandboon.co.uk/subscriptions**

*** This call will cost you 7 pence per minute plus your phone company's price per minute access charge.**